POTEET VICTORY

POTEET VICTORY

VICTORY

J. Robert Keating

atmosphere press

CHAPTER 1

A Painting Called Renegade

Poteet Victory is staring at his canvas and thinking about his Cherokee grandmother and *her* grandfather. He is thinking about the story he had first heard when he was a small boy. He had replayed it in his mind at least a thousand times. It is a tale of injustice that still riles his blood. But for now, he is considering how that tragedy plays out in paint and color on the canvas before him. He is finalizing his thoughts when he hears his name being called on the gallery's intercom.

He turns toward his phone and answers, "Yeah?"

His assistant says, "I have a Judy Hightower on the line from, uh... It's some production company in Los Angeles. She wants to come by tomorrow morning. She says she wants to talk to you about your family."

"Hmm. I guess that's okay," Poteet says as he continues to stare at the blank canvas. "I'll be here. Jus' tell 'er that we don't open 'til nine."

"Okay."

CHAPTER 2

Judy Hightower

The next day, Poteet reviews his work in progress as he thinks about the story he's telling with his painting. He is pleased with the cut and stature of the Indian that dominates the canvas, but he knows how the quiet peace of this work is about to change.

In his mind, Poteet thinks that the painting should call for only dark colors, but he had allowed small patches of turquoise and gold to sneak through. He had also painted a large portion of the background white. He is thinking about how to tone that down when he hears footsteps on the stairs and female voices.

He turns to see his gallery assistant and another woman enter his studio. The woman he doesn't know appears to be in her mid-thirties and is wearing a navy skirt, a white blouse, and a dark-red belt. The skirt was tight enough to reveal a nice figure but long enough to say, "I'm here for business."

His gallery assistant gestures to the woman and says, "Poteet, this is Judy Hightower. You know, she called yesterday."

"Sure. Come on in."

Ms. Hightower walks in and says, "I'm sorry to interrupt..."

"No problem. I have people in here all the time."

As the gallery assistant takes her leave, Ms. Hightower steps slightly forward. With little or no facial expression, she continues, "I want to know if you are who I think you are."

Poteet chuckles but doesn't respond.

Somewhat off balance, Ms. Hightower asks, "Is Willie Victory your grandmother?"

Poteet tilts his head and stares for a couple of seconds before answering, "Yes."

"I thought so."

This curious conversion and line of questioning is causing Poteet to wonder.

Ms. Hightower continues, "Did she write an article for *True West* magazine."

"Oh... She wrote that a *long* time ago."

"She did. But anyway, I started looking into her which led me to you, and I became interested. So... Anyway, I was in the area and thought I'd come by."

"Okay," Poteet responds, still confused.

"I've seen your website and your paintings there." She smiles and nods. "I looked around downstairs before coming up here, and I love your gallery"—she takes a moment to look around—"and your studio. It seems so comfortable."

"It is," Poteet says as he crosses his arms.

"I had that question about Willy Victory and just needed to be sure about your connection to her." She points to the easel closest to Poteet and says, "That face is very strong."

Poteet begins to relax and turns to look at his painting. "It is, but there's more I'm gonna do to it. This one's about my family."

"I see—a connection to your roots."

"It is, an' I probably won't sell it."

"Huh."

"Some paintings I jus' do for myself."

"I like the Native American look I see there."

"My grandmother was full-blood Cherokee," Poteet explains.

"I figured something like that, which only increased my interest in you."

"So..." Poteet says. "Maybe I need to tell you this... Southwestern was all I did when I first got out here."

"Makes sense."

"After several years of that, I changed to doin' mostly abstract."

"I saw both styles downstairs. I like all of it."

"An' so... For the past couple of years, I've been doin' more Indian paintings."

Judy stares at the work in progress and nods slightly. "I hope I have a chance to see that when it's finished."

"I'll be through with it in a couple of days."

She continues to stare and then says, "I won't take any more of your time."

"...no problem."

"So... I'll report back to my boss about coming by today."

With a more serious look, Poteet asks, "So, who'd you say your boss is?"

"I don't think I said. But... It's Elliott Jacobs."

Poteet cocks his head. "Of course, I know of Elliott Jacobs."

"It's actually Sizzling Rain Production Company, and we're a subsidiary of Jacobs Films."

"Okay."

"But I'm working directly with Mr. Jacobs on this project."

Poteet nods slightly.

"And... I think he'll want to come with me next time. We'll see." She turns to go but stops at the double doors to say, "I'll let you know when we're coming back."

"Okay," Poteet says and stares at the double doors. He listens to her footsteps fade.

CHAPTER 3

Elliott

By late morning, Elliott Jacobs and Judy Hightower are taking the turn into the first courtyard entrance from Canyon Road. Elliott notices the "Victory Contemporary" sign across the plaza and realizes they have reached their destination. He looks around to notice all of the art galleries in the immediate vicinity.

As they step out of the rented limousine, the chill of the early Spring air causes Judy to tighten her coat and move quickly toward the gallery entrance. Before they can even take two steps inside, they hear a loud, "Mr. Jacobs!"

They turn to see a trim, middle-aged woman approaching. She has kind eyes behind her dark-rimmed glasses, and she's wearing a warming smile. It's hard to not notice her flamboyant dark-black hair.

Her eyes sparkle as she says with a Southern accent, "Welcome to Santa Fe."

Elliott returns her smile and says, "Thank you."

She holds out her hand and says, "I'm Terry."

He reaches out and receives a soft handshake. He bows slightly and says, "I guess that makes you Terry Victory."

"It does."

He looks more carefully at Terry with masculine approval and notices her turquoise jewelry. It's conspicuous and oversized like everything else about Mrs. Victory. He can't help but like her.

She turns toward Judy, who offers her hand and says, "Hi. I'm Judy. I was the one who came by to meet Poteet the other day."

Terry smiles and reaches out to shake. "I'm sorry I missed you. I'm here four days a week, and that was one of my days off."

"Sure. I understand. I wasn't here long, and your assistant took good care of me." She continues, "And now I'm back." She looks over at Elliott. "This time I brought Elliott with me."

"An' we're so glad you did," Terry says and steps back. Her smile remains. "I assume you came to see Poteet."

"Yes, of course, but we came to meet you too," Elliott explains.

Terry bows her head slightly. "Thank you, Mr. Jacobs. I am honored to meet you."

Elliott looks at Terry and says, "One of these days, I want to talk to you about Poteet. I'm sure you have some special insight there."

Terry chuckles. "Oh yeah... In my twelve years with 'im, I've gotten to know 'im pretty well. An' I think I've heard most of his stories by now." She points. "He's upstairs if you wanna talk to 'im."

"Do you mind if I take a look around your gallery first?" Elliott asks.

"No, of course not. I think you should." With enthusiasm, Terry gestures to indicate the room they are in. "Everything in *here* is Poteet's." Turning and with a sweeping movement, she adds, "We show our other artists' work in these rooms."

Elliott nods as he glances around. He says, "Judy mentioned the mixture of Native American themes with his

8

abstract painting style."

"Yes, sir. Once he gets started, I never know what's gonna show up on his easel. He gets somethin' in his head, ya know... An' then, there it is. But I like 'em all. I really do."

Judy's eyes widen as she steps toward the finished painting she had seen as a work in progress the last time. The changes seem violent, and she wonders what Poteet was trying to say. Part of the answer comes when she reads the name posted underneath. It says, "Renegade." No price is given. She nods slightly as she moves closer to study the detail.

On the other side of the room, Elliott steps toward a painting that catches his eye. The colors are hues of red on a background of various shades of gray. He's drawn to its beauty, and it seems so different. As he continues to stare, he thinks it looks like flowers, and they seem to include the full spectrum of everything red.

The placard on the wall reads, "Early Summer Roses $9,200."

Elliott turns to stare out the glass door. He strokes his well-groomed beard as he thinks about where the painting could go in his own house.

A dog appears and begins to bark. Terry says gruffly but lovingly, "Hush, Honey." She points at her guests while speaking to the dog, "That's Mr. Jacobs an' this is Judy. An' you need to be nice to 'em. They're here to talk to Papa."

Elliott and Judy both smile at the grandfatherly reference.

Terry picks up the dog and holds him out to Elliott. "This here's Honey Badger, an' he thinks he needs to protect me from y'all."

Speaking to the dog, Elliott says, "It's okay. We're not really that dangerous." He then reaches out to pet Honey Badger, who quickly warms to him and gives a friendly lick in return.

"See anything you like?" Terry asks.

9

Judy immediately thinks, "Yes," but remains quiet.

Elliott answers, "Yeah, I really like the red roses."

"I like that one too," Terry replies.

As he looks from painting to painting, he says, "Growing up in New York City, we had access to museums with some really great art."

"I'd say you were very lucky, Mr. Jacobs. We didn't have that where I grew up."

"We took field trips to some of the art museums. But since then, I've only been back—maybe once." He shrugs and then looks at Terry. "My interest from an early age was film."

"Lookin' at all the movies you've made, Mr. Jacobs, that doesn't surprise me a bit."

Elliott turns back to look at the red roses before saying, "I guess I'm ready to meet Poteet now. You say he's here?"

"Yeah. He's right upstairs." Terry puts Honey Badger down and looks at Elliott in a way that says, "Follow me." She takes steps toward the next room.

Honey Badger gives a couple of barks to no one in particular, before turning away.

Judy continues to study the painting named *Renegade* until she is required to fall in behind Terry as they climb a nearby flight of stairs.

Elliott follows, noticing that there are paintings everywhere. The ones he's seeing along the stairway have been signed by someone other than Poteet Victory. At the second-floor landing, he pauses and notices what appears to be a *collection* of paintings on the wall across the room. One has a white background with a red square in the middle and a dot just below. It's unusual, and for some reason it speaks to him.

He then turns away from the paintings and notices a set of narrow double doors partially open at the end of a short hallway. Terry moves easily to the doors and pushes through. She says, "Mr. Jacobs an' Ms. Hightower are here."

"Come on in," echoes from inside.

Elliott smiles and steps in to see Poteet at work. The studio is light and cool. The smell is of fresh paint and coffee. Two easels dominate the room—each holding a painting in some stage of completion. The studio looks very much as he had imagined from the way Judy had described it. Even at age seventy-two, Poteet looks strong and has the full head of dark hair Elliott had seen on the website. He observes that a flat-file cabinet with drawers serves as Poteet's painting table. The cabinet is covered with jars filled with brushes, tubes of paint, and painting knives. A sheet of paper on top of the cabinet serves as the painter's palette, and it matches the colors on the nearest easel.

The room has a fireplace in one corner stacked with boxes and papers. There are two windows on adjacent walls. The studio is comfortable and warm. It seems to Elliott to be the perfect place for an artist.

Poteet takes note of the perfectly cut business suit being worn by Mr. Jacobs. It is unusual to see that style of garb in Santa Fe. Poteet extends his hand and says, "I'm Poteet Victory."

Elliott responds in kind. "I'm Elliott Jacobs."

Judy steps forward and offers her hand.

Poteet says, "Nice to see you again, Judy." He turns back to Elliott. "You've done some great movies, Mr. Jacobs."

"Thank you, and please call me Elliott."

"Sure," Poteet responds. "Terry an' I watched some of your movies here recently—knowin' you were comin'. Of course, most of 'em we'd seen before."

"I've got a fairly long history in the business."

"Yes, you have. You've done some great work."

"Thank you for that. I've been very fortunate to work with some great people. But, you know, I'm always thinkin' about my next project."

Poteet smiles. "I'm sure it's like painting. You never know when that next idea will hit ya."

"Yeah. It's very much like that. And then, the research begins. And right now, I've got the bug to do something *real*. It seems to be what the public's demanding. So many of the successful series for the past few years depict actual history; and I'm drawn to that myself. When it's history, it's real characters, real stories, real places..."

"Sure."

Judy steps forward and speaks to Elliott. "I told Poteet about finding him because of that article." She turns to look at Poteet and says, "At Elliott's suggestion, I was reading old issues of *True West* magazine."

"Your grandmother's story is very compelling." Elliott explains, "And it's compelling because it's real. It's where truth is better than fiction. And yeah... The Marvel movies have been good, but how many more superheroes like that can you create. Star Wars and Star Trek... Those have been great too, but they've lost much of their punch. It's always safe to do another one. But face it, they're not fresh anymore."

"They lost me some time ago," Poteet admits.

"And that's why we're here," Elliott says as he points at Poteet. "I'm told you have a remarkable story."

Poteet raises his eyebrows and replies, "I do have a story."

"Oh, it's remarkable," Terry says with a devious smile.

Elliott chuckles and looks over at her. "That's what I'm hoping for." He turns to Poteet and says, "But anyway... Thanks for allowing us to come by today. I hope we didn't disrupt your schedule too much."

"...not at all," Poteet says as he gestures with a quick look around. "This is where I am seven days a week."

"Looks like a good place to be."

"It is."

"Poteet *loves* to work," Terry says as she turns toward the double doors. She adds, "I'll leave y'all to talk."

As Terry is walking out, Judy takes a cautious step forward, timidly raising her hand. Looking at Poteet, she says, "...the painting called *Renegade*—the one you were painting the other day."

"Yes."

"I see conflict there. I see violence. And the red over the eyes... It's kind of hard..."

"You're not wrong."

"You said the other day that it says something about your family."

"It does."

Elliott's eyes narrow and he cocks his head as he watches Judy and Poteet.

Judy adds, "I couldn't tear my eyes away. I'm so glad I got to see the final work."

"I'm glad it speaks to you."

Elliott straightens up to say, "I like your art. I really do. But I'm not really an art guy."

"Not everyone is," Poteet says and shrugs.

"I went to some museums when I was in school, but that's about it. I got interested in film. And since then, that's what I've always done."

"Sure. But I think film is very similar to painting. It's art." He shrugs. "It's being creative. It's looking for that next kernel of an idea."

"Yes, of course."

"But art's always been an important part of *my* life. From as far back as I can remember, I liked to draw."

"I would have expected that."

"I met Harold Stevenson when I was young, an' he helped me a lot."

"I don't know about Harold Stevenson."

"If we talk very much about my background, you will. He

was my mentor an' an important influence in my life."

"I'll want to know more. But... To get back to your work, I have a question about a painting." Elliott turns to point in the direction of the double doors. "It's one I noticed from the stairs. It's on that wall you can see from there, and it looks like it's part of a collection."

"Right. It is. Those are the originals in my abbreviated portrait series."

"I read on your website about those. They represent people, I think."

"You're right. They do."

"The one that caught my eye had a white background, a red square in the middle, and a black dot."

Poteet chuckles. "That was my very first abbreviated portrait. It started it all, an' I had no intention of introducin' a series or doin' anything like that. I wanted to create a white painting, which I did. I painted the red square. An' on a whim, I added the dot. When I looked at it with the dot, it hit me. I thought, "I know who that is."

"Well, who is it?"

"...can't tell ya."

Elliott chuckles.

"...takes the fun out of it. But you'll figure it out."

"Maybe."

"Those on that wall are the originals. I think we've got nineteen now, an' we sell 'em as prints in two sizes."

"Interesting," Elliott says and stands straighter. He likes what he's seeing of this man, Poteet Victory. But he wants to know as soon as possible if they're on to something significant with him.

CHAPTER 4

Tell Me a Story

Elliott's smile disappears as he turns to look out the west window. He says slowly, "I don't want to sound rude or abrupt. And... I've enjoyed meeting you."

Poteet steps back slightly and folds his arms.

"I need to know right away if there's anything here for us," Elliott says. He then looks at Poteet and cracks a smile. "Don't get me wrong. I already know you're a fun guy and a great painter."

Poteet lets his arms drop, and his eyes soften.

"In fact, there's a painting down there I think I might want to buy."

Poteet's smile returns. He replies, "Hey. Great. We can sure help you with *that*."

"And I may need to have that one with the red square too. I can put it in my office."

"I haven't seen your office, but I can tell you right now... You do need that one. An' you'll understand why, once you figure out who it is."

"We'll see."

"I'm jus' tellin' ya..."

Elliott chuckles. "But... Like I was saying... I need to know if there's anything here for us."

Poteet nods and says, "I understand."

Elliott pauses and fixes his gaze on the window again. After a moment, he turns to Poteet and says, "Tell me a story."

Before Poteet can even respond, Elliott adds, "Tell me a story about something you've done that's different." He looks away. He turns back. Animating his speech with his hands, he says, "Yeah...something that's special...something that's unique...or *exciting*."

Poteet turns to look at his painting in progress before turning back to Elliott. He nods and lifts his right hand slowly. With his index finger extending, he says confidently, "Here's one."

Elliott's eyes light up, and he finds the gesture to be humorous. He says, "Okay..."

Poteet smiles slightly and begins, "I had gotten on a plane in Dallas an' was headed for New York City."

"Okay. New York City...not very Native American but a good start."

Poteet chuckles and focuses on Elliott. "Ya know, I told you about Harold..."

"Right—your mentor?"

"I was a model for 'im when I was in high school."

"...a model. Hmm. So, Harold was a painter too."

"Yeah. He was a great painter—one of the best of his generation."

"So, how does this fit into New York City?"

"I'll get there, but you gotta know about Harold an' the modelin' job first."

Elliott shrugs and responds, "Okay."

"I posed, an' he made sketches of me."

"And you were in high school?"

"I was. An' he used those sketches for his series of paintings on Alexander the Great."

"Hmm. Interesting."

"So... Like I was sayin'... On my trip up to New York City..."

"Was this while you were still in high school?"

"No. This was... I was like thirty-somethin' years old by then."

"Okay."

"So... On my trip up there..." He looks at Elliott and adds, "This is when I was startin' at the Art Students League."

"Oh! I know about the Art Students League. It's that building down on West Fifty-Seventh Street, I think."

Poteet perks up, and he looks at Elliott. "Most people wouldn't know that."

"Well, most people didn't grow up in Queens."

"I see. So, you probably would know."

"Yeah."

"But anyway... I was tellin' you about the trip."

"Right."

"Uh... I got on the plane in Dallas."

Elliott chuckles. "So, we're still getting on the plane."

"An' I mean, it was *really* hot. An' I had on a Western straw hat, ya know."

"Okay?"

"So, I'm sittin' on the plane, an' I'm sittin' right beside this guy. We introduced ourselves. He was a Wall Street broker. An' I told 'im what I was doin'... that I was goin' up there to go to art school. So, we get to LaGuardia, ya know... We get off the plane, an' I shook his hand. An' I said, 'Nice meetin' ya.' An' he said, 'Well... So, what are ya gonna do now?' An' I said, 'Well, I'm gonna go meet Andy Warhol.' 'Cause Harold had called Andy, ya know."

Elliott cocks his head and focuses more closely on Poteet's expression.

Poteet continues, "So, this broker said, 'Oh, yeah?'"

Elliott smiles.

Poteet chuckles. "An' I said, 'Yeah.' He said, 'Well, I'll tell you what.' He said, 'I've got to go into Manhattan anyway.' He said, 'You're a student. You don't have any money.' He said, 'I'll pay for the cab fare to take you over to Andy's.' I said, 'Okay. Great.' So, I get in the cab with 'im, an' I give the cab driver the address to The Factory."

"Right, The Factory—Andy Warhol's studio," Elliott states for clarification.

"Yeah. An' uh..." Poteet chuckles. "So... We pull up there, an' I get out. An' I shake the guy's hand again. I said, 'Thanks a lot. I really appreciate the ride.' But he said, 'Well... Uh... We'll just wait on ya. Maybe Andy won't be here.'"

Elliott and Judy begin to chuckle.

"An' I said, 'Oh, he'll be here.' He said, 'We'll just wait.'"

Elliott and Judy continue chuckling.

"I said, 'Okay.' So, I go up to the door. An' the doorman's there, an' I tell 'im who I am. I said, 'Andy's expectin' me. If you'll go get 'im, I'll just wait right here.' The doorman said, 'Okay.' So... In a few minutes... Well, here come Andy—with his hands in the air and a big smile on his face, sayin' 'Hey... Great!! You're here!'" Poteet lifts his hands—shaking them to demonstrate.

Elliott and Judy laugh.

"I look over, an' the guy in the cab was doin' this." Poteet puts his face in his hands. "After a moment, he looks up with a big smile, an' he can't... He can't believe it. He *cannot* believe it. But the reason... Andy was... Uh... Well, Harold did that series of paintings on Alexander the Great an' all that. Well, ya know, he did 'em over in Paris. But... He tol' me... He said, 'You became very famous.' An' I said, 'Why's that?' He said, 'Well, in Europe, it's not like in America.' He said, 'Sometimes the models are more famous than the artists.' So, when he called Andy, ya know... He told Andy I was comin' up there. An' Andy was tryin' to put 'im off, sayin', 'Oh, I don't know...' Harold said, 'No, Andy. This is the boy that modeled for Alexander.' So, Andy said, 'Well, send 'im over.'"

Elliott chuckles and then asks, "Did you really meet Andy Warhol in New York City?"

"Yeah. I met 'im at The Factory."

"And you went inside?"

"Sure, many times."

"Did you go to parties there?"

"No. I was in New York City to learn to paint, an' I had to have a job too. I didn't have time for parties."

"You know, Andy Warhol and The Factory were a big deal. I feel like the artists who were in New York City at that time set the tone for the sixties. It set the tone for much of what changed in our culture. In my mind the impact continues to this day."

"Maybe. I hadn't really thought of it like that."

"Oh yeah. Bob Dylan was a part of that. Some people say that Dylan and Warhol competed over who would be the leader of the New York City art scene. Of course, they were both a big deal in their own right."

"Sure."

"But they did compete for real over a girl named Edie Sedgwick. She was an actress and had starring roles in several of Warhol's films. Along the way, she fell in love with Bob Dylan, which caused Warhol some problems. Plenty has been written about that."

"It's funny you should mention Edie Sedgwick."

"Why is that?"

"Because... She was a very close friend of Harold's."

Elliott squints and moves closer. "Harold who?"

"My mentor, Harold Stevenson."

"Hmm... Really?"

"Yeah. At least, that's what Harold always told me. An' I don't think he had a reason to lie about it."

Elliott nods and says, "Edie was young and beautiful... Like I said, she was in Warhol's movies. She was a socialite with plenty of money. She was *Life* Magazine's 'Girl of the Year' back in the mid-sixties. She was a New York City girl. She was cool. She was hip. She was sexy. Her pictures were all over the place. You know, that makes an impression on a young man coming of age."

Judy smiles and looks away.

"An'... Harold was in the middle of all that," Poteet says. "Edie an' him were friends—very good friends. He tol' me a lot about 'er."

Elliott looks at Poteet. "It's been rumored for years that she was the inspiration for Bob Dylan's song 'Like a Rolling Stone.'"

Judy edges forward.

"A lot of people say that. I don't know... But when I hear that song, I can believe that it was about Edie Sedgwick. She *was* a 'little rich girl,' you know. And once she started running with Warhol, she had to learn how to 'live out on the street.' I don't *really* know that Dylan wrote that song about her, but it definitely fits."

Judy says, "I know that song."

Elliott smiles and says, "You're young, but *everybody* knows 'Like a Rolling Stone.' And then there's 'Positively 4th Street.' It's another Dylan song where Edie's name often comes up."

"You seem to be an expert on Bob Dylan songs," Poteet suggests.

"I'm not. But I've studied the culture. Like I said, I think it set the tone for the sixties, and that *is* interesting to me. But with the song 'Positively 4th Street,' I never thought it was about Edie. I never thought Dylan would feel that kind of hatred for her. He broke off the relationship, so she was the one who had every reason to be bitter. Especially, since she claimed to be carrying Dylan's baby."

Poteet steps up. "Because of Harold, I've always been curious about Edie Sedgwick." He pauses then continues, "And from articles I've read and the movie, I think Edie fell apart after Dylan left 'er."

"And..." Elliott responds. "That's why I've thought for a long time that the song was actually written about Dylan's relationship with Andy Warhol—not Edie or even the journalists who often criticized him. Not many would agree, but it makes complete sense to me. The hate-filled lyrics always seemed inspired by the bitterness one can feel for a competitor—or you could even say an enemy. And I think Andy Warhol was that artistic competitor. It seems clear that Dylan and Warhol didn't like each other, and Edie fueled that fire." Elliott looks at Poteet and continues, "Just listen to the lyrics more carefully the next time you hear that song."

"I will."

"...interesting," Judy concludes.

"Yeah," Poteet adds. "Harold was around all that, but we never talked about Bob Dylan or the lyrics to his songs."

Elliott nods and then returns to the topic, "...your trip to New York City. That's a great story."

"It is," Judy agrees.

"But is it all true? Like I said, I'm looking for true stories."

Poteet steps closer and assures his guest, "Yeah, it's true."

"How could I possibly know?"

Poteet stiffens as he answers, "Look it up."

"How would I do that?"

"Check out the movie *Heat* that Andy made."

Elliott nods and says, "Okay."

"Harold was in that one. I don't think he had a big part, but he was in it."

Elliott pulls out his phone and starts punching the screen.

Poteet turns back to his table, scans his paint options, and reaches for a tube. He squeezes a small portion onto the paper and begins to mix the new with the old.

Still turned away from Judy and Poteet, Elliott proclaims, "Well, I'll be damned."

Judy's eyes sparkle above a sweet smile.

Poteet chuckles.

"There it is," Elliott says as he turns and points at his phone. "You were right. It says, 'Harold Stevenson.'" He shakes his head and remains quiet for a moment. "So, this Harold Stevenson was your mentor."

"Yeah," Poteet says softly. "...an' my friend."

"Wow."

"Yeah, he was from Idabel, but ended up in New York City at a young age. He was there the whole time Andy was. They were associates but not great friends."

"They must have been close enough for Harold to talk Andy into meeting you that day."

"Yeah. They were. Because... When Andy first got to New York City, Harold was already established. So, Andy wanted to be around 'im. In fact, Harold helped Andy get started. Harold had the connections—galleries, museums, ya know... An' Harold brought Andy into that. Harold always knew Andy had talent."

"He was right about that."

"The difference was... Andy was a promoter." Poteet shakes his head. "Harold really wadn'."

Elliott chuckles. "So, obviously Harold was well aware of what Andy Warhol was doing with film at that time."

"Of course. Sure. But I don't think he was too impressed. Harold wadn' that impressed with Andy's art in general, ya know." Poteet picks up his painting knife and starts mixing. "But I've seen some of Andy's movies myself, an' I'm not that impressed either."

"To tell you the truth, I agree with you," Elliott confesses.

"Some are better than others. But his best ones weren't very good. I've probably seen 'em all. When you're into film like I am, you look at some pretty obscure stuff. I've looked for redeeming qualities in those Warhol movies, and it's just not there."

"Yeah."

"Even so, Warhol had a following, and he had his lineup of..." Elliott uses his fingers for an air quote. "...stars." He looks at Poteet and says, "...like Edie Sedgwick."

"Right," Poteet says softly.

"And there were others."

Poteet turns toward Elliott and says, "Harold told me that Andy could get those high-society rich girls to do that for 'im."

"That's right. They wanted to be movie stars, and Andy seemed to be the ticket. He even had a house band. They were called The Velvet Underground. I think they had a hit or two. It was a crazy time."

"Yeah," Poteet says and looks over at Elliott. "An' a lot of that was still goin' on while I was there. I didn't see most of it. But some of it, I did." Poteet turns with a loaded knife to his painting.

Elliott nods and says, "I find all that fascinating."

"Yeah. It was an interesting time to be in New York City."

Elliott watches Poteet apply the paint and asks, "So, is that the end of your story?"

"Yeah."

"Like I said... It's a good one, and I believe it's true. It changes who I think you are."

Poteet chuckles. After a moment, he says, "But, there's somethin' else...?"

Elliott grins and says, "I thought that was the end."

Judy smiles in anticipation.

"Not quite," Poteet says. He looks at Elliott and then Judy.

Elliott gives a nod.

"Like I said, it was hot summertime when I got on the plane in Dallas."

Smiling, Elliott shakes his head and says, "So, we're back in Dallas."

"Yeah. An' I had on that cowboy hat—a straw hat. An' it was a funny thing... Because... That very day when I met Andy at The Factory, he was gettin' ready to go to a party."

"Yeah?"

"...a *cowboy* party."

Elliott chuckles and asks, "So, did he borrow your hat?"

"Yeah. I didn't need it."

All three laugh.

"So, I guess you didn't go to the party."

"No. I had to get settled into this place I'd rented an' get ready to go to art classes the next day."

Elliott and Judy turn to acknowledge Terry, who is walking into the room. She says, "I heard y'all laughin'."

"Poteet's keeping us entertained," Elliott turns to say.

With a total straight face, Terry says, "Oh yeah, Mr. Jacobs, Poteet's real good at doin' that."

"I'm finding that out."

Terry nods.

Elliott says, "I asked him to tell me a story."

Terry looks at Poteet. "Which one did ya tell 'im?"

"...about meetin' Andy in New York City."

Elliott chuckles.

She smiles. "That's a good one. But Mr. Jacobs, there's plenty more where that come from."

Elliott shakes his head. "I don't know how you can beat that one."

She shoots a questioning look at Poteet.

He answers her expression, "He already knew a lot about The Factory an' Andy an' all that."

Terry nods.

"He even knew about Edie."

She turns to Elliott and asks, "Did you know about Harold?"

Poteet intercepts the question and answers, "No. But he's seen some of Andy's movies. An', ya know, Harold was in some of those."

Terry says, "Yeah, that's true." Looking at Elliott and then Judy, she asks, "Can I get you anything? Coffee? Some water?"

Elliott answers, "No. I'm fine, thanks."

Judy shakes her head.

"Can I at least get you chairs? I can't believe Poteet didn't offer."

"No, we can't stay. We've stayed longer than I had planned. I've got to get back. I've got some people to see this afternoon about another project. My plane's at the airport waiting for us right now. I could only spare enough time for a quick stop on my way back from the East Coast."

"We hoped you'd stay longer."

Elliott looks down and shakes his head. He looks up and says, "...not this time." He looks at Poteet. "I needed to meet Poteet to see if there was any potential."

Pushing the envelope, Terry asks, "Well..."

"Yeah. I'll come back. After that story, I've *got* to come back. But I need to start from the beginning next time."

Poteet shrugs and says, "Sure."

"But... I don't want to waste your time—or mine." He turns to look at Poteet, then back to Terry. "It's about whether I think this works, you know, for a film. It's a high bar, and I think you knew that."

"We do," Terry says and smiles.

"Okay then, we should probably get underway."

Poteet and Elliott step toward each other for a parting handshake.

Poteet reaches for Judy's hand. They shake and smile.

Terry and Judy head for the stairs.

Elliott turns to say, "Thank you," as he follows the women out.

Downstairs, Judy walks over to the *Renegade* painting to get a last look. She tries to decipher decades of Poteet's family history from what she's seeing.

From the front door, Elliott says, "You like that one."

"I do. He was working on it when I was here before." She points to the lower section of the painting. "And this part... I'm trying to understand it. He's done something to the texture of the canvas. And also... The images and the colors here are totally different. To me, they seem to go back to ancient Native American themes. It's an interesting mix."

Elliott nods and looks more carefully at the painting. After a moment he says, "It catches your eye."

"It does. And it says something about Poteet's family history. He told me that."

Elliott takes a quick look before turning to give Terry a parting wave.

Once in the waiting limo, Judy turns to Elliott and asks the obvious, "What'd you think?"

After a moment of consideration, Elliott replies, "He's not what I expected."

She chuckles and asks, "Do we come back?"

"Oh yeah, we've got to come back."

Judy relaxes, believing that her hunch was right about her boss's likely interest in Poteet.

As the limo pulls out into the traffic on Paseo de Peralta, Elliott is thinking about the significance of meeting Poteet. He wonders whether Poteet's story is Native American enough for what he'd been hoping to do. At this point in his life, he'd been wanting to "give back" and had a heart for helping Native Americans. In the past, he had worked on movie sets on Indian reservations and had witnessed the hopelessness of those conditions. Poteet was certainly interesting, but he might not have the right background to accomplish what he wanted. He would need to follow up with that on his next trip.

CHAPTER 5

The Indian Side

Honey Badger knew that something was up. Mama had been working at her computer but had mostly been looking out the window.

Terry was anxious to see their guest again. Mr. Jacob's office had called yesterday and asked if he could come by. When she saw his limo, she jumped up quickly and headed for the front room. As he walked in, she said, "So, you're back."

"I am."

"We must not have bombed out completely."

"Not at all," Elliott says as he closes the door. "Nice to see you again, Terry."

"Le' me tell ya somethin'," she says with an attitude. "When ya come into *this* gallery the second time, you begin to feel like family to me, an' I'm gonna give you a big hug." Her arms go around Elliott, and she gives him a peck on the cheek. He smiles. With satchel in hand, he awkwardly reaches around Terry and manages to brush a kiss on her neck.

She moves back and then takes steps in the direction of her office. "Come on. You can put your coat down in here."

Elliott follows, thinking about the warm welcome.

Terry points to a large leather chair. "Put your coat right there."

28

Elliott removes his coat, places it on the chair, and sets his hat on top. He stands and notices the room. It's obviously an office—not large but adequate, with a computer prominently sitting on a glass table in the middle of the space. Beyond that, it looks like an extension of the art gallery. One wall is covered with small paintings. They remind him of the larger ones he'd seen from the top of the stairs. All the walls are covered, which gives the room a sense of sophistication and fun. He wishes *his* office was more like this one.

As Terry moves around behind her computer chair, she says, "Poteet's up there paintin'. He'll be glad to see ya. I'll come up an' look in on y'all after a while. Sometimes Poteet leaves things out of his stories, ya know."

"Sure," Elliott says, grabs his satchel, and heads for the stairs. As he's walking up, he's thinking about how to approach the subject of Poteet's connection to the oppressed Native American tribes—wondering if there's anything there at all.

Poteet turns to see Elliott, who had announced his presence with a tentative, "Knock, knock." They smile, shake hands, and Elliott sits on the stool Poteet had brought out earlier.

"Sorry about the last-minute decision we made yesterday to work Santa Fe into our schedule. But I've been in New York City again, and I thought I could take a few minutes..."

"No problem. I'm usually here, an' it happens all the time."

"Well good... There's an important topic I want to cover with you, and I hoped we could do it today."

"Fine."

"But before we get into that, I want to tell you that you were right about the white painting with the red square and black dot. I figured it out. Well... There were some pretty big clues. But yeah, I *need* that for my office."

Poteet chuckles. He then says, "I knew you would, an' we

can take care of that for ya. We sell prints of it in two sizes. Terry can show you that later."

"Okay," Elliott says and reaches into his satchel. "I brought a recorder with me this time." He holds it up and glances around at the worktable right behind him. He asks, "Can I set it here?"

"Sure," Poteet says as he turns back to his painting table and palette. "Do you mind if I continue to paint?"

"No, not at all. I'll enjoy watching." While he's setting up the recorder, Elliott says, "After last time, when we talked about your trip to New York City, meeting Andy Warhol, being at The Factory and all... I wished I'd recorded that."

Poteet turns to his painting with his knife in hand and says, "We can talk about those things again if you want."

"We'll need to. But I want to talk today about your Native American roots."

Applying the paint, Poteet says, "Okay."

"I must admit, I'm having a hard time seeing how your New York City experiences turn into a Native American story. It's definitely not what I had pictured when we got interested in you."

"I don't know what to tell ya. It's just my life, ya know," Poteet says and shrugs.

Elliott turns on his stool to squarely face Poteet. Leaning back against the worktable with his hands clasped on his stomach, he looks up at the ceiling. After a moment, he says, "I didn't find much on this, but I know you did a project with the University of Oklahoma—some years ago. I think that it had to do with your Native American heritage."

Poteet turns toward Elliott and says, "Yeah."

"So, what was that about?"

After setting his knife down on the painting table, he says, "The Trail of Tears."

"So, why did you do that?"

"People don' know anything about it. Most haven't even heard of it."

"So, you wanted to tell that story—the Trail of Tears story."

"I did. That's *exactly* what I wanted to do."

"Were you able to?"

Poteet takes a deep breath before answering, "...not like I wanted."

"I detect some frustration."

"Some people would say I'm bitter."

"Are you?"

"Maybe." Poteet picks up his painting knife, turns to the sheet of white paper that is his palette, and continues, "I was born in 1947. An' when I was growin' up there in Idabel, I remember that Indians were terribly discriminated against." He stops mixing his paint and looks over at Elliott. "They really were." He turns back to his palette. "My mother was not Indian, but she was dark. She had black hair, an' everybody thought she was Indian." With knife in hand, he turns toward his painting. "But Daddy *was* Indian. He was Cherokee an' Choctaw. An' that made us different for some reason. I didn' get it. Yeah, I can remember... I didn' understand what that was all about. Discriminatin' against Indians an'..." He shakes his head. "An' ya know, those Indian boys I grew up with... They were very guarded." He turns to look at Elliott. "They were." He turns back to his palette. "Most of 'em grew up quiet. Yeah. They didn't speak much until you got along with 'em. An' then, they were a barrel of monkeys."

Elliott smiles and lets Poteet continue.

"But I could go with either side. I could go with the Indian boys an' talk to them. Or I could be with the white boys. I jus' kinda went back an' forth, ya know. It didn' faze me—maybe that was because I was just *part* Indian. I don' know. But I knew it bothered them."

"So, early on you saw people that you cared about being discriminated against."

Poteet turns to Elliott to answer, "Yeah. I did. An' I can tell ya... I didn' like it. I didn' like it at all. 'Cause I knew it was part of my heritage."

"So... With your Native American background, I can understand your interest in this history."

"Right."

"So, what can you tell me about your experience at the University of Oklahoma and what you were trying to accomplish there?"

Poteet sets his painting knife down and looks toward the window. He says slowly, "At that time, I'd had some success with my painting career." He turns and reaches for a rag. He starts cleaning his hands. He looks over at Elliott and continues, "I guess I just started thinkin' about my family an' my background."

"So, how did that get you hooked up with the University of Oklahoma?"

"If you wanna know about all that, then we've gotta go way back."

"Okay."

Poteet looks over to stare out the window again. After a moment, he begins, "J.C. was my grandmother's father—my Cherokee grandmother's father. An' the reason he never signed up with the Dawes Commission was because..." He sets the rag on his painting table. "When he was a little boy, him an' his brother witnessed their parents bein' killed by renegade white men. He said that him an' his brother were in the pig pen lookin' out through the slats."

"That's awful."

"Yeah. An' he, ya know... I mean, who wouldn't? J.C. hated the white man after that."

"Of course."

Poteet continues without the hint of a smile. "I had an uncle. His name was C.C. Victory. He was Vice-Chief of the

Cherokees for twenty-two years. An' he had gone to J.C. He said, 'J.C., you really need to sign up.' J.C. said, 'No. I don't trust anything the white man does.'"

"And you can definitely see why he would think that."

"So, J.C. never signed up. But I mean... Who could blame 'im?"

"Your family's probably not over that yet."

"...not completely. No."

Elliott says, "There's a rumor of a murder in my family history—back in Ohio. I remember when I first heard about it, and it kind of takes you back."

"It does. And that's what I've been dealin' with. I think the painting will help."

"And what happened in my family is nothing compared to what happened to yours."

"I don't know about that. But I do know that mine is still pretty fresh—even after all these years."

"I'm thinking that this is probably the family history Judy was trying to see in that painting she called *Renegade*."

"It is."

"For Judy to be so moved, you must have captured the emotion of that attack in a significant way—in your painting."

"It all came rushin' back as I was doin' it. An' I told 'er I jus' did that one for myself."

"I see. I'll mention that she needs to listen to the recording of this discussion."

"Okay. I think she'll be interested."

Elliott nods and says, "I've been wondering... You've been using the word 'Indian.' I've been saying 'Native American.' So, what should I say?"

"American Indian."

"So, you prefer 'American Indian.'"

"Yeah. I do. *You're* native American."

"Hmm. I guess so."

33

"Right. The ones I know call themselves American Indians."

"Okay. I'll start saying that," Elliott replies and leans back against the table. After a moment he looks at his watch and immediately reaches for the recorder. He says, "I've got to go. I've got to get back, and I'm pretty sure my car's waiting for me out there. This was supposed to be just a quick stop."

"I don't know if any of this helps."

While putting the recorder away, Elliott says, "It did. It helped a lot. It's another powerful dimension to who you are. And I think it's a big deal."

"I don' know. But... I'm glad you could come by." Poteet smiles and then the smile fades. He says, "But... Thinkin' about my project for the Indians..." He stops and looks away. He sighs.

"It bugs you," Elliott observes.

"I try to avoid talkin' about the OU part of it."

"I see."

"That's where the frustration is."

"We'll avoid that if you want."

"Maybe someday, we can..." Poteet's voice tapers off.

As Elliott hoists the strap of his satchel over his shoulder, he says, "I really do hope to stay longer next time."

"You *should* stay. You'd like Santa Fe."

"I will. But for now, I've got to go." Elliott stands. They shake hands, and he heads for the double doors. As he's walking out, he looks more closely at the paintings on every wall. He now can tell which ones are Poteet's. He likes the Native American themes and is drawn to the lines, the bold colors, and the traditional symbols in Poteet's work.

Out in the bright sunshine of a beautiful mountain spring day, he sees his driver sit up to start the car. As he is being driven away, Elliott reflects on his meeting with Poteet. He knows that Poteet is the real deal, but he still wants to know more. He thinks about Poteet not being on the tribal rolls and wonders if that will be a problem.

CHAPTER 6

The Fifth

Terry looks up and practically shouts, "Elliott!"

He chuckles as he watches her quickly stand and rush over to greet him.

She grabs his hand but keeps moving in for a hug. After a moment, she backs away and says, "I lost track of the time. I've been busy. I've got some people interested in buyin' some art, an' I'm tryin' to get what I sold yesterday boxed up an' out the door."

"Please... Don't let me interrupt."

"Oh, you're not interruptin' a thing," she says as she waves the thought away with her hand.

Elliott smiles but doesn't move.

Terry points to the stairs. "I told Poteet you'd be comin' by. He's expectin' ya."

Elliott grins and says, "I hadn't mentioned this before, but we have friends who are collectors of yours."

"Oh?"

"Yeah. ...the Kleppers—Pam and Jim Klepper."

"You're kiddin'."

"No. They've been talking about their trips to Santa Fe for years and asking us to come with them. We just discovered recently that they have several of Poteet's paintings."

"Yeah. They do."

"So... When Judy brought the Willy Victory article to me and we made the connection, I thought that it might be time for me to make a trip."

"I see."

"I've talked with the Kleppers about Poteet, and I've talked with them about you."

"This is about Poteet. It's not about me."

Elliott snickers and adds, "But they wouldn't tell me everything."

Looking at Elliott out of the corner of her eye, Terry asks, "Whadaya mean?"

"So, now I'm genuinely curious."

"...about what? What wouldn' they tell ya?"

Elliott moves closer. "Like..." He says quietly, "Like... You're the fifth wife."

"I am. An' I have been for nearly twelve years. None of them others lasted that long. An' I'm the last. I know Poteet. An' at this point in his life, he don't want another woman. He jus' wants to paint."

"I think I can believe that." Elliott says and turns to look directly at Terry. With added volume, he adds, "But I want to know how you and Poteet got together."

Terry chuckles.

"So far, no one's willing to tell me the story—except something about the Pizza Hut. Surely there's more to it than that."

"Yeah. There's more."

"And they say I need to hear it directly from you."

"I guess."

With a slight smile, he adds, "I think I'm going to find the romantic piece I'm looking for right here in *your* story."

"Well... Maybe... But... Ya know, Poteet's a freakin' encyclopedia of romance."

Elliott laughs. "*Now* we're getting somewhere."

She says confidently and with a nod, "Yeah. It's true."

He chuckles.

"I'll even tell you about them others, at least what I know. But they're distant memories for Poteet now. They're no threat to me. Poteet's glad to be rid of 'em."

Elliott reaches into his satchel for the recorder. He says, "You know, I'll be recording these conversations."

"Right. Poteet tol' me about that."

"I'll just set it right here," Elliott says as he moves the recorder in front of Terry.

She pushes back with eyes wide. "You mean you wanna record *me*?"

"Yeah," he says matter-of-factly. "It's no big deal."

She raises her eyebrows and nods slightly. "Okay. If you say so." She sits and points at the second chair at the table. "If we're gonna talk, you can sit right there."

After settling in, Elliott says, "So... They tell me that you met Poteet at the Pizza Hut in Idabel."

"I did."

"So, you didn't know Poteet before that?"

Terry sits back, crossing her arms and looking at the recorder. She pauses for a moment before saying, "I knew Loretha an' that she had a brother. But I didn't know *him*."

"And, Loretha is...?"

"Poteet's sister."

"Okay."

"An' I knew Rowland."

"And Rowland is...?"

"Loretha's husband."

Elliott nods. "Poteet's brother-in-law."

"Yes. An' I knew Rowland an' Loretha's son, their daughter, her daughter, ya know. But I didn' know Poteet."

"...because he was older?"

"Well, no. He's younger than Loretha, but... From me, he was... He's ten years..."

"...ten years older than you?"

"Yeah. I was born in '57, an' he was born in '47."

"So, you didn't know him, but you knew of him."

"Well, he wadn'... He wadn' ever there. An' uh... It is strange, ya know, the chances of us *not* knowin' each other... It's just unbelievable. Because he would come in, an'... Ya know, his best friend, Wayland O'Rear... Well, they had these wagon races. ...out there at the ranch."

"Okay."

"An' I mean, it got really wild. An' it was jus' *really* fun. It was real fun to go to."

"...with real wagons?"

"Yeah...wagons an' horses. An' then they'd have the relay races. They'd run their horses an' then jump in the pool an' swim the pool, ya know..."

"Sounds like fun. An' even with all this happening, you never met Poteet."

"Right. But I can tell you what I had on that day. It was back when Rocky Mountains was in style, ya know—those tight, Rocky Mountain jeans. Mine was bright yellow, an' I had a shirt on that had that yellow in it."

"Hmm."

"An' I was about as big around as my finger. I was skinnier then. An' uh..."

"Okay. So, you remember that day, that event, what you wore..."

"Yeah. I remember what I wore, but I didn' see him. An' I ended up gettin' hooked up with a *goofball.*"

Elliott and Terry laugh together.

"...a total idiot. Yeah. An' I'm here to tell ya, *that one* got a little western." She smiles. "I was mean. I had to put the fear of God in that one."

They laugh again.

"So how long after that was it before you and Poteet met at the Pizza Hut?"

Terry sighs and ponders. "Oh! It would've been probably twelve to fifteen years. Yeah. Cause uh... Yeah. It was probably twelve..."

"*Twelve to fifteen years...?*"

"Right...'til he come into the Pizza Hut that day."

Elliott's eyebrows rise, and he stares at Terry without speaking.

"Actually, the day before I met 'im, I was workin' at the salon. Okay? It was Tanya, my really good friend, the owner of the salon, an' some others that was there. I said to 'em, 'Y'all come here,' 'cause I saw 'im. He was in that little black XLR Cadillac." She moves closer to Elliott and speaks as though she's confiding in him. "An' he had a *woman* with 'im." She backs off and changes to her normal voice. "Poteet an' her was like goin' into the bank—or maybe the drugstore or somethin'. I said, 'Come here an' look at this good-lookin' guy.'"

"Really?"

"Yeah."

"That was the day before?"

"Oh... Now that I think about it, it could've been two or three days before."

"And you didn't even know who he was."

"I didn'."

"So, when he came into the Pizza Hut that day..."

"Actually, he was already there when I come in. He must've been in the back 'cause I was up at the salad bar an' hadn' seen 'im. An' I was tellin' all my friends, 'Y'all come on down an' lemme do your hair,' an' all that stuff. 'Cause I was gonna make me some money an' get out of there. I thought, 'I'm gonna go to Hollywood, an' I'm gonna do hair for the rich an' famous. An' if anybody can pull this off, I can.' Those were exactly my thoughts."

Elliott chuckles under his breath.

Showing no sign of being offended, Terry sits up and gives Elliott a completely serious, stone-faced look. "Ya know, ya have to have a dream." She sits back and adds, "An' so... Anyway, he was walkin' out with that same woman I'd seen 'im with. An' when she got out the door, he come over to me an' said, 'Where do you work?'"

"I tell you... I was stunned, but I said, 'Shag Rat Salon.' He said, 'I'm gonna come see ya.' I said, 'Okay,' an' I'm thinkin'..." Terry stops and shakes her head. "But I didn't know what else to say. I mean, I'm thinkin', 'This guy that I saw in that car is gonna come see *me*.' So, later that afternoon... I'd been out runnin' an errand... I was jus' gettin' back in my car, an' I saw Poteet again. He come out the door, an' he said, 'You wanna go to lunch tomorrow?' An' I thought, 'Yeah.' So, I said, 'Yeah.'" She looks at Elliott, "I said, 'But call me.'" She leans forward. "I gave 'im a way out, Elliott, 'cause, I'm thinkin', 'You really wanna go to lunch with *me*?' Because... Ya know... Poteet is *so* good lookin' an' all. An' I'm thinkin', 'Wow!' Because... Ya know, it was a big deal. It made my heart flutter an' all that stuff. It caused my stomach to go crazy an' everything. Anyway... An' when I told 'im to call me, he said, 'No.'" She nods slowly. She looks at Elliott and says, "He stood up to me right off the bat. He said, 'I'll pick you up at twelve o'clock.'" She looks away for a moment and then back. "An' I thought, 'He jus' told me what *he's* gonna do.' An' that was *real* unusual for me, because *I* was usually the boss."

"Huh."

"That was our first lunch date, November the 12th, 2008." She smiles and says, "An' then he asked me out *again*..." She leans back, raises her hand, and shakes her head. "An' I had several boyfriends at the time."

"You were 'dating around,' I guess."

"Oh yeah... I mean... To me, they were jus' like a game. Yeah. I mean... I didn't really like any of 'em very much. I didn' care whether they liked me or not. But... Then Poteet come along an', ya know... He's... I was totally..."

"Right," Elliott says and nods. "So... You went to lunch that day. And then what?"

"Actually, we went to lunch, an' then he took me back to the salon. An' about, like two thirty or somethin'—maybe three... I think I had an appointment at three or somethin'— with somebody. An' I was doin' hair, an' here he come back in. He handed me one of those Trail of Tears cards, an' he had his phone number an' his email on it." She leans forward to say, "I couldn't believe he'd gone to his ranch an' then come back to town to give that to me." She sits back and stares for a moment. "Okay, Elliott," she says before pausing again. She then admits, "I knew *nothin'* about computers. Okay. I mean... I'd *never* messed with 'em. But I thought, 'Man, I don' want to call 'im. 'Cause that...'" Her eyes narrow as she looks at Elliott. "Mama taught us to not *ever* call a guy. Let the guys do the callin'. So,' I thought, 'But I could email 'im—an' tell 'im I enjoyed lunch.'"

"Right."

"An' I did. I figured it out on my brother's computer. My brother an' my mom was in Texarkana, an' so Michael wadn' there to show me how to do it. But I figured it out, an' I thanked 'im for lunch an' told 'im I enjoyed it. An' I think I even put everything in capital letters."

They both laugh.

"Anyway... Yeah. An' then, uh... I think I might have given 'im my phone number in that email. An' um... So anyway, uh... Yeah, the next day we went to lunch again, an' he'd been to the gym. An' Elliott..." She pauses with a grin. "My friend Sylvia... She talks really, really slow. An' she, ya know... She come in, an' I was goin' to lunch. No... I'd jus' got back from lunch, I believe. But... Anyway, she come in the salon..." Terry stands and walks to a drawer a few steps away and pulls out an article of clothing. "An'... If I remember correctly, Poteet had been to the gym. Okay?"

"Yeah."

She holds up a pair of pants, looks over at Elliott, and says, "An' he wore these M. C. Hammer pants to the gym."

Elliott shrugs. "Okay. Yeah."

"If I remember right, these are the ones he had on."

Elliott chuckles. "The very ones?"

"Uh-huh."

"And you've kept them all this time?"

"Yeah. An' I remember what I was thinkin'? I'm thinkin' 'I ain't crazy about 'em'"

Elliott chuckles again.

"Ya know... Even in ol' hick southeast Oklahoma ten years ago, it was kind of weird to wear these," she says as she holds up the pants again.

They laugh, and she puts the pants back in the drawer. She sits down and says, "So anyway... I introduced Poteet to Sylvia, ya know. So... Sylvia looked at 'im an' said in her slow way of talkin', 'Terry, he's real cute an' everything, but I don't like his britches."

Elliott and Terry burst out laughing again.

"She said this right in front of 'im. An' I didn' know what to say. I thought, 'I don't like 'em either, but I don' wanna tell 'im.'"

Elliott shakes his head and says, "Funny." Still smiling, he asks, "I guess that didn't scare him off."

Deadpan, Terry answers with a pronounced drawl, "Guess not."

They laugh again.

"No, it didn't—not at *all*." She moves closer and lowers her tone. "An' by the third lunch date..." Her eyes get big, and she backs away. "He started talkin' about gettin' married." Her eyes get even bigger. "An' buildin' a *house*."

"Had he talked to your mother by then? I mean... I've heard that he talked to your mother early on."

"Right. He did. He met my mama on the second date."

"That seems soon."

"Well, he took me back, an' we were in the..." She stops and gazes into the distance before saying, "Nobody was at the salon, so we were sittin' on the sofa. No... Maybe that was the first date." She pauses. "I remember he was dressed up. Yeah, he looked real good—wearin' a white shirt, starched trousers, his boots an' uh..." She pauses again and raises her finger. "I think he kissed me on the first date. Yeah. I think he did."

"Oh, really?"

"Yeah. An' then, on the second date he took me back, an' we were sittin' there on the sofa. He said he wanted to meet my mom. An' I said, 'Really?' An' he said, 'Yeah, I wanna meet your mom.' He said, 'When can I do that?' An' I said, 'Well, they're in town.' Because they lived out—like twenty miles out in the country. An' so, my brother an' my mom were in town. An' I said, 'Lemme call an' see if Michael will bring 'er by here.' So, I call. An' sure enough, here they come in a little bit. An' with him meetin' my mom..." Terry sits forward and smiles. "He's told everybody. He said my mama was the reason that he married me."

"I've heard that."

"Yeah. Because mama was thirty-four years old when my daddy passed away, an' she never knew another man. Ya know... She raised four kids, an' Poteet really respected that with her."

"How could you not?"

"An' so, anyway... An' then... The third date, he was talkin' about gettin' married. An' that's, ya know... I'm thinkin', 'Whoa...'"

Elliott smiles.

"But I had... I had several boyfriends an' none of 'em knew that I had the other."

"You mentioned that."

Her smile fades. "I mean, that's terrible of me to be that way, Elliott."

He shrugs.

"So, I had to get rid of 'em. I had to get rid of *all* of 'em. I mean... I thought, 'This is the... I can't chance... Because I can't... I don' want my phone ringin' an' me scared they're gonna call me when I'm with 'im, ya know.' 'Cause, I knew where I wanted to be. An' that, to me, was just unbelievable. Because, ya know, I'd never had anybody affect me like he did. An' I'd dated guys with money. Ya know, some people say, 'Well, it was the money...'" She looks over at Elliott and explains, "'Cause Poteet does have money." She looks away and then back. "But I've told 'im a hundred times... I'd live under a picnic table with 'im."

They both laugh.

"It's funny. Yeah. But I would. That's how I feel about 'im. An' uh... I mean, the money's nice, but *I would*... Whatever it takes, ya know, because I have so much respect for him." She looks at Elliott and smiles. "But yeah..."

"It must have sounded silly—talking about getting married on the third date."

"It did. It caught me totally by surprise."

"And these were lunch dates."

"Yeah."

"So, what then?"

She raises her hand like she's swearing on a Bible. "You may not believe this, but it's absolutely true."

Elliott nods and says, "Okay."

"So, I went home, an' I asked God to show me a sign—to jus' make it so plain that even *I* could understand it. An' the *very next mornin'*... I wasn't even thinkin' about Poteet or nothin'. An' the very next mornin' is when that truck backed out right in front of me. An' there was that big emblem. I had to stop. I *had* to stop, an' I knew..."

"...because the truck was in the road. You couldn't get by?"

"Right. It wasn't like it was a highway. It was just a paved road, but it wasn't... Ya know, it was just a country road. An' I knew the ol' boy... I went to school with the ol' boy that backed out in front of me. Orajohn Brewer was his name."

"I guess you were fortunate to not run into him."

"Well, I was goin' slow, ya know. I was goin' slow 'cause I was drivin' the back roads huntin' for a deer on my way to work."

Elliott chuckles. "Really? ... hunting for a deer on your way to work?"

"Yeah. If I'd see a deer, I'd shoot 'im an' put 'im in the trunk. An' that helped me afford to eat."

Elliott sits back and stares at Terry—thinking about how different their lives had been.

She continues, "But anyway... When that truck backed out, ya know, I *did* have to stop. But I was... I mean, it wasn't like a sudden stop or nothin'. But then I saw that emblem."

"What emblem?"

"The one I saw on Poteet's card—the one he give me with his phone number an' email on it—the one that said 'Trail of Tears,' ya know. I told you that he gave me his card."

"Right... So... The truck you stopped for on the road had 'Trail of Tears' written on it?"

"It did. But it had that design too. That's what I'm tryin' to tell ya, Elliott! It had the Trail of Tears logo right on it."

"Wow. That *is* amazing."

"Yes, it was," Terry says, and her friendly smile turns down.

Elliott gives her a moment.

"I had prayed for a sign that I couldn't miss. An' He gave it to me. With that truck, He gave me a sign," Terry says as she removes her glasses and sets them down. She wipes her eyes as Elliott watches. Still holding her glasses in her lap, she adds, "Orajohn had worked for Poteet at the ranch, an' Poteet had sold Orajohn that truck."

"What a coincidence."

She puts her glasses back on and sits up straight. "It wadn' a coincidence, Elliott. I mean, it *wadn'* a coincidence at all." She shakes her head. "It was a sign. It was the sign I had prayed for, Elliott. I mean... 'Cause Orajohn was... This was down there by Hayworth where I'm talkin' about, an' Poteet lived out there on the other side of Idabel."

"I get how you would see it like that."

"Yes. Exactly. So... It was all supposed to be, ya know."

Elliott nods and asks, "So, when did you tell Poteet you were willing to marry him?"

"Well," she says and smiles. "When he first mentioned it, it was like..." She hugs herself with both arms. With her smile growing, almost giggling, and staring dreamily into the distance, she answers, "I didn't know really what to say." She drops her arms and sits forward. "I didn't. 'Cause here I thought, 'Man, I gotta get rid of all these others.'"

"You mentioned that..." Elliott says, and they both laugh.

"Yeah. An' I hate to tell you this... An' please don't put this in any damn movie... But, I even had an engagement ring from one of 'em."

Elliott chuckles and notes, "And even with a ring, you were still 'dating around'?" This time using air quotes...

"Yeah. An' the one in Arkansas had no idea about that or anything else. I mean... An' we'd been datin' off-and-on for about a year. So, it was... I mean, I had to... I was in... I was kind of in a mess."

"And *that's* what was going through your mind when

Poteet was talking marriage."

"Oh yeah. I'm tellin' ya. I was thinkin', 'How am I gonna get outa all this?' But when I saw that sign on the side of that truck, I thought, 'I gotta do whatever it takes. I jus' gotta do it.' An' I mean, I always..." She stops and shakes her head for a moment. "I never was one for a confrontation. An', ya know, I just... I didn't really like 'em, but I didn' like hurtin' anybody's feelings either." She looks away. "But I don't know why I was worried. They really didn't care—probably. Well... One of 'em kinda got a little mad. Well... They both kinda got mad, but... They was blessed they didn't end up with me, I'm tellin' ya. 'Cause I never would've been good to 'em." She turns to look at Elliott. "Ya know it? I wouldn't of..." She sits back and then continues, "But anyway... Yeah... An' so, I got rid of 'em. I had to." She shrugs. "An' I did."

"Okay."

"An' then... Let's see... I believe it was the day before Thanksgivin'. An' Poteet said, 'Why don't you jus' come out here to the studio.'" She pauses to get Elliott's attention, leans forward, and says quietly, "...an' bring some clothes." She hugs herself again, looks starry-eyed at the ceiling, and says with a high-pitched wavering voice, "An' I'm thinkin' 'Oh, my gosh... Oh my gosh...'"

Elliott smiles, and his eyebrows lift.

Terry unwraps her arms as she continues with the delicate, high-pitched voice, "An' so, I did."

"You must have been nervous."

"I was. I really was."

"But you went."

"Yes. I went anyway. And... The next day we got up, an' we went to Mama's house for Thanksgivin' dinner. An' uh... After that, ya know, we've never been apart."

"Nice story."

"But I ain't through," she says, almost singing the words.

"Okay."

"Mr. Jacobs, you need to know this about Poteet."

"What's that?"

"On our first date..."

"Yeah?"

"Ya know, that first time... When we went to lunch..."

"Yeah?"

"Well, Poteet told me that he was abstinent."

Elliott looks over the top of his glasses at Terry and stares.

"Yeah, you heard me," she says, and they chuckle.

"But why? I thought he was a walking encyclopedia of romance."

"You'll have to ask him about that," she says and they laugh.

"Okay. I guess I will."

Terry is still snickering as she says, "Okay. I didn' even know what that word meant. I had no idea."

Elliott chuckles.

"I had to go home an' look it up."

They laugh.

Terry sits back and says, "Elliott, I'm tellin' ya... I was a mess, an' I think you sorta understand. But I'm *so* much better today. I mean it. I try not to say anything ugly or hateful or have anger an' resentment in my heart an' all that stuff."

"Good for you."

"But I was a little mess. Okay? ... *straight out mess*. I was... I was Momma's black sheep. Yeah. But Poteet took that chance on me. An' I'm so blessed. I'm *so* blessed."

"Do you think he knew?"

"He *had* to. I mean everybody in the county knew I was a mess. It wadn' like I was tryin' to be an angel. There was nothin' angelic about me. I was just fun-lovin'. I had a good time pretty much everywhere I went. An' I mean... I was... I did a lot of things that I certainly am not proud of today."

"Well, haven't we all?"

"Yes. An' thank you for sayin' that." She gives Elliott a nod. "But I've done more than most, an' he still took a chance on me." Terry reaches for a tissue, removes her glasses, and dabs around her eyes again. As she puts her glasses back on, she continues, "An' I'm tellin' ya... He gained my respect, because I'd never seen anybody quite like him, ya know. I just had *not*. He was educated. He's very good lookin'. He's strong. I never even knew that people like that were out there. I didn' know I wanted him, 'cause I never had anything—anywhere close to that, ya know." Terry dabs her eyes under her glasses. "I wanna tell ya, Elliott. My life hadn' been easy."

"I've gathered that."

"But yeah, I've been broke in my life. So broke that I had to..."

Elliott sits back.

"Yeah, I could go the Easy Mart an' get a quarter honeybun. An' then, I could go down to Save-A-Lot an' put a quarter in the Coke machine. So... For fifty cents, I had a meal to eat."

"...not much of one."

"That's what I mean. But that's how broke I've been. I mean, I've seen days like that."

"I'll admit. I've never been that broke—not even close."

"Right. But Elliott, that *was* my life."

"I believe you."

"Right. But I wadn't about to ask nobody for no money. I can tell you. I just... I wouldn't do it. But I will tell you... When I was goin' up to take those state boards, ya know... This is before Poteet an' I got married. An' he... He come by the salon, an' he said..."

Elliott interrupts, "So... You had to take a test for your hairdresser's license?"

"Yes. An' I didn' know how I could do it, ya know. I had a

car. I had a little Honda Accord. An' anyway... He said I could drive his car. An' I said, 'Oh, no, no.' Ya know, I wadn' comfortable with doin' *that*. An' this was not long after we'd just had our first date. I don' know exactly, but I wadn' stayin' out there with 'im or nothin' like that. But he handed me an envelope. An' I thought, 'What is *this*?' 'Cause he knew I was gonna go to Oklahoma City, an' I had to take a model. I had to take someone I could do their hair, ya know. You have to take someone with you, an' you have to stay all night. An' I had saved up, I think, a little money from workin'. An' I wadn'... My mama... I wadn' about to ask my poor little ol' mama for... I wouldn't do that. So, he handed me this envelope. Well, I had worked late that night. I think it was dark when I was leavin'. I opened it up, an' I couldn' believe it." She sits up, her eyes widen, and she shakes her head. "He'd given me *ten* one-hundred-dollar bills to go to Oklahoma City." She sits back, still shaking her head. "I'd never had anybody give me that much money—*ever* in my whole life. No way! I couldn'... I mean, I jus' could *not* believe it."

Elliott nods.

Terry looks at her computer screen. And without thinking, she jiggles her mouse. "But man, you talk about a blessin'..." She stares at the screen, and a smile begins to materialize. She moves her hand away from the mouse and looks up. She continues, "An' uh... I remember..." The joy of the memory is obvious on her face. "We went shoppin', an' I got to buy my little granddaughter somethin' for Christmas."

Elliott smiles. "Poteet was generous with you—even then."

She nods slowly. "He was." She breathes deeply. "An' when you've been broke—as broke as you can be, you realize how..." She shakes her head. "Ya know, somethin' like that is a huge deal—a *huge* deal. An' I mean, I jus' never had anybody treat me that good." She sits up. "An', I'm thinkin', 'Wow.'"

"Right."

"But we got it done."

"Okay."

"An' I'm talkin' about the state boards," she says as the corners of her mouth turn up slightly. "Because he helped me."

Elliott nods and starts to speak as Terry says with new energy, "Christmas. It was Christmas..."

Elliott sits back to listen.

She grins. "Yeah. An' it was just a couple a weeks after that."

He smiles.

"We weren't... Ya know, we weren't married yet, but we came to Santa Fe."

"Okay."

Her face lights up, and her eyes sparkle. "Oh, my goodness, I was just like... blown away." Her voice reveals the excitement she remembers. "We did the Canyon Road walk on Christmas Eve, an' the snow... It was big. We stayed over here in a friend's condo, an' it was snowin' *so* hard. We had rented a car in Albuquerque an' drove up here. That night we went to dinner at the Coyote, an' that's when I met Chris an' Heidi. An' then there was Luis. Jose Luis was there, an' that's one of their friends. An', of course, I was a nervous wreck—meetin' all these people that Poteet had known for all those years an' been friends with, ya know. Everything was happenin' just so fast. But... Anyway... It got to snowin' so hard after we got to the Coyote that we had to park the car down there on the street an' *walk* to the condo. Because it couldn't go up the hill." Her eyes widen as she leans forward and looks at Elliott. "An' I'll tell ya somethin' else."

He smiles.

"Let's see," she says as she glances up. "That night at the Coyote..." She taps her fingers on the desk. "I'm thinkin'... Uh... That bill was like four or five *hundred dollars!* An' I'm thinkin'…" She gasps as she sits back and draws her hand to her chest. After a moment, she leans forward, smiles, and says, "Elliott, I'm talkin' Sonic girl here."

They laugh.

"I'm thinkin'… I mean, I've seen times that I was *blessed* to be able to get a Sonic cheeseburger. So, he took me to town an' bought me some boots, ya know—the warm boots. An' he bought me some coats—at these high-dollar places. Elliott, I never had anything like that—*in my life,* ya know. An' he paid all this money for these things. An' I'm thinkin', 'It's just like Cinderella.' Honestly, I felt like Cinderella. An' that's the truth. I thought, 'I've found the love of my life,' an' that's *all* I was thinkin' about. I wadn' thinkin' about his ranch, his money, or nothin'. That wadn't even in there for me. So, on the fifth of January we went to Arkansas to get married. For our two witnesses, it was my mom an' my brother. Ya know, Michael knew Poteet. He'd been goin' to the gym with Poteet for a while."

"You mentioned that."

"In fact, that Thanksgivin' Day, Michael was the one that told us at dinner that Poteet was a famous artist. An' I thought, 'I didn't know *famous.*' I didn't know about that. I knew he was an artist, 'cause I'd been seein' him do his work, ya know. I saw his work out there at the ranch. But I thought, '*Famous?*' I had no idea what status he was. But it all jus' felt like a Cinderella story for me. It really did. It felt like the prince had put my glass slipper on." She nods. "Honestly, Elliott, it did."

"I believe you. Sounds like a Cinderella story to me too."

She holds up her hand and index finger as if to say, "…one more thing."

"Okay."

"When Poteet an' I first got married an' I was goin' to the grocery store, he tol' me, 'You don't have to buy off-brands.' Because… Man, all my life I'd bought off-brands. An' with

Poteet, I got to go to the grocery store an' buy *Del Monte*—an' all these other high-dollar brands."

They both crack up.

"That's funny," Elliott eventually says.

"An' then, ya know, it all changed to organic."

They laugh again.

"An' you know about that."

"Oh, yeah. We do it too."

"So... We moved out here, an' we had to work to get everything done, ya know." She looks around. "We didn' even have any of this office stuff in here. We found us a desk somewhere at the secondhand store. Anyway, I wouldn't..."

"Well, it's a great place now. That's for sure."

"Oh, yeah. So, we opened those doors on February the fourteenth."

"Right after you were married?"

"Yeah. An' that first day, it was cold an' snowin'. It was 2009 an' not much was happenin' out here. But that day... An' I mean... I didn' even really have decent clothes to wear, ya know. I think I had on blue jeans an' a sweatshirt. An' that day we opened the door..."

"...right here?"

"Yeah...right here. An' I had seen these people out walkin' around, like the day before. I talked to 'em an' found out they were from Oklahoma. They was from Tulsa. Well, I'd been out here like a little over a week, an' I'm thinkin', 'Oklahoma people feel kinda like kinfolks to me.' Ya know, I'm kinda... An' here my family was seven hundred fifty miles away. An' so, anyway... I'd met 'em an' thought the world of 'em an' everything. An' then, that day we opened the door. Like I said... It was cold an' snowy. An' I look up." She points. "Right here at this window, an' I see 'em, all four of 'em—two couples walkin' in. So, I run out there, an' I hug their necks. 'Cause I was happy to see 'em."

"Yeah?"

"An' that day, I sold the biggest painting in the gallery. It was Poteet's, an' I sold it for $31,500."

"Good start."

"I'm tellin' ya... An' I'm thinkin', 'I believe I like this job.'"

They laugh together.

Buoyantly, she adds, "I can do this."

They laugh some more.

Still smiling, Elliott watches Terry—waiting for whatever is next.

She sits back and says, "An' that's the end of my Cinderella story."

"So... You lived happily ever after."

"Well, I can't say that. Ya know, we have our days..."

"Sure. Who doesn't?" Elliott says and nods quietly. After a moment he adds, "That's quite a story."

"It is. But that's jus' what happened."

Elliott continues to sit as he thinks about what he could do with this very unusual Cinderella story. He eventually says, "Well, thanks for telling me."

Sitting up straight, Terry says, "I like to tell it."

Elliott chuckles and stands. "I think it's time for me to go see Poteet."

Remaining seated, Terry says, "I'll check in on y'all after a while. I've got a few things to do down here first."

Elliott looks at Terry, nods, and grabs his recorder. He then reaches for his satchel and heads for the door. Instead of going immediately to Poteet's studio, he walks outside to make a call. When he has Judy Hightower on the line, he says, "I just talked to Terry about how she and Poteet got together."

"Oh yeah?"

"And you won't believe it. I got it recorded, and you've got to listen to it."

"Of course."

"It's good. It's amazing. And... I just wanted to tell you that your instincts on Poteet have been right so far."

"Thank you."

"That's it. I'll talk to you later."

"Okay. Bye."

CHAPTER 7

Early Life

Poteet is applying paint to one of his canvases, when he hears a knock. He turns to say, "Come on in."

Elliott pushes through and smiles. Poteet grabs a rag to wipe his hands. They greet each other with a handshake.

Elliott shows the recorder to Poteet and sets it on the table. Poteet nods his approval.

As he fiddles to get the recorder going, Elliott says, "I just had a nice chat with Terry."

"Oh yeah? Wha'd y'all talk about?"

"...children, failed marriages and some about you."

Poteet smiles and says with a questioning tone, "...failed marriages?"

Elliott chuckles and says, "Yeah."

"Well, I'm an expert on that."

"I know. And I know she's the fifth. I asked her about that." Poteet shakes his head.

"Don't worry. It was all good. But I think I need to hear more—particularly your side of the story."

Poteet chuckles to himself and moves to retrieve his painting knife.

"But we can do that at another time. I have a different

agenda for today."

"Okay."

"As I mentioned last time, I want to know more about your life as a kid."

"Sure."

"But, before we get into that, I've got to tell you about what's happening on my end."

"Okay."

"Well... We have a meeting every week where we talk about stories, storylines, and anything we might have working. So naturally, we've talked about you. And there's a lot of interest in your story." He looks at Poteet. "But still, we've got a long way to go. We've not committed to anything yet."

"Sure."

Elliott sits on the stool Poteet had placed for him earlier.

They both turn to look at Terry as she appears at the double doors.

She asks, "Can I come in?"

Elliott turns and answers, "Please join us."

As Terry sits by the fireplace, she looks at Poteet and says quietly, "Elliott knows the Kleppers."

"Pam and Jim?" Poteet asks with his face showing surprise.

"Yeah."

He turns to look at Elliott who smiles and nods confirmation.

Elliott explains, "I'd already heard about you from them. And then... When Judy verified the connection between you and Willy, I had to come."

"I see," Poteet says as he nods. He then adds, "Okay."

Elliott looks at Terry and then at Poteet. He asks, "Are you ready to proceed?"

"Sure."

Elliott glances at his notes before saying to Poteet, "I heard you had it pretty rough as a kid."

"I did."

"...and you were born in Idabel, Oklahoma?"

"I was, an' I was lucky to even survive my first day," Poteet says and sets his painting knife down.

"Oh yeah?"

"The doctor that delivered me... He induced labor, an' actually I was a month early. I don't know why he did it. I asked Mother about it, an' she said, 'I can't remember why.' But..."

"Wadn' he a drunk?" Terry asks.

Elliott chuckles.

"No."

"Oh, okay. I thought that doctor was a drunk."

"No... No, he wadn'. Uh... But... Yeah... 'Cause, when I was born, I was hemorrhagin' out of my... Mother said. '...my eyes, my ears, my nose, my mouth...' So, they rushed me over to Texarkana to a larger hospital, an' uh... That doctor told 'er over there... He said that it's a wonder that the doctor that delivered me didn't kill me."

"That's a rough start," Elliott notes.

"It was, an' it happened again about two years later. I mean, the bleedin' part."

"...you mean, bleeding from your nose and ears and all that?"

"Yeah. When I was two, my uncle dropped me on my head."

"Huh. It's a wonder you're okay."

"At that time, the doctors didn't know how I'd be."

"I understand."

Poteet turns to pick up his painting knife and continues, "But anyway, we didn' have much of a family. My Mother... She, ya know..." He shakes his head. "So... When I was young,

I hardly knew my dad. He left when I was five."

"What was his name?"

"Ed."

"Speaking of names, I was told that you added 'Victory' to your name at some point."

"I did. 'Victory' was my Cherokee grandmother's family name, an' there wadn' anyone on that side to carry it on. So... Ya know... All my life I'd been Robert Lee Poteet. I just added 'Victory' to that."

"Is your name then: Robert Poteet Victory?"

"Legally, I still have 'Lee' as a middle name. So, actually it's Robert Lee Poteet Victory."

"I see."

"It was my cousin Beth. She suggested that I do it. I liked the idea, so that's what I did."

"Okay...makes sense. I wondered how that happened. It doesn't matter. I was just curious."

"Sure. I'll admit that it's a little unusual."

"Right. But, back to your immediate family..."

"Okay."

"We were talking about your father."

"Right. When I was five..."

"So, he and your mother got divorced?"

"Yeah, they did."

"And then, your father wasn't around."

"Right. He wadn'. An' ya know, I held that against 'im forever. But as I got older, I started to realize that, ya know, he fought in World War II. He had PTSD. 'Cause Mother told me that... She said, 'Ya know, your dad was never the same after he come back from the war.' An' he became an alcoholic. He died when he was 52, just from drinkin' too much. An' then... Mother started livin' with this guy. Uh... He was pretty much an alcoholic himself. He was a bootlegger."

"...a bootlegger?"

"Yeah." Poteet says and chuckles. "An' uh... This one house we lived in... Ya know, there'd be guys pullin' up late at night. They'd go out there an' unload the whisky. But Mother... She told me... She said, 'Now, you don' ever tell nobody nothin'. You don't know anything.' She said, 'Cause some of the feds may ask you questions, but you don't tell 'em nothin'. An' uh... So, they had this thing in the house, like in this room here." Poteet uses his painting knife to point generally at the floor. He then walks to the door behind his easels and points through it. He says, "You'd go around the corner, an' that was the bathroom." He walks back to his painting table and continues. "Well, in the bathroom was a big full-length mirror, an' uh... If you got that mirror open, that whole wall was full of whiskey bottles."

Elliott chuckles.

"...yeah, whiskey bottles. An' the only way you could get to it. You had to come in this room..." He points again at the floor. "...an' pull that plate aside." He points at the wall. "You'd stick an Allen wrench in there an' turn it. An' that would open it."

"Like the plate on an electrical outlet?"

"Uh-huh. But you could do that, an' the mirror would open."

"Wow."

"An' we had the feds come out there more than once when I was little, an' they'd ask me questions. An' I'd go, 'I don' know. I don' know.'"

"I guess you probably knew more than what you..."

"Oh, I knew all of it."

Elliott and Terry laugh.

Poteet chuckles.

"So, they never found the hidden closet?" Elliott asks.

"Nope—never found it."

Elliott grins.

"Boy, they searched everywhere too. Ya know, we had a

barn out there. An' they searched that... But naw, they never... They never found anything."

"That's pretty sophisticated."

"Yeah, it was. An' he never got caught either. They caught a bunch of 'em around there, but they never caught him," Poteet says and chuckles. "Yeah... I was... I was a little outlaw an' didn' know it."

All three laugh.

Poteet turns to mix paint on his palette.

"With all those law enforcement people coming into the house... I mean, that must've been frightening for a little kid," Elliott says.

"Well... Actually, it wadn'. 'Cause I never... Ya know, there was never any reason for me to be... Ya know, at that age—to be afraid of a cop."

"Yeah?"

"'Cause... Like the police in town, I knew 'em all."

Poteet turns to his canvas and starts applying the paint.

"Well, I'm surprised it didn't frighten you anyway. It just seems like all that activity and... Surely, they were coming in with guns drawn, and..."

"They did."

"But you really weren't frightened?"

"No, I don't ever remember bein' frightened."

"Huh."

"No. It was... It was like... I was just *bewildered*."

Elliott chuckles and Terry smiles.

"Ya know... Lookin' around, goin, 'What the hell?' Yeah... But I knew that somebody was gonna get in trouble if they found that whiskey."

Elliott nods.

Poteet turns to his painting table and palette. He says, "Or, if I talked about it or anything..."

Elliott nods and says, "That seems like a lot of responsibility for a kid."

"I guess it was, but I never thought about it in those terms. But... Ya know... If they'd a busted him, they'd a busted Mother too."

"That's probably true."

"An' I never thought about it like that."

"So, you lived at the house where your mother was—with the bootlegger?"

"Sometimes I would be there. But sometimes... I stayed at the house that Mother owned there—that her an' Daddy had built... But, she didn' live there."

"Oh, I see. She lived with the guy at his place, and you lived at her house. So that's how you kind of lived away from her."

"Exactly. An' I would... I'd stay there by myself, ya know— as a little kid."

Terry adds, "... when he was just five years old."

"Yeah. It was a strange situation. It really was." Poteet turns away from his painting to face Elliott. "Mother would give me money every now an' then, but I knew she couldn' help me much. 'Cause the guy she was with wouldn't let 'er, ya know."

"Hmm... So, to get help from your mother, she had to do it—kind of on the sly."

"Yeah... Yeah she did." Poteet sighs. "Yeah, she did. When I was little, I could be gone for days, an' nobody'd even ask, 'Where's he at?'"

Terry adds, "...like seven years old."

"Yeah, I could be gone for days."

"I can't imagine," Elliott responds.

Terry says, "I can't either."

"Well, lookin' back on it, I can't either. An' I remember...a lot of my friends, ya know, they'd have to be home. We'd be out playin' an' stuff..."

"Sure, when it was getting dark or something like that."

"Yeah. An' I remember thinkin', ya know, I wish I had a

family. 'Cause they'd go home to their families, an' I didn'. I'd just go home. Ya know, one Saturday we decided to go explorin' back in the woods, an' everybody got lost. We all got lost. An'... 'Course, the parents were goin' crazy. The cops were lookin' for us an' everything. An' uh... We found our way back. All the parents were there." He shakes his head. "But... Mine wadn'. I jus' walked on home."

"That's sad."

"I can remember when I was little. Uh... If I got hungry, I'd jus' go knock on somebody's door. Everybody knew me. An' I'd say, 'I'm hungry. ...got anything to eat?' They'd always be friendly. They'd say, 'Oh yeah. Come on in.'"

Elliott takes a deep breath and then asks, "Did your mother try to protect you by getting you out of the bootlegger's house? Was that what that was about?"

"No."

"So, it was your choice to leave."

"Yeah. That's the way it was. Naw, she didn't try to get me out of it. It was... Ya know, it was my choice. An' she was all right with it. Like I say, we never were that close. I think I was probably a big inconvenience—for her. Ya know."

Elliott shakes his head and stares at Poteet's painting in progress. After a few seconds, he says, "Someone mentioned this, and I wanted to ask you about it."

"Okay."

"It was when you were five, I think, and you..."

"Yeah. When I was in the closet?"

"Yeah. I think so."

"You're talkin' about seein' Jesus?"

"Yeah. Do you remember that?"

"Yeah, I remember it. I really have a good memory—especially for things when I was young. I don' know why, but I jus'..."

"Your mother had given you the Bible, right?" Terry asks.

63

"Yeah. She had given me that Bible, an' it had pictures in it. Soon after she gave it to me, I saw Jesus in my closet." Poteet nods and adds, "I remember it clearly."

"So, you really did see Jesus in your closet?" Elliott asks.

"I did."

"I would guess that something like that would make an impression."

"Yeah, it did."

"Did it change your life?"

"Lookin' back, I'd say 'Yeah.'"

"Hmm... Like how?"

Poteet stares out the north window for a moment and then says, "Among other things, it caused me to think about the spiritual side of my life. An' to tell you the truth, that's been a meaningful journey for me. An' uh... I think it's an important part of life that people should look into."

Elliott nods.

They hear noise downstairs. Terry stands and heads for the door. She says, "I need to see who's here."

Elliott says, "Sure," as she walks by.

Poteet continues, "An' ya know... No one ever took me to church. But I'd show up—every Sunday mornin'."

"Would you really?"

"Oh yeah—at all the different churches in town."

"At what age?"

"I don' know...five, six..."

"When you were five or six years old?"

"Yeah."

"And that's when you were on your own—roaming around town."

"Yeah, I'd go to church. Uh... I used to love to go to the Presbyterian Church 'cause they'd let me ring the bell."

Elliott smiles.

"It'd lift me completely off the ground, ya know." Poteet

chuckles. "I'd go to that one. I'd go to the Methodist Church. I'd go to the Baptist Church."

"Hmm..."

"They all knew me."

"Yeah? ...like, to Sunday school? Would you go to Sunday school? Or would you go to the whole thing?"

"I'd go to Sunday school. Yeah. That's mainly what I did—was go to Sunday school, an' uh... Yeah. So, it's kind of been with me throughout my whole life, ya know. I was exposed to it then. An' uh... Yeah... Like I say, I can't remember anybody ever takin' me to church or Sunday school. I'd just get up an' go."

"Hmm... That's very unusual."

"I guess it is."

Elliott sits quietly for a moment before saying, "I don't know why I thought of this, but did your mother get child support from your father?"

"No. She didn'."

"Seems like she would have."

"He wouldn' a paid it."

"You told me that they went through a divorce."

"Yeah."

"It must have all been legal."

"It was. But, ya know... Back then, they didn' enforce those laws like they do today. An'... But yeah... I mean, he could've helped us, but he didn'. An' uh... Yeah... I think that's one reason why she hated 'im, ya know."

"Yeah."

Poteet shakes his head and adds, "'Cause he didn'... He didn' help his children."

"Yeah. I can see that. It seems to me that you could have been angry about your father not coming around, after the divorce."

"Yeah... I was angry."

"He could have come around."

Poteet says slowly, "Yes... He could've."

"Alright... So, tell me. Where was your dad from?"

"Uh... He was born there in Oklahoma—way up in the mountains. It was near Wright City, which is probably about... I don' know... close to forty miles away. An' back then, people didn' get very far out of their hometowns, ya know."

"Yeah."

"A five- or ten-mile radius was about as far as people traveled."

"I guess that's true—and especially up there where he's from."

"Yeah. But Grandpa, my father's father, he was Choctaw. I never did know 'im. He died before I was born. He wadn' full-blood, but he was Choctaw. Ya know, I've got the court records from 1902 where his family... Ya know, you had to appear before the Dawes Commission to be put on the tribal rolls."

"Right."

"My dad's family tried to get on, but their claim was rejected. One of 'em that went had blue eyes or somethin' like that."

"Hmm."

"But... A lot of 'em didn' wanna get put on the tribal rolls. 'Cause then, they would've become wards of the state, an' some didn' want that."

"I see."

"But my sister knew my dad's father." Poteet smiles. "She was five the last time she saw 'im, but she still remembers 'im. She tol' me, 'He had the biggest damn corral I've ever seen.' My grandfather had horses in the mountains up there. Once a year, they'd round 'em up. That corral was where they'd bring all the horses. They'd put 'em in there, brand 'em, an' get 'em ready to sell."

Elliott turns to notice Terry peeking through the door. She

smiles at Elliott and walks in quietly.

Poteet looks at her and asks, "Well, did ya sell somethin'?"

"No, but I think they'll come back. I just got that feelin' from 'em."

When Terry is seated, Poteet continues, "They met when my mother was sixteen. Daddy had joined the CCC."

Elliott nods and looks away. "I think that was a government program—started during the depression."

"Yeah, it was. So, he joined that, an' they stationed 'im down there at Idabel. An' Mother said... After school, that her an' her sisters would stand out there an' watch the CC boys come marchin' by, ya know. An' I guess Mother picked out Daddy—he was a good-lookin' guy. An' she told her sisters... She said, 'I'm gonna marry that guy right there.' An' she did."

Terry says, "She was a hellion, wadn' she, Poteet?"

"She sure was."

"I mean, she shot two men."

Elliott's eyes get big and Terry laughs.

She continues, "Yeah. An' there ain't no tellin' how many she whipped."

"Oh, yeah..." Poteet says. "She was bad. She was bad for a woman. I mean... Men were afraid of 'er."

Elliott asks, "And the guys she shot?"

"Well... One of 'em was my dad. She shot him."

Terry starts to chuckle.

"An' uh..."

Elliott asks, "Did she kill him?"

"Huh-uh... Didn' kill 'im. An' uh... This other guy... I don't..."

Terry continues to chuckle.

Elliott thinks it's funny too.

Poteet grins and then begins to chuckle himself.

Soon, all three are laughing.

Terry grins and says, "Elliott, you're dealin' with outlaws here, boy."

Their laughter notches higher.

CHAPTER 8

Cafe/Beer Joint

Elliott turns to Poteet to say, "Thinking about our conversation the other day..."

"Right."

"I can see that you're very connected to your Indian heritage."

"I am. An' I've always known who I was."

"Okay," Elliott says and looks away for a moment. He smiles and adds, "I've wanted to ask you some more about that. But right now, I want to know more about what you just said about your mother."

Poteet and Terry chuckle.

Terry says, "You didn' mess with Dorothy."

They all laugh.

Elliott says, "I guess not. But what I wanted to ask... It's about your dad... Was the shooting before or after their divorce?"

Terry and Poteet chuckle.

Poteet answers, "After."

"So, he'd come around?"

"Yeah."

"I guess he shouldn't have," Elliott says with a smile.

With a sly grin, Poteet responds, "Probably not."

All three laugh again.

"So... What do you remember about your father? I know he left when you were five."

"Yeah."

"You probably have some impressions or memories of him."

"Well..." Poteet looks at the floor and then back at his painting on the easel before saying, "Thinkin' about those early days... I really don't remember much, 'cause he was always gone."

"So, even before they were divorced, he wasn't around— much."

"No. He was always... He was pipelinin'. An' uh... I remember... When I would see 'im, I was... Ya know, he was my daddy, an' I was crazy about 'im. But I didn't see 'im that much."

"So... After the divorce, your mother must have provided food for you?"

"She did."

"Even though you lived apart, and her bootlegger boyfriend didn't allow for her to give you money..."

"Right."

"...food would somehow show up at the house?"

"No—not really. But she always had a little café down on Skid Row. An' uh... It was a café an' a beer joint, ya know. So, I would... Like, when I was in school, I'd go eat down there. But, talkin' 'bout my mother... She was tough, but she had to be. She owned that beer joint an' all."

"I guess that's true."

"But I... Ya know... Growin' up down there, I saw violence all the time...guys fightin' an' shit...*all the time*. Yeah. That was a rough place."

"I'm sure it was."

"But it wadn' all bad. ...bein' round there—down on Skid Row an' all, when I was little. I met a lot of colorful characters. An' I remember some of 'em."

"Oh yeah?" Elliott responds and chuckles.

"An' the other kids didn't get to do that."

"True."

"But yeah... I..."

"I guess, it all contributed to your background."

"It did."

"...and your understanding of the world."

"Yeah... An' I remember... There was a soldier who come in there one day in uniform, an' he was eatin'. So, I sat down an' talked to 'im. An' when he got ready to leave, he asked for a pencil an' a piece of paper. So, I gave it to 'im, an' he wrote a passage from the Bible. It was Matthew 6:6. He handed it to me, an' he said, 'You remember this.' An' I didn' know. So, I said, 'Okay,' an'... So, I took it back, an' I showed it to Mother. She had a Bible there, an' she opened it up. An' I don' know why he did it, but that's the passage that says, 'When you pray, pray in secret.' Ya know, this is between you an' God. An' it said somethin' about, 'Go into your closet.' Well, that kind of meant somethin' to me, because of that experience, ya know, that I had—in the closet."

"Yeah."

"But I never saw that guy again. Mother didn' know who he was."

"Huh..."

"An' there was this other guy. He was an' ol' black man, an' his name was Julius. I don' remember his last name. But ol' Julius would come in there. An' I remember Mother tellin' me. She said, 'You ever talk to Julius?' An' I said, 'No.' She said, "You oughta talk to 'im.' So, I did. I'd go back there an' sit down with him, an' I talked to 'im—a lot. Ya know, every time he'd come in, I'd say, 'Hi' to 'im or sit down an' start talkin'."

"Hmm."

"An' uh... Yeah... He told me that he could remember his mama pickin' cotton. She was holdin' 'im with one arm an' pickin' cotton with the other. An' he was actually livin'... Yeah... as a slave on a plantation."

"...as a slave?"

"Yeah, there's not many people who can say they actually knew a slave."

"No. Huh-uh," Elliott says quietly.

"Well, I did. I knew 'im. I knew ol' Julius."

Elliott nods. "Well... What did he tell you?"

"I don't... I can't... I was so little. I don't remember."

"Yeah, 'cause you were... You had to be just what? ...five, six, seven—years old."

"I don' know. At that time, I was probably... I don' know—seven or eight."

Elliott closes his eyes and looks up. After a moment, he says, "Well, the Civil War started in the mid-1860s or so. I'd say, he had to have been born in the early 1860s, or more like the late 1850s."

"Yeah. That's probably right."

"And this was the mid-fifties when you were talking to him, right?"

Poteet nods.

"So, he *was* old—maybe not a hundred yet, but probably pretty close."

"Yeah."

Elliott adds, "But I'm pretty sure I've never talked to anybody that had ever been an actual slave."

After a moment, Poteet says, "Yeah... I mean, at the time, I didn'... It didn't register on me, ya know. I really didn' understand anything about slaves, slavery..."

"Yeah. You were young," Elliott says and brings his index finger to his lips. He narrows his eyes, cocks his head, and looks to the side. He looks back at Poteet and asks, "Did she have a separate room for her African-American customers?"

"She did," Poteet answers and nods. "It was a separate room. But Mother wadn' prejudiced. She wadn'. She was not a prejudiced person."

"But on the face of it..." Elliott says, cocks his head, and shrugs. "She had a separate room for African Americans." He lifts his chin, and stares down his nose at Poteet.

"You couldn't call her a racist, because she wadn'—at all. In Idabel, Oklahoma, it was the custom at the time. Ya know, she was jus' tryin' to scratch out a livin'—pretty much like everybody else. An' white people wouldn' a come in there if it hadn' been that way."

"No, they probably wouldn't have."

"They wouldn't have. But it didn't keep me from goin' in there an' talkin' to Julius."

"That's true, and I think that speaks to your claim of her not being prejudiced. She wouldn't have promoted your friendship with him if she had been."

"I think that's true. That's exactly true."

Elliott nods and seems to be somewhat relieved. "So, you mentioned characters you met at your mother's cafe. Were there others?"

"Oh yeah... Sure... One of 'em was an ol' Indian chief. He come in there one day... An' uh... His name was John Tonika. An' he was a hundred an' four years old. An' that man had the biggest nose I've ever seen on a human being."

Elliott and Terry laugh.

"An' I'm not shittin' ya."

They become animated with their laughter, and Poteet joins in.

Poteet eventually says, "Yeah..."

The comment seems to make the situation even more comical. After a few moments, he adds, "Yeah, I talked to him too."

Elliott makes a loud sigh as the humor ebbs.

Still buoyed by this thought from the past, Poteet adds, "Yeah. ...ol' John Tonika."

Elliott takes a deep breath and says, "Wow..."

"He was a Choctaw," Poteet notes and grabs his cup. He asks, "How about some coffee?"

As he's considering a cup, Elliott thinks about Poteet's tough early life. It wasn't about life on a reservation, which was disappointing. But it was certainly a hard upbringing. It was a struggle. It was a fight. It was tough every day. And... It was so different from his own early-life experiences.

CHAPTER 9

Grandma

Regarding the coffee, Terry responds, "No, thanks."

Poteet looks at Elliott and says, "I make good coffee."

Elliott cracks a smile, "You talked me into it, I guess. Thanks."

Poteet heads into his little kitchen and starts making noises. He yells, "Elliott, do you like cream and sugar?"

"No—just black." Elliott then turns to Terry and asks quietly, "Did you know about all this Indian stuff?"

She nods. "Most of it. I knew about his interest in the Trail of Tears, of course. He's always talked a lot about that."

"He's mentioned the Trail of Tears to me, but he won't say what happened to him at the University of Oklahoma."

"There're several reasons for that. I think he mostly wants to leave that behind 'im an' move on."

"I hope he'll open up to me at some point. I get the feeling that's an important part of his story."

"It is, for sure," she says and turns to look at Elliott. "But that'll be up to him to decide."

"Of course."

They sit quietly and listen to the sounds of clanking cups and a machine making coffee.

After a few moments, Terry breaks the silence, "I've been thinkin'."

Elliott turns to Terry with a curious look.

"You an' Poteet have been talkin' about his childhood."

"Yeah."

"An' it was tough, jus' like you said. But he did have some family around."

Elliott turns his gaze away for a moment before saying, "I know he had his mother and his sister."

"Right—an' his grandma. I know he would sometimes stay with her when he was little."

Poteet walks out with two unmatched ceramic cups filled with steaming coffee and says, "Yeah, I was close to Grandma." He sets one down on the table next to Elliott and one on his painting table. "I still think about 'er a lot. An' she was always good to me. She was one of those hard workers, ya know."

"Did she live in Idabel?"

Poteet nods and says, "Yeah." He takes a sip and sets his cup back down. "Yeah, she was born in the 1800s an' came to Oklahoma in a covered wagon. She had four daughters. My mother was the youngest. An' yeah, I think about 'er often. She was probably one of the most practical people I've ever been around."

"What about your grandfather on that side?"

"Well... Way before I was born, her an' her husband got divorced. I never knew what the deal was about that. He lived there in the town. He was actually the Fire Chief. An' uh... That man never spoke to me." Poteet looks at Elliott. "Now, idn' that weird? I mean, I look back on it, an'... I'm thinkin', ya know... There I was, his grandson, an' he never spoke to me."

"You mean, never?"

"Huh-uh... No. An' I... Still to this day, I'm thinkin', 'What the hell's wrong with him?' Ya know?"

"Yeah. I agree with that. Yeah. I mean, that *is* totally weird."

"But yeah... I remember when he died... My mother told me about it. She said, 'You gonna come to his funeral?' An' I said, 'Well, hell no. Why would I? I didn't even know the son of a bitch.'"

"Hmm."

"But, thinkin' about my grandmother..."

"Yeah?"

"She'd get up every mornin' at four o'clock, rain or shine or snow or whatever. An' she'd go out there an' milk two... two or three cows—by hand. An' then... If I was around, I'd get to churn the butter."

"I guess you liked to do that."

"Mmm... Most of the time I did. But she was tight with a dollar. Whoo!" Poteet says and chuckles.

Elliott and Terry snicker and chuckle too.

Elliott says, "Well, she worked hard to get it."

Still chuckling, Poteet says, "Yeah, she did."

Terry says, "I know you asked her for a penny one time."

"Yeah. I wanted a penny, so I could run down to the store to get me a sucker. She wouldn' give it to me."

Terry laughs.

"I hadn't earned it."

Terry says "Yeah," and Poteet chuckles. She continues, "From what Poteet's told me 'bout 'er, she loved animals."

Elliott grins.

Poteet smiles. "An' just about any animal that I wanted... Well, she'd get it for me. I remember... When I was real little, uh... She bought me a pig—a white pig."

Elliott laughs. "Did you ask for a pig? "

"I guess. His name was Blue Boy."

Elliott repeats, "...Blue Boy."

"So, when Blue Boy was little, she'd let me bring 'im into

the house, ya know."

"Yeah?"

"An' then he got started growin', an' I'd ride 'im around in the front yard. An' when he got big... Well, she wouldn't let me bring 'im into the house anymore. An' that pissed me off."

Elliott chuckles.

"But... An' then, I don't remember what happened to 'im. I think, one day he was jus' gone, ya know. She didn' tell me."

"Do you remember having any bacon?"

Poteet grins and says quietly, "Yeah."

Elliott and Terry laugh.

"An' uh... She didn't like horses, 'cause they'd bite the cows."

"I didn't know that."

"Yeah. So, she didn't..."

"So, horses and cows can't be in a pen together?"

"No... She'd... No... But I remember havin' rabbits. I had hamsters. I had guinea pigs, ya know? An' I... I think that's an important part for a kid too. Uh... Because you have to take care of 'em. That teaches you responsibility, an' I think she may've known that."

"So, your grandma was a good influence on you."

"Yeah, she was. Yeah. 'Cause she was real calm. Ya know... She didn't get upset."

"Hmm."

"So... If I needed to be punished, she'd... We had a willow tree out in the backyard, an' I'd have to go out there, an' uh... She'd say, 'Go out there an' cut a switch.' So, I'd cut a switch. It might be a little ol' bitty switch."

They all laugh.

"I'd bring it back in... 'No, no—not big enough. Go get me another one.' An' uh... An' when she started to whip me, I'd jump in the bed an' pull the blanket up over me. Boy, she'd just whip that blanket. An' I'd holler." Poteet looks at Elliott with a smile. "Ya know, I didn' feel nothin'."

They chuckle and laugh.

"But she... Yeah, she wadn' tryin' to hurt me. She never did... I think the maddest she ever got at me... Was... Ya know, she had milk cows. She was pretty particular about her milk cows. Ya know, she didn' want 'em to get upset, 'cause it affected the milk. An' uh... She caught me one day... 'Cause they'd be out there layin' down chewin' their cud."

Elliott grins.

"An' I'd sneak out there an' jump on 'em."

Poteet, Elliott, and Terry laugh again.

Chuckling, Poteet says, "Boy, she tore my ass up for that. Yeah, she didn' like that one bit."

Elliott sighs from the laughter.

"I remember one time we were... We were pickin' blackberries. An' I was a little bitty shit. I don't know how old I was. I know I wadn' in school. An' uh... But I remember this very clearly. Over there where we lived it was kind of swampy. Ya know, a lot of water an' stuff. An' uh... These water moccasins would get over there in the blackberry patches to catch birds. The birds'd come down to get the berries. But I remember... I do remember this. I can still see it in my mind— that there was a water moccasin an' he was coiled up. An' I was lookin' at 'im. I didn't know what it was. An' I remember he had his mouth open. It was just pure white. An' I was like, gettin' closer an' closer. An' I was just about to reach out an' touch that snake. Grandma grabbed me by the back of the neck. She said, 'No! That's a snake. You can't do that.'"

"Wow," Elliott says. "That was a close call."

Poteet chuckles and shakes his head. "My grandma... She'd say she was afraid of snakes. But I guarantee... You give her a hoe, an' she'd attack a python."

All three laugh.

Terry says, "Tell 'im 'bout that ol' turkey."

79

Elliott chuckles.

"Wadn' it a turkey?" Terry asks.

"Oh yeah, the turkey... Yeah. Grandma had... Ya know, we had a barnyard, but she always had all kinds of animals. An' uh... I wadn' very old." He chuckles. "But... I had to worry... Every time I'd go out in the barnyard... We had a big ol' tom turkey."

Elliott and Terry begin to chuckle.

"An' that son of a bitch would chase me..."

Elliott's chuckle turns into a laugh.

"An' I was scared of 'im. An' uh... But one day I made up my mind. I thought, 'All right, I've had enough of this.'"

Elliott and Terry grin.

"So... I picked up a rock—a pretty big rock... An' I went out there. An' boy, here he come after me. He run right up to me, an' I went, whack!" Poteet demonstrates with a swipe of his arm. Grinning and chuckling, Poteet says, "I hit him right in the head."

All three laugh.

Still chucklng, Poteet says, "...knocked 'im down, ya know. An' uh..."

Elliott asks, "...didn't kill him though, I guess."

"I didn't kill 'im. Then uh... So... He run around there for a few days with his ol' head hung over."

Elliott and Terry chuckle.

"Grandma said, '...wonder what's wrong with that turkey?' I told her... I said, 'I don' know.'"

Terry, Poteet, and Elliott all laugh.

Terry says, "She probably knew, Poteet."

"But I'll tell you what... He never come after me again. An' that was the end of that."

Elliott sighs and says, "Whoa..."

"But... Grandma didn't need much."

"Oh yeah?" Elliott asks softly.

"She was pretty self-sufficient. She raised her own food... ya know. She was... always... She was the one who'd get up— four o'clock every mornin'... go out an' milk the cows, an' always... I mean... flowers, all over the yards, ya know. An' she was always doin' somethin'... But, one day she sold her cows."

"Hmm..."

"She was like eighty somethin' years old."

"Well, you can't blame her for that."

"That's true, but she didn' slow down much. An' one day she was up on a damn step ladder—hangin' wallpaper..."

Elliott grins but says, "Oh my gosh!"

Poteet chuckles. "An' she fell off."

Trying to throttle the laugh, Elliott tries to empathize by saying, "Oh, no."

"An' broke 'er hip..."

Elliott dials up the concern, "No..."

"An everybody said, 'Well, that's... That'll probably be the end of Ms. Davis.' Yeah... But, in a few months, she's around an' back at it again. She didn' have a hip replacement or nothin'."

"It just healed?"

"I guess. Yeah." Poteet chuckles. "She was..."

"She was quite a woman."

"Yeah, she was. Like I said, I still think about 'er a lot."

Elliott nods.

"Yeah... Grandma... You never could tell about her. You couldn't ever tell if she was serious, or... She was always real dry, ya know... My mother finally got 'er into a nursin' home. She didn' wanna go, of course. But they finally got 'er into one. An' Mother said she was sittin' there one day—out front. An' somebody come up an' saw Grandma sittin' there an' said, 'Ms. Davis... I didn't know you were here in the nursin' home.' She said, 'Nursin' home! Hell, I thought I was at the court-house.'"

Elliott laughs hard. And then, Poteet and Terry laugh just as hard.

When he catches his breath, Elliott asks, "So how old did she live to be?"

"...'bout ninety."

"Hmm...ninety."

"Yeah... An' a funny thing..."

Elliott chuckles.

"Ya know, she hadn' been in the nursin' home that long, an' Mother says that she was out there one day... Mother's name was Dorothy. She said, 'Dorothy, ya know, I think I'll just go ahead an' die.' She said, 'Oh, don't talk like that, Mom.' An' she said, 'Well, I ain't gonna get any better.' She said, "I think I'll just go ahead an' die.' An' uh... Mother didn't think much about it. But... About two days later, she died."

"Huh..." Elliott responds.

"An' this nurse that was out there... She said, 'You know, she didn't act like there was anything wrong with 'er.' ...said, 'She'd asked me if I'd get 'er a glass a water.' She said, 'Yeah.' So, she went to get her a glass of water. She said, 'I came back, an' she was dead.'" Poteet looks at Elliott and asks, "Now, idn' that somethin'?"

Elliott strokes his beard and adds, "...makes you wonder."

Poteet nods. "Yeah. Grandma was good to me. I'd stay with 'er some. But mostly I stayed at Mother an' Daddy's house."

CHAPTER 10

Abandoned?

Elliott thinks about growing up in New York City and even being in Los Angeles. He says, "...seems like that would've been dangerous for a kid."

"Yeah, it does. Ya know, I think... Especially today, you hear about all these children who get molested an' all." He shakes his head. "I must've had a guardian angel, 'cause nothin' like that ever happened to me."

"Hmm."

"Nothin'... I mean, bein' out there—all alone. But, no..."

"It was a different time."

"Yeah. It was a different time, an' a whole different world. Ya know, nobody locked their doors. When you... When you'd take your car to town or whatever, nobody even took the keys out of their cars."

Elliott doesn't respond but looks down at a pad of notepaper he'd brought with him. After a moment, he says, "Your grandmother was around. You could always go there. Your mother was there. You could go and eat at her bar."

"Yeah—on Skid Row," Poteet says.

"...on Skid Row, yeah. Um... It doesn't quite fit the picture of 'abandoned' to me. Can we really use that word?"

"Uh... I don' know. But... Like I say, I could be gone for three or four days, an' nobody'd even ask, 'Well, where's he at?' ...ya know."

"Right. That's true," Elliott says. He takes a moment and then nods slightly. "Yeah, that sounds a lot like 'abandoned.'"

Poteet shrugs.

"It does to me," Terry says.

Elliott chuckles. "By the law, by any definition... That's 'abandoned'—for a kid. It really is."

Poteet says, "Yeah. I think so. I jus' don't think Mother really cared that much...ya know? But I know I didn' have a childhood like everybody else did."

"Yeah. If you could be gone for days..."

"No, they didn' care. But... Yeah, my childhood was..." Poteet winces slightly. "I can look back on it, an'... I always say that there was two things that kept me sane back then. I always had a horse, an' I could keep that at Grandma's as long as it wadn' around her cows. An' then, there was art. 'Cause I was always into art—drawin' pictures. An' uh. It really did keep me sane."

Elliott nods, then looks down again at his notes. He says, "Changing directions a bit here..."

"Okay," Poteet replies and reaches for his painting knife.

Elliott scratches the back of his head. "How did you adapt to being an American Indian, and did you think about that very much?"

Poteet starts working with his palette. "Ya know, as we got older... Uh... About the time that I graduated from high school, things had started to change quite a bit in that regard. There wadn' so much of that. But when I was younger, there was a lot of it. An' uh... But yeah... Like I said, I knew it was part of my heritage."

Elliott nods and says, "We've talked about the Trail of Tears."

"Yeah," Poteet replies and turns toward his painting.

"...and your interest in that."

"Right."

"Another phrase that's sometimes used is 'forced assimilation,' where they forced the tribes to come together."

"Right."

"...and how they forced those people into Oklahoma Territory."

With an edge, Poteet adds, "Yes. And some still haven't assimilated."

Elliott nods and says, "And I think I know what you mean. You're talking about the reservations and how tough it is for the people there—still."

"Yes. Exactly."

"So, it makes me wonder about your father's family. It seems like they must have assimilated pretty well."

"Uh... I don't think I'd say, 'pretty well.' No..." Poteet looks out the window and says, "No... I think... Yeah... They figured out how to make it." He turns back to Elliott. "But... Like I say, my father's family... They lived way back up in the mountains. They kind of kept to themselves an' lived off the horses they could sell."

"Well... I mean... To me, that seems like they assimilated."

"Yeah, sort of... I think it was more like figurin' out how to survive."

"I think that's fair. And then, your father... And he's not that far, generationally, from the ones who were forced into this." Elliott pauses and stares in the direction of Poteet's latest painting. "So, maybe it was the army..."

"Yeah, I think so."

"And then, he needed a job when he got out, and he went to work where he could."

"Yeah. That sounds right."

"He adapted."

"An' he was good at what he did," Poteet says. "He worked all over the world."

"I don't think I knew that."

"Yeah, he did. He sure did. He worked on buildin' pipelines all over the world. I got into some of that too—when I got outa high school. But, talkin' 'bout my dad... Throughout his whole life... I'm sure he was discriminated against, as an Indian. But I didn't discriminate against anybody—Indians, blacks, the poor kids... I didn' care."

"From all I can tell, that seems to be true."

CHAPTER 11

Fourth Grade

Poteet reaches for his painting knife, starts mixing paint on his palette, and says, "An' I remember... There was this kid... An' he was probably the poorest kid in school."

A smile begins to form on the movie maker's face, but it fades as he thinks about some kid being considered "poor" by Poteet.

"All the other kids made fun of 'im. An' uh... So, I got to talkin' to 'im, ya know. An' uh... He asked me if I wanted to come over to his house one day after school. An' I said, 'Yeah, I'll go.' So, I go over there. They were just dirt poor, ya know. An' I remember... He asked me to stay an' eat dinner with 'im. An' what was served there was cornmeal mush. It was just cornmeal with hot water, ya know. That's what they had for their supper that night. An' I sat there an' ate with 'em. It's hard to imagine people bein' that poor."

"Coming from a kid who was abandoned, that says a lot."

"Yeah, I suppose so." With a loaded knife, Poteet turns to his painting. "But... If every kid in that school had done what I did, they'd a had a different outlook. I can guarantee you... You wouldn't a looked at 'im like that again. He couldn't help it."

Elliott nods. "I'm sure that's true. There's a lesson in there..."

"He was kind of a rebel too. I remember, he..." Poteet chuckles. "He, uh... This was long, ya know, before... I think it was in the fifth grade, he showed up with a Mohawk haircut."

All three laugh.

Poteet says, "Anyway... I jus' thought I'd tell you that, 'cause... Yeah, I didn' discriminate."

"Okay."

Poteet shows a devious smile and continues, "But I did have other issues. An' I was kind of a... An' I don't really know why I was. But... I was a rebellious sort of kid. An' I always had problems with authority. An' I think, it's because, ya know, authority is sort of linked to masculinity." He looks at Elliott. "Ya know what I mean. An' that's a proven. Uh... An' I think it was because my dad was never around, an' I sort of resented it, ya know."

"I've detected an issue there, I think."

Terry chuckles.

"So, I gotta tell ya this."

Elliott nods and says, "Okay."

"It was when I was in the fourth grade."

"Hmm..."

Terry crosses her legs and sits forward. She says, "I know this one."

"Like you might expect, I was always drawin' pictures. An' I had this teacher. She couldn' even teach today, she was so damn mean. An' I remember her makin' fun of kids. An'... I always had a soft spot in my heart for poor kids, ya know, like the one I was jus' tellin' you about."

"Right."

"An' she'd make fun of 'em. So I detested her. She didn't like me either, 'cause she knew I didn' like her. She'd catch me drawin' a picture, an' she'd come up behind me an' hit me in the head with a ruler. An' that just made me more determined. An' I remember... There was some function at school that one night, an' uh... She had a bran' new '57 Ford. An' I practically destroyed that car—that night. I did. I knocked out all the glass in it, flattened all the tires, scratched it all up an' uh..."

Terry grins.

"And it was brand new?" Elliott asks.

Poteet nods. "...brand new. An' uh... Uh... They... There wasn't such a thing as, ya know, like counselin' or anything back then. They just kind of looked at me like, 'Ya know, this kid's got a problem. Look out for him.'"

"Did they know you did it?"

"Yeah. Yeah, they knew."

"So... What happened?"

"Nothin'."

"How does nothing happen to you"—Elliott starts to chuckle—"when you destroy somebody's car?"

"I don' know. But nothin' happened. I remember gettin' called into the... This was in grade school, ya know. An'... I got called into the office, an' the principal talked to me there. An' then, they took me over to the high school, an' I had to talk to the superintendent. An' uh... I think they just said, 'What are you gonna do with 'im? How you gonna punish 'im?' An' uh... I guess they didn't have an answer. So, they didn't do anything to me. They jus' kind of left me alone, ya know? But I... I kind of had that reputation." He chuckles. "An' so... They kind of gave me a wide berth after that."

"Huh."

"An' uh..."

"Did you continue to have that teacher?"

"Uh... Yeah, I did."

"Really?" Elliott asks.

"Yeah, they didn't even take me out of that class."

Terry shakes her head as the beginning of a laugh escapes.

Elliott says, "Well, I'll be damned."

"No, they didn't—come to think of it. I... It's funny that you mentioned that, 'cause I never really thought about it." Poteet looks away and says quietly, "So why didn't they take me...? Why didn't they put me in another...?"

Elliott asks, "Yeah... Why?"

"Probably, 'cause nobody else would take me," Poteet says and laughs.

"Huh... I'm sure that was it. But it seems like she would have really been hard on you—after that."

"Actually, she wadn'."

Elliott chuckles. "Then maybe that's it. Maybe she didn't want anything like that to happen again."

"Yeah... I think they thought, ya know, 'This little shit right here, now...'"

Elliott and Terry laugh.

"...you better watch him. But... Ya know... It was just... I jus' had so much anger—towards her. An' I... I probably jus' had anger—period."

Elliott nods and says, "I just... I think if that happened today..."

"Yeah?"

"You'd go someplace," Terry says.

"Yeah, they'd put you in a school or somethin' like that," Poteet suggests.

Elliott says, "I think they'd put you in juvenile detention or maybe a mental institution. They'd do somethin' to ya."

"I would think so."

Elliott continues, "You wouldn't just show back up in class like nothin' had ever happened."

All three chuckle.

After a moment, Poteet adds, "I know it."

Elliott glances at the recorder and then his notes.

Poteet turns back to his palette.

Elliott sets his notepad down and looks at the floor while stroking his beard. The break in the conversation doesn't feel uncomfortable to him but rather needed, after the last story.

Terry watches Elliott and wonders what he's thinking. After what he'd just heard, he could have come to the conclusion that Poteet is just crazy. Or he might not even believe these bizarre stories at all. She wouldn't blame him.

Elliott looks up at Poteet and then at Terry before saying, "Somewhere in there, high school—maybe it was junior high... At some point you got hooked up with your mentor."

Relieved, Terry thinks, "Well, he hasn't walked out yet."

CHAPTER 12

Harold

Poteet answers, "Yeah, Harold."

"Right..." After a moment, Elliott recalls, "Stevenson. Yeah, Harold Stevenson."

"Right," Poteet confirms and then lifts his knife from the sheet of paper that serves as his palette. He turns to Elliott. "I met Harold when I was young. I think I was around eleven or twelve. He was livin' in Paris, France. Well, he lived in Rome an' different places. I don't really remember where he was livin' then. But, uh... He would come in every summer, 'cause his mother an' father lived there—an' his brother. An' uh... He'd come in, an' he'd usually spend a couple a months. An' he would jus' find some place to paint. An' uh... My mother... Harold was in town at that time. So, she took me over to the studio. An' he... uh... Ya know, all mothers think their children are precocious. So, she wanted to show 'im these drawings that I'd done—ya know, these horses an' stuff. An' uh... He was really nice. I mean... Yeah... He got down on the floor with a piece a chalk an' drew the anatomy of a horse—ya know, the skeletal anatomy of a horse. An' he tol' me... He said, 'I can see that you've got talent, but...' He said, 'You can't draw the outside unless you know what's goin' on—on the inside.' An' I always remembered that. An' he was absolutely right. Yeah... Knowin' the anatomy of an animal is paramount to drawin' it. An' uh..."

Terry interjects, "His father was a veterinarian."

"Uh-huh..."

Elliott asks, "So, how did Harold become this big deal artist in New York City?"

"Because..." Poteet replies. "An' he says this in his biography. He says, 'I was a serious artist when I was five years old.' An' he was."

"How do you do that?"

"Well..."

"He was just gifted," Terry explains.

"Yeah. He was gifted, an' he followed that track. He was born to be an artist. He knew it at five, an' he was a great one."

"Do you feel like you were born that way?"

"Oh, absolutely!" Poteet says as he looks squarely at Elliott. He then turns to his canvas and continues, "So... With Harold, his parents got 'im the materials that he wanted. An' he would do these paintings of people an' things. An' they'd say, 'Well, there's Harold—the little artist.'"

"So, he just followed that track?" Elliott asks.

"Yeah, he did. An' he had a scholarship. They gave him a... I said, 'How'd you get a damn scholarship to OU?'"

"He got at scholarship to the University of Oklahoma?"

"...an art scholarship. An'... But he never finished. It bored the shit out of him. An' uh... He just went to New York, ya know..."

Terry says, "Tell 'im 'bout the girl that you went to school with when you were in the third grade. Ya know, when you were supposed to draw somethin'." She looks at Poteet and asks, "Wadn' it a horse?"

"Well, we were supposed to draw an animal. An' she said, uh... She said, 'I drew a dog, an' it looked like a box with ears on it.'"

Elliott laughs and then Terry joins him.

"An' she said, 'An' you turned in one, an' it was this horse runnin' across the pasture with a mane flowin' an' every-thing.'"

All three laugh.

Elliott says, "So, the talent was showing through."

"Yeah...even at an early age," Terry adds.

"But the reason for that was... It's because, I did it all the time. I remember gettin' Superman books. An' I'd draw... I'd draw every frame in the damn comic book. I would..."

"Wow."

"Yeah, I'd... I did it all the time. It's what I wanted to do, so I did it. But... Yeah... When I started gettin', ya know—older, I jus' became real independent."

"I'm sure you didn't get much encouragement with your art."

"Naw..."

"But there wasn't anyone to say you couldn't do it, either."

"True."

"No one even showed up for his high school graduation," Terry points out.

Elliott shakes his head.

"Yep. They didn'," Poteet confirms. "An' like... Every sporting event that I was ever in, nobody came."

"Not even your mother...?"

"Nope."

"And she was right there in town."

"Yep, she was."

"I mean... I can understand, say a stepfather..."

"Uh-huh..."

"But I would think... Your mother..."

"Uh-huh..."

"... would've been there," Elliott says and shakes his head.

Poteet nods. "That's just how it was."

"That kind of neglect had to be rough."

He shrugs. "I adjusted."

"How do you even do that?"

"There were other folks in town that helped me."

"Like who?" Elliott asks. He pauses, then adds, "Who would do that?"

"The Chastains... The Chastains helped me."

Elliott wondered about these people and wanted to know more. They must have been saints. He didn't think he knew anyone who would take up the cause of a rebellious boy who'd had little or no adult supervision his whole life.

CHAPTER 13

Ranch Life

Elliott says, "Tell me more about the Chastains."

"They lived on a ranch outside a town."

"...and they helped you?"

"Yeah. I don't think I was quite twelve yet. But Mr. Chastain was an older guy. He was probably in his... I think he was sixty-five when I met 'im. An' his wife... They'd never had any kids, so maybe that's why they sort of took me in."

"I see."

"But I think my sister had gone out there an' ridden some of his horses or somethin' like that. An' I started goin' out there. He jus' took me under his wing, ya know, an' taught me a lot—taught me a lot about horses an' cattle. So, I'd go... I stayed out there a lot. I'd spend nights out there, an'..."

"So, was that near where you lived?"

"Mm-hmm. He lived right outside of town. An' uh..."

"So, you could walk there?"

"No, I couldn't walk. Uh... I had to either get a ride out there, or... If I'd ridden my horse home, I'd ride him."

"Okay," Elliott says and thinks that the Chastains were good people who probably had a very positive influence on Poteet's life.

"But... What Mr. Chastain wanted me to do was to become a roper. An' I remember he bought... To start me off, he bought goats, so I could rope 'em. But I kept tellin' 'im, I wanted to get in the ridin' events. He'd say, 'No, no, no, no. I don't want you in the ridin' events. You'll get hurt.' But... What I wanted to do was ride the bulls."

"...bull riding?"

"Yeah. That's what I wanted. So' I just kept houndin' 'im about it, an' uh... I'd seen a setup someplace where you could practice ridin'."

"Oh?"

"Yeah. You attach ropes an' springs on four corners of a 50-gallon drum. An' it's suspended from poles. An' then you get on it, an' somebody shakes it, ya know. So, I talked 'im into to makin' that thing."

"Really."

"Yeah, he made it for me. He did."

"Even though he didn't want you to ride..."

"Yeah. I guess he didn' mind me practicin'."

"Maybe he hoped that'd be enough."

Poteet chuckles. "An' I didn't tell 'im that I was gonna get into bull ridin', 'cause he'd a been tryin' to talk me out of it. So, I didn't tell 'im. But he was always right there to sort of oversee the whole thing."

"Okay. So, you uh... You got into bull riding?"

"Yeah."

Elliott draws back and thinks that Mr. Chastain was probably right about getting hurt. He takes a deep breath and reflects, "So... You rode that barrel thing to practice."

"Yeah."

"What else?"

"I rode some horses that bucked a little bit. But... Nothin' that you could..."

"I don't see how that prepares you for riding a bull."

"It dudn'. Nothin' does. Believe me, *nothin'* does."

Elliott chuckles and shakes his head.

"Because... Even that barrel, it's... No... Ridin' a bull is... Especially back then, ya know... Boys today... They've got a lot of people coachin' 'em—ya know, people who've been there before. I didn' have any of that. But yeah... So, I went over to this rodeo, an' uh... I walked around there an' ran into this one bull rider. He was over there rosinin' up his rope. I was thirteen. These guys were in their 20s, an' uh..."

"So, this was full-blown rodeo?" Elliott asks.

"Yeah."

"This wasn't like junior rodeo...?"

"Nope."

"...or anything like that?"

"No, this was full-blown," Terry says. "These were big, fifteen-hundred-pound bulls."

"So, this bull rider... I asked 'im, I said... Uh..." Poteet chuckles. "I said, 'Would you let me borrow your spurs? I'm in the bull ridin', an' I don't have any spurs.'" Poteet chuckles again. "An' he said... He said, 'Man, I ain't gonna give you my spurs.' An' I said, 'Well, I really could use 'em.' I said, 'I don't have any, an'...' An' uh... So, I guess he felt sorry for me. So, he finally said, 'Okay, I'll loan you my spurs, but I'm gonna go with ya. I'm gonna watch you 'cause you ain't gettin' off with my spurs.'"

Elliott, Terry, and Poteet laugh.

Terry then says, "He thought you was gonna swipe 'em."

"Yeah. An' uh... That... That bull fell with me. An' uh... I stayed on 'im. He got back up an'... An' uh... Oh, I mean, everybody was goin'... The whole audience was goin' nuts, ya know, because... An' that... That cowboy run out there in the arena an' grabbed me... An' uh... He was jus' proud of his part of it, ya know."

Elliott chuckles.

Terry says, "An' you won the entire rodeo—bull ridin', didn' ya?"

"Yeah."

"Really?" Elliott asks.

"Yeah."

"...at age thirteen."

"Yeah..." Terry says.

"I can't imagine."

"...even with all those grown competitors," Terry tells Elliott.

He shakes his head and says, "Wow."

Poteet smiles but says, "It was stupid."

Elliott and Terry laugh.

"But ya know... That's what we did."

"Would your friends...?" Elliott asks. "Would they do the same thing?"

"Oh, some of 'em... Yeah. I had... Yeah. I had a couple of friends that did it too. Yeah."

"Were they out there that night?"

"No... No."

"So, you... Just on your own..."

"Yeah. An' I jus' said I wanted to do it, an'... Yeah, I don't even remember how I got over there. I couldn't..."

"You couldn't drive," Elliott notes.

Poteet laughs and repeats, "Yeah. I couldn't drive."

Elliott chuckles.

"I guess I hitched a ride with somebody—over there."

"Did you have to pay some money to enter?"

"Uh... Yeah. There had to have been an entry fee."

"I'll bet."

"An' I don't remember how I got that money either. Uh..."

"Did you win money that night?"

"Yeah, I did. I forget how much it was. I know I won a buckle."

"Sounds like you needed to win some spurs."

"Yeah. I didn' *win* any, but I bought some."

Elliott thinks it's funny and asks, "With the money you won?"

"Yeah, I did. I went an' bought a pair. I sure did. Yeah. I remember the guy I bought 'em from. He just laughed his ass off."

"Huh."

"'Cause he had a store, an' he was sellin' 'em, ya know."

Chuckling, Elliott says, "Yeah."

"I said, 'All right, here's the money. I'm gonna buy these spurs with some of the money I won." An' I told 'im, I said, 'Easy come, easy go.'"

All three laugh.

"He just thought that was hilarious for some reason."

"Did he know that you'd won?"

"Oh yeah."

"... the bull riding?"

"Yeah. Well... Obviously, it's a small town. Everybody knew it."

"Oh."

"Ya know... Everybody knew," Poteet says and laughs.

"Huh... Then, it was kind of a big deal."

"Yeah, it was, but... I don' know. It was hard for me to stay focused on anything—when I was young like that."

Elliott nods and chuckles and then stares at Poteet for an uncomfortable few seconds. He looks at Terry and cocks his head slightly. Smiling, he says to Poteet, "I've enjoyed listening and laughing. But I *have* to ask, 'Are these stories real?' I mean, destroying your teacher's car in the fourth grade with no repercussions and then winning a bull-riding contest at age thirteen..."

Terry watches Elliott carefully.

"I've never heard stories like that. Can they really be true?'"

Before Poteet can answer, Elliott continues, "It makes me even wonder about meeting Andy Warhol in New York City. It's all pretty outrageous."

Without showing any emotion, Poteet says, "Yeah. It's all true."

Looking over his glasses, Elliott follows, "...even the Warhol stuff?"

"Oh, yeah. I knew Andy."

Elliott nods.

"But I'm sure you'll want to verify what you can," Poteet says. "An' I know you've got people who do that."

"I do. And they will. But I just want to know now, and I want for you to tell me. If this is fiction, it's still entertaining. And I'm okay with that. I present fiction all the time. I just need to know which it is."

"Sure, I understand. An' uh... I'm not offended that you'd ask. My life's been unusual. I get it. But yeah... I assure you. It's all true."

Terry sits forward and says, "I call 'im Forrest Gump all the time, with everything that's happened to 'im."

They laugh.

"Yeah. I can identify with Forrest Gump. But really..." Poteet smiles and looks at Elliott. "I can tell you that my memory is... It's good but not perfect."

Smiling, Terry says, "I dunno why ya think he's makin' it up. To me, it all sound jus' like 'im."

Elliott chuckles and picks up his recorder. He pushes a couple of buttons and says, "I think that's enough for today."

Poteet nods and says, "Okay."

Terry stands and asks, "So, whadaya think?"

Elliott turns to her without a hint of a smile and says, "I don't know." He looks away for a moment and then back. He adds, "It's a different story than I had expected. I think you know that."

Poteet turns to rearrange his painting table.

"It's not a bad story. It's just different." Elliott looks at Terry and then at Poteet. He looks back at Terry to say, "You know, I was expecting a Native American story, and it is. But then, it isn't. It's got that component for sure, but..." He shakes his head slightly. "To describe Poteet within the frame of Native American, or I should say 'American Indian,' doesn't nearly complete the picture."

"You got that right," Terry says.

Poteet leans on his painting table to observe the discussion.

"My friends used words like 'historical,' and even 'genius' to describe Poteet. I was drawn to those words and that character, but I'm not seeing those qualities." Elliott looks over at Poteet, who hasn't changed his expression, and then continues, "I think I'm seeing 'historical.' Yeah. But not as I expected. I'm seeing him as New-York-City historical... Culturally historical... I don't know. The word that comes to mind for me so far is: 'Rebellious.' He had a problem with authority when he was young. It's even what *he* says."

"Yeah. He did," Terry agrees.

"Another word that comes to mind is 'humorous.' And I never expected a Native American artist in Santa Fe, New Mexico, to be this funny."

Terry chuckles. "You're right about all a that, an' I get what you're sayin'. But I think those other words are right too. The thing you're gonna begin to understand about Poteet is the word 'genius.'"

Elliott looks over his glasses at Poteet and then back at Terry. "Sorry. I've not seen that."

She nods confidently. "You will. I'm tellin' ya... You will."

Elliott chuckles. "But you know... I do recall my friends saying that they were"—with fingers up for air quotes—"'entertained' by Poteet."

Terry and Poteet chuckle.

Elliott nods and says, "That part of it... I get it now."

They all laugh.

Elliott says, "I've got to go." As he reaches for his recorder, he explains, "This had to be another quick stop. This time I'm traveling to New York City, and I've got a meeting this evening."

Terry stands and says, "Okay, Elliott, you're gonna miss us."

He turns to her and smiles. He then picks up his satchel and looks at Poteet. He says, "I hope you didn't take what I said the wrong way."

Poteet shakes his head and waves off any concern. He explains, "I learned how to take criticism a long time ago."

"I don't think I even meant to be critical."

"I get it. I really do. I didn' even take it as criticism. No. I'm fine."

Elliott nods. They shake, and Elliott heads for the double doors.

Terry follows him out, wondering when they'll see him again. She watches as he climbs into the waiting car.

Elliott still has a smile on his face as he settles in, thinking about all the crazy stories. One thing for sure, he's been enjoying his visits to Santa Fe.

CHAPTER 14

"I Was Very Independent."

As Elliott walks along Alameda Street, which follows the Santa Fe River near the gallery, he notices the gathering clouds and the precipitous drop in temperature. The short walk had been invigorating, and the sweet smell of pine was in the air. But, he'd been thinking that he'd made a mistake by not wearing his jacket.

He is relieved when he crosses over the river and begins walking up Canyon Road. He walks into the gallery with his satchel in one hand and a stand for the recorder in the other.

Terry is quickly front and center to greet him. He sets his bag down and his recorder stand on top of it. She gives him a friendly hug and a kiss. They move apart, and she says, "So good to see you again."

He smiles.

"What's it been? ...about a month?"

"Yeah. It was mid-April, I think."

"They tell me you're stayin' overnight this time."

"I am. I've checked in at the La Fonda Hotel. It's a nice place."

"It is. An' it's hard to get in there."

"I guess I should be grateful."

"I think you'll like it. It's downtown, an' their restaurant's good."

"I haven't had a chance yet to try it."

She points. "Poteet's up there, an' he's expectin' ya."

"Sounds good."

She says, "I'll be up there soon."

"Great," Elliott says. He then grabs his things and heads for the stairs. As he walks through the double doors, Poteet is right there—standing right in front of him and crouching over his large worktable.

Poteet looks up and says, "Hey. I'm glad you're back." He extends his hand, and they shake.

Elliott smiles and says, "Sure. I look forward to coming now. I'm ready to have some fun."

Poteet chuckles. "I may not be everything you expected, but... At least, I'm not boring."

"No, you're not boring. But... Like I said, I'm still trying to figure you out."

Poteet looks down at the pieces of wood he is fashioning into a frame. He explains, "I've got an idea for a painting, so I've got to get a canvas ready."

Elliott asks, "Is it okay if I just stand over here by the door?"

Poteet quickly looks at the situation and says, "Sorry. I meant to have your stool out here."

"That's fine. I can stand."

"No, I'll get it," Poteet says and heads for his kitchen. He returns with stool in hand and glances at a spot close to the door. "We'll set you right here—it'll give you a little more room."

"Sure, that will be fine. Thanks."

Poteet moves back over to his frame project.

Elliott looks at the recorder stand he's holding. Awkwardly, he digs out his recorder and sets his satchel on the floor.

Poteet says, "If buildin' this frame is a problem, I can do it later."

"No. It's not a problem. I like to see you work." Elliott then lifts the recorder stand to show Poteet. "...glad I brought this. Looks like I'll need it today." He points. "My recorder will work better over here than on your table."

Poteet nods and looks at Elliott. "Sure. Jus' set it anywhere. An' I'm kind of surprised you don't have a whole crew of people for that."

"I've thought about it, and I've talked with my staff. Right now, we prefer a casual approach, and we think what we're doing is working. We want you to feel completely at ease."

Poteet nods again.

"And I think you are comfortable. Later on... If we decide to take the next step, we'll need to move crews in, of course. Even then, it depends on the story we decide to tell."

"Sure."

"And if we get that far, we'll need to sign some contracts."

"I understand," Poteet says and turns back to his frame pieces. "So... In that case, I'll keep doin' what I do."

"Cool," Elliott says and then fumbles with his tripod—extending the legs, attaching the recorder, getting the recorder turned on, and setting the stand in a strategic location. When all seems to be in place, he asks, "How's this?"

Poteet looks and replies, "That's fine."

"And I could send someone else to do the interview, but I'm a hands-on person. It's the way I've always worked. I've got to get into the details of a story, before I feel comfortable with it. I don't want surprises. I don't want to ask, 'Why the hell didn't we know that?' Particularly, when the subject is real, like you—a living person." He nods. "There can be blowback. There can be skeletons, if you know what I mean."

"Oh. I promise ya. There's plenty of skeletons in my closet."

Elliott grins. "As long as we know about 'em, that's okay."

"I ain't holdin' back."

Elliott chuckles. "I believe that, and that's why I'm here—besides the fact that I like it here. I like you and Terry. I like hearing your stories. We've laughed a lot. And I've gotten to the point in my career where I can do what I want to most of the time." He shrugs.

"We're enjoyin' it too," Poteet says and reaches for a piece of the frame. "I've enjoyed talkin' to you, an' we *have* laughed a lot. Terry even says that about our sessions."

"And... I feel like I'm just getting to know you and your story. I'm intrigued still. I want to know more. I'm learning, and I've got questions." Elliott glances over at his notebook to make the point.

"Sure. I'll try to answer," Poteet says and reaches out for another piece of frame.

After a moment, Elliott says, "I've spent some time listening and cataloguing our conversations."

"Okay."

"I know you had all kinds of family problems."

Poteet sets the pieces of the frame down, looks at Elliott, and says, "I did."

"Right. So, I've been wondering how you got along with other kids—like kids your own age, kids in your classes."

Poteet extends his arms, leans on the table with both hands, and looks out the window in front of his table.

Elliott continues, "Did you have friends?" He pauses. "And how did you do in school? Did you make good grades? ...bad grades?"

"Ya know, I always got along great with my classmates an' everything. I remember... When we got to the seventh grade, I was voted 'Most Popular.' An' in the eighth grade, I was voted that again."

"Really?"

"Yeah. Oh yeah. So, I didn't have a problem with other people. I think it was just this authority thing, ya know. That's what it was."

"You were a rebel."

"Yeah. I guess so. I think it was more about bein' independent though. I'd been on my own for so long, an' I could think for myself. An' uh... That made it difficult for me... I mean, I had a real hard time followin' somebody else's stupid-ass ideas."

Elliott laughs and responds, "I might call that wisdom."

Poteet chuckles. "I think most people would call it 'bein' hard-headed.'"

Elliott laughs again and says, "Well... That's probably true. Although, I think the 'wisdom' aspect really is a factor."

"Maybe. But I had to make my own decisions. I didn' have a choice. I had to decide some things early on. I mean... I could've dropped out of school at any time. But I knew that I couldn't. I jus'... There wadn' anybody tellin' me I couldn't. I jus' knew that I couldn'."

"Because you wanted to make something of yourself."

"Yeah."

"In order to get established and get ahead, you needed to go to school."

"That's right. But I never would really apply myself. I remember... I had friends that'd say, ya know... 'How in the hell can you come in here an' you do so well on tests? I know you didn' study.'" Poteet looks at Elliott. "I cannot remember ever takin' a book home—from first grade to twelfth grade. I mean, the only studyin' I would do would be in class. An' that was it."

"So, you did well in school."

"I did."

"...and you had friends."

"Yeah. I did."

"And your interest in art continued."

"Sure. It's what kept me sane."

Elliott chuckles.

"I think he doubts jus' how sane you were," Terry says as she walks in. She points toward the hall and adds softly, "I overheard..."

Poteet smiles.

After Terry is seated, Elliott says, "I want to follow the art track, if you don't mind."

Poteet nods and says, "Sure."

"So, when did you see Harold again?"

Poteet stares in the direction of his partially open double doors, "I think I was sixteen, an' I was rodeoin'. Harold loved rodeos, ya know. An' uh... So, he come up to me after the rodeo, an' we kind of got reacquainted. He said, 'I remember you.' An' I said, 'Yeah, I remember you.' An' so he tol' me... He said, 'Well, I'm gonna be here this summer, an' I'm gonna do a series of paintings on Alexander the Great.'"

"Right. You mentioned that in our first meeting," Elliott says.

Poteet steps closer to the worktable near Elliott and begins looking through a stack of papers. He pulls a magazine out of the stack and hands it to Elliott. He says, "They sent this to me. There's an article on Harold in there."

"Thanks," Elliott says as he takes the magazine from Poteet. He looks at it and reads the name, "...*Oklahoma Today*."

"Yeah. They called me for a quote. I'm in there."

"I'll read it."

"I think you'll like it."

Elliott glances through the magazine before putting it in his satchel.

Holding up the beginning pieces of a frame, Poteet continues, "But, yeah... Harold mentioned the Alexander the

Great paintings he was gonna do. He tol' me... He said, 'I need a model that can handle a horse—*in the studio*. We've got to bring the horse into the studio.' An' he asked, 'Could you do that?' An' I said, 'Well, it depends on the horse, I imagine. But yeah, I can do it.' An' we did. We worked that whole summer doin' that. An' then... I mean... 'Cause he was constantly talkin' to me, ya know. I'd go out there after school an' spend an hour or so... But yeah... That went on, an' he did those paintings. An' then, he come back the next year, an' we did the same thing. An'... By the end of that... Ya know, listenin' to 'im talk about art an' what it meant to 'im an'... It's... I knew right then I wanted to do that."

Terry looks at Elliott but points at Poteet, "An' ya know... Poteet was very famous in Europe."

"Right. He mentioned that. So... Those paintings must've been fairly well known."

"Yeah," Poteet responds.

"At least, in Europe..."

"Right. Harold had a great career goin' over there."

Elliott watches Poteet hold the pieces of the frame together as he wonders about the significance of Harold Stevenson in Poteet's life.

CHAPTER 15

Lightnin' Billy

"Did I mention that Sharon and I had dinner the other night with the Kleppers?"

"No."

"I asked them, 'What are your favorite Poteet Victory stories?'"

Poteet chuckles.

"Well... Pam said, 'Ask him about Lightning Billy.' So... I did a search, and I saw a painting of Harold's called *The Eye of Lightning Billy*. That's an unusual name. So, I wondered if that's what she was talking about."

"I think she was probably talkin' about Lightnin' Billy—the guy. An' the fight I had with 'im that night."

Elliott looks at Poteet over the top of his glasses and says, "...could be. So, you and Lightning Billy had a fight."

"Yeah. An' he was a mean son of a bitch. Everybody in town was scared to death of 'im, ya know. I mean, he'd maim you." He looks at Elliott. "I knew one guy..." Poteet nods and says slowly, "Lightnin' bit his nose off."

Elliott's eyes get big, and he stares at Poteet.

"Yeah...bit another guy's ear off."

Elliott draws back. He exhales and responds, "Oh, shit."

"Yeah. An' he was bigger than me," Poteet says and sets his partially-assembled frame aside. He also sets his hammer down, turns toward Elliott, and leans sideways against the table. With a serious demeanor, he says, "An' he was a very striking person, physically. I think that's why Harold liked 'im."

"And... Harold painted this guy—this guy you fought?"

"He painted his eye—a really big painting of his eye."

"Huh...just his eye."

"Yeah. But Lightnin'... He liked to bully people—especially younger boys. But he never really bullied me, until that night. I remember... I had a date, an' we pulled up right there in town. I parked the car. An' when I got out, he was standin' there. He come up to me, an' said somethin' about, 'Well, there's a pretty boy' ... or somethin' like that. An' he grabbed me an' just started slappin' me. An' when he did"—Poteet makes a fist—"I jus' went POW! I hit 'im as hard as I could, an' the fight was on—right there in town, on Main Street."

"Wow."

Poteet chuckles. "Yeah. An' uh... Boy, we fought for a long time. We caved in the whole side of a car parked there next to us. Yeah. 'Cause, I mean, we were... He almost had me knocked out at one time. He had me on the trunk of the car. An' he was laughin'. An' uh... He said somethin' to me. An' I... I jus'... Ya know... shook the cobwebs out. An' I remember, I come up off the car an' hit 'im right under the chin. An' uh... He was... Ya know... I... I didn' have too many marks on me. But he had a bunch, 'cause I'd cut 'im. I was a much better boxer than he was. An' he went crazy. An'... He grabbed me an' got right at my face. ...tryin' to bite me."

Elliott whispers, "Oh shit."

"...like an animal. An' I just kept fightin' 'im, ya know. An' finally, he'd had enough. An' uh..." Poteet chuckles. "But... He looked bad. I saw 'im the next day, an' he saw me. An' I wondered, ya know, 'Do you wanna start this again?' But no. He didn' want to. His eyes were black, an' he had cuts all over. An' uh... Harold found out about it. An'... It jus'..." Poteet shakes his head and takes a deep breath. "Harold... He was jus'... He was so upset, because..."

"...at you or Lightning Billy?"

"Both of us."

"Because he liked you both."

"Yeah."

"He didn't want to see you fighting each other."

"No. An' he called me. He said, 'When you get off work, I want you to come out here to the house'. An' I said, 'Okay.' So, I get out there, an' there's Lightnin' Billy. An' Harold said, 'You two sit down right here.' An' he said, 'I love both of you, an blah, blah, blah...' An' he said, 'Don't do this. Don't *do* this.' An' uh... He said, 'There's a rodeo tonight.' He said, 'You two... I want you two to go to the rodeo together.'"

"An' I'm thinkin', 'Ya know, this is gonna be great,'" Poteet says sarcastically.

Elliott chuckles.

"An' uh... I said, 'Okay. Let's go.' An' he was as nice to me as he could be. I never had another problem with 'im—never had a problem. But yeah..."

"Whatever happened to Lightnin'?" Terry asks.

"A young boy shot 'im. He was bullyin' 'im. An' the kid pulled out a pistol an' killed 'im. Right down in Tom, Oklahoma. 'Cause he was doin' the same thing to that boy that he tried to do to me."

"Wow. Did the boy go to jail?" Elliott asks.

"No."

"...because it was self-defense?"

"Yeah. Everybody knew Lightnin's reputation. They were glad he was gone."

"I can imagine. So, what if he'd beaten you to a pulp that

night—bitten your nose off or worse?"

"Hmm. I don' know—never thought about it. I mean... I knew it was possible... I mean, it was a tough fight."

"And it sounds like he was that close to doing that very thing."

"Yeah. But he was that close to gettin' his head beat in the concrete too. It went back an' forth. An' anybody who watched that fight would've thought, 'I don' know who's gettin' the best of who right here.'"

"Wow."

"I knew when I walked away... I thought, 'All right. I'm tellin' ya, I won it.' 'Cause he didn't want any more of it."

"You mentioned you were a better boxer than he was."

"Right."

"Where did you learn to box?"

"From my friend, Wayland." Poteet smiles as he says, "All the girls wanted to be *with* him an' all the boys wanted to *be* him."

Elliott chuckles. "Sounds like an interesting guy. Was this in high school?"

"Yeah. He was older, but we were friends. He was a two-time Golden Gloves boxin' champion, an' he was my boxin' coach."

"I see—sounds like you needed that kind of training."

"I did. An' ya know, I saw all those fights in Mother's beer joint. I didn' wanna be that guy on the floor gettin' his brains bashed in."

"Right."

"An' there's no way I could've fought Lightnin' without..."

"Of course."

"An' Wayland... He drove a great car too..."

"Okay. What'd he drive?"

"...a Corvette."

Elliott chuckles and smiles. "Very cool—every high-school-kid's dream!"

"Yeah. An' by the time I got to high school, he was already out."

"You mean, graduated?"

"Yeah, but he wanted to hang with me, an' he wanted me to hang with him. An' yeah... It was kind of unusual."

"Well, maybe you'd been independent for so long, you might've been on the same maturity..."

"Well, I was more mature than he was."

Elliott laughs. He then says, "But even at that, a lot of parents would say, 'He's too old. You can't hang out with him.'"

"So, who was gonna say that to me?"

"No one. And of course, that's the point."

"But he was... He was very talented, an' I respected that."

"Sure."

"But... He was devious, too."

Elliott smiles. "Okay. Tell me about that."

"Well. Like if it was Friday afternoon an' a nice day, he might call the school an' tell 'em he was my uncle or somethin'."

Elliott chuckles.

"An' he'd tell 'em... He'd say... There was, like an emergency in the family. So, he'd come down there an' pick me up. An' boy, we'd take off to the beer joints."

They both laugh.

"I'll tell you what we did..."

"Okay."

"There used to be a beer joint there—between Broken Bow an' De Queen, Arkansas. An' it was right there on the river—below the bridge down in there. It was called the Choctaw Club. An' this son of a bitch was the most western place you've ever seen in your life. An' there... I mean, anything went."

"By 'western,' you mean as in 'wild' west—emphasis on the 'wild.'"

"Yeah—western. Boy, an' I mean. Uh... Ya know, gam-blin'..."

"...illegal, obviously."

"Oh, yeah... An' Wayland... Uh... People don't believe this, but I'll tell you it's true. 'Cause I was there, an' I saw 'im get in thirteen fights in one night... one night! I mean, they didn't last long. Like... Wayland'd hit 'em, an' they were out. But yeah, somebody'd say somethin'—playin' poker...somethin' go wrong an'..."

"Sounds like you were living on the edge back then."

"I was. An' it's a wonder me an' Wayland hadn't got killed over there."

"Sounds like it."

Poteet takes a deep breath and says, "I'll tell you another thing about high school."

"Okay."

"It's about Vietnam."

Elliott nods and then replies, "Sure. You were just a little before me, but it was a big deal back then."

"It was."

"It shaped our generation," Elliott says and remembers his own close calls with the draft. He was in college when the lottery numbers were drawn. It was one of those things. If your draft board got to your number, you were gone. The night of the lottery, the pundits were saying that his number would probably get him drafted. As it turned out, it didn't. With Poteet bringing it up, he wondered about Poteet's experiences with the draft and the military.

CHAPTER 16

The National Guard

"But... Early in high school...Ya know, Vietnam wadn' even a thing in Idabel. Hardly anyone thought about it."

"It was going on," Elliott notes.

"Yeah, but nobody... I mean... It was like off the radar. Nobody much..."

"There weren't as many troops there at that time. And that was probably four or five years before it was ever an issue for me."

"That's right. An' that made a big difference," Poteet says. "I think it really got cranked up about '66 to '67."

"Yeah. I think that's about right."

"So... I had a couple of older friends, like Ernie Coleman—two years older than me. An' he was in the National Guard. An' ya know, I'd see the guard boys, an' I'd think, 'Man, I'd like to wear that uniform.'" Poteet laughs. "So, I joined the Guard. ...in high school."

"Hmm."

"An' uh..."

Terry asks, "Did you consult anyone about that? Did you talk to your mother? Or..."

"Naw..."

"You just went an' joined."

"Yeah. I just went an' joined. 'Cause they were tryin' to, ya know... They were tryin' to recruit guys at that time. But... By the time I graduated from high school, you couldn't even get in."

Terry says to Elliott, "The National Guard wadn' full time, ya know."

"Right."

"You'd go once a week or once a month..."

"...once a month," Poteet says. "Yeah. An' I remember... They came an' got me. It was a big forest fire up there by Beaver's Bend. This was in '66, I think. An' I was in class that afternoon. These MPs come down there an' said, 'We gotta go, man. ...callin' in everybody. We gotta go fight this forest fire.' But we didn' know a damn thing about fightin' a forest fire."

Elliott chuckles.

"Damn near got burnt up too."

"Well, I'd think it could've been dangerous, if you didn't know what you were doing," Elliott says.

"We got down in this valley. An' uh... We were tryin' to light these backfires, ya know. An' before we knew it, we were surrounded by flames. An' everybody was disoriented. An' uh... They were hollerin', 'Go this way. Let's go that way.' An' I... Like I say, I wadn' very good at takin' orders. I just took off on my own an' ran right through it. I got out of it. Everybody got out of it. But it... It was a pretty close call. Man, I didn' wanna do that again."

"I'll bet."

"But back then... I couldn't... I could not wait to get out of Idabel."

Elliott nods.

"I graduated that one night, an' the next day I left town. I went... I went off on a pipeline, an' I worked with my dad."

"Huh... So, you spent some time with your dad when you got older."

"Yeah, I did." Poteet nods. "An' I was what they call a swamper. My dad was a tractor driver. Ya know, he was drivin' a side boom. A side boom is... It's like a big D8 Cat with an arm on it that lifts the pipe up, ya know. My job was to... When they needed another joint of pipe... Well then, I'd have to run in front of that tractor up to where the pipe was, an' hook it up, an' run back, an' set it in. An' this was like—all day. An' Daddy'd been all over the world doin' this—South America... the Middle East... Africa... all over the place."

"Do you think he liked it?"

"Uh..." Poteet looks up and shakes his head slightly. "I don' know. He was very good at it. I remember my uncle tellin' me... He said, 'He was the best. He was the best operator he'd ever seen.'"

Elliott nods and asks, "How was it—working with your father?"

Poteet takes a moment and then says, "An' so, yeah... I got to know 'im a little bit."

"Seems like you might have made up for some lost time."

Poteet gives a slight shrug. "Yeah, I guess. But that first job we were on together... I was only there two months, an' then I had to go to basic trainin'."

"Oh."

"But then... After I got out, I worked a couple more jobs with 'im. But... Ya know... My impression of him, by that time... I'd grown up, an' I could actually look at 'im objectively. An' I... I jus' knew that he was..." Poteet stares at the wall and says slowly, "Ya know, he had a big problem." He looks over at Elliott. "He was a raging alcoholic. He would be drunk twenty-four hours a day, if he could stay awake."

"That's sad."

"An' that's why he died early."

Elliott nods.

Terry stands and says to Elliott quietly, "I think I hear

someone." She points downstairs.

When the doors are closed behind Terry, Poteet says, "But, Daddy's got one brother who's still alive." He looks at Elliott and grins. "His name is Bill... An' he was always a hippie, ya know?"

Elliott chuckles and says, "Oh really?"

"Yeah. An' he still is."

"...a hippie?"

Poteet chuckles and says, "Yeah... Bill, he had... He had an *aversion* to work."

Elliott laughs. "Where does he live?"

"He lives up in Oregon."

"Oh, okay. ...good place for a hippy, I think."

"Yeah. He was out here—I don' know, about three or four years ago—had his wife with 'im, an' they were in a travel-trailer thing."

"Yeah?"

"An' he uh..." Poteet chuckles. "I forget where he was. I think it was up in Colorado or somethin'. An' he sent us these pictures." Poteet laughs. "Because he went into this... Ya know, Kampgrounds of America or somethin' like that."

"Oh yeah?"

"An' anyway, he'd... Somebody was standin' there. An' they got into a gunfight." Poteet laughs again.

Elliott grins and draws out, "Oh no."

"Not with him, but..."

"Oh..."

"But they shot up his trailer." Poteet laughs harder. "He showed me the bullet holes—in the trailer."

"Damn."

Still laughing, Poteet says, "Yeah."

"You don't think of that kind of thing in an RV park."

"No, you don't."

Poteet continues chuckling and turns back to his frame

building task. "Sorry for that diversion. I thought you might want to hear about Uncle Bill."

Elliott chuckles and says, "Yeah. That's a good story—ol' Uncle Bill."

Poteet shakes his head, smiling.

"So..." Elliott says, looking down at his notes, "You were working on a pipeline with your dad when you got called up."

"Right. It was the summer after I graduated. An' yeah, after two months they said, 'We need you down in Fort Polk, Louisiana.'"

"Okay."

"It was basic trainin', but I was ready. I had hauled hay part of that summer, an' then I went on up to Pennsylvania to work on that pipeline, ya know. An' uh, those were tough jobs. So, by the time I got to Fort Polk... Like I said, I was ready. An' man, it was hot! Whoo! Ya know, the humidity... An' uh... It didn' bother me, like it bothered a lot of 'em though. An' I remember standin' in a formation... An' that was the only time I was in the Army where they'd let you take your trousers outa your boots an' roll 'em up. An' uh... take your shirt an' untuck it an' roll up your sleeves. Because it was jus' that hot. An' I remember..." Poteet chuckles. "We'd be standin' there, an' you could hear somethin' go 'ker-plop.' An' it was one a those ol' boys that was laid out, ya know. ...from up North. ...somebody from up there."

Elliott chuckles.

"An' there was pay phone booths, ya know, at the PX."

"Yeah?"

"An' every night, there was jus' like a line a mile long—for each one of 'em."

"Yeah?"

"An' I was never in one of those lines."

Elliott laughs. "Oh, I didn't think you probably were."

"No, I wadn' in 'em."

"I imagine a lot of 'em had girlfriends or..."

"Yeah."

"...wives or..."

"Yeah."

"...something or other—and mothers."

"I remember one of the things that I thought was strange, but... This was mostly in basic trainin', ya know—inside the barracks." Poteet looks at Elliott. "You've been in Army barracks, I'm sure. Where you've got a bunk here..." He points. "...an' one up here."

"Right..."

"Yeah. You know, lights out at ten o'clock an' all that shit. An', you'd be lyin' there, tryin' to go to sleep, an' you'd hear these ol' boys cryin'. The first time I heard it, I thought, 'What the hell?' I mean..."

Elliott chuckles.

"Ya know... I mean, that never entered my mind—cryin' for home an' shit. I thought, 'What the...'" Poteet chuckles. "So, I remember that. Because, I thought, 'Maybe somebody's...'" Poteet looks at Elliott and shakes his head. "When I first heard it, I thought, 'Maybe somebody's hurt or somethin'?' Then I realized... 'Nope.' An' I just found that so strange. It was just so foreign to me. I couldn'..."

"Yeah. That wasn't you."

"No. Not at all... Cryin' for *what?*" Poteet adds, "That wadn' me."

Elliott shakes his head.

"An' I was a terrible soldier. I mean, I had a real problem with authority."

"Yeah. I think we've established that."

"An' I was always in trouble. Always. An' I remember, we was goin' off on one of these three-day things, an' it was cold, an' it was rainin'. I had a hangover really bad, 'cause we'd been out partyin' the night before. An' so, when we got to where we was goin', they told us, 'Everybody, get off the truck.' So, everybody bailed off but me. An' I told 'em, 'No, I'm not gettin' off.'" He chuckles. "So, that was the Sergeant. He said, 'You better get your ass off.' An' I said, 'I ain't gettin' off.'"

He looks at Elliott to explain, "Ya know, it's cold, an' it's rainin'."

Elliott starts chuckling.

"I said, 'I ain't gonna do it. Nope.'" Poteet grins. "An' so... The Sergeant goes over an' gets the Lieutenant. The Lieutenant come over there an' tol' me to get off the damn truck an' I told him, 'Hell no.' An' so... Then they went an' got the Captain. Well... With the Captain was the Battalion Commander. He was a Major or Lieutenant Colonel or somethin'."

"They got the brass..."

"Right. So, he come up there an' give me a cussin' an' tol' me to get my ass off that truck. An'... They already had me carryin'... Ya know, to punish you, they'd make you carry this... It's called a Browning Automatic Rifle. An' it weighed about... Shit, I don' know what that thing weighed—probably twenty pounds—or more. An' uh... They already had me carryin' it. So, when he told me to get off the truck, I just walked to the back an' threw the rifle down in a mud puddle right there in front of 'em. It got mud all over the Captain an' the Battalion Commander."

Staring in disbelief at Poteet, Elliott says, "Oh shit..."

"An' they just turned around an' walked off. An' I thought, 'I'm goin'. I'm sure I'm goin' now.' 'Cause they kept threatenin' to send me to Vietnam, ya know. An' uh..."

"Seems like that might've done it."

"Yeah. An' I did that again when we was over at Fort Chaffee. We used to have to go over there for two weeks. It was summer camp."

"I'm surprised you weren't in Vietnam."

"Me too..." Poteet says and picks up the frame that's

beginning to look finished.

Terry walks in and asks, "Don't you think we oughta have Elliott over tonight for cocktails an' dinner?"

Elliott looks at Terry and says, "That sounds like too much trouble."

"Oh no. It's not. We've got a little Mexican food place just around the corner that Poteet likes. We can either go there or just pick somethin' up."

Elliott nods and says, "I can do that."

"We can have a couple of drinks an' then decide what we wanna do."

"...sounds good."

After settling the evening's plans, Terry moves to her seat.

Poteet gestures to Elliott and says, "Lemme tell ya about Jackie Stewart."

Elliott chuckles and says, "Okay."

Terry's face lights up.

"Jackie was a friend of mine. An' uh... They came to 'im. He was a platoon leader—platoon *Sergeant*. An' uh... They came to 'im an' said, "We wanna put *him* in your platoon. An' if you can make 'im behave..."

Elliott starts to chuckle and asks Poteet, "... to put *you* in his platoon?"

"Yeah. They said, 'If you'll do that, we'll give you another stripe.'"

Elliott can't help but laugh.

Without cracking a smile, Poteet continues, "He come to me, an' he said, 'Man...' He said, 'You've gotta help me out here.' An' I said, 'Well...' An' Jackie, he was a good friend of mine. I said, 'Oh, I'll do what you tell me to do. But I ain't listenin' to those other mother fuckers.'"

Poteet and Elliott laugh.

"So, I did what he tol' me to do. An' he got his stripes."

Laughing, Elliott says, "Damn... Wow."

"Yeah."

"An' Jackie an' Poteet are still friends today," Terry says with a smile.

"Oh yeah... We are."

As Terry watches Elliott's eyes move from Poteet to his notes, she's thinking about him coming over and what she needs to do to prepare for that.

As he's moving around behind his worktable, Poteet says, "Excuse me. I've got to get connected up here."

Elliott and Terry watch Poteet move his worktable forward enough to allow him to open the door behind the table. He steps out through the narrow opening to a balcony and turns on an air compressor he keeps out there. The compressor connects to a nail gun he uses to nail the canvas material to his frames. He moves the hose from the compressor through the door to the worktable where he's been building the frame. He closes the door as much as he can. He places a piece of canvas over the frame and begins to inspect the fit.

As he positions the canvas, he says, "Ya know, when I first went into the service, my MOS was Field Wireman. An' they had me climbin' poles."

"Hmm..." Elliott responds.

"But each week, there was like three hundred of us in this group, an' they tested us on different things. An' uh... It seemed like every week I was the top guy. An' I'm thinkin', 'How the hell do I know this stuff. I don' know this stuff.'"

"What kind of stuff?"

Poteet looks at Elliott but doesn't answer immediately. He eventually says, "It wadn' stuff you could study for, ya know. An' uh... So, we'd done that for about two months an' then..." He chuckles. "...one day these MPs pulled up, an'... Ya know, in a jeep... An' they went over an' talked to our Lieutenant who pointed at me. An' I thought, 'Oh, shit.'"

Elliott's face brightens, and a smile begins to form.

"An' I'm thinkin' 'So, what have I done this time?' Well, the MPs walked over to me an' introduced themselves, an' they said, 'Hop in the jeep. We're takin' you over to this place. An' I'm thinkin', 'Yeah, great.' An' uh... So, we pull up to this buildin'. It was a one story, low-slung buildin'. It had ten-foot-high concertina wire. All the windows were blacked out an' they had bars. An' I thought, 'Hell, they're gonna throw my ass in the brig.'" He chuckles. "An' so... They said, 'Get out an' go in.' They watched me go in, an' this Captain met me at the door. An' what it was... It was about encrypting an' decrypting messages. What I was scorin' high on was abstract reasoning."

Elliott gives a high-pitched, multi-note affirmation of understanding, "Ohhh..."

"So... Yeah. That's what I did. I'd decode messages. An' that's... 'Cause that's what they were testin' for. ...to see who, ya know, they could find."

"So, once you got into that, it seems like you would have really progressed through the ranks."

"No. Well... I did that at Fort Leonard Wood, Missouri. An' so, when I finished my trainin' up there, I got sent back down to my home unit. An' we didn' have any of that."

"Oh. Of course..."

"An' they had me doin' shit like runnin' wire an' climbin' poles again."

"If you'd been full-time Army," Terry says, "they'd probably put you right into that."

"Yeah, they would've."

"But you had to be in the unit where you lived."

"Mm-hmm... But... Also, I was an E2 after six years. The lowest rank you can have is E1. That's when you first sign the papers. Right then, you're an E1."

"Yeah?"

"So..."

Elliott chuckles as he says, "So, you didn't progress very far."

"No, I didn'. I got to PFC one time. That's Private First Class. That's an E3, an' that's the highest I ever got."

Elliott says, "Then you got knocked down, I guess."

"Yeah, I did."

Elliott and Terry laugh.

Poteet joins in the laughter and says, "Man, I was horrible."

Smiling and chuckling, Elliott looks at Terry and says, "He *was* horrible."

"I'm tellin' ya..."

Elliott asks Poteet. "So, you were in for six years?"

"Yeah. When you sign up for the Guard, it's six years." Poteet looks toward the window and shakes his head slightly. He says, "Yeah. I don' know how..." After a moment, he continues, "Well, I do know... I do know how they didn' send me to Vietnam."

Elliott chuckles and says, "I'm curious..."

"It was because of my cousin. He was the first Sergeant, an' he knew what was goin' on. So, he'd go in there an' plead my case, ya know. 'Cause he told me... One time, he said, 'I didn't do it for you.' He said, 'I knew your mother would whip my ass.'"

Elliott cracks up.

Poteet and Terry join in—partly laughing at Elliott's reaction.

After they gain composure, Poteet adds, "Yeah, she probably would've."

Elliott laughs again.

Terry says, "Yeah, I'm sure she would've."

Still chuckling Elliott says, "Wow, that's funny."

Poteet adds, "Yeah. Nobody messed with Dorothy."

Elliott nods, and Poteet chuckles.

"Did the National Guard do anything for you art-wise?" Elliott asks.

"No... I can't think of a thing. No... It didn't." Poteet takes a deep breath and says after a moment, "Well... One thing, I guess, it probably did do is... It did teach me a little discipline—self-discipline, ya know. 'Cause... I mean, you had to have that."

Terry points at the shelves on the studio's west wall and says, "Do you see how neat these all are—an' orderly. It did teach 'im that."

Elliott chuckles and looks at Poteet. "I guess you learned something."

"Yeah. After six years, I can stack paint boxes."

Elliott and Terry laugh.

As the laughing dies down, Terry watches Elliott, who seems to be enjoying himself. She thinks they'll have a good time this evening at the house. She'll find out from one of their collector friends what Elliott likes to drink, and she'll leave early enough to make sure she's prepared.

CHAPTER 17

Fighting to Make His Way

Elliott eventually says, "I'm trying to get a handle on the post-high-school period of your life, Poteet."

"Okay."

"Your timeline is a little hard to keep track of right through here."

"Yeah." Poteet nods. "It is... It is for me too."

"You graduated from high school in '66. You left. You went to Pennsylvania."

"...on pipeline."

"Your dad was up there. You worked for a couple of months. Then they sent you to..."

"Fort Polk."

"...Fort Polk for basic training."

"Yeah."

"...which was six months."

"Yeah. I was there for... What..." He looks away. "Two an' a half months..."

Elliott squints and cocks his head. "Only two and a half months?"

"An then I was transferred up to Fort Leonard Wood, Missouri..."

"Oh. Okay."

"...for another two an' a half months—somethin' like that."

"Alright. That helps."

Poteet picks up his stretching tool and grabs a piece of canvas with it. While stretching the cloth he says, "Ya know... There was somethin' else I was thinkin' about."

Elliott and Terry turn to listen.

"When I first got out, ya know, from trainin' in the Army. An' uh... I was in, probably the best shape of my life. An' I went to work down at the Lone Star Army Ammunition plant, about ten miles west of Texarkana. There was an ol' boy that worked there while I did, an' he was a damn bully to most people. An' uh... He was on the crew I was on, an' he was always bullyin' people around. An' I don' know... It was just one of those times, when I went, 'You know what? I've had about enough a you.' So, me an' him locked up to fight."

"He was a lot bigger than you, wadn' he?" Terry asks.

"Oh, yeah. An' I kicked the shit out of 'im. An' uh." Poteet laughs. "An' I remember... It was the next night at work... We'd all gone into the break room, an' that was the talk of the place."

Elliott nods and says, "I can imagine."

"They'd say, '...you hear about this? ...about that fight last night? That little guy jus' beat the *shit* out of that big guy.'"

Terry chuckles and smiles.

Poteet looks at Elliott to explain, "You know I have this thing about authority."

Elliott grins. "Yeah. I know about that."

"Well, ya know... Seein' somebody be a bully all the time... I got a thing about that too."

Elliott nods slowly, staring at the floor. He looks up and starts stroking his beard. After a moment of looking toward the window, he says, "I've been thinking about this."

"Okay."

"It's the fighting part of your life."

Poteet nods but remains quiet.

"There's a part of that that makes me uncomfortable," Elliott says and shakes his head. "I'm not a guy who's been in fights. I didn't have to fight to survive or protect myself. I didn't see fights where guys were injured and maimed. My friends didn't have to do that either. The environments I was always in were safe and controlled—at school, in the neighborhood, when we were out as a family... And I guess I didn't see myself having to fight, unless I would have been drafted or something like that."

"Of course."

"And... I can see that it was different for you. You knew you'd have to fight to survive."

"I did."

"And it really wasn't even a question."

"It wasn't."

"You knew the situations you'd be in."

"I did. I'd seen it. I'd grown up with it."

"Right. And that's something different than I faced."

"Sure."

"I didn't ever see myself as soft or weak. I played and competed in sports, and I held my own. At one time, I was considered one of the better athletes in my class. As time went on, I got the film bug and became less interested in sports. That's just how it was."

"I understand."

"So, when I think back, athletic competition was about as close as I got to fighting. I mean, I fought with my brother, but nobody ever got seriously hurt. But, back to you... You knew you'd have to fight, and so you wanted to be good at it. You had a coach, Wayland..."

"Yeah."

"And he taught you how to fight."

"He did."

"So, you knew how to fight. You didn't mind fighting. In fact, you seemed to like it."

"Maybe... I don't think that's totally true."

"Yeah, that may not be fair."

"There was a time in my life... Uh... When I was younger, I got in a lot of fights."

Terry says, "He was usually fightin' somebody bigger."

"Right," Poteet agrees. "Sometimes I was standin' up for somebody else."

"...like your fight at the ammunition plant."

"Yes. Exactly," Poteet says and nods.

Elliott sits forward, holds up his hands and then brings them down to rest on his thighs. "But... My point here is... Sometimes, certain people *have* to fight. You were one of those people."

"Yeah. I was, an' I knew that at a very young age."

"You learned how to fight, and you took pride in that."

"Yeah, I guess... But I'd also say this... Nobody can know for sure that they won't need to defend themselves sometime—especially in today's world."

"That's true. And... I'd have to say I'm not prepared to do that. We have security at the studio, but... You never know."

"That's what I'm sayin'."

Elliott nods slowly and then looks at Terry. "I've watched you, and I think you take pride in Poteet's ability to defend himself and you."

"I do. Yeah... Of course, I do. An' I'll tell ya, Poteet's had to defend me right here in this town—right here in Santa Fe, New Mexico. He defended me."

"Really?"

"An' nobody's ever stood up like that for me before."

Elliott notices the tears in her eyes. He pauses before saying, "And, you're proud of him for doing that."

Even through the tears, she speaks up quickly and loudly, "Yes I am. I'm very proud that he did that for me—very proud."

Elliott nods. "Like I said, I'm trying to figure this out for myself. Fights, fighting, fighting as a skill... You know, you see it in movies. But that's usually about cops or military or gangs and those kinds of things." He turns to Poteet. "But this is real life, and that's an important part of who you are."

"It is. An' it always has been."

"I think I'm educating myself enough to appreciate that aspect of your life."

Poteet continues nodding but remains quiet.

"When you roll that into everything else about you, it makes you quite the superhero."

Poteet looks down, shaking his head.

"And... I don't really know how all this fits the image of what I expected to find here. I'm not saying it's bad. I'm just saying it's unexpected."

With energy, Terry sits forward to say, "Tell you what, Elliott. He's my superhero."

Elliott smiles and looks at Terry. He says, "And I totally believe that."

Poteet chuckles.

After a moment, Elliott asks, "So, where were we?"

Poteet and Terry wait for Elliott to lead the conversation.

"Oh! We were talking about your life after high school, and you were just telling me about the fight at the ammunition plant."

"Well..." Poteet pauses long enough to grab another piece of canvas, stretch it, and nail it to the frame.

Elliott watches carefully and comments, "That will be very strong."

"That's the way I do it. I don' want it comin' apart in just a few years."

"It looks to me like it could hold for centuries."

"I expect for it to."

"You do quality work."

"That's all I know."

Elliott nods and then says as a reminder, "...ammunition plant?"

Poteet looks up to say, "After I left Lone Star, I went back to workin' on pipelines."

"Seems like you were just knocking around—going from one job to another at that time."

"I was. But usually, the pipelines didn't last that long."

Terry stands and holds up her index finger. She points downstairs and walks out.

Poteet grins and says, "I remember one pipeline job I was on."

Elliott chuckles and replies, "Okay?" knowing that another story is coming.

Poteet inspects his frame and then sets it on the table. He looks over at Elliott and says, "I wadn' but about, oh gosh... maybe nineteen or twenty. So, me an' these two other guys left Oklahoma, an' we went down to Mississippi. We didn't have any money. An' I remember..." He chuckles. "We got down there, an' uh... One of these other boys was an Indian boy. Me an' him was pretty good friends. An' when we got there, we had ten dollars." Poteet begins to chuckle. "This little Indian boy told the other one... He said, 'Ya know, you've been carryin' that money the whole time.' He said, 'Lemme carry it for a while.' An' he said, 'Well, all right.' An' uh... So, when we got there, we checked into this ol' hotel. We had the money for that, an' then we had the ten dollars. An' uh... So, we said, 'We're gonna go get somethin' to eat. An' he said, 'You sons of bitches better not spend all the money.' So, the first thing we did... We went out an' bought a fifth of Wild Turkey."

Elliott and Poteet laugh together.

"An' yeah... We ended up in a... a VFW or somethin' like

that. Yeah... Anyway, we picked up these ol' gals an' went with 'em."

Elliott chuckles.

"But I had worked for about two days. I mean, it was kind of like... It was gettin' cold, ya know. The weather was gettin' cold. An' it was... Man, we had really shitty jobs. 'Cause we were jus' kids, ya know. So... I mean, back then... I forget what the wage scale was, but it wadn' very much in Mississippi."

"Oh yeah, I'm sure."

"An' uh... So, I'd worked about two days. An' I come back into the hotel that evenin', an' I'm covered in mud, ya know. An' I'm walkin' down the hallway, an' I walk by this room. I jus' sort of glance in, an' there was two women. One of 'em was standin' there with nothin' on the top."

Elliott laughs.

"An' I'm like..." Poteet chuckles. "...an' I'm walkin' on by an' she hollered at me. She said, 'Hey... Uh... You wanna have sex?'" He chuckles again. "An' I'm like..." Poteet starts a backward motion with his arms and legs. With a smile, he says, "...backstroke."

They both laugh.

"I said, 'Yeah.' Shit."

Elliott sighs and mumbles something.

Poteet laughs. "An' uh... But she was... I thought she was old then. But she was probably... I don' know... maybe forty."

"Yeah?"

"But there was another one—a young one. An' she was like my age. She was eighteen or nineteen. An' uh... So... Ya know, I was talkin' to 'em. We talked there for a while, an' they had somethin' to drink. So, we was drinkin'. An' uh... So, I got over by the young one, an' I said, 'You wanna do this?' She said, 'Yeah. You got any money?' I said, 'No. Shit, I ain't got any money.' She said, 'You don't?' I said, 'No, I just went to work down here.' She said, 'Well, I'll loan you the money.'" Poteet laughs hard.

Elliott asks, "Were they prostitutes?"

"Mm-hmm. Yeah, they were. An' uh... So, she loaned me the money."

They chuckle and laugh.

"She gave it to *me*, an' I gave it back to *her*. An' uh... But she said, 'Oh, I have to do it that way.' She said, 'I can't do this for nothin'.' I said, 'I understand...'"

Poteet and Elliott laugh.

"An' then, this went on for... I don' know, a couple of days. An' uh... She said, 'Why do you have to go out there an' do that?' I said, 'Well, I mean, I gotta... I gotta make some money.' An' she said, 'Well... Ya know... I'll take care of all that.' She said, 'You don't have to go to work.' An' uh... I said, 'Okay.'" Poteet begins to laugh. It gets to the point where he's laughing so hard, he can hardly say, "I quit workin." He then adds, "An' these other two guys... It pissed them off *so* bad."

Elliott laughs.

"They called me all kinds of names. I said, 'Well, you'd a done it too—you assholes.'"

They both laugh.

After the laughing settles down, Elliott says, "Wow."

"Yeah," Poteet says and chuckles. "Yeah, that was funny, when I think about it."

Elliott shakes his head and says, "And this happened—just out of the blue?"

"Yeah, I didn't know... But..."

"Wow."

"But she... Yeah... This one, she really liked me." Poteet tapers off, "Yeah, she jus'..."

They both laugh.

Elliott mutters, "Shit..."

"That didn't last long though. I don' remember... But it didn' last very long at all... I know I got tired of it."

"That's a story I've never seen or read or heard, where a

prostitute loans a John the money." Elliott shakes his head. "Chalk another one up for the 'Unusual' column."

Poteet chuckles and says, "I'll admit it was unusual."

Elliott asks, "And that was in Mississippi?"

"Yeah—McComb, Mississippi. I got tired of that an' came back to Oklahoma. Yeah... But I'll never forget it."

"I'll bet," Elliott says, chuckling. He then breathes deeply trying to remember where they were. He tries to bring the conversation back by saying, "So... During that period of time, I get the impression you worked pipeline jobs whenever you could."

"Yeah, when I could. It's how I could make the most money, an' I'd go all over—Pennsylvania, Mississippi, Michigan..."

"Any of the other jobs stand out for you?"

"Yeah. There was one, I'd been workin' up in Pennsylvania... An' uh... We'd finished that job an' there was a job goin' on in Mississippi."

"...not the same job you just mentioned."

"No. That was a different one."

"Okay."

"An' it was a non-union job. Which... Ya know... Uh... I knew my dad was involved with all this union bullshit, ya know."

"Huh."

"I mean, he had a reputation. So... I go down to this job in Mississippi. An' uh... I knew there could be problems, 'cause we were havin' to cross a picket line to go to work."

"Oh, I see."

"An' there'd been quite a bit of violence down there already. An' I jus' thought, 'I'm not gonna get involved in that.' So... I was in my motel room—one night. An' somebody knocks on the door—about midnight. So, I get up, like an idiot, an' go over to open the door. An' there's a guy standin' there—in a suit with a pistol."

Elliott's eyes pop open.

"An' this guy said, 'Get back in there an' sit down.' So I'm thinkin', 'What in the hell's goin' on?' So, I sit down, an' uh... He sits across the room, an' he tol' me... He said, 'Uh... You're Robert Poteet.' An' I said, 'Yeah.' An' he said, 'You're the one I'm lookin' for.' An' he said... 'You...' An' I forget how he said it, but he said, 'You... You non-union assholes' or whatever... He said, 'Ya know, y'all have killed a couple of our guys, an' we're jus' gonna return the favor.' An' I said, 'Wait a minute! What are you...? Why are you...?' But... All the time I knew what it was about. 'Cause, Daddy's name was Robert also—Robert Edward."

"They called him Ed though. Right?"

"Yeah. An' uh... An' I said, 'You got the wrong guy.' I said, 'You're lookin' for my dad.' An' uh... I said, 'I know what's goin' on here. You got his name off of some news report or somethin'.' But I said, 'Man, I'm only nineteen years old.' An' so... He's listenin' to me. An' I said, 'It's not me—who you're lookin' for. It's not me.' An' I said, 'Plus, my daddy... He's not even on this job. He's somewhere else.' I said, 'He's not even around here.' An' uh... So... He... He said, 'Okay. Get up. We're goin' over here to the motel office, an' I'm gonna see how you signed in.' He said, 'If that says Ed Poteet on there...'"

"That would be very frightening."

Poteet chuckles and continues, "I said, 'Okay.' So, he put the gun in his suit pocket an' put it in my back. We went over to the motel an' woke the guy up. An' he said, 'Let me see the register.' He looked at the register, an' sure enough, ya know... So then, he marched me back over to the motel room an' come back in the room with me. An' he told me... He said, 'Okay.' He said, 'I believe what you're tellin' me.' He said, 'But don't you think you can go to the police or anything—about what's happened here tonight.' He said, 'If you do, I'll come back an'

I'll kill you.' He said, 'When the sun comes up in the mornin', you get your ass outa here.' An' I said, 'You don't have to tell me twice.'"

"So, obviously..."

"Yeah. By the time the sun was up, I was way on down the damn road. An' that was like the last pipeline job I did, at least for a while."

"So, then what?"

"That's about the time I went to Southeastern University."

"Is that in Oklahoma?"

"Yeah. It's in Durant. An' that was in 1968. I remember that."

"...must've been pretty soon after your basic training then."

"Yeah, it was." He turns and stares out the window. "No. No, because my basic training..." He nods. "All of that was in '66."

"Okay. So... basic training, ammunition plant, pipelines, and then college."

"Yeah, I think that's what I did for a couple of years."

"You must have made enough money—to go to school?"

"Yeah, I did. But when I was at Southeastern, I didn't even try. I was jus' there to party. I joined a fraternity. It was the Sig Taus. An' I remember, there was one semester I got into a fight every weekend—that whole semester...every damn weekend—with somebody."

"You must have wanted to."

"I must have. Ya know, I'd always tell myself, 'Well, I didn't start it.' Yeah, you did."

Elliott chuckles and says, "Maybe you were trying to hone your fighting skills."

Poteet cocks his head and takes a deep breath. "Maybe I was." He shrugs. "Maybe subconsciously I was. I'm sure I didn't think of it like that. But... If you've got that attitude, you'll find someone to mix it up with."

"Maybe these other guys were trying to home their skills too. Or maybe they were testing the waters and trying to see just how tough they were."

Poteet shrugs again. "You could be right. But regardless... If you're in that frame of mind, you'll definitely find a fight."

Elliott nods slowly and then says, "So, you went to Southeastern for a year?"

"Let's see... Let me get this timeline again... I was there a year an' a half. An' then I went off pipelinin' that summer. An' I remember this. Yeah. It was in 1969... I was workin'. An' I think we were in Michigan, where all of us guys, young guys, ya know, were stayin' in this motel—two or three to a room."

"Mm-hmm. Sure. ...on per diem."

"Yeah. An' I remember... We were kind of up on a hill. An' at the bottom of the hill there was a little store an' a gas station. An' I had walked down there, 'cause I saw all these vans, an'... Ya know, with the flowers on 'em, an' all this crap..."

"Oh...like hippies."

"Yeah. They were hippies. An' uh... They were all young people, so I started talkin' to 'em, ya know... I ended up talkin' to this girl, an' I said, 'Where you goin'?' She said, 'Oh, there's gonna be a big festival up in New York—at Woodstock.' An' uh... I said, 'Really?' She said, 'Oh, yeah, there's gonna be bands an' all these people.' An' she said, 'Come go with us.' An' I said, 'I'd love to, but I gotta... I'm workin'. I gotta do this job.'"

Elliott rubs his forehead and closes his eyes. He says, "Hmm... Woodstock."

"But yeah, that's..."

"Do you wish you'd gone?"

Poteet shrugs. "Naw, I don' know."

Elliott laughs.

Poteet chuckles and says, "I never thought that much

about it. But yeah. That's..."

"Woodstock... That's pretty significant."

"Yeah, it was. It was—when you think about it."

From downstairs, they hear, "Poteet, I'm leavin'. Y'all come soon."

Poteet looks at his watch and then yells down to Terry, "We'll close up." He then looks at Elliott and asks, "What if I take you by your hotel, an' then we'll go to the house?"

"If you don't mind, that would be great."

As they walk out, Elliott is looking forward to a good time at Poteet and Terry's—also thinking he'll need to be careful about saying too much once they start drinking. He doesn't want to mislead anyone about their prospects.

CHAPTER 18

The Fight in New Orleans

When Poteet and Elliott enter the house, Honey Badger is there to greet them—jumping, barking, and trying to be noticed.

Terry says, "Hush, Honey. You leave Elliott alone."

Elliott leans down to give the dog some attention. He looks up at Terry and says, "I love your pool. Do you get to spend much time out there?"

"Well... With that cover, I'm surprised you could even tell it's a pool."

Elliott chuckles.

"But yeah... Poteet had it built for me about a year ago, so last summer was my first time to use it. An' I *love* it. I really do. It's my favorite place, an' I'm so lookin' forward to summer now."

"I can see why—looks like a great place to spend some time."

"It is. Lemme tell ya." She points to a club-style chair by the kitchen island and says, "You can sit there."

Elliott sits and pulls out his recorder. He shows it to Poteet, who nods.

Poteet says to Elliott, "We heard you liked gin an' tonic."

"I do."

"Can I make you one?"

"Sure."

Poteet moves to the other end of the island, where he makes drinks for everyone.

When they're all seated, Elliott raises his glass. When the other glasses are lifted, he toasts, "To Poteet and Terry and their gracious hospitality." They touch glasses and drink.

Poteet says, "I've got one."

Terry smiles.

They lift their glasses.

Poteet says, "To all our friends that are gone, an' all the friends that we know, an' all them lucky sons of bitches that get to meet us."

All three roar.

They drink, and Terry shouts a high-pitched, "Woooo!" She says, "Let's do that again."

"I like that one," Elliott says.

Poteet smiles and looks at Terry. "Really...? Again...?"

She nods with a grin.

Poteet looks at Elliott. He lifts his glass. Poteet and Terry lift their glasses.

Poteet says again, "To all our friends that are gone..." He stops and looks first at Elliott. ...then at Terry. "...an' all the friends that we know..."

Elliott says, "Okay."

"...an' all them lucky sons of bitches that get to meet us."

They break up again, and Terry gives another, "Woooo!"

"Awesome," Elliott says as he straightens up in his chair. "I've got to remember that."

Terry says, "One more time."

"Well, I'm not gonna say it again."

"No. I mean, jus' drink."

Elliott laughs again.

They touch glasses and take another drink.

"Yeah!" Terry says loudly and with a big smile.

Elliott asks, "Is that a Harold Stevenson thing?"

"No, that's mine," Poteet answers.

"Well, I've got it on tape." Elliott says and chuckles. "I'll be able to learn it and use it."

Terry sighs and stands. She then grabs some snacks to bring over.

Poteet and Elliott aren't shy about digging in.

Terry says, "We can talk about what we're doin' for dinner later. We might wanna go to our little neighborhood Mexican place over here. It's pretty good, idn' it, Poteet?"

"Yeah. It's good." With a straight face, Poteet looks at Elliott and says, "Earlier today... When we were talkin' about fightin'... An' you asked me, was I out lookin' for it?"

"Yeah."

"An' I'd have to say, 'Yes an' no.'"

Elliott chuckles.

"An' that probably dudn' make any sense. But I'll tell you how one of 'em happened."

"Okay."

"When it started, I was drivin' by. I wadn' even there. When I pulled up, this friend of mine was fightin' two guys. So, I get out. An', ya know, I *had* to get involved, which..."

"...being two against one?"

"Yeah. So anyway, this guy that my friend was fightin'... uh... He got really hurt. So, both of us got locked up that night. An' uh... So, we were both charged with aggravated assault an' battery. Anyway, I got out of jail an' my trial was comin' up in a few months, an'... So I went off—workin' on a pipeline. I'd worked all summer an' then come back for that trial. An' all the money I'd been tryin' to save, I had to pay the attorneys, ya know. An' I got sentenced to a year in prison."

"Wow! Did you serve the sentence?"

"No. My attorney got 'em to suspend it, an'... But that judge was really pissed off. He said, 'I'm gonna tell you somethin'.' He said, 'If you get in trouble one more time...' He said, 'If I catch you jaywalkin', your ass is gone.' An' I said, 'Don't worry about it.' I said, 'I'm not even gonna be here.' An' so, I left the next day an' went down to New Orleans to work on a pipeline. I'd been down there jus' one day, an'... Uh... We'd gotten off work an' all these guys decide they wanna go down to Bourbon Street. So... We did. We had a few drinks. An' I remember... We'd been into a... Uh... Oh... What's the name of the club? Uh... Pat... Uh..."

"O'Brien's?" Elliott guesses.

"Yeah, Pat O'Brien's. An' I remember... I had a big hurricane." Poteet indicates the size of the glass with his hands.

Elliott chuckles and says, "Yeah, they're big there."

"An' we were out on the street. It was really crowded. An' uh... Ya know, there's clubs everywhere. We're walkin' down the sidewalk." Poteet takes a deep breath. "An' this black guy come walkin' out of this club an' he was kind of... He wadn' lookin' where he was goin'. An' the guy in front of me shoved 'im away, ya know. Well, the guy turned around, an' he thought it was me, an' uh..."

"The guy in front of you actually shoved this guy."

"Yeah. But the black guy thought it was me."

"Okay."

"An' uh... So, he started cussin' me, ya know. An' he come up an' I said, 'Look man, I didn' do it.' I said, 'Somebody else shoved you. It wadn' me.' An' uh... He just kept cussin' me, an' uh... I was tryin' to walk off an' I'm thinkin', 'Ya know, that son of a bitch is gonna come up behind me.' An' so, I told 'im— two or three times, ya know. 'Jus' leave me alone.' I didn' want any trouble. I couldn' afford any trouble. But he jus'... He just kep' on comin'. So, I went up there an' turned the corner. An' when I did, I backed up against the wall. I still had the..."

"Oh...the hurricane glass."

"Yeah. I had it in my hand. An' I thought, 'If that son of a bitch comes around that corner...' I was also thinkin' 'Damn, I can't do this. Ya know, I can't. Because, if I get in trouble...' Anyway... I hoped he'd go on, but he come around the corner instead. I dropped the hurricane glass, an' I knocked his head off. He hit the ground right there on the concrete. But he jumped right back up. So, I knocked 'im down again, but the guy jus' kept comin' at me. An' I thought, 'Ya know, this guy's got to be on drugs or somethin'. An' so, I knocked 'im down the third time. An' boy, when I did, I got right on top of 'im, an' I just pounded his ass. I knocked 'im out, an' blood was all over the place. An' uh... Within seconds, here come two cops."

"Oh no."

"An' yeah, they come right up an' grabbed me. An' uh... This one cop... He was a coonass." Poteet starts talking with a Cajun accent. "He said, 'What's your name, boy?' An' I said, 'Poteet.'" He looks at Elliott. "Well, Poteet's a Cajun name. An' the cop said, 'Poteet? Is that right?' I said, 'Yeah.' He said, 'I'll tell you what you do, Poteet. You get yo' ass out of here, an' don't you come back.' An' I said, 'Yes, sir.' An' I did. I left. But ya know... I'm tellin' ya. I wadn' lookin' for it."

"No. Sounds like you weren't. There was too much on the line for you at that time."

"Right. Exactly. But... I think you jus'... I think it's a vibe— a vibe you have, ya know."

"I guess. So, other people who are inclined that way can see it in you."

"Yeah. You... You somehow draw it to you, ya know. An' I thought about it. 'Cause, I wadn'...'" He shakes his head. "That was the last thing... I mean, I had just gotten out of jail."

"Yeah. You didn' need that."

"Huh-uh. 'Cause if they'd a locked me up down there, with

that suspended sentence hangin' over my head... I'd a gone to prison."

"You're lucky not to be in jail!"

"I know it."

"I'm not just saying that, Poteet." Elliott shakes his head and adds, "You really are lucky."

"I know it. But yeah. I..."

"That was a really, really... really close call. It seems like you've walked a fine line your whole life."

"I'm with ya," Poteet says and chuckles. "Yeah... When I think about some of this shit I've been in..."

Elliott chuckles.

"It's 'Wow!'"

"Yeah," Elliott responds, shaking his head again—thinking about Poteet's many near disasters. But he knows from experience that "near disasters" and "great escapes" are what the public's looking for in a film.

CHAPTER 19

The Jobs

"So... At some point I decided to do somethin' else. I never really liked pipelinin' anyway. But... I thought, 'There's better things in life...'"

"Okay. So, then what?"

"So, then I came back to Idabel an' went to work for Mr. Hill."

"What kind of business was that?"

"It was a department store. It was the clothing business."
Elliott nods.

"He was a good fellow, an' I worked for 'im for a while. It got to where he really depended on me, an' everybody shopped there. I mean, *everybody* shopped there. An' uh... I was a young guy an' clothing styles changed around that time—ya know, the hippy thing an' all..."

"Sure."

"An' I was up on all that stuff. So... He got to where he would take me to market with 'im every year, so I could pick out the clothes, ya know. He... But I was always too antsy. I jus'..." Poteet shakes his head and takes a drink. "Jus' workin' for him didn' appeal to me." He shrugs. "An'... I told Mr. Hill that."

"Okay."

"So... I decided, 'Well, I'm gonna go back to college.' I'd already been to Southeastern, ya know."

"Which didn't do much for you."

"Right. I just partied. But I enrolled in some classes at Texarkana."

"Did you keep working at the department store?"

"I did. An' uh... Mr. Hill couldn't get over it. He said, ya know, 'I don' know how you do it.' He said, "You work here. You go to school in Texarkana—part-time. You play in a band on the weekends. An' you tol' me you're a straight-A student. How the hell do you do all that?'" He chuckles. "An' I said, 'I don' know, Eual. I jus'... I don' know.'"

"It seems like that was a productive time for you," Elliott notes.

"It was, but... After a while, I had a proposal for 'im."

"Which was..."

"He owned his buildin' an' then another one—just a few doors down. It was smaller. An' it would have worked for what I was thinkin'. Uh... I said, 'Why don't you let me put in a jeans store?'" Poteet nods and takes a drink. "An' this is like, late '69-'70, ya know."

Elliott chuckles. "...a jeans store?"

"Yeah... An' that's when all that shit took off! I mean..."

"Yeah, it did."

"An' I kept askin' 'im, ya know, 'Lemme do that.' An' then... He thought about it, an'... An' then he told me... He said, 'No, I don' think so.' He wouldn't do it."

"You must've been disappointed."

"I was. An' that's when I told 'im I was gonna quit an' go to OU."

"How'd he take it?"

Poteet laughs. "Not so well. An' so... He had a deal for me. He said, 'If uh... If you'll work one more year, I'll pay your way through school—at OU.'"

"Sounds like a pretty good offer."

"But, I said, 'Nope. I ain't got time to do that.'"

"If Mr. Hill would have agreed to the jeans store...?" Elliott asks.

"I would've stayed. But I had told 'im... I'd said, 'I want somethin' of my own. I don' wanna jus' work for you, ya know.' I said, 'I want somethin' that belongs to me.'"

"So, you wanted him to be your partner."

"Yeah. An' I'd a done it fifty-fifty with 'im."

Elliott nods. "Looking back, I'll bet he wished he would've done it."

"Yeah, probably."

"I think you'd have made it work."

"I would've."

"It would have been a good business."

Poteet takes a shot of Tequila and says, "But yeah... I left the department store an' went to OU. At that time, I knew someone at Conoco Oil who tol' me... He said, 'If you'll get a degree in petroleum engineering, I'll get you fixed up with a job.' So, I thought, 'Yeah, that's probably a good idea.' So, my first year at OU, I was an engineering major. An' I absolutely hated it—just hated it. I hated to go to class. I didn't like doin' all that shit. It wadn' what I wanted to do. So, the next year when I came back, I jus'... I thought, 'No. I'm gonna get a degree in art.' So, I changed my major to art."

"I assume you liked that better."

"Yeah, I did. But I had to work. I had to pay my bills."

"What kind of work did you do there?"

"I sold shoes. I sold women's shoes at this mall."

Elliott chuckles.

"An' uh... I didn't get paid a salary. I worked strictly commission—ten per cent. I worked part-time, an' I was the top salesman in four states."

"Nooooo..." Elliott says and laughs.

"Yeah." Poteet laughs too. "Yeah, I was. But... A woman... She'll work you to death—tryin' on shoes."

"Yeah?"

"She'll say, 'I want that one, that one, that one, an' that one in a 7B.'"

Elliott chuckles.

"We sold men's shoes too. But we didn' sell near what we sold in women's... When a man comes in, he'll look around at the shoes an' go, 'You got that in a 10D?' We'd tell 'im, 'Yeah.' An' he'd say, 'Okay, I'll take it.'"

Elliott chuckles and says, "Right. That's exactly what I do."

"An' I remember one time, an' it was when I was at OU... I had lost my grandmother's phone number, an' it was when you used to call the operator to get the number, ya know."

"Yeah, I remember."

"So, I called..." He laughs. "an' I said, uh, 'I need the number for Willie Victory, in Oklahoma City.' An' the operator said, 'Is this a man or a woman?' ...which I thought was kind of weird. An' I said, 'Well, it's a woman.' An' I said, 'That's my grandmother?' She said, 'That's your grandmother?' An' I said, 'Yeah.' She said, 'That's my grandmother, too.'" He chuckles.

"Noooo..."

"She was my cousin. Yeah."

"Now that's wild."

"It is."

"Did you know her?"

"I knew she existed."

"Okay."

"But I didn'... I hadn' met 'er."

"Wow," Elliott says and shakes his head. "So, you were calling Willie."

"Yeah. We talked occasionally. An' I don't remember what I was callin' about at that time. I jus' remember the part about my cousin."

"Sure. But it shows that you did have a relationship with Willie, and you called her occasionally."

Poteet shrugs and says, "Yeah. I called 'er occasionally."

Terry brings over some more chips for the bowl.

Poteet says, "But, after bein' at OU for a while, I was at a point in my life where I jus'... I didn' feel like I was makin' progress, an' I jus' wanted to do somethin', ya know. Jus' goin' to school an' all this stuff was like, yeah, yeah, yeah. But I wanted to have an adventure."

Elliott smiles. "So, what does that even mean?"

"Well... I'd seen a travel brochure, ya know. It was while I was at OU. An' uh... I think there was a travel agency in the Student Union there. I can't remember for sure, but... It got me to thinkin'."

Elliott smiles.

Poteet looks at Elliott's empty glass and asks, "How about another gin an' tonic?"

"Sure."

Poteet grabs the empty glass and stands.

As he walks away, Elliott says, "Tell me about this travel brochure."

From the other end of the kitchen island, Poteet says, "It was for Hawaii."

Elliott chuckles. "So, you decided to go to Hawaii."

"I started thinkin' about it. So, at the end of the semester, me an' Ron Clark opened a night club in Idabel. It was called Friends. Later it was called the Red Barn, an' it burned down. But that summer..."

"You opened a bar?"

"Yep."

"For a summer job?"

Terry giggles.

"Yeah."

Chuckling, Elliott says, "That's pretty aggressive."

"I guess. Our band... Yeah, we played there."

"You mentioned something earlier about a band?"

"Uh-huh."

Terry says, "But the Red Barn, it was... It was pretty salty, wadn' it, Poteet?"

"Uh-huh."

"An' what I mean by salty, I'm talkin' 'bout... Ya know... It could get rough."

Poteet nods and says, "Yeah. It did."

"I mean...lots of fights," she says and turns to look at Poteet. "It was right out there on the curve, wadn' it, Poteet?"

"Yeah. But..."

"...right there. It's when you're goin' into Idabel."

"Yeah."

"What instrument did you play?" Elliott asks.

"Piano. An' uh... I taught myself... I've always been, ya know, artistic in different ways. But... I remember when I was little, we had this old upright piano. My mother would play it, 'cause she taught herself to play. My older sister taught herself to play. An' so, I thought, 'Well, I don't see why I can't do that.' So, I taught myself to play."

"Hmm."

"Did y'all lease the club?" Terry asks.

"Yeah. But I don't remember, ya know... I'm sure it wadn' that much."

She asks, "Did you have to have licenses to do all that, or...?"

"No."

"I guess you didn't—back then."

"Naw. But after that summer, I never played again."

"Huh... So, did you make money?" Elliott asks.

"Yeah. We made a little money—not much. I'm sure I'd hoped to make more."

"Did you bounce while you were there?" Terry asks.

"Well, I... All of us guys in the band... Ya know, if somethin' started... Yeah, I had some fights."

"I figured that," Terry says, smiling.

Elliott lifts his hand with his index finger extended. "There it is. You had to fight to protect your business."

"I did. An' I'll tell you who one of 'em was. It was Bob Franklin."

From the way Poteet had said the name, Elliott knew it would get a reaction from Terry.

Startled, she sits up and asks, "Who?"

"Bob Franklin."

Terry draws back and asks, "My friend?"

"Mm-hmm."

"Oh, I love Bob Franklin."

"We were friends too, but he got a little rowdy in there one night."

With a pained look, Terry asks, "What happened?"

"I hit 'im, an' it was too hard. It sounded like a damn gun went off." Poteet smiles and then slams his fist into his open hand. "Pow! An' uh... Yeah."

"Well... I know he recovered," Terry says reassuringly.

"He did. But he shouldn' a gotten rowdy that night."

"I suppose so."

"I remember one time that summer I got cut really bad, an' uh... It was in a fight. An' so, I was in the hospital at the emergency room there in Idabel." He points to his face. "I think it was over here, an' it was cut all the way down, so you could see the skull an' all. So... A nurse an' a doctor come in. An' the doctor says, 'Oh yeah, we gotta sew that up.' An' he says, 'So we're gonna have to shave your eyebrow off.'"

Elliott chuckles.

"An' I was like, 'No! You ain't doin' that. No.' 'I'm too vain for that. No. Hell no. You're not...'" Poteet begins to chuckle as Elliott begins to laugh.

"So, they say, 'Well... We don't have a choice. We have to.'" Poteet reaches for a chip. "An' I say, 'Call *my* doctor.'"

Terry snickers.

Still holding the chip, Poteet continues, "Now this guy had been my doctor, since I was that tall, ya know." He holds his hand out to indicate a small child.

Elliott nods.

With perfect timing, Poteet adds, "An' he was the town drunk."

Elliott bursts out in laughter. He then says, "That's where she got that about the doctor—when you were born, I think."

"So... He shows up at the hospital. An' he tells 'em, 'No... We're not doin' that to that boy.' An' he sewed me up without shavin' it off."

"Wow!" Elliott says.

"Yeah, an' he was drunker'n shit."

Elliott cracks up.

After a moment Poteet adds, "He was as drunk as I was."

Terry asks, "Who was this?"

"Dr. Hale."

Elliott says to Terry, "So his *regular* doctor was the town drunk."

Chuckling, Terry responds, "Yeah."

Poteet adds, "But he was also the best doctor in town—drunk or not."

Elliott shakes his head, grinning.

"He really was. He was the best, an' he had known me... I mean, Mother started takin' me to 'im when I was just a little bitty shit, ya know. He'd known me my whole life."

"That's funny."

Poteet smiles and chuckles to himself.

CHAPTER 20

Hawaii

"So... You were saying that you were ready for an adventure."

"I was. I really was."

"And it looked like that adventure might include Hawaii."

"I guess. Ya know, I kept thinkin' 'bout that travel brochure."

"I can see why you'd want to go there."

"Yeah. An' I think it was my early upbringin'... I knew that I wadn' afraid to jump out there an' do stuff. Ya know, I never had been. An' there wadn' anybody tellin' me, 'You can't do this, an' you can't do that. You shouldn' do this, or you shouldn' do that.' I kind of had to figure that out on my own."

Elliott nods and says, "I know... You did."

"So, when I bought my plane ticket, I had three hundred bucks in cash left over. But... I mean, in 1970, ya know, that was..."

"Yeah. That was quite a bit," Terry says.

Elliott nods. "Yeah. It was."

"But on the way over there... Uh... I flew out of L.A., an' it's a six-hour trip, ya know. An' this steward kept comin' by. He was givin' everybody champagne, an' then, *he* started drinkin' it."

Elliott laughs.

"He got drunk. An' so, he just gave everybody a whole magnum. So... By the time I got there that night, uh... When I landed... We'd had to fly into Oahu, an' then I caught a smaller plane over to Maui. An'... When..." Poteet chuckles. "When I was gettin' off the plane... It was late at night, ya know. An' I was already walkin' out of the airport, an' I thought, '*I lost my damn money.*' An' I... So, I went back in... An' there was no way. I mean... It was jus' gone. An' I thought, 'Boy, I'm in a hell of a shape here now.'" He laughs quietly. "...out here on an island. ...out in the middle of the Pacific Ocean, an' I don't have a damn dime."

Elliott begins to chuckle.

"An' I don' know anybody. So, I thought, 'Well, I can't stress over it right now.' So... I had long hair, an' I had a backpack. So, I walk out of the airport. An' the road to Maui... It was five miles, an' it was all dirt—at that time. So, I walked out there, an' I thought, 'I don't even know where I'm goin'.' An' it's just pitch black, an' I thought, 'To hell with it.' So, I jus' walked over to this field, threw my backpack down, an' went to sleep."

"Damn," Elliott mutters.

"I woke up the next mornin'"—Poteet says and laughs—"an' I didn't have any water on me, an' all these cars had been drivin' by. I had dirt all over my face. An' uh... So, I didn't really know, but... Back then, they *hated* hippies over there. I wadn' a hippie. I jus' had long hair, 'cause I'd been playin' in a band an' everything. So... There wadn' anybody gonna pick me up. But it was a good thing, 'cause... Durin' that five-mile walk, I got my head cleared, an' I figured out what I was gonna do. So... When I..." Poteet chuckles. "...I got there, I asked somebody... I said, 'Where's the Welfare office?' An' so, they pointed me to it, an'... I went in there, an' there was a Hawaiian lady who interviewed me. An' she said, 'What happened?' So, I told her exactly what happened. An' she said, 'Well, ya know... We've got a special relief fund for people that are stranded here, if you haven't been here for more than forty-eight hours.' She said, 'Do you have a copy of your plane ticket?' An' I did. I said, 'Yep. Here it is.' I said, 'I just got in last night.' An' she asked me... She said, 'Where you from?' An' I said, 'Oklahoma.' An' she said, 'Are you Indian by any chance?' An' I said, 'Yeah.'"

"What I didn' know was that Hawaiians feel like they're Native Americans, too. An' she said, 'Well... If anybody needs help, it's you.' An' I said, 'I agree with you.'" He chuckles. "So, she gave me... Uh... She fixed me up with all these food stamps, an' then she gave me one-hundred-twenty bucks in cash."

"She had cash?" Terry asks. "... that amount of cash?"

"Yeah, she did. An' she gave it to me. An' uh... So, I walk out of there about an hour later, an' I don' know where I'm goin'. Yeah. I'm jus' walkin' down the road. I figured somethin' would turn up."

Elliott and Poteet laugh.

"So... Sure enough, here comes this old boy in a '41 Chevrolet, ya know—one of those big ol' Al Capone-lookin' cars. So, he pulled over. I wadn' hitchhikin' or nothin'. An' I walked up to the car, an' he says, 'Hey. ...you like a ride?' An' I said, 'Sure.'"

Elliott begins to grin.

He said, 'Where you goin'?' An' I said, 'I don' know.'"

Elliott starts to laugh—low in volume and low in tone.

"He said, 'Okay.' So, we take off, an' we don't get very far before he says, 'You like my car?'"

Elliott chuckles.

"I said, 'Yeah, I like your car.' He said, 'You like to buy it?'"

Elliott laughs.

"I said, 'Sure. Whadaya want for it?'" Poteet laughs.

"He said, '...a hundred fifty dollars.' An' I said, 'No man—

can't do it.' I said, 'I got a *hundred* dollars.'"

Elliott chuckles.

"I had a hundred twenty, but I wadn' gonna cough it all up. An' he said, '...a hundred dollars?' I said, 'Yeah.' He said, 'Okay.' So, he turns the car around. We go back to the courthouse, an' he signs this thing over to me. I give 'im a hundred bucks, an' he walks off. I get in the car an' start drivin'. I think, 'Ya know, this ain't so bad.'"

Elliott starts laughing again.

"About two hours before, I was absolutely destitute. An' now, I've got some money in my pocket. I got a new car." Poteet chuckles. "But yeah, I kept that old car the whole time I was there. It never failed to start. An' it was jus'... Ya know, those old cars back then... They were so damn heavy."

"Yeah."

"I had this drunk native run into the front of it..."

Elliott chuckles.

"...comin' down the mountain, an' it just tore the hell out of that little ol' Japanese car."

Elliott shakes his head laughing.

"An' it jus' knocked the headlight out of mine." Poteet laughs. "An' uh..."

Terry asks, "Could you sleep in it?"

"Yeah."

"On the beach?"

"Yeah. I called it my mobile home."

Elliott chuckles.

Poteet explains, "I took out... I took out the back seat an' put in some apple crates. I had food an' everything in there. An' uh... I stopped at this one place, 'cause I saw these bananas growin'. So, I snuck out there an' stole a big stalk of 'em. An' I brought 'em back an' put 'em in the car. I hung 'em from the headliner."

Elliott grins.

"I'd be drivin' down the road an' everybody'd be pointin' an' laughin' at me. But I didn' care." He pauses, then continues. "But yeah... An' when I slept in the car, I wouldn't go to the same place twice."

"That seems smart," Elliott observes.

"So, one night I pulled out into this field. An' what I didn't realize was... This was a sugar cane field. An' I didn' know that they burned those damn things. An' that's what happened to me. 'Cause, when I woke up, there was fire all around me. An' I thought... I was disoriented, an' I thought, 'What the shit?' Ya know... What...? I couldn' remember which direction... So, uh... Anyway, I started the car up an' just drove through it."

"You drove through the fire?" Terry asks as she leans forward.

"Hell yes."

"Oh my gosh."

"What else you gonna do? I mean..."

"That'd scare ya," Terry says with eyes wide.

"Yeah. It did." Poteet chuckles. "Yeah, that was... So, I'd been there about, I think. ...about three months, ya know—sleepin' in the car. Sometimes I'd sleep on the beach, an' uh... But I've thought about this too."

"What's that?" Elliott asks.

"Even when I realized I was broke there... When I first got off the plane in Hawaii..."

"Yeah?"

"It never entered my mind to call anybody."

Elliott nods.

Poteet chuckles and says, "Naw. It never did. It never entered my mind. I always knew that I could figure out somethin'. An' it was lucky for me that it was a five-mile walk into town. Because... Walkin' that five miles, I figured it out, ya know."

"Yeah?"

"I thought, 'Hey. I'm lucky I'm not in a foreign country.' 'Cause I knew... I thought, 'Shit, I'm still in the United States of America.'"

Elliott says, "It makes a difference."

Terry brings over some fresh vegetables with dip and asks, "How did you make enough money to live?"

"Well... From workin' for Eual Hill, I had unemployment. But it was only like $30 a week or somethin' like that. But I got by. I... I wadn' hungry."

"What did you think of Maui?" Elliott asks.

Poteet smiles and shakes his head. "Yeah... Unless you actually see somethin' like that... 'Cause I remember... I jus' couldn' believe how beautiful it was. Ya know, you're standin' up there on those mountains—lookin' out over the ocean... that beautiful blue ocean, an' WOW! I kept thinkin', 'I ain't goin' back.'"

"I know you had to do somethin' to make some money," Terry mentions again.

"I did. An' I began to figure that out too. One of the things was... I saw that they were buildin' a new Sears store there, an' I got interested. So, I went in there—where all the construction was goin' on. An' I saw what they were tryin' to do... I noticed that they had these displays they were tryin' to put together. Well hell... I'd worked in a department store. I knew... So, I asked... Uh... Would they hire me? An' they said, 'Naw. ...can't hire you with hair like that. No. ...can't do it.' An' I said, 'Well, I'll tell you what... I've been sittin' there watchin' these guys over here, an' they don't have a clue what they're doin'. I guarantee you I can put it together.' An' he said, 'Okay then, put it together.' So, I put it together, an' he said, 'Okay, you got a job.' But he said, 'You can't work here.' He said, 'I'm gonna put you out...' So, they put me out in this damn buildin' all by myself."

Elliott and Terry laugh.

Terry says, "...to hide you."

"Yeah... An' uh... So, I did that for a little while... made a little money, ya know."

"I guess this trip to Hawaii came after you'd finished with the National Guard," Elliott asks.

"Almost..." Poteet says and chuckles. "I know when I left OU... Uh... I think I had one... one or maybe two more Guard meetings I had to make—for my discharge. But... I jus' went ahead an' went to Hawaii anyway. I jus' went AWOL, an' I said, 'Screw it. Come get me.'"

With a straight face, Terry says, "See, I didn't even know that part—'til jus' right now."

Astonished, Elliott says, "I think I know enough about the military to know that going AWOL is a big deal."

Poteet nods and says, "It is."

Elliott shakes his head. "That goes under the 'Rebel' column, I think."

Poteet chuckles and continues, "But I knew... I jus' didn' think they would charge me. 'Cause I only had two months left, ya know. I just took a gamble an' said, 'I ain't comin'.' An' I didn' either. So..."

Terry is gasping for air and staring at Poteet.

"But..." Poteet chuckles. "I'm the only person that I know... Because... When it was time to get out, they wanted you to re-up, ya know. Because... They've spent all these years trainin' ya."

"Sure."

"I'm the only one that I know of, that they never did ask."

Elliott and Terry howl. Then Poteet joins in the laughter.

Terry says, "They were sick a you."

Poteet chuckles. "Yeah, they were. An' I think they were glad that they didn't ever have to see me again."

Elliott says, "Maybe the AWOL was a win-win for *everyone*."

"I'd say that it was."

After she catches her breath, Terry says, "So, you worked for Sears."

"Yeah, for a little while."

"Then what...?"

"Well, I came into town one night to wash my clothes..."

"Oh, I've heard this," Terry says and sits back—smiling.

"...an' I was sittin' in the laundromat, an' I was the only person in it. I'm readin' a book, an' uh... So, I see somebody comin' through the door. I look up, an' there's this guy. An' I mean this son of a bitch looked like he's Schwarzenegger. I mean, he was..."

Elliott grabs his drink and sits back.

"Yeah. He had a big, long black beard, long black hair. ...no shirt. An' uh... He come walkin' over to me, an' I'm actin' like I don't even see 'im, ya know. I'm just readin' the book. But he stood right in front of me. So, I look up. An' I said, 'How you doin'?' An' uh... He said, uh, 'How long have you been here?' I said, 'You mean, in the laundromat?' An' he said, 'No, no, no—on the island.' I told 'im, I said, 'Oh, 'bout three months.' An' he said, uh, 'Well...' He said, 'It's about time you got here.'"

Elliott laughs.

"An' I said, 'What are you talkin' about?' An' uh... He said, 'Well, we've been prayin' you in here.' An' I said, 'Really?' He said, 'Oh, yeah.' An' he told me... He said, 'We live right around the corner. There are several of us over there.' An' he said, 'What we do is, we... To make money to sustain us... We print these T-shirts for local businesses. An' the guy that was doin' all of our design work... He left.' An' he said, 'We don't have anybody to do the designs.' He said, 'You are an artist, aren't you?'"

Elliott laughs.

Poteet looks at Elliott and says, "He actually asked me that question."

Still laughing, Elliott asks, "How would he have any idea?"

"I don' know. An' I said, 'Well, yeah.' He said, 'No, you're the guy.' He said, 'We've been prayin' for you.' He said, 'Come around here to our place an' meet everybody.' An' I thought..." Poteet shrugs. "An' I thought, 'Okay, let's go.' So, we walk around the corner, an' this guy's name was John. So, there was John, Joseph, James, Joshua, an' Jeremiah. An' they believed..."

"Those were their real names?" Elliott asks.

"Yeah—their real names. An' they believed... They really believed that Jesus was hoverin' in a spaceship..."

Elliott cracks up.

"...gettin' ready to descend, ya know. He was comin' back an' uh... But that's... That's what they believed. An' I thought, 'What the hell.'"

Elliott shakes his head.

"I didn' care. I really didn'. But, he tol' me. He said, 'I really can't pay you.' Uh... He said, 'But I can give you room an' board.' He said, 'You can have a place to sleep an' enough to eat.' An' he said, ya know, 'You can come in an' work on a design an' have the rest of the day to do whatever you want.' I thought, 'Hell, that's a pretty good deal.' So, that's what I did."

"Hmm."

"But I learned... I didn' know how to silkscreen. But, uh... They had this one boy from California, an' I guess he'd learned it there. But they were good at it. So... I learned basically how it was done, ya know. An' it was all done by hand. They were printin' 'em one at a time."

"Did you ever figure out what made this guy think you were the one?"

"Huh-uh."

Elliott shakes his head. "Even with all the time you spent with 'em..."

"Huh-uh. I mean... He come around to the laundromat an' found me."

Elliott chuckles and picks up a piece of celery.

"But there was a lot of crazy shit goin' on back then, ya know. We had this one guy that would come by, an' uh... He claimed he was from Venus."

Elliott begins to laugh as he lowers the celery into the dip. Terry asks, "What was his name?"

"Omar."

"Omar. That's right. I remember now."

Poteet smiles. "An' uh... I mean... But he would come in with these, ya know, typed out things an' tell us... He'd say, 'These are from Venus.' An' actually, his little publication had all kinds of interesting shit in it. An' uh... I never really questioned it much. I just kind of went along with the whole deal."

Terry says, "Wasn't there one guy there who was very famous—a publisher or somethin' like that?"

"Oh yeah. I can't remember his last name. His first name was Ron. But I remember... When I first walked in there, he was sittin' in a chair. His hair was all dirty an' oily. An' uh... This went on for a couple of days. So, I finally asked somebody, I said, 'What's the deal with Ron over there?' He said, 'Oh, you don't know?' An' I said, 'No.' I said, 'What is it?' He said, 'Well, he was the editor of *Surf* magazine.'"

Poteet dips a carrot into the sauce, looks at Elliott and continues, "Ya know, *Surf* magazine was a big publication at that time. This guy tol' me. He said, 'He OD'd on LSD, an' it burnt his mind up.'"

Elliott shakes head.

"I mean, he could not function after that, an' uh... This guy said, 'Oh yeah, he's been that way for a couple of years.'"

"But they allowed him to live with 'em," Terry says, wondering.

"Uh-huh. Yeah. For some reason... I never did figure that out either. But yeah... I lived with John an' his friends, an' we got along okay."

"So, you found these guys..." Elliott says and pauses. "Well, I guess they actually found you."

"Right. They found me."

Terry stands and says, "Excuse me," and disappears into another room.

"So... You learned how to do silkscreening."

"I did, an' that's how I got off the island."

"Okay. So, how'd you do that?"

"Well... I printed up some T-shirts. I got some money from somewhere to do it, an' I took 'em down to Lahaina where... That was the city, at that time, ya know, where everybody went. An' I jus' walked down the streets of Lahaina sellin' 'em. An' I made enough money to get me a plane ticket out of there."

"By that time, you were ready, I guess?"

"Yeah, I was. I remember... Back then, ya know, you could buy land, an' it wadn'... It wadn' that expensive. An' I started thinkin' 'bout buyin' some."

"Hmm... That would have been a good idea."

"Oh man, yeah! An' that was my plan. It's what I intended to do. I wanted to make enough money to get back over there an' buy some land. But I never made it."

"So, that's pretty much the end of the Hawaiian story, I guess."

"It is, but I wanted to tell you this too."

"Okay."

"An' it's what I was thinkin' about spiritually at that time."

"Okay. We discussed some of what was going on with you when you were very young."

"Right. An' the spiritual side of my life has always been important to me."

Elliott nods. "You know, as a Native American..." He takes a short breath and shakes his head. "I mean, American Indian..."

Poteet nods slowly.

"I don't think I'm surprised at your interest in spirituality—especially since you're an artist."

"Yeah. I don' know. But... When I was in Hawaii, I became friends with some other young people who were also searchin' spiritually. An' they kept tellin' me about this guru, ya know, that they were followin', Guru Maharaj Ji. An' uh... I'd already learned how to do Transcendental Meditation. An' they said, 'Oh, we got a better one.' ...a better meditation. So, I got to goin' to these meetings where they'd have these Mahatmas, an' they'd talk about the Guru. An' uh... So, when I finally left Hawaii... The first place I went was to L.A. to that ashram out there."

CHAPTER 21

T-Shirts

It was intriguing to Elliott to learn that Poteet's first stop on the mainland was an ashram. He sits up to ask, "So, you were interested enough to go right there?"

"Yeah. An' uh... At that place, we'd have to... Ya know, we'd listen to these Mahatmas. They'd teach us all day long. An' uh... So... At some point, I decided. 'I've had about enough of this.'" Poteet chuckles. "'Cause we'd have to get up, like at 3:30 in the mornin'. An' we'd sit on the wooden floor an' eat this stuff—out of a bowl."

Elliott sits back.

"An' uh... I thought, 'Yeah...' I kind of enjoyed the teachings, but I thought, 'Nah, this ain't for me. I need to get out of here.' But... I'd noticed that there'd been some others who said they were gonna leave. An' uh... Well, they didn' want ya to leave, so they'd come an' talk to ya. They wanted to keep ya there. So, when I got ready to go... I didn' have much. I just packed my stuff an' started walkin' out. I said, 'I'm leavin'.' They said, 'Well, wait a minute.' An' I said, 'Nah. An' don't try to stop me either. That's...' An' they didn'.""

"So, the Maharaj Ji, the ashram, and the meditations didn't do anything for you spiritually?"

"No. Not really. But... When I left, I thought, 'I'm *not* goin' back to Idabel.'"

"That doesn't surprise me."

"But... I was familiar with Dallas an' I thought, 'I'll jus' go to Dallas an' see if I can't print T-shirts there.' So... That's where I went. I guess I had some money, 'cause I rented this really cheap little place. I mean it was just a dump, an' uh... But anyway, I set up a little work area in there where I could print T-shirts."

"... very entrepreneurial."

After a moment, Poteet continues, "I had no transportation, ya know. But I met this girl who lived down the street, an' she let me borrow her bicycle. I still had long hair an' everything, an' I always wore cutoffs. Sometimes I'd wear a shirt, an' sometimes I wouldn't. But I'd get her bicycle an' ride to Greenville Avenue there in Dallas. That's where all the clubs were—the bars an' all that. So, I'd jus' stop in... An' uh... This is hard to believe..." Poteet stops and looks at Elliott. He says, "But there was nobody that could print T-shirts in Dallas at that time. Nobody was doin' it. Ya know, the craze started in California, an' then Hawaii picked it up. So... I mean, I got there, an' it was exactly the right time. Yeah. It was *exactly* the right time."

"What an opportunity."

"'Cause, I could go into any bar—practically any restaurant, any club—walk in an' say, 'Would you like to have some printed T-shirts?' An' I'd carry one or two samples with me. They'd go, 'You can do that?' 'Oh yeah, I can do it.' An' uh...I'd tell 'em how much it'd cost. An' they'd say, 'Well, what are they gonna look like?' An' I had a little drawing pad, an' I'd draw out some little design an' say, 'Somethin' like that.' An' they'd say, 'Oh yeah, I like it.'"

"You'd just think of it on the spot?"

"Yeah. An' uh..." Poteet chuckles an' says, "So... I

mean...What gets me... Lookin' back on it... I know how I looked. But I never had one person question my veracity—not one."

"That *is* amazing."

"An' I'd make 'em give me half the money up front. 'Cause I'd take that money an' go buy the T-shirts. An' uh... No one ever said, 'Well, I don't trust you' or 'No, I can't do that.' Naw... not one time. An' uh... That in itself was a miracle."

"I'd say they wanted the T-shirts..."

"They did."

"... and they were willing to roll the dice on you."

"They did. An' then... That thing just mushroomed so fast. 'Cause I... I got so busy, I mean I was... Back then, I was probably makin'... I don' know... $300 a day—just doin' that. An' uh... So, then more business started comin' in—an' even more business. An' then... By that time, I was able to buy a car, an' I rented a building—a cheap building. An' I started, ya know... I'd hire this guy. An' then, we'd get busier, an' I'd hire somebody else. An', one day some guys come in an' told me... They said, ya know, 'We've heard about you'. An' uh... They were from Chicago. They said, 'We've developed this machine that will print these shirts, an' it'll print seventy-two dozen, four-color an hour.'" Poteet looks at Elliott and says, "That's a lot a T-shirts."

Elliott nods and responds, "...sounds like a lot to me."

Poteet's stare intensifies and he says slowly, "Seventy-two dozen in an hour."

"Right. That's a lot of T-shirts."

"So... They said, 'We want you to try it an' tell us what you think.' An' I said, 'Great. Set it up.' So, we set the thing up, an' I ran it for... I don' know—a month or two. An' they come back an' said, 'Whadaya think?' An' I said, 'I want it. Yeah, I want it.' So, I bought that machine from 'em. An' then, boy... Once I bought that thing, I started doin' all these big companies. I started doin', ya know, all these—like CBS Records, Arista Records. I mean I'd jus' go... I can't even think of all of 'em. But once they knew that I was the guy, I mean it was..." Poteet shakes his head. "An' every week, we'd be doin' a promo for some artist."

"It seems like those companies would have been head-quartered in Los Angeles."

"They were."

"But they knew of *you*..."

"Yeah. I mean... They'd just call me an' say. 'We're sendin' you artwork, an' we need this many T-shirts.' An' I'd say, 'Okay.'"

"Huh."

"An' then, ya know, I started doin' T-shirts for the artists, like Willie, Wayland, Jerry Jeff Walker. Oh gosh... After a while they didn' even go through the record companies. They'd jus'... They did it themselves. 'Cause they could sell 'em."

"Sure—at concerts."

"Yeah. An' that's when all that started."

"Huh. ...interesting."

"But yeah, I did that. An' I remember doin' all these T-shirts for Bruce Springsteen. The record company said, 'This is a new artist we really think's gonna be hot.'"

Chuckling, Elliott says, "I think they were right."

"Yeah. They were right. An' I did all the groups... I mean, they were just too numerous to even... Seems like I did everybody's."

"That's pretty cool."

"It was."

"So, did the artists ever come around?"

"Some did. An' I partied with 'em."

"Huh."

"An' I look at Willie Nelson... Ya know, Willie would drink Lonestar Beer or somethin'. But... A lot of those others that were around there, like Wayland... David Allen Coe an' all of them... They did go off the deep end, but... Willie never did. He never did."

"By 'deep end,' you mean drugs?"

"Yeah, drugs..."

"...and alcohol?"

"Yeah, an' alcohol—the whole deal. ...but not Willie. He's still out there doin' it."

"Yeah. He is."

"Of course, he loves to smoke pot. He loved to smoke pot more than he did to drink."

"That's his public image, I think."

"Yeah. But it's not just a public image. From what I know of 'im, that's how he is."

"Okay."

"An' I remember... ZZ Top come in one time."

Elliott chuckles.

"Yeah... Billy Gibbons come in, an' he had his girlfriend with 'im. He wanted to get 'er set up in the T-shirt business. He asked me... He said, 'Could we see how you do it?' I said, 'Sure. Come on in.'"

"Really?"

"Yeah. I don' know if he ever did it or not. But yeah, I didn' care. No, I was really fortunate... I was at the right place at the right time."

"Yeah. You were."

"But I... I sure didn' think it would take off like that."

"You were a successful entrepreneur at a young age."

"I was. But... I didn' think of myself like that. I jus' thought I knew of a way to make some money. It caught on, an'... No, I never... An' I was at the right age to do it, too, ya know—in my 20s. Yeah... I had the stamina then."

"Okay, so you were very busy printing T-shirts and making money in your twenties. I'm a bit lost on how that turns into an art career in Santa Fe."

Terry reappears. The men watch as she quietly sits back down.

Poteet turns back to Elliott and responds, "Painting is what I always wanted to do, but it took a while for me to get there."

"I can understand. Looking at where you started."

"Yeah. That was some of it."

"But... What about Harold? Did you ever see him?"

"...not too much. But back then... Back durin' the sixties an' early seventies... He did some *really beautiful* paintings. That was his 'golden era,' as far as I'm concerned. An' Harold *did* have talent. He was a *great* painter, ya know. I may have told you that he was considered the best of Peggy Guggenheim's stable of painters at that time."

Terry interrupts to say, "Yeah. An' the paintings of some of those artists sell for tens of millions of dollars today."

"Really."

"Yeah—Robert Rauschenberg, Jackson Pollock, Max Ernst, Jasper Johns..."

"They do." Poteet agrees and nods. "So... Back in 2006, one of Jackson Pollock's paintings sold for a hundred forty million. Yeah—a hundred forty million dollars, an' Harold was considered to be better than any of 'em. But that's another story."

"Wow. That's big time."

"It is."

After an uncomfortable few seconds, Elliott says, "I have to admit that I'm not familiar with those names."

"If you're not a serious collector, you wouldn' necessarily know of 'em. But they're huge."

"I clearly get the dollars—tens of millions and more that their paintings are worth today. Wow."

"Yeah."

"And so... Obviously, Harold was very talented to be considered a part of that group," Elliott observes.

"Right. He was. An' he had his own style. But... I mean, as he got older, his work got so homoerotic that it didn' appeal to me. An' truthfully, it didn' appeal to most anybody."

"I don't think you've mentioned that."

"Yeah, he was that way. But to answer your question... We did reconnect when I got back from Hawaii an' lived in Dallas."

"Okay."

"So... He called me one day, an' uh..."

Elliott grins.

"I'd made some trips to Idabel, an' I'd seen 'im. He said, 'Are you comin' in this weekend?' An' I said, 'No. I wadn' plannin' on it.' He said, 'Well, I really wish you would.' He said, 'There's a writer from *Esquire* magazine, Dotson Rader, that's comin' down an' he's gonna do an article on the Wright City Rodeo.'" Poteet looks at Elliott. "It's supposed to be the oldest rodeo in America, an' uh... So, Harold said, 'I'd like for 'im to meet a real cowboy.'" Poteet smiles and says, "An' that wadn' his intention at all. But I said, 'Well... Yeah... If you want me to, I'll come down.' So, I did. I drove to Idabel that afternoon. An' so, when I went into his house, an' he introduced me to... Uh... Uh..." He looks at Terry.

"Dotson," she says.

"Dotson Rader," Poteet repeats and nods to Terry. "An' then he said, 'An' the photographer that's doin' all the photos for the magazine is Tony Snowdon.' An' uh... I said, 'Hi, Tony.' An', ya know, he said 'Hello' to me. I could tell he was an English guy. So, Harold said... He said, uh, 'Dotson an' I gotta run to town an' do somethin'.' He said, 'You sit here an' talk to Tony 'til we get back.' I said, 'Okay, no problem.' So, I sat there, an' we talked for over an hour. An' uh... So, Harold an' Dotson come back in an' Harold was just grinnin', an' he said, 'Well, how did the conversation go?' An' I said, 'It went great.' He said, 'Well, you know who this is, don't you?' An' I said, 'Well, yeah. That's Tony Snowdon.' He said, 'No.'" Poteet chuckles. 'This is *Lord* Snowdon. This is Anthony Armstrong Jones from the Royal Family.' An' I said, 'No shit.'"

Elliott and Terry laugh.

"So, they all got a big kick out of that. Tony did, too. But me an' him became friends. So... Harold... He got me aside, an' he said, 'Ya know,' he said, 'I told Tony that you've got this T-shirt manufacturing place, an' uh... He said he wants some T-shirts really bad for the Royal Family.' An' uh... I said, 'Well, I can do that.' An' he said, 'But he's leavin' on Sunday.' Well, this was Friday afternoon. So, I said, 'Harold... There's... I couldn't possibly get those done.' He said, 'Oh, you have to. You jus' have to.' He said, 'I promised 'im that.'"

Elliott begins to chuckle.

"I said, 'What the hell?' So, Harold tol' me... He said, 'Their club is called the Ya-Ya Club.' An' he drew it out—like a..." Poteet looks up and says, "It looked like a Coca-Cola logo. But Harold said, 'This is what it needs to look like.' An' uh... I said, 'Well, hell, I'll have to go back right now.' An' he said, 'Yeah, you've gotta go back.'"

Elliott laughs.

Poteet starts to chuckle. "Harold said... 'But...' he said, 'You meet 'im at the press room at DFW.' An' he gave me the time Sunday afternoon. He said, 'Now, when you go up there, he's gonna send one of his minions down to you. An' they're gonna say, 'Well, jus' give me the T-shirts, an' I'll give 'em to Lord Snowdon.' He said, 'Nope. No, no.' He said, 'You insist that they go get Tony an' bring 'im down there.' But he had told Snowdon the opposite story. He said, 'Oh, there's no way.'"

Elliott grins.

"He said, 'There's no way he could do that.' He said about me, 'He'd love to at some time, but there's...' So, he was playin' both of us, ya know."

Elliott chuckles.

"So, I did 'em. I got 'em, an' I had 'em ready. So, when I

got to the airport... Sure enough, somebody come an' said, 'Yeah... Well... He'd love to have 'em. So, jus' give 'em to me.' An' I said, 'Nope. Absolutely not. Now, you go get 'im. You tell 'im it's me an' to come down here.' So, in a few minutes... Well, here he comes—jus' smilin', an' laughin', an' everything. An' he said, 'What are you doin'?' I said, 'I got your shirts.' He couldn' believe it. He kept shakin' his head. Then, we both knew that Harold had done this to us. But... He tol' me... He said, 'Ya know...' He said, 'I don't make friends very readily.' He said, 'But, I'm gonna tell you...' He said, 'Wherever I am...' He said, 'I don't care if it's Buckingham Palace...' He said, 'I'm gonna be pissed off at you if you don't come see me.'"

Elliott chuckles.

"He said, 'You do that.' An' I said, 'All right, I'll do it.' But I never did."

"Well, it's obvious that you and Harold were close, even at that time—if he'd play a practical joke on you like that."

"Yeah, we were friends. But Harold was a very funny person when you got to know 'im. He was funny as hell."

Elliott nods and removes his glasses. He sits quietly for a few seconds before saying, "But, getting back to the T-shirt business..."

"Okay."

"How did that play out?"

"Well... Like I said, I'd done some work on some small runs for Coke an' some of these other big companies. An' since Frito-Lay was headquartered right there in Dallas, they heard about me. An' so... One of their people come by one day, an' he said, uh, 'Could you run us off, like, I don' know, twenty-four dozen of...' I think it was, 'Chester Cheetah.' An' I said, 'Yeah... Sure.' So, I did that order for 'em. An' then, they'd come back with small orders... An' then, they hit me with that big one."

"...big one?"

"Yeah. Their guy... He come over... An' the next thing I know, I've got a purchase order for a million shirts."

Elliott drops his head with his mouth open. Looking over the top of his glasses, he says, "...a million T-shirts?" He straightens up and stares at Poteet for a moment before admitting, "I guess you know... That's hard for me to believe."

Poteet smiles and continues, "It's actually hard for me to believe too. But this guy... He said, 'Do you think you can do that?'"

Elliott chuckles.

"An' I said, 'Yep. I can handle it.' An' so, I called Fruit of the Loom, 'cause I knew I could get their shirts cheaper, ya know. An' uh... So... I made an appointment with the President, an' I went up there. I did put on a suit, but I still had long hair. An' uh... So..." Poteet chuckles. "I finally got into his office. He was a real nice guy. We talked there for a little bit, an' he said, 'Well, I know you came all the way from Dallas to talk to me. So, what can I do for you?' An' I said, 'Well, I've got this purchase order from Frito-Lay for a lot of shirts, an' I jus' need to make sure I can get 'em on the delivery schedule I need an' everything.' He said, 'Okay.' He said, 'Well, how many shirts do you need?' I said, 'A million.' He said, 'What?'"

Elliott and Terry chuckle.

Smiling, Poteet says, "I said, 'I need a million of 'em.' He said, 'Hold on a minute.'"

Elliott grins.

"So, he got on the intercom, an' he said, 'You guys get in here.' So, in a few minutes, here come all these guys—all these executives come walkin' in. He said, 'Tell 'em what you told me a minute ago.' I said, 'You mean about the shirts?' An' he said, 'Yeah.' I said, 'Well, I need a million of 'em.' An' they all started laughin'. An' I said, 'What's so damn funny?'"

Elliott starts laughing.

"An' uh... So, this President... He said, "Oh no..." Poteet

chuckles. "He said, 'Son, we're not laughin' at you.' He said, 'Nobody has ever ordered a *million* shirts before.' He said, 'Nobody.' He said, 'We don't even have a million shirts.' He said, uh..."

Elliott continues to laugh.

"'I'll tell you what, though,' he said, 'that's a legit purchase order.' He said, 'You don't worry about it.' He said, 'I'll get in touch with Hanes an' some of these other mills,' he said, 'We'll get you your shirts." An' uh... I said, 'Okay.'"

Winded from laughing, Elliott says, "Wow!"

"An' he did, too. He got me the shirts," Poteet chuckles and says, "but I had people tell me years afterwards... When somebody'd ask 'im about T-shirts, he'd say, 'Don' ask me.' He'd say, 'Ask that boy down there in Dallas, 'cause he knows more about T-shirts than anybody I've ever seen.'"

Terry, Elliott, and Poteet all laugh.

"But that million-shirt order burned me out. I mean..."

"I can see how that could happen," Elliott says.

"I... I still wanted to paint. But I was so busy with the silkscreening that I couldn't do it. An' I'd had several offers to sell my company, an' uh... So, after that Frito-Lay thing... Ya know, I was only... How old was I? ...twenty-eight, twenty-nine—right in there. Yeah."

"That was young."

"Well... We ran that machine around the clock. We'd have to run a day shift for all of my other orders—the bars an' all that stuff. An' at night, we'd run Frito-Lay. That's all we'd run—all night long. An'..."

"This was in an un-air-conditioned buildin'. Wadn' it, Poteet?" Terry asks.

"Mm-hmm."

She says, "...no air—an' in Dallas, Texas...in the summer-time."

"Yeah. But that wadn'... That didn't ever bother me too

much. But... What would happen was... Ya know, at least two or three times a week... Well, I'd get a call at two in the mornin' or three in the mornin', 'Hey, the machine's broke down. Somethin's wrong.'"

"An' I'm the only guy that can fix it. So, I'd have to get up an' go down there an' take care of that problem. An' uh... Then, I'd look at my watch, an' it'd be like five thirty or somethin'. I'd go, 'What the hell?', ya know. So, I'd just stay up the whole damn night, an' then start all over again. So, by the end of the Frito-Lay thing, I was done. I thought, 'Well, I made some money, an' I'm done.' An' uh... So, I called this guy that had been wantin' to buy me out, an' I said, 'You wanna talk about this?' An' he said, 'Yeah.' He said, 'I can be there by noon.' I said, 'Well, come on over.'"

"So, he come by, an' we went down to this Mexican restaurant. An' uh... Before we even got our food, I made the deal with 'im. I said, 'You wanna buy this?' He said, 'Yeah, whadaya want for it?' So, I told 'im. He counter offered, an' I said, 'You got a deal.'"

Terry asks, "How much did you end up sellin' it for?"

Poteet looks away for a moment and then says, "Ohhh... At that time, it was... There was a lot of other stuff involved too— a lot of different equipment things. I don' know... After all the equipment an' everything was sold, maybe two hundred."

Elliott and Terry both say, "That's a lot of money."

"An' I'd already made a lot of money. But ya know... What he was really buyin' from me... 'Cause he had one of those machines, too. He bought his after I did. So, what he was really buyin' from me was my client list."

Elliott nods and says, "I understand."

"That's what he wanted. But I look back on it, ya know, an' uh... I was twenty-four when I started that, an'... I don' know... It seemed like an opportunity to make some money."

"Sure. But... You worked...? What...?"

"Yeah, I worked all the time. When everybody else was out partyin' an' doin' everything... I was workin'."

"You had your wild-and-crazy moments, for sure. But you were able to focus, and you were willing to work hard."

"I had to. I didn' have a choice."

"You had a choice. You could have walked away. But you didn't. You chose to be successful, and that's one of the things I like about your story."

Poteet nods.

"So, your hard work paid off, and you built a good business—at a young age."

"I did." Poteet chuckles. "But it all started by goin' to Hawaii, ya know."

"Yeah. You took a chance."

"I did. But I wadn' so glad when I got off that plane drunk. That was..."

Elliott laughs.

"But I still think about the price of land over there on Maui. It was cheap."

Elliott nods.

After a pause, Poteet adds, "It's not now."

"Yeah, right... So... If you would've gone back and purchased some land, do you think you would have still pursued art?"

Poteet sighs. He then replies, "It's hard to say." He shakes his head. "Probably... No. I would've. 'Cause I was into it by then. Even when I had the T-shirt company, I would do paintings, ya know—when I could."

"You were doing the art for the T-shirts. Did that help?"

"Hmm. I was doin' those designs, which was kind of fun, but it wadn' what I really wanted to do. An' yeah, I've thought about it."

"I see."

"But I don' know if I even wanna see Maui again. 'Cause...

When I was there, it was *so* pristine."

"Have you ever had any contact with any of those people you lived with?" Terry asks.

"Huh-uh. I never did." He shakes his head. "But I did find out about this one. He didn't live there with us. Well, he did for a couple of weeks, but uh... His name was Joe Ritchie, an' Joe was funnier than shit, an' uh... I saw a thing on TV... He became a Jack Nicholson impersonator."

"Really," Terry says, chuckling.

"Yeah. ...in Hollywood. An' he looked jus' like Nicholson too."

Poteet laughs and continues, "But the rest of 'em...? No, I never did see any of 'em. Uh... But that big guy I was tellin' you about... His name was John, ya know. But... Years later, when I had my T-shirt company, somebody... An' I can't remember who it was..." Poteet turns his head and stares at the wall. After a moment, he says, "It was that clothing line. Ya know... Uh... It was Faded... something..."

"...Glory? Faded Glory," Terry assumes.

"Yeah, that was it. An' they were doin' some kind of promotion."

"Yeah. They're still out there."

"So, this guy come to me, an' I was printin' T-shirts for 'em. An' we got to talkin'. An' he said, 'Yeah...' He said, 'We tried to get this guy from Hawaii, ya know. We heard he was really good.' An' I said, 'Who was it?' He said, 'John Scofield.' An' I said, 'I know 'im. That's the guy I learned from.' He said, 'Oh my God, really?' An' I said, 'Yeah.'"

"Was that the guy who came to you in the laundromat?" Elliott asks.

"Mm-hmm. An' uh... So, this guy said, 'Yeah, we brought 'im up to New York City...' He said, 'An' he was absolutely *nuts.*'"

Elliott chuckles.

"I mean... He said, 'He offended everybody in the factory.'"
Elliott's chuckle turns to laughter.

"Ya know..."

Terry asks, "Was he that way when you knew 'im?"

"No," Poteet says, "It sounded to me like he was on drugs or somethin' because... He said, 'What company is this?' They said, 'This is Faded Glory.' An' he said, 'Oh, "F" Old Glory.'"

"Oh, my goodness!" Terry responds.

"I know. So, they said, 'We couldn' get 'im out a there fast enough.' But... Yeah... So, that was the only thing I ever heard about him. An' it sounded like he had lost it, ya know. He wadn' like that at all when I knew 'em."

"Have you ever tried to find 'im on social media?"

"Yeah. ...nothin'."

"He's probably not with us anymore."

"I don' know—maybe not."

Terry sits up and says, "I'm hungry." She looks at Elliott. "You ready to get somethin' to eat?"

Elliott shrugs. "Sure."

"Poteet?" Terry asks.

Poteet looks down at his drink and says, "Why don't you two go. I'm not that hungry."

Terry looks at Elliott and says, "Poteet's mostly a homebody. He'd rather jus' stay here most of the time. That's jus' how he is. Now me... I could go out every single night."

Elliott smiles and says, "At one time, we were out most nights but not so much anymore. I appreciate my time at home now."

"So, whadaya think, Elliott? How 'bout some Mexican food?"

"Sure. I'm in."

As they're walking to Terry's Escalade, Elliott feels almost disoriented. He'd had certain preconceived notions about this

Native American painter. The fact that he'd built a successful business and sold it for big money didn't fit. It was confusing—or maybe it was just the alcohol.

CHAPTER 22

The Hooker, the Dancer, and NYC

Elliott says, "I guess that's the one you built yesterday."

"It is. An' I'm tryin' to visualize the painting I've got in my mind."

Elliott sets his satchel down and begins digging through it. He says, "Thanks for having me out last night. It was fun."

Terry smiles and says, "It *was* fun."

"And I got some good stuff on tape too—all the stories about Hawaii." Elliott chuckles.

"I guess Uber got you back to your hotel alright?" Poteet asks.

"They did."

Terry sits in her regular spot.

When Elliott's recorder is running and positioned, he says, "Through everything we've talked about so far..."

"Yeah?"

"You were single."

"I was."

"Did you ever consider getting married? You haven't really mentioned anyone you were just crazy about."

"No... Well... Ya know, I dated girls all my life, but... I didn' ever wanna... I knew I didn' wanna get married an' possibly have a child an' not have a way to support it—because of what I'd lived through."

"Sure."

"An' so, I actually waited. I was almost thirty years old when I got married for the first time. An' uh... She was an ex-hooker that had cleaned up her act."

"And you knew all that, I guess."

"I did."

Elliott turns to Terry and asks, "Does it bother you for us to talk about other women?"

"No. I've already heard it."

He turns back to Poteet. "So, about this ex-hooker..."

"Yeah... A friend of mine introduced me to 'er at a softball game, an' uh... She was real cute, an' he tol' me the story. He said, 'She's really... She's changed her life, an' she's in a Christian school' an' all this. An' so, we got married, an' that lasted... It didn' even last a month." He shakes his head. "An' I jus' walked out."

"So what happened—to cause you to..."

"We were jus' arguin' about shit all the time. An' I jus', ya know... I wouldn' tolerate much of that in any kind of relationship. An' so... I started datin' this other girl. She was a dance instructor, an' uh... So, we dated for a few months, an' she wanted to get married. An' I thought, 'What the hell?' She was a really good dancer, an' that was when disco was real popular, ya know?"

"Yeah, okay."

"An' uh... She had a dance partner. He was a black guy—a gay black guy. An' man, those two together were just unbelievable to watch. An' so, the Playboy Club put on this contest all across the United States, in each city where they had a Playboy Club... An' there was one in Dallas, so I talked 'em into enterin'. I said, 'Y'all gotta go do that.' An' sure enough, they won it. An' all the winners got to go to L.A. to compete for the championship."

"So, did you go?"

"Oh yeah. But ya know, I was sort of like a third wheel, because all of *their* expenses were paid."

"Hmm."

"Mine wadn'. But I had more fun 'cause... Well, I got to meet Hefner. An' all the Bunnies were there too, an'..."

Poteet and Elliott chuckle.

"Yeah. An'...So, we had lunch out there—outside. It was... He had wild animals an' shit runnin' around out there."

"Yeah. The grounds are beautiful, but it is strange."

"Yeah. An' uh... When I met 'im, he had on his..."

"...robe?" Elliott asks. "That's what I'm picturing."

Poteet chuckles and continues, "So... That afternoon they said, 'Okay everybody... We have to go practice.' Well... I didn' have to go practice. I stayed there, an' I was out there in the pool with the Bunnies."

Terry sits up and says, "Ya gotta know that's where"—she points at Poteet—"that's where he'd be."

Elliott asks, "Were you tempted to have some *special fun* that afternoon with the bunnies? If you know what I mean."

The corners of Poteet's lips turn up and into a wicked smile. "I was married, ya know. I couldn't do anything."

Elliott chuckles and says, "I get the feeling that this is a sanitized version of what went on there that day."

"I wouldn' say I wadn' tempted."

"I would think so. Here you are—every young man's fantasy. You're at the Playboy Mansion—no one else around except the bunnies."

"Well... There were others around but not many. The dance contest was the main event that day, and those people had left. So... Yeah... It was mostly jus' me an' the bunnies out by the pool."

"That's what I'm saying."

After a moment, Poteet chuckles and answers, "Yeah... I was sure talkin' to 'em."

"I'll bet."

"And I don't know how much this has to do with you becoming who you are. But it's just too juicy of a scene to not put it in your movie. To me, it probably falls under the 'Forrest Gump' heading that Terry talks about—how so many unusual things happen to you."

"It *is* probably that."

"But... The Playboy Mansion, just you and the bunnies out by the pool, a dance contest... Wow! That would be fun."

"I guess."

"I might even be able to use some contacts I have to actually shoot those scenes at the Mansion." Elliott stops to stare into the distance. After a moment, he continues, "But I'm sure there'd be trademark issues with Playboy."

Poteet nods and responds, "Probably."

"Who knows how that might work out. But... If we did that scene, I'd play up the temptation angle and create some tension." Elliott nods slightly and then holds out his left hand, palm up. "Here's the good-looking, *married* Poteet being tempted by the beautiful, sexy bunnies in their tiny bikinis. It draws you in." The other hand extends out—palm up. He adds, "And then here's Poteet enjoying the banter, the suggestive looks, the innuendoes, the revealing poses, the soft but 'innocent' touches... I could go on. You know what I mean."

"I do. I wouldn' say it wadn' kind of like that."

Elliott laughs and reacts, "It would be a fun scene."

Poteet chuckles. "An' then one night, they had us all goin' to a hockey game. An' uh... So... We all showed up, an' they introduced us to the owner, Jerry Buss..."

"...a very well-known southern California guy."

"Yeah."

"He also owned the Lakers."

"Right. An' so, the Kings, the hockey team, had seats for everyone that night. An' when we got there, they said, 'Okay everybody, find your seat.' An' uh... Well, I didn't have a seat. An', they said, 'We don' have a seat for you.' An' I said, 'Well, I'll jus'... I'll jus' do somethin' else.' An' Jerry Buss asked me... He said, 'You don't have a seat?' An' I said, 'No.' An' he said, 'Well, you come sit with me.' So, I went up there, an' I sat right beside Jerry Buss, in his suite... no kiddin'. An' uh... When we were up there, he said, 'You want anything?'"

Elliott chuckles.

"...like a drink or, uh... You want somethin' to eat?' I said, 'Like what?' An' he said, '...anything. Whadaya want?' So, I jus' sat up there an' ate an' drank with Jerry Buss."

"What a perfect way to top off that Playboy episode... Here's Poteet Victory, the Native American painter, sitting with this icon of professional-sports ownership in his owner's box, watching a game—eating and drinking it up. I see us panning out on that very scene to end the episode." Elliott shakes his head for too long. He chuckles and adds, "That's so 'Poteet.'"

Terry looks at Elliott and says dryly, "When I call 'im Forrest Gump, you can see why."

"I know. I get it. I even said that."

"Right. And it's totally appropriate."

Poteet snickers and says, "Yeah. My wife an' her partner didn't win it, but they came in third."

"Really...?" Elliott says and chuckles.

"Mm-hmm."

"That's really good."

"Yeah... But I'll tell you why they didn' win it. Her partner... He wanted to wear these... Remember genie pants—real blousy pants."

"Oh yeah. Terry showed me a pair of yours."

Poteet chuckles and then looks at Terry.

She grins and responds, "You know, those ones I have in the office."

"Right. But anyway... I tol' 'im, I said, 'Man, they're not gonna be able to see you movin' in those pants.' But... He wouldn' listen to me. An' when they got out there to perform, I thought, 'Yep, you really screwed up.' An' he did. But they did get to go on TV—not then. It was later. Ya know, there was a TV show called *Dance Fever*."

"Yeah, I remember."

"An' they did win that. Yeah... Yeah, they did."

"Well, even with the genie pants they won third. That's really good."

"Uh-huh. Yeah."

"I think you were right about the pants though."

"I was, an' I knew I was right about it, but... Yeah, I get to tell people I was at the Playboy Mansion. An' yeah... I met Hugh Hefner."

Elliott chuckles.

"So, I stayed with 'er about a year, but it wadn' workin' out. An' then, I thought, 'I gotta go.'"

"And this all happened about the same time you sold your T-shirt company?"

"Yeah. That's right."

"And then, you had all this money."

"I did."

"So, then what?"

"I started goin' to Vegas quite a bit." He pauses and nods before saying, "An' I'll tell you this."

"What's that?"

"I lost a lot of money out there."

Elliott chuckles. "So, you gambled a lot."

"Yeah. An' uh... Oh shit, I used to bet... What was it? I'd bet... I'd bet... sometimes—$20,000 a day. Yeah... I remember one time... I bet twelve football games at $1,000 each an' lost all twelve of 'em."

"Oh, wow. That's really poor luck."

"Yeah. But I... I came to my senses. I talked to a guy that befriended me—an ol' man that was... He was kind of like a mentor to me, 'cause he was an ol' rag man out a New York."

"Rag man?"

"Yeah—clothing salesman, an' I'd sold clothes back in Idabel."

"Right."

"An' uh... He knew me when I had the T-shirt company. An' I told 'im... I said, 'Yeah... Shit... Man, I screwed up. I've lost all this money.' An' he said, 'No. That's exactly what you should've done.' He said, 'Ya know, the first time you make money like that...' He said, 'You don't appreciate it.' He said, 'Jus' go out there an' blow all of it.' He said, "'Cause the next time, you won' do that.'"

Elliott chuckles.

"An' I think he did learn his lesson," Terry says.

"'Cause... For me to bet fifty dollars on a football game's a big deal."

"Yes, it is," Terry confirms and walks out.

"Well, let me just throw this in," Elliott says to get their attention but then stares past Poteet. After a moment he adds, "I like the idea of the Las Vegas scenes. I like the glitz and the lights. I like the contrast between small-town Oklahoma, where you grew up, and Vegas. I'd round it out by showing the differences between your being a high-roller and being a barefoot-boy, hand-printing T-shirts in a Hawaiian commune. It really highlights the broad range of adventures you've had."

Poteet chuckles.

"And I like your newly rich, bad-luck, losing-all-your-money escapades as well. Again, it shows the richness of your experiences—and even at such a young age."

Poteet nods and then points at Elliott. He says, "An' this is relevant."

"Okay?"

"It's about the paintin' part."

"Okay?"

"So... While I was blowin' all my money..."

"Yeah."

"I figured out what I wanted to do. I said, 'Let's get serious about this art thing.' An' the only way I could see to do it was to go to New York City."

"So, the dream of going back to Hawaii to buy land turned into let's get serious about art."

"Yeah. That was it. Yeah."

"...and to go to New York City."

"Yeah, yeah. That's pretty much what was goin' through my head. But... I didn' know a soul up there, an' I didn' know what the hell I needed to do. But anyway, I went up there an' went over to the Art Students League. There was a bulletin board, an' I put my name on it, ya know. You could put on there, 'I need a place to stay.' So, I did that, an' went back to Dallas. Not long after, I got a phone call, an' there was this girl. She said, 'Yeah... We're like three blocks from the Art Students League, an' there's several of us livin' here—in this walkup. It's in Hell's Kitchen.' An' uh... She said, 'Yeah, I've got a room that's comin' up.' An' uh... I said, 'Okay, I'll take it.'" Poteet turns to Elliott. "I told you about my trip up there."

Elliott chuckles. "You did... great story!"

"So... My first day in class... Ya know, they wanted us to bring a portfolio, an' I didn' have one. An' I'm lookin' at what these other young people were doin', an' I thought, 'Man, I gotta get my shit together. They're so much better than me.'"

"It was a challenge."

Poteet nods. "Even then, I knew you either rise to the level of the competition, or you don't. An' if you don't rise to that level, you don' make it. Well, I set my mind to makin' it, an' I did. Ya know, I did. 'Cause while they were all out there partyin', I was in there paintin'. But, for a while, I mean... I didn'... I didn' have any money. But yeah, on the street you could get a slice of pizza for a quarter back then. An' I lived on that for about two weeks." Poteet laughs. "But then, I got a job. I apprenticed with this illustrator. His name was Vincent Topazio an' he was really, really good. He did book covers. He was an illustrator for *Playboy*. He did a lot of movie posters— *lots* of movie posters. An' I worked on those with 'im."

"Yeah?"

"The way he would do it is... Ya know, they'd call 'im an' say, 'Vinny, this is a new movie gettin' ready to come out.' An' they'd tell 'im what it was all about. So, he would sit down with just a magic marker, an' do these different drawings. An' then, we'd go into these studios, an' he'd say, 'Here's my ideas.' An' they'd start sayin', 'Oh yeah, I like this one, I like that one.' Ya know... An' then we'd go back an' put the thing together."

"Huh..."

"He made a lot a money. Yeah. But I never saw 'im again. He was a nice guy. But then, somebody tol' me 'bout a company downtown that did reproductions of old masterpieces. An' they hired a lot of people out of the Art Students League. They tol' me... They said, 'But, you gotta be a pretty good painter.' So, I went down there, an' uh... The guy... I talked to the guy. He said, 'Okay.' He said, 'Here you go.' He set up a painting right there, an' he set me up a canvas. He said, 'Paint it.' So... I did, an' they hired me. An' uh... Yeah, an' I did that for a while. We did the... Like these old Venetian paintings... We did Chinese watercolors. Like I was sayin'... We did about everything."

"I'm sure you had to learn a lot of different techniques to do that."

"Oh yeah, I did."

"Did you like painting in watercolor?"

"Oh, I mean, ya know... To me, I just got to play around with all of it."

"Uh-huh."

Poteet turns back to his canvas.

"Did you always know that you wanted to go to the Art Students League?"

"No."

"So—what made you go there?"

"I don' know. I guess I just started readin' about it. I'd... I'd seen some of these artists that were really famous. An' I'd see that they'd studied there. So, I thought, 'Hmm.'"

"Did you have to be accepted? Or was it hard to get in, or...?"

"No... 'Cause the Arts Student League is not an accredited school."

"Hmm."

"No. An' it's practically free. Yeah. It cost like thirty bucks a class or somethin' like that. It didn' cost much."

"Really?"

"Yeah. It's subsidized. I don' know who..."

"Huh..."

"No, I mean... If you go there, you don' have to... They don' care if you go to class or anything. You don' get any grades."

"So...no grades?"

"It's jus' for serious art students that wanna learn."

"I haven't been by there to notice, but... Is it still there?"

"Oh yeah. ...right there on fifty-seventh. It's an old building, of course. I forget... It goes back to like nineteen hundred or somethin'."

"I believe that."

"An' it's... like, dark in there. Uh... An' I remember the classes, like life drawing class or especially the painting classes. We'd have live models."

"Oh yeah?"

"We'd have easels set up, an' we'd have to rotate every day, because... If you were in the very back, you really couldn't even see the model."

"Hmm."

"But... Actually, it was a good exercise for me. 'Cause, I'd have to walk up to the model, look at it, an' try to keep that in my mind. I'd paint what I could remember, an' then walk back up there. But then... Day after day, I'd rotate up another row, another row, another row. An' finally, I'd get to the front row, ya know. But yeah, it was a pretty good exercise for me—studyin' the model—really learnin' how to study it. An' then, goin' back an' paintin' what I saw."

"Did they rate you at all?"

"Nope. But they had some great instructors, an' I learned a lot from 'em. This one instructor... Yeah... He was a great painter. An' he said, 'You're really not painting until you learn how to paint wet on wet in oils.' An' he was right. He was absolutely right."

"Is that what you do?"

"Yeah. Oh yeah..."

"...wet on wet. So, they sort of mix?"

"Yeah."

"...and it changes the color?" Elliott asks.

"Yeah, sure. I think half of painting is learnin' how this stuff works. 'Cause, when you first start painting in oil... I mean... It's intimidating, 'cause you don't know how this is gonna work with that an' that an' that. But..."

"So, there's a lot to learn."

"Yeah. It's a steep learnin' curve—very steep."

CHAPTER 23

Harold in New York

"I was studyin' at the Art Students League, an' I had a job. I was kind of established when Harold came back to New York. He'd been livin' in Paris, ya know. He called me right away to tell me he'd moved back. So, one day he called. He said, 'What time do you get off?' An' I said, 'Oh, 'bout four o'clock.' He said, 'Well, I want you to come up here on the Upper East Side.'" Poteet looks over at Elliott and explains, "There was an Indian princess... She really was. An' she was from India. An' I knew who he was talkin' about. Her name was Bachu. An' uh... He said, 'We're havin' a cocktail party, an' I want you to come up here.' An' I said, 'Oh Harold, I got paint an' shit on me.' He said, 'Oh perfect.'"

Elliott begins to chuckle.

"He said, 'Come on up here—jus' like that.' I said, 'All right.' So, I get up there, an' uh... He took me into this one room. There were several people sittin' around. An' uh... There was this one guy that was an Englishman, very dapper, ya know—with a monocle an' all that. So, Harold... He said, 'I want you to sit here an' meet these people.' He said, 'I'll be back in a minute.' So... He set me right down by that guy with the monocle."

Barely perceptible, Elliott says, "Yeah?"

"So, I started talkin' to this guy, an' uh... I don' know. I talked to him probably five minutes, an' I said, 'Could I see that monocle?'"

Elliott begins to chuckle.

"An' everybody in the room jus' *died* laughin'. So... Here come Harold around the corner. He said, 'Yeah, I bet 'em all ten dollars you'd have that monocle in five minutes.'"

Elliott and Poteet laugh together.

"But... Ya know... The art scene then was so..." Poteet shakes his head. "I had a conversation with this artist yesterday. He was a sculptor an' he had taught at the Cooper School of Art up in New York City, an' we were talkin' about that. He was sayin' 'Yeah, when you were there...' He said, 'It was... It was pretty exciting in the art world.' An' I said, 'Yeah, it really was.' Because most of it was concentrated down around Soho. An' this was the time of Warhol an' all those guys. But now..."

"Was that the tail end of Warhol and that group of artists?"

"No—not really. I'd say it was right smack dab in the middle of it. I think Andy died in '85."

"So... New York City and the Art Students League... Seems like a good place for studying art—and especially at that time."

"It was, but... I think back on it... I think, 'Man...'"

Elliott chuckles.

"I think, 'You were ballsy to do that. You didn' know anybody.'"

"Yeah."

"...didn' have a job...didn' know what I was gonna do. It was a step of faith. I've had three of those, an' goin' to New York City was one of 'em."

"If you don't mind... What were the other two?"

"Goin' to Hawaii was one. New York City was second. An', comin' out here was the third."

With a sly grin, Elliott says, "I thought maybe your University of Oklahoma project would be one of 'em."

Poteet chuckles and shakes his head.

"Are you ready to talk about that yet?" Elliott asks.

Poteet turns to look at his blank canvas. He shakes his head slowly and replies, "...not really. It'll put me in a bad mood for sure."

"Okay then, let's not do that. I didn't come out here today to be in a bad mood."

Poteet chuckles and offers, "Maybe sometime..."

Elliott looks at the ceiling for a few seconds to think about this project Poteet won't talk about. He knows it had something to do with the Indians and the tribes. If he could confirm what that was, he might be able to make this whole thing more appealing to himself and to his partners.

On the other hand, he wondered, "Could Poteet's reluctance to talk about this be a lingering liability issue?" He certainly hoped not. Something like that could derail everything he'd done so far with Poteet and Terry. But for now, he looks at Poteet and says, "New York City."

Poteet turns around to face Elliott and smiles.

"In New York City you got some help."

"I did."

"You knew Harold, and he had contacts."

"Right."

"And that turned out to be significant."

"It did. So... One day he asked me... He said, 'How much do they pay you?' He was talkin' about painting the reproductions, ya know. An' I said, 'They don't pay very much.' An' they didn't. An' he said, 'I've got a really good friend that owns a really nice restaurant right down in the theater district.' An' uh... He said, 'I think I could get you a job there.' He said, 'Would you like to do that?' An' I said, 'Yeah, if I'd make more money, yeah.' So... He called the owner, an' he tol' me... He said, 'Okay, you gotta be down there tomorrow—for an interview.' He said, 'So dress nice an' stuff.' An' I said, 'Okay.' So... I went down there, an' the owner wadn' there. An' I was talkin' to some of the waiters. I said, 'Well... What are they gonna have me doin' around here? ...washin' dishes?' He said, 'I don' know. We don't need any more waiters.' An' then... I guess the guy who was the assistant manager come up. He said, 'No, no, no.' He said, 'No. You're the new maître d'.' An' I said, 'Me?' He said, 'Yeah, you.' I said, 'Okay.' So that was great. It was an easy job."

Elliott chuckles.

Terry walks in and sits.

"Ya know... *All* the stars, Broadway stars, movie stars... They all came in there. Yeah... An' it was called Curtain Up. You had to come through me—to get in there. So, I met all these people, an' uh... Ya know... What was funny, though, was... Uh... When I'd start talkin' to 'em, they'd wanna jus' ask me another question or somethin'. An' I started thinkin'... 'Man, I'm a popular guy aroun' here. Everybody wants to talk to *me*.' Well, what they were doin' was... They were practicin' my accent."

Elliott and Terry laugh.

"After about two weeks... 'Cause everybody that worked there was in the performin' arts, ya know. Hell, everybody talked jus' like I did." Poteet waves to no one and says, "Hey y'all!" in his best southeastern Oklahoma accent.

Elliott chuckles.

"Yeah. It was good. It was a good job for me, 'cause, I met *so* many people—a lot of famous..."

"I think I might've been in there a time or two," Elliott says. "It was way back when. And it might have even been while you were there."

"I was there in the early to mid-eighties."

"That's about the same time."

"But... We had lots of famous people come in."

"...like Al Pacino," Terry says.

Poteet adds, "Pacino, Robert Duvall, uh... Tennessee Williams, an' uh... We had many, many more."

"I'm sure."

"But yeah... Tennessee Williams... Ya know, He was a flaming gay guy, an' he uh..."

"...the playwright?"

"Yeah. Ya know. ...*Cat on a Hot Tin Roof, The Glass Menagerie, A Streetcar Named Desire.* Yeah. He wrote those. An' Harold knew 'im very well. But he got to where..." Poteet sighs. "Ya know... Every time I'd walk by 'im, he'd try to grab me by my ass or somethin'."

Elliott grins.

"An' I finally told 'im, I said, 'Tennessee, you jus' gotta knock that shit off—now. I'm tellin' ya, I'm not gonna put up with that anymore out of you.'"

Elliott chuckles.

"The owner there... His name was Bob Neihaus, an' he was connected somehow with the shows an' the actors. I think he may have done some Broadway in his time, ya know."

"Hmm."

"But the building Curtain Up was in... It was called Manhattan Plaza."

"Yeah. I remember."

"It's subsidized housing for anybody in the performing arts, an' I thought that was pretty cool."

"Right."

"Yeah. It's a forty-somethin'-story building an' right there in the theatre district."

Elliott nods. "...right there on West Forty-third, I think."

"Right. So, we had a big rush *every* night before the shows..."

"I'll bet."

"...an' after. There were lots of people that came in there—lots of people. An' I mean, it was all the actors. It was *the* actor hang out, ya know." Poteet chuckles. "I think I was the only person who worked there that wadn' in the performing arts."

"...makes sense."

"Yeah. Everybody else was a, ya know, singer, dancer, actor... Everybody was an aspiring somethin'. But there was only one of those people that I ever saw afterwards, an' I've seen him a lot..."

"Oh?"

"He was a comedian, an' he was a bartender when I was there. His name was Allan Havey, an' I've seen him in some movies."

Elliott's face lights up. "Of course, he's been all over the place."

"Right. But... All the rest of 'em... I never saw any of 'em again. Yeah... never did. But Allan, he made it."

Elliott nods.

"An' uh... Another famous person came in there a lot. It was Harry Reasoner, an' he was datin' some actress that lived there. So, he would come in Curtain Up—around noon. An' he would have three martinis." Poteet holds up three fingers and repeats, "Three. An' you could see... I could see... 'Cause you'd see 'im on TV, ya know. He was always so deadpan an' everything."

Elliott laughs.

"Hell, he was drunk. He was. He was drunk. I know he was. 'Cause he'd leave there, an' I'd see him on TV an hour or so later, I'm like, 'Damn.' But yeah..."

Elliott chuckles.

"An' I saw this while I was workin' there at Curtain Up."

"Yeah?"

"It was the first time I ever saw anybody get killed—like murdered."

"Oo..."

"Yeah. It was in the summertime." Poteet removes the top from the tube and squeezes out some green paint. He continues, "An' uh... The restaurant had an outdoor area, an' I'd have to, ya know, walk down through there—askin' people, 'Is everything okay?' Or whatever." He sets the tube of paint back on his table and picks up his painting knife. "An' I heard this guy screamin'. I looked up an' he was across the street, but he was runnin' towards us. It was at night, ya know. An' there was two guys behind 'im." Poteet begins mixing the paints on his palette. "An' I mean, it was right there—jus' the next buildin' over. They finally cornered this guy, an' they were hittin' 'im. Hell, I thought they were hittin' 'im with sticks, 'cause it was 'pop,' 'crack,' every time they'd hit 'im." With a loaded painting knife, Poteet turns to his canvas and says, "So, I run over. An' when I got up there, I could see they were hittin' 'im with machetes."

Elliott and Terry say in unison, "Oh my god."

Poteet turns to Elliott and says, "Yeah. They killed 'im. An' uh... This... One of 'em turned around an' saw me. An' he actually pointed an' said, 'Get 'im.'"

Elliott responds, "Oh shit!"

Poteet turns back to his canvas and begins applying the paint. He says, "But I jus' started backin' up. 'Cause the restaurant was right there—full of people, ya know. Then finally, they jus' took off. They took off runnin', an' uh..."

"Did they get caught?"

Poteet turns to Elliott to answer, "Yeah. The cops caught 'em. They sure did."

"...that night?"

"Yeah. Yeah, they caught 'em. 'Cause they knew which direction they were runnin', ya know. 'Cause they came an' interviewed me. They said, 'Wha'd you see? What happened?' An' I told 'em."

"I never saw anybody get killed," Elliott says. "But... Yeah... New York City can be a rough place."

Poteet turns back to his canvas and says, "An' I saw plenty of that."

"But... New York City has a good side." Elliott thinks about growing up there, the fun he had with his neighborhood friends, and the love he felt from his family.

CHAPTER 24

The Business of Painting

Poteet turns to the sheet of paper that is his palette for more paint. "It was great for me when Harold was there. He'd take me places—nice restaurants. I remember a Chinese place called Pearl's, an' he would take me there. They treated 'im like royalty."

"Sure. I know of Pearl's. It's got a great reputation."

Poteet turns to his painting. "But he would teach me things. An' he must have liked to do that."

"...like, painting things?"

"Yeah. But mostly on the business side—the painting business." Poteet continues to paint as they talk. "Like one day he called me an' he said, 'What are you doin' Saturday mornin'?' I said, 'Oh nothin', I guess.' An' he said, 'Well, I want you to go with me—over here to this place.' An' he tol' me... He said, 'It's for this Greek shipping magnate. I'm doin' portraits of everybody in the family.' An' he said, 'I'm workin' on this one of this young boy right now.' An' he said, 'Come over an' go with me.' An' I said, 'Okay.'" Poteet smiles. "So, when we get there, ya know, the boy's there, an' Harold tells 'im... He says, 'Okay... Well, you can get back over there where you always are in that chair an' sit down.' An' he had the painting covered up. So, he pulls his thing back. An' I'm lookin' at it. An' I'm thinkin', 'Well, what are you gonna do to it? It's already done.'"

Elliott and Terry chuckle.

"An' he sits around there an' just plays with the background an' shit, ya know. An' this goes on for about thirty, forty minutes, an' then he tells the boy, 'Okay, that's all we can do today.' ...covers it back up. An' when we left, I said, 'What were you doin'?' An' he said, 'I wanted you to see this.' He said, 'Don't let anybody ever see how easy this is.'"

Elliott laughs, and so does Terry.

"It was a good lesson—a *good* lesson. An' he said, 'Don't...' He said, 'No, no, no.' An' it happens all the time to me. 'Cause people come in here an' ask, 'Well... How long does it take you to do somethin' like that?' An' I say, 'Oh my God'—ya know."

Elliott smiles.

"It could take weeks an' weeks."

Terry nods and says, "I've seen 'im do that."

Elliott chuckles.

"An' I can do it in two days. Ya know..."

Elliott sighs.

"But if you make it look too easy..."

"Yeah. They don' wanna pay for it."

"Huh-uh."

"I think that translates to other businesses as well," Elliott suggests.

"Yes, it does. It sure does."

"You don't want to make it look too easy."

"It's pretty obvious with a lawyer," Poteet says.

Elliott and Terry break up laughing.

"You can see they ain't doin' nothin'."

Elliott and Terry continue to laugh.

"...chargin' ya a damn arm an' a leg," Poteet says and begins to laugh himself.

When Elliott's and Terry's laughing finally stops, Terry sighs.

Poteet chuckles. He then says, "But, there was another lesson he taught me."

"Okay."

"Ya know, I painted a lot at the Art Student's League. An' after a time, I had some paintings I wanted to sell. So, I got 'em in a gallery an' felt pretty good about it. Not long after, I got with Harold an' I said, 'I wanna take you down to where I'm showin'.' He said, 'What? What are you talkin' about?' I said, 'No, we're goin' to the gallery.' He said, 'Don't you dare.' He said, 'You stay away from that place.' He said, 'Don't even... Don't even walk past it.' An' I said, 'Why?' He said, 'Because...' He said, 'That's one of the biggest no-no's there is in this business. It can destroy the relationship between the artist an' the gallery. No. You leave them alone.'"

"Interesting. I'm surprised at that," Elliott remarks.

"Yeah. I was too. But... I've remembered that. So, I don't... I don't call an' ask anything."

"He doesn't," Terry confirms.

"Well, ya know... You talk about Harold not being a good businessman, but in that sense..."

"Oh yeah, an' in other ways too..."

"When it came to the art business..."

"Yeah."

"...and being a painter and selling..."

"Yeah. He knew about that part. An' I'll tell you another thing he taught me, which I've gone against an' learned the hard way—a few times. He said, 'I don't care who they are, don't you ever *give* a painting to somebody. 'Cause once you give 'em a painting, they'll never buy one from you.'"

"Huh."

"An' it's true. I've had that happen."

"Huh. You'd hope... You give somebody a painting...

They'll like it so much they'll buy others."

"Right. But it dudn' work that way. It was a good piece of advice. I'm sure Harold learned these kinds of things over his career."

"Yeah—the hard way, like you say."

"Yeah."

"Is there anybody who's been more influential in your life than Harold?"

"Nope. He's the one. An' uh...not only in art but in other things as well. Ya know... He jus'... Harold had a different way of lookin' at life than most people. His whole thing was about the beauty. Uh... Somebody asked 'im back in the sixties about life an' death an' everything. An' he said, 'Ya know, I really think that God gives everybody the time to do what they were sent here to do.' He said, 'Like a young poet, he'll have time enough to express the beauty that he sees in life.' An' he said, 'An' I'm the same. That's what I was put here for.' An' he said, 'When I get to the point of where I can't do that... Then I'll die.' An' that's exactly what he did. Exactly. Because he had quit painting. An' then... Shortly afterwards, he died. But Harold... Yeah, Harold was... Ya know, you learn a lot from somebody that's traveled the world—bein' with all the dignitaries an' celebrities that he associated with."

"He was a man of worldly experience."

"I know you've been all over the world yourself—makin' movies."

"Yeah. I have."

Holding his painting knife, Poteet turns from his canvas to face Elliott. He says, "But Harold... He never was... Uh... He was always humble about it. I mean, it never was a big deal to him—the fame, the connections..."

"He was an interesting man," Terry adds.

"I've been callin' 'im 'a Great American Treasure.'"

"You have," Elliott says. "And I'm beginning to see why.

Speaking of great American treasures, I heard that you met Elizabeth Taylor."

Poteet says, "I did," and turns to his palette.

"Her career was just ahead of mine—generationally speaking," Elliott notes. "And I never had an opportunity to meet her."

"Yeah. It was when I was datin' this actress in New York—when I was up there at the Art Students League, ya know. An' uh... Her good friend was this gay guy, an' he was Liz Taylor's hairdresser. An' so, when she was doin' that Broadway play, *The Little Foxes*... Well, he asked... He said, 'Do y'all want to come back an' meet 'er?' We said, 'Yeah. Sure.' But that guy... An' I can't remember his name, but uh... He was sayin' that, ya know, he traveled with 'er everywhere."

"Of course. A star like that would always take her hairdresser with her."

"I guess. But anyway... He said he was out with her all the time in New York, an'... He said he'd never seen 'er pay for a meal—ever. He said that a lot of the time they didn' even wanna bring 'er the check. An' she'd say, 'Oh, bring me the check.' So, they'd bring the check, an' she'd sign it. She'd hand it back to 'em. An' that was..."

"It was an autograph. It's proof that she was there."

"Yeah. Exactly."

Elliott smiles. "They cared a lot more about an autograph and maybe a photo than they did about getting paid for a meal."

"Sure. Jus' think..." Terry says. "If Liz Taylor came into your restaurant..."

"Yeah. You'd frame that one, I promise you," Elliott says and then closes his eyes. He scratches the top of his head, repositions his glasses, and says to Poteet, "Thinking about New York City, the Art Students League, and everything that went on there..."

"Yeah."

"You didn't have money. You had to work."

"Right."

"Basically, you had to survive somehow."

"I did," Poteet says and nods.

"But... From what I've been hearing, I think you consider those the good times."

"I do," Poteet says as he turns back to his palette. "An' those *were* the good times. Ya know... You look back on your life... Those *are* the good times. I mean... It was tough, an' you never knew what was around the next corner. But that was sort of the excitement of the whole thing for me. It was a part of growin' up."

Elliott nods and says, "I agree with you. I remember my early days the very same way. And I had some great friends back then... We were all just scaping by, but we were all in it together—it seemed."

"Yeah. Things are great now, but there was somethin' special about jus' gettin' started."

Elliott thinks back about his early days in southern California. He was fortunate to be able to go to school in L.A. He'd had a leg up on anybody who hadn't. He remembers that first job. It was creating storyboards. He was fortunate to get that job, and it kicked off his career. After a moment, he says, "I've got another question about Harold."

CHAPTER 25

He'd Make a Dollar

"Was he promoting you to go to New York City?"

"No. That was all my idea."

"But once you decided to do it, he helped you out?"

"Yeah. He said, 'Well... If you're gonna go, then you might as well know the right people.'"

"An' Harold did help Poteet," Terry says.

"So... Thinking about how we'd present your story... I think Harold is a character we could create some great subplots around."

As he paints with broad sweeping arcs, Poteet says, "I don't know what you're thinkin', but I imagine you could. He lived all over the world. He knew kings an' queens. He knew the rich an' famous of his time. He hung with infamous scoundrels. He was a great painter. An' he was on the forefront of the sexual revolution." He turns to Elliott to say, "Ya know, he was out of the closet by the late fifties."

"Huh..."

"An' uh..."

Terry leans forward to say, "There's a biography about 'im you could use for reference."

"Somebody wrote a book about Harold?"

"Yep."

Elliott smiles and says, "Hmm. That's something to think about. It really is. For a successful series, you need interesting characters that have stories of their own."

"Well... There's plenty there with Harold," Poteet says.

"That's for sure," Terry adds.

"An' we stayed in contact. He thought I was young an' didn' know what I wanted to do. But once I locked in with art... Then, he was all behind it, ya know."

"I'm curious now about those Alexander the Great paintings," Elliott says.

"Okay."

"Was it a series, or was it just one painting?"

"No. Well yeah... Uh... There was one big one, an' he did several smaller ones. But that one big one... Yeah... 'Cause... To me, his heyday... I thought he did the most beautiful paintings in the sixties an' seventies. An' that was when he did those. An' that big one... It was beautiful."

"Poteet..." Terry says.

Elliott and Poteet turn.

"I mean, I would love to know where that is."

"I would too," Poteet says, nodding.

"Maybe someday they'll find it," Elliott suggests.

"I'd love to see it again," Poteet says. "Maybe somebody at the Guggenheim will look for it. It would be a great addition to their collection."

"You mentioned something about Guggenheim and Harold..."

"Oh... Harold had a long an' very colorful history with 'em—with Peggy Guggenheim an' her cohorts back in the day."

"Huh..." Elliott says. "I've done some reading on mid-century art, and Peggy Guggenheim's name comes up a lot. Her life was exciting but tragic. Did Harold know her?"

"Yes—very well."

"Did the Guggenheim Art Museum show his paintings?"

"Oh, yeah. But he became very controversial."

"In what way?"

"It was about his painting, *The New Adam*. An' now, that may be his most famous one."

"What did it look like?"

"It was a giant painting of a nude Sal Mineo."

Elliott's eyes widen.

"An' when I say 'giant,' I mean it was really, really big. It's like forty feet wide an' ten feet high. You can imagine how jarring a giant nude-male painting would've been back in the sixties."

Elliott chuckles and says, "Yeah—shocking, to say the least."

Without commenting, Terry stands and walks out.

Poteet continues, "But Harold... He got a lot of publicity... Ya know...It sort of made 'im famous, an' it should've. He was a great painter. But they kicked *The New Adam* out of the show. It made 'im mad, an' he went to Paris. Ya know, he became very, very famous there."

"Maybe they were more accepting of his controversial ways."

"Yeah... In Paris... I think you're right. They *were* more accepting. An' they liked where he was taking the art world."

"What do you mean?"

"Gigantism."

"What's that."

"Well... He noticed that some people would go into art galleries an' some wouldn't."

"Sure."

"So, he started paintin' big, so that people would have to see it. An' that's why he hung that painting on the Eiffel Tower."

Elliott cocks his head and asks in disbelief, "He hung a

painting on the Eiffel Tower?"

"Yeah. An' it stopped traffic," Poteet says and laughs. "They had to get the government involved." Poteet laughs again. "It was like forty feet tall."

"...forty feet tall!"

"Yeah. He really wanted to make a statement."

"So... What did this giant painting look like?"

"It was El Cordobes, the bullfighter."

"And this bullfighter was known in Paris?"

"Oh yeah. He was world famous. An' he was the first athlete to ever make a million dollars a year. He was in *Life* magazine for that."

"Hmm. I sort of remember something..."

"Harold knew 'im, an' he was a big fan. But... In the painting... All you could see was, like three quarters of his face."

"Yeah?"

"You could see his outfit, the cap he wore, an' then his shoulder. The costumes they wore were colorful, an' Harold gold-leafed the thing. So, when you saw it, it was vibrating in the wind. Yeah, it got people's attention."

"Was that the largest painting he ever did?"

"Probably," Poteet replies and smiles. "'Cause, it was huge. But... I mean, one of his regular paintings could be twenty feet long, Ya know... fifteen feet. That wadn'..."

Elliott turns to gaze out the west window and repeats under his breath, "Harold stopped traffic at the Eiffel Tower." He looks over at Poteet. "I worked on a movie in Paris years ago. We shot some scenes around the Eiffel Tower, and I'm just trying to picture how that would work."

"He said it caused a hellava traffic jam."

Elliott chuckles and nods. He says, "I'll bet it did."

"But Harold... He brought new thinking. He was very original in what he did."

"I think you called it gigantic-acism."

"Gigantism."

"Gigantism," Elliott repeats. And he then asks, "And that was *his* idea?"

"Yep. No one had ever done that before."

"You can't help but appreciate that kind of creativity. Everyone in the fields of artistic endeavor is always searching for a new way, something different, a new angle, a new approach..."

"Yeah. An' he did that. Yeah... An' I mean, it was somethin' we always talked about. An' I don' know what makes people artistic. Ya know, I've read stories about people like David Bowie an' the Beatles. They were art students. Yeah. They were failures at it..."

Elliott chuckles.

"...but they were art students."

"I remember hearing that about John Lennon."

"Yeah. David Bowie was too."

"Okay."

"Yeah. An' uh... I think those things translate very easily between, ya know, the performing arts, an' then the visual arts."

Elliott turns to look at his satchel on the floor. He says, "By the way, I read that article about Harold."

"What'd ya think?"

As he's reaching for his satchel, Elliott says, "It was great." He pulls out the magazine and sets his satchel back down. He stands, lays the magazine on Poteet's worktable, and opens it to the article. He says, "An' yeah. It's just amazing to me... In the article it talks about how Harold, uh... He had a studio down there on Central Avenue—across from the theater."

"Yeah, that was... Uh... when he was very young."

"Oh yeah. ...ten years old. I think it says."

"Yeah. Well, he was on his career path well before then."

"I understand. And we've talked about that."

"Right."

"And this says, 'He opened his studio, and he would do portraits.'"

"Yep."

"...for a dollar."

"Yeah. He was a professional artist when he was ten," Poteet says with a laugh.

"That's amazing."

"It is. It really is. If you're like that, you're just born with it. It's, uh... Ya know... Nobody encouraged 'im to do anything like that."

"Well, I wondered."

"Yeah."

"I mean... It seems like... To do something like that, you'd have to get some help—get encouragement from your parents or something."

"Oh, I guess, ya know..."

"...to even..."

"They just allowed 'im to do it, I think."

"Yeah, And, if he's selling his portraits and making a dollar, then..."

"Yeah."

"He could probably pay his rent."

Poteet chuckles.

Elliott begins to chuckle. "I'm guessing that the second story of a building down there in Idabel wasn't very expensive."

"They probably gave it to 'im anyway—whatever it was," Poteet says.

"They may have."

Poteet walks over to see the magazine. Looking at a large photo on one of the pages, he points and says, "Yeah, I was right there in that studio when he was doin' those portraits."

"Hmm."

"He did a series called 'The Great Society.' It was back in the sixties. He painted a hundred portraits of just common everyday people, ya know." Poteet points at the second page showing Harold and an unfinished portrait of a man. He says, "That was the doctor that delivered me. Yep, sure was—Dr. R.D. Williams."

"Hmm." Looking at the picture of Harold, Elliott says, "He was obviously young then. Was he..."

"He was like thirty-one, thirty-two—somethin' like that. Yeah. An' that's when Harold an' I... That's when we really got to know each other."

"Was that about the time he was painting you?"

"It was. It was after the Alexander series, but one of the hundred was of me."

"Hmm. And so, all the people... Most of them were..."

"...from Idabel. 'Cause everybody knew Harold, an' he'd say, 'Why don't you come out to the studio an' lemme jus' do your portrait real quick. Ya know, I'm doin' this series...'" Poteet looks at Elliott and says, "An' of course, everybody came."

Elliott nods.

"An' he didn't care who you were or what you looked like or any of that. He'd just..."

"So, doing a hundred portraits wasn't any big deal for Harold?"

"No. Not at all. He had such a great eye, ya know. Harold could jus'... I mean, he didn' struggle with the likeness or anything. He jus'... Yeah... He had a great eye. I watched 'im do many portraits. He had a real talent for that."

Elliott nods slowly and says, "So, we know Harold made money when he was very young. Did he make money through his adult career?"

"Harold made a lot of money. But he... He didn't think in

those terms. He was totally unconcerned. I mean, he jus'...
Money jus'... Yeah... Especially back in the sixties an' seventies,
he made a ton of money. I don' know what he did with it—
gave it away, I imagine. Ya know... That'd be something he'd
do—give it away. But yeah..."

"Wouldn't you have to be concerned about paying your
rent?"

"Yeah. He'd do that. But he wadn' a businessman. He didn'
try to accumulate anything."

"Huh," Elliott says and holds up the magazine. "Do you
mind if I keep this a little longer?"

"No. Go ahead."

"I'd like to read it again."

"Sure," Poteet says and shrugs. "It's funny how your life is
sort of a mosaic, an' I think it was that way for Harold too. Ya
know, I look at it that way." He stares out the north window
and shakes his head. "I've learned... I've learned some things
about the way I paint," Poteet says and then pauses. He
continues, almost like he's angry, "Don't take the mistakes out.
Use 'em. Make 'em work for ya." He moderates his tone to say,
"Sometimes I think a painting has a mind of its own, an' you
jus' follow it. An'... I think that's the way life is. Sometimes you
jus' have to go with the flow."

Elliott nods without knowing it.

"An' sometimes that takes faith." Poteet walks into his
kitchen and quickly returns with a painting with two horses
in the foreground. He shows it to Elliott and says, "When I
started... This wasn't really what I had in mind. But I went
where it took me, an' that's what I've learned to do."

They turn to see Terry walk in.

Poteet lays the painting on the table. All three gather
around. Poteet says, "Ya know, I get real tired of lookin' at
traditional paintings." He smiles. "I get bored with 'em real
fast. An' I can go either way. I can do realism, or I can do

216

abstract. This one here's more realism, but I still try to keep it loose, ya know."

"Yeah. That's beautiful," Elliott says.

Poteet shrugs and then nods. He says, "I like the way it turned out. People come in here an' go crazy over paintings like this."

"So, what is it that they like so much?"

"It's the landscape, I think. It's the horses in the foreground."

"I like the way it comes into focus here"—Elliott points at the painting—"at the horses."

"Right. An' that's sort of the secret to painting. Uh... Because the way you naturally see somethin'... Like... If you focus on somethin', everything out in the periphery is gonna be blurred a little bit. An' only that center of interest, what you're starin' at, will be sharp. So, you have to keep that in mind when you do a painting. Ya know. I sort of exaggerate it. But I like for a realism painting to look about halfway abstract."

"I've heard that about Rembrandt's style."

"You're right. That's how he painted."

"Is that what you've always done?"

"No—not really." Poteet picks up the painting and returns it to his kitchen. Terry and Elliott sit.

As Poteet walks back in, he says, "When I started, I was totally Southwest. As time went on, I threw in more abstract influences. An' then, I switched to mostly abstract. I had my reasons, an' mostly it worked out."

"Sure."

"An' something you'll notice about people that collect art... Their tastes will change as time goes on. An' uh... I've noticed that about myself too. Some of the artists I used to really be enamored with, I'm not anymore. An' some of 'em I didn' like, I do now. But jus'... Your tastes change—whether you're a painter or a collector."

"You can say the same about movies, like with this 'real-life' concept thing I'm interested in now. I didn't care a thing about history when I was young. It was all about car chases, fights, guns, knives, fast sex—the more, the better."

"Sure."

"But man... I've seen enough of that."

"Me too!" Terry adds.

"Where are the nuances? Where are the subtleties? All this action bullshit is boring. It's predictable. It's formula. At my age, I've got to learn something. I've got to be informed. My intellect has to be tweaked and advanced somehow."

"Right on, Elliott," Terry encourages.

Poteet smiles and reaches for a tube of paint from the collection on his table.

"The really great films are deep. They have meaning. They touch you. And that's what I'm looking for."

Poteet squeezes some yellow paint onto his palette.

Elliott explains, "I guess I needed to get that off my chest."

Poteet chuckles. He then turns to Elliott. "But I agree. You can't really argue against any of that."

"Okay. So... There's something else I've been thinking about."

"What's that?"

"It's about artists in general."

"Okay."

"I'm thinking... And this would be about painters... sculptors... musicians, I guess."

"An' what is it that you're wonderin'?"

"I think about them as being kind of mellow and low key and not as likely to get upset about things as your average person."

Poteet smiles and says, "Oh... I've known so many artists who are just neurotic as hell."

Terry sits up to agree, "Yeah... That's true."

"Oh yeah. I don' know about musicians, but painters an' sculptors are terribly neurotic. Yeah. You need to rethink that."

"Okay," Elliott says and chuckles. "I learned something today."

CHAPTER 26

The Big Hoax

"Well, here's somethin' else you need to know."

"Okay."

Poteet picks up his painting knife and starts mixing paint on his palette. He says, "It's one thing I've always said about art. An' I've had heated discussions with other artists about it. An' it's about modern art."

"Okay."

"I think it's the biggest hoax ever perpetrated on the American people—or the *world* for that matter. It really is."

"That's a big statement."

"It is. But the more you learn about it, you start to see it."

"Explain that a little bit to 'im," Terry says, "'cause, I didn't get what you meant when you first said that to me."

Elliott looks at Terry and asks, "Do you know what he's talking about?"

"Yeah."

Poteet turns to his painting. As he begins to apply the paint, he says, "Well, it's when I was goin' to school there in New York. Harold an' I were walkin' down the street in Soho, an' I jus' mentioned to him... I said, 'Ya know, Harold, I jus'... I don' get it.' An', he said, 'What?'" Poteet turns and looks back at Elliott. "An' I said, '... modern art. I don' get it.'" Poteet turns to his palette to refill his knife. "I said, 'Ya know, I can look at a painting, an' then I look at all the art-speak written about it. An' I can only think, 'That's bullshit.'" He turns with a loaded knife and continues, "I said, 'I don't see it.' I said, 'I'm a semi-intelligent person—semi-educated. An' I don' see it.' An' he said, 'Well, you know why you don't see it?' An', I said, 'No. Why?' He said, 'Because there ain't nothin' to see.' He said, 'It is what it is. An', it ain't nothin' else. I don' care what anybody says about it.'"

"That's interesting," Elliott responds. "I'm not sure what I think about that point of view."

Poteet turns to his palette for more paint. "An' he tol' me somethin' else. It's related to... It kind of explains it, I think."

"...about modern art?"

"Yeah." Poteet turns and begins to apply the paint. "So... When Harold was young, like it was in the sixties. An' he knew all of these people. I mean... He was, ya know, part of their peer group—Jasper Johns..."

Terry says, "...Rauschenberg an' those others I was talkin' about."

"Right," Elliott says and nods.

Poteet stands, grabs a rag, and cleans his knife. He sets the knife down and turns to Elliott. He continues, "Rauschenberg, Pollock, all of 'em. Harold knew 'em well—ran around with 'em. An' uh... 'Cause I asked 'im 'bout what they were doin'. I said, 'Well, what about somebody like, I don' know, Jackson Pollock.' An' he said, 'Oh, I'll tell you about Jackson Pollock.' He said, 'Pollock was a notorious alcoholic an' womanizer.' An' he said, 'Ya know... When I first met 'im, he was paintin' these little landscapes.' He said, 'They weren't very good, an' uh...' But he started datin' Peggy Guggenheim. Well... At the same time he was with Peggy, so was this other famous artist. Well, he's famous now—named Max Ernst. An' uh... Harold said he was at the party one night... An' uh... Ernst an' Pollock didn't like each other, but..."

"Because," Terry explains, "they were both havin' an affair with Peggy."

Poteet looks at Terry, nods, and says, "Right. Yeah." Poteet picks up his painting knife, points it in the general direction of Elliott, and continues, "Harold says they got into an argument, an' he heard Max Ernst tell Pollock... He said, 'Ya know, Pollock, you'd be better off if you jus' put those canvases on the floor an' *threw* paint on 'em.' An' Pollock said, 'Well, by God, I will.' An', he did. That's when he started doin' those drip paintings. An' he was still..." Poteet turns to his palette. "Ya know, nobody knew 'im. But... Peggy Guggenheim, bein' Peggy Guggenheim, started placin' those drip paintings strategically in museums. An' she did the same thing for Max Ernst. The rest is history."

Terry says, "...priceless. Today those paintings are priceless."

Poteet looks up from his palette to say, "They are. An' that's exactly how that happened."

"Hmm... Seems like Harold was in New York City at the right time," Elliott suggests.

Turning to his canvas, Poteet responds, "He was..."

"I get the feeling that those artists... And maybe it's still that way. But, that group of artists... They were considered almost like rock stars."

As he applies the paint, Poteet says, "Oh yeah. Absolutely. An' if Harold had played his cards right... I mean, he would've been a bigger household name than Jackson Pollock."

"...or Andy Warhol," Terry adds. "Peggy Guggenheim was the key. Harold should have stayed closer to her. He could have been right there with 'em."

"So... From what you're saying and from what I've read, Peggy Guggenheim was the kingmaker of her day in the art world," Elliott says.

"She was," Poteet responds.

"She was very wealthy..." Terry injects. "She had her favorites an' those were the ones who got their paintings hung in the art museums—the Guggenheim and several others."

"Yeah," Poteet confirms.

Terry stands and turns to leave. She says, "I'll be downstairs if you need me."

Elliott smiles and then says to Poteet, "But, what surprised me about her is how much older she was than Harold. I mean, she really was of a different generation."

Poteet cocks his head and says, "I didn' know that."

"She was born in 1898."

"No kiddin'?"

Terry stops at the door, turns around with a startled look, and says, "Really?"

"Yeah."

"She was a lot older than I thought," Poteet says.

"Yeah. She was thirty-one years older than Harold."

"Huh..." Terry says to herself as she continues out the door.

CHAPTER 27

The Art Landscape

Poteet is genuinely surprised by the age of Peggy Guggenheim relative to Harold. He tries to recall the conversations he'd had with him about Peggy and the other artists he'd known in New York City. He quietly states the obvious, "So... Harold was the young guy."

"He was."

Poteet nods slowly and says, "Warhol an' Stevenson were the young generation of the artists in New York City at that time."

"I think they were."

"So... I think knowin' the difference in the ages helps me put it in a better perspective. I know Harold didn' get along with 'em."

"He didn't get along with any of 'em?"

"It's what he tol' me. But he went to their parties an' hung out with 'em."

"Huh."

"Yeah. I think they tolerated 'im, but they never really accepted 'im, ya know?"

"Why?"

"He was... Well, he was gay, for one thing. But... As an

artist, he was havin' success. I think they were jealous. No one had ever done what Harold did with his gigantism movement."

"So, gigantism was having an impact."

"Yeah... Because... When they did that big show with the Guggenheim in '62, he was the star. He really was. Ya know... Nobody knew who Warhol was. He was in the show, but... No. Then you get the new guy, Harold. Well, I mean... His painting was fuckin' huge—forty feet long."

Elliott chuckles as he says, "Yeah...forty feet long and a nude male. That had to have stunned the patrons."

Poteet chuckles as he continues to paint. "But he made the biggest mistake he ever made when he pulled out of that show." He turns to face Elliott. "'Cause they told 'im, 'No, we want *you* in the show. We jus' don't want *that* painting.'"

"I see," Elliott says quietly.

"He could've... His painting, ya know, the *Eye of Lightnin' Billy*... He'd already done that one. He should've... Ya know, he could've put that in there. But it just pissed 'im off when they rejected *The New Adam*. So, he pulled out of the show."

"I think that haunts you."

"It does. An'... Hey... Harold an' I talked about it—many times. Ya know... He said 'Yeah. It's... It was...'" Poteet shakes his head. "He agreed that everything would've been different. An'... Not only did he pull out of the show. But then, he started bad mouthin' all the critics, an' he caught a lot a shit for that."

"Okay."

"Yeah. Sometimes, he was his own worst enemy. He really was."

"I mean, that sounds a little rebellious."

"Yeah."

"Maybe that's why you and he got along?"

Poteet chuckles under his breath.

After a moment, Elliott says, "The *Oklahoma Today*

magazine article cited other paintings. One was the *Eye of Lightning Billy* that we've talked about."

"Right."

"And uh, the hundred portraits. It said that Harold was commissioned by the United States government to do those."

"Right. He was."

"So... At some point, the University of Oklahoma decided they wanted those portraits for their museum."

"Yeah."

"But they're missing *one*."

Poteet smiles. "Yeah, they are. An' it bugs 'em."

Elliott chuckles. "So... What do you know about that?"

"It's me." Poteet points to his small kitchen. "An' I've got it right in there."

Elliott laughs.

"Yeah." Poteet chuckles. "They know I've got it, an' they've asked me several times about it."

"Don't give it to 'em."

"I'm not," Poteet replies with a smile. "Ya know, it's advertised as 'The Hundred Faces.'"

Elliott chuckles and says, "But it's only ninety-nine."

Elliott and Poteet laugh together.

Elliott says, "That's funny."

Poteet looks over at Elliott. "Do ya wanna see it?"

"Sure."

Poteet heads toward his kitchen and says, "I think I can find it." He soon returns with a large roll of papers.

Elliott stands and watches as Poteet inspects layer after layer of the roll. Eventually, a portrait is revealed within the stack.

Elliott's face brightens as he looks at the portrait. He says with a smile, "That's cool."

"Yeah, that's..." Poteet moves in closer to review the painting. "He did this in 1965, an' that's how he did all of 'em."

Elliott repeats softly, "'65."

"Yeah."

"You were eighteen?"

"Mm-hmm... Yeah..."

"Can I take a picture of that?" Elliott askes as he reaches for his phone.

"Yeah... Here. Let me move it," Poteet says as he reposi- tions the papers to remove the portrait from the stack. "Uh... He actually did two of me at that time, an' this was the first one. It was before I went to the Army. An' when I got back, he did another. 'Cause... He said, 'You're a different person now.'"

Elliott studies the painting and remarks, "That's really beautiful."

"Oh, Harold was a great..."

"That *really* is a beautiful painting."

"Yeah, he was a great artist, I mean. He had a great eye, ya know."

"That's an amazing portrait," Elliott says. "I think I've got a whole lot better feel for him now."

Poteet looks again at the portrait and nods gently.

"So, what paint did he use?"

"Oil."

"It's an oil painting."

"It's oil an' charcoal."

"Oh, okay. Was it typical for him to use charcoal?"

"Mm-hmm."

"...do the outline and then add color."

"Yeah."

"I think he did a great job on your eyes."

"Yeah. He could capture a person really quickly. Throughout my whole life, he did paintings of me. I've got one at home that he did in '91. But I... He did some in the '70s. The ones that he did in the '80s got burnt up."

"Gosh."

"Yeah, I know. They burned in his studio."

"That's sad."

"Yeah. An' I don't think he did any more of me—in the 90s." Poteet places the portrait back in the stack of papers and begins rolling it up. He says, "It's like I've been sayin', Harold was a *great* painter."

"Yeah. But sometimes you have to see it—to fully appreciate that kind of thing."

"Sure," Poteet quickly agrees. "He was a great painter, but he was a great man too. He was a great friend. He was very generous. He was kind. He was funny. Yeah. Harold had a great sense of humor. An' he didn' mind helpin' people."

Elliott nods.

"An' that reminds me. I'm gonna start usin' this too. Because he... I have people come in here an', ya know, they've got children an'... 'Oh this child is really artistic. An' what advice would you have?' Harold said somebody asked 'im that. 'What advice could you give me?' An' he said..." Poteet pauses to set the roll of papers on the table. He says in a loud voice, imitating Harold, "'You tell then *hell no*. You *cannot* do that.'"

Elliott starts to chuckle.

"'That is completely out of the question. You're crazy, an' I will not support that.' Harold would say, 'Do *everything* you can to discourage 'em. An'... If that dudn' work, then they're an artist.'"

Elliott laughs and then Poteet laughs.

"He said, 'You don't have to tell an artist to be an artist. They're gonna be one.'"

"I guess so."

"So... I thought, 'Yeah, that's a good idea.' Just tell 'em, 'Absolutely not,' an' 'You stay away from this.'" Poteet laughs and continues, "So... While we're talkin' 'bout Harold, I should tell you this."

"Okay."

"It's more about his opinion on modern art."

"Okay."

"It's Harold's view an' mine too."

"Alright. Let's hear it."

"Well... Modern art, I mean, to me, should always express what's goin' on socially, economically, politically, all these things."

"Okay, that makes sense."

"So... Not too long before he died, Harold was doin' an interview, an' he had a great response, I thought. Somebody asked 'im, 'Well, whadaya think about modern art?' An' he said, 'Like who?' An' they said, 'I don' know—maybe Warhol or somethin'. He said, 'Well, that ain't so modern is it? ...anymore?'"

Elliott laughs.

"So... I read this book called *The $12 Million Stuffed Shark*. It's about Damien Hirst. The book was very enlightening, 'cause it talks about... An' I can't remember this guy's name. He discovered Jasper Johns an' all these other artists... Castelli. Yeah. Castelli was his last name. What Castelli would do back in the sixties. He would find these young artists—these artists he thought were talented, an' he'd put 'em on a stipend. But part of the deal was... Whatever they painted belonged to him. So... I mean, he became so wealthy. But if you were in that stable of artists—of Castelli's artists... Well hell... I mean, you became famous. He made everybody famous. An' now, there are certain collectors that can do the same thing. If they buy a piece of art from, like an up-an'-comin' artist... Well... Overnight, they're just... ya know. I mean... It's jus'... Their career is made. It's what they call bein' branded—as an artist. Once you're branded... Well hell... I mean, the sky's the limit."

"I get that. It's about becoming known. And it's about promotion. You've got to do that in my business too."

"Right."

"And you've mentioned that Andy Warhol had good business sense."

"Oh yeah. He did. Harold tol' me this story about Andy promotin' himself. He said, 'Well, ya know what Andy did, don't ya?' An' I said, 'No.' He said, 'Well, when he was in college... Uh... Every year, the Rotary Club would have a little art show. An' all the little old ladies an' everybody would put their paintings in there. So, Andy did a painting of a guy pickin' his nose.'"

Elliott chuckles.

"It was a big painting. An' the Rotary Club rejected it. They wouldn' let 'im show it. So, he jus'... Oh, man... He jus'... Ya know, Andy jus' started callin' all the newspapers an' radio stations an' everything. He got this big furor goin' about the painting. An' so... Finally, the Rotary Club said, 'Look... We'll let you display it.' An' they did. An' there was a line a mile long for people to get in to see this stupid painting. An' that's the truth."

Elliott chuckles again.

"But Harold... Yeah, he said, 'Ya know, Andy figured out that controversy will make you famous.' An' he kind of built his whole career on that idea."

"Huh."

"If you ever saw Andy in some of those ol' interviews, you'd think, 'What an airhead.' Ya know, he jus'..."

"I remember seeing an interview of Andy Warhol on TV," Elliott says. "But it was a long time ago."

"An' he was real deadpan in those things. I remember when he did the Campbell's soup can an' the Brillo boxes. They were interviewin' 'im, an' the guy said, 'Andy... People say your work is senseless an' trite. Whadaya say to that?' An' he'd go, 'Yeah. Yeah.'"

Elliott chuckles.

"He'd say, 'Do you intend to do more?' An' Andy'd answer,

'Uh, Yeah.' I mean... But... Ya know... Knowin' 'im on a one-to-one basis, he wadn' like that at all. That was all a show. I mean... So, he knew what he was doin'. He wanted to be a freak, so people would notice 'im. He didn' wanna be, ya know, a down-to-earth type of person. He wanted to have that persona about 'im. An' he... He did it."

"...seems like it worked."

"Oh, yeah. Andy was a great businessman. He really was. He knew how to make money, an' he made a bunch of it. But no... He set out to do that. But... Personally... I really never thought much of Warhol's art. He... Andy was anti-painting. He, uh... I don' know... Most of his art was just silkscreens an' stuff like that. Andy was more into the image itself rather than the quality of the piece, but... I'm very concerned about the quality of anything I paint, an' Harold was too."

"...a different emphasis."

"Right. But... Andy became famous, an' he created a brand. He did. An' his paintings... Every time they go to the auction, they're bringin', ya know... One that sold for twenty million two years ago, it's forty million now—fifty million. 'Cause... People with a lot of money like to buy art... Those paintings are a very stable thing to put your money in—instead of stocks or whatever."

"Yeah. I'm sure they're a good investment."

"Yeah—especially the big names. An Andy Warhol painting will never go down. An' neither will Rauschenberg's or any of those. I mean, they'll always... They're gonna bring more money as time goes on, ya know... Eventually, they'll become almost priceless."

Elliott closes his eyes and pushes back his hair with one hand then the other. He says, "I should have bought more art."

Poteet chuckles.

Elliott continues, "So... I know when you made your first trip to New York, uh... Andy Warhol met you."

231

"Uh-huh. ...for art school."

"...and it's a really funny story about the guy on the plane." Poteet chuckles.

"But, um... Did you hang out much with Warhol?"

"Not really... I mean, I'd go over there. But... No... I wadn' cut out for that. An' I never really wanted to be a New York City artist. That wadn' my thing. I mean, I was fascinated with it—just watchin' it. But... Yeah... I was there to learn to paint, an' I had to make money to pay my bills. But... Ya know..." He chuckles. "Bein' an art student... An' the first person you meet in New York City is Andy Warhol..."

Elliott grins.

"I mean, that's pretty heady stuff."

Chuckling, Elliott says, "Yes, it is."

Poteet laughs.

"And Andy was willing to do that for Harold."

"He was."

"And then, Harold came back and was in New York City most of the time you were in art school there."

"Yeah, he was."

"Uh... Was he hanging out with Andy?"

"No. An' I got the impression he wadn' all that crazy about Andy."

"They'd already had a falling out?"

"Well, I don't know if they were ever great friends."

"Okay."

"I mean, that's kind of the way it seemed..." Poteet clarifies.

"I see."

"Uh... Ya know, he... Harold never was a big gossip—talkin' about people an' all. But he would say things to me like, 'Well, ya know... If you've got a good idea... Don't let Andy know, or you'll see it next week out on the street.'"

"Did *you* learn much from Andy?"

Poteet shakes his head and says, "No. Not really. But I think I taught him a lot."

With a surprised turn of his head, Elliott asks, "How's that?"

"...silkscreen printing. He was messin' around with it, but he wadn' very good at it."

"Huh."

"Ya know, I'd already built that T-shirt company an' knew all about silkscreen printing. I had even become pretty good at doin' a four-color process."

"That sounds like it's hard to do."

"It was. But I could do it. An' Andy was tryin' to get better at jus' doin' the simple things. He had a lot of technical questions, an' I always tried to help 'im. Over time, he got better with his technique, an' he used silkscreening a lot in his art."

"He was fortunate to have you around there."

Poteet nods and says, "We didn't collaborate on anything. I wanna be clear about that."

"So, you must have known Andy pretty well."

Poteet shrugs and says, "I knew 'im."

"Huh..."

"But... Harold didn't have much positive to say about Andy. An' I think a lot of it was because of Edie Sedgwick. Harold an' Edie had been inseparable. Edie wanted Harold to marry 'er. I mean, they were together all the time. But she became a heroin addict, an' I really think he blamed Andy for her death. Ya know, she did OD on heroin."

Elliott whispers, "Wow."

"An' I... I was jus' readin' between the lines on that."

Elliott whispers, "Yeah." He nods and says in his normal voice, "So, I was wondering, uh... You know... You said that Edie wanted Harold to marry her."

"Uh-huh."

"...full well knowing that he was gay?".

"Yeah. He'd tell me that she wanted to be with 'im all the time, ya know... It's what he tol' me—back in the sixties. He was... He said, 'Oh God... I've got this woman that wants to get married, an'...'" Poteet chuckles.

"Really?"

"Yeah. But... Back then, I didn' have any idea who she was."

"Well... I told you I knew all about Edie Sedgwick, but that's because I was there—in New York City at the time."

"Sure. But... Bein' in Idabel, I had no idea."

"She was the toast of New York City, and... I mean, she was really beautiful."

"Of course, I know all of that now. An', ya know, when they did that movie about 'er, Harold was kind of hurt."

"I watched that movie."

"But..." Poteet explains, "Harold was talkin' to me about it, an' I could tell it hurt his feelings. He said, 'There's no way you could do a movie about Edie Sedgwick without talkin' to me.' He said, 'I knew 'er better than anybody in the world. An' no one ever even called.'"

"...interesting," Elliott says and remembers some of the photos of Edie Sedgwick that made such an impression on him back in the day. Some of those images are still fresh in his mind. She was older than him, but her photos always seemed so youthful—so vivacious, so pure. He didn't care to think of her any other way.

"She was hangin' around Andy," Poteet says, "so she could be in those stupid movies he made."

"Yeah... Evidently so." Elliott glances down at his notes. "But, something else..."

CHAPTER 28

The Cultural Icons

"I've been doing some more research on Warhol and The Factory. I think I told you why—about setting the stage for the cultural changes of the sixties and so on."

"Right. An' I get that."

"Again, much of it had to do with Bob Dylan and Andy Warhol."

"Yeah... But about Harold an' Dylan..." Poteet shakes his head. "The celebrity part... Harold jus' didn' get into that. None of that impressed 'im. He uh... Ya know, he was livin' at The Dakota when John Lennon lived there—back in the day."

"Harold lived at The Dakota?" Elliott asks with a surprised look on his face.

"Yeah," Poteet answers. "I did too—for a short time, but that's for another conversation."

Elliott chuckles and says, "You? You lived at The Dakota?"

"Yeah... But when Harold lived there, you could lease the apartments. Now, I mean, you can't do that. But uh... Yeah..."

"Harold Stevenson lived at The Dakota," Elliott repeats softly, "when John Lennon lived there."

"Yeah. He did. An' he tol' me... It was a funny story, because... Uh... Him an' Lennon were on the elevator together.

An' ya know, they introduced themselves. An'... So... At a later time, Harold told one of his nieces about living there."

"Okay..."

"An' she asked, 'Have you ever met John Lennon?' An' he said, 'Who's that?'"

Elliott laughs.

"An' she said, 'One of the Beatles,' ya know. He said, 'Well, I ran into this one guy in the elevator...said his name was John Lemon or somethin'.'"

Elliott chuckles.

Poteet says, "An' there's another story..."

"Okay."

"He was in a restaurant, an' the Beatles come in. An' they... I guess Harold had a big table or somethin', an' they wanted 'im to move."

"The Beatles—all four of 'em?"

"Yeah."

For clarification, Elliott repeats, "So... Harold was at this restaurant. He had a table, and they wanted to sit where *he* was?"

"Yeah. An' he... He said, 'Well, this is *my* table.' Ya know. He wasn't impressed at all. Celebrity jus' didn' impress 'im. It didn't. Ya know... He was so unique in that respect."

"Well... Did he move?"

Poteet chuckles and shakes his head. "I don' remember if he ever said."

They both laugh.

When the laughter dies down, Poteet continues, "But, regarding Edie's death an' Andy—an' Harold. Throw Bob Dylan in there too." Poteet looks down and shakes his head. "It turned into a tragedy for Edie. She got hooked on heroin, an' she died at age twenty-eight of an overdose. It was sad an' it tore Harold up. I know it did. An' Harold tol' me... He said... 'Andy Warhol was the biggest damn heroin dealer in New York city.'"

"Noooo..."

"Yeah. An' Harold said, 'Andy wouldn't sully his own hands with it, but he didn' have to. All his minions sold it for 'im.'"

Elliott sighs and shakes his head.

Poteet continues, "An' I know... Jus' knowin' Harold an' the way he'd talk about it, I think he held that against Andy."

"So, Harold wasn't into the drug scene."

"No. Harold didn' get into that. Now... He'd drink ya under the table, but he didn' do drugs."

"Did Andy have any family around? Did Harold ever talk about that?"

"Yeah, ya know... He tol' me about Warhol's mother. She would uh... He said he'd seen 'er. She would come to New York to visit Andy, an' he said she was an absolute lunatic. An' he said that sometimes... Sometimes she'd just go nuts, ya know. He said that nobody really knew it, but he witnessed it. Yeah."

Elliott says quietly, "Maybe he feared that he would turn out that way too."

"Maybe he did. An' he looked jus' like 'er. He really did. But... Andy had a fascination with death. He always did. Harold brought it to my attention. An' I started seein' it in some of his art. His silkscreens would be of, ya know... I remember one was this car wreck that had killed these people. An' the series he did on it... It was just a repeat image."

"I see his art that way, and I've been paying more attention lately. He often repeated the same image."

"Yeah. But also... Death was a common theme for 'im. An' for 'im to die the way he did, I mean... He practically killed himself—checkin' into some obscure little hospital under a fictitious name. Ya know... Like Harold said... He said, 'Basically, he died of neglect.' He laid right there in that bed. An' nobody checked on 'im, an' he died."

"That's sad."

"But, ya know... Harold had a weird fascination too, I mean. Uh... I know he certainly wadn' afraid of death, but... He was involved with this young guy in New York that was nothin' but a psycho. An' I tol' 'im one day, I said, '...you know what? You're gonna keep foolin' around, an' that son of a bitch is gonna kill you.' He said, 'Oh, that'd be a marvelous way to die.' An' I thought, 'Really?'"

"...strange."

"I remember one time he was talkin' to me. He said, 'Somethin's really botherin' me.' An' I said, 'What is it?' He said, 'I had the strangest dream.' He said, 'I don't know why it's botherin' me so bad.' So, I said, 'What was it?' An' he said, 'Well... It was this old man an' this ol' woman. An' they were fightin' each other, ya know, like to the death. ...to determine which one was gonna live.' An' uh... I said, 'Harold, that's you.' Ya know, 'cause he was gay. I said, 'Sounds to me like you've got one side of you pullin' against the other side.' He was like... 'Ya know...' an' his eyes got big. He said, 'Yeah, you could be right. You could be right about that.' An' I think I was, I mean..."

They hear Terry calling up from the first floor. She yells, "Poteet, I'm leavin'."

Elliott looks at his watch.

Poteet shouts back. "Okay. I'm right behind ya."

"Yeah, I know it's time. It's past time," Elliott admits. He reaches out to get his recorder and gather his notes. He stands, and Poteet steps toward him for a parting handshake. Elliott holds on to Poteet's hand for too long. His gaze narrows, and he says, "I remember now."

Poteet's smile disappears, and he drops Elliott's hand. His eyes narrow.

"I've been trying to remember the name of the artist who worked with Andy Warhol."

"There weren't that many."

"Right. And I just thought of it."

Poteet lifts his eyebrows and says, "I think you're more into art than you led me to believe."

"Not really. Like I said, I'm into culture."

Poteet nods but doesn't reply.

"But the artist I was trying to think of..." He strokes the beard on his chin. "I think his name is Bos-ki-ot or something like that."

Poteet nods.

"So, do you know of him?" Elliott asks.

"Sure. Jean-Michel"—he pauses, then adds—"Basquiat. Yeah. Andy made 'im famous."

"I think you're right about that. And even with my level of understanding, I can tell *his* paintings. They're pretty rough."

"Right. He was becomin' famous while I was in New York City. He made his name with graffiti."

"I remember that. I remember seeing that graffiti around the city when I was back there visiting my parents. It was news for a while. He got everybody's attention, and I think he even did it under a different name."

"Yeah, he did. He painted the graffiti under the name SAMO."

"That's right. I remember now."

"It was him an' another guy," Poteet recalls. "He was doin' it when I was at the Art Students League."

"Huh."

"But it was Jean-Michel who had the career. I don't remember what happened to the other guy."

"Yeah. And I think Mr. Basquiat made a lot of money from those paintings."

"He did. An' Andy did too."

"Huh. I guess that's the way it works."

Poteet nods. "Ya know, Jean-Michel died at a young age too."

"I don't think I knew that. I guess his paintings have probably increased in value since his death."

"Oh, yeah. They're in the millions. He had the good fortune to meet Andy Warhol one night in a café. Andy was in there with his manager. So... Basquiat comes up to their table an' says, 'Would y'all like to buy one of these?' He wanted ten dollars apiece for some small drawings. So... Andy bought a few of 'em. An' he told Basquiat to come see 'im."

"So... He must have, I guess."

"He did. An' if it hadn' been for Warhol, you never would have heard of Jean-Michel Basquiat. It's what I've been talkin' about. Andy branded 'im."

"Yeah. Teaming up with Andy Warhol... I'd say he got a nice endorsement there."

"Have you ever seen the movie, *Basquiat*?"

"No, I didn't know there was one."

"Oh yeah. An' it was a good one. David Bowie played Andy Warhol."

"Really?"

"Yeah."

"That's probably a pretty good likeness."

"It was. Yeah. Bowie had him down—ya know, his mannerisms an' everything. It was good."

"Huh. I'll have to watch that. Was it all pretty much true, as far as you know?"

"As far as I know, yeah. He'd go into a cafe or somethin' an' take the ketchup an' the syrup, an' pour it on the table an' start drawin' these faces an' shit." Poteet begins to chuckle. "He'd get kicked out of restaurants, ya know." Poteet's chuckle turns into a laugh.

Elliott laughs and says, "I'm sure. Wow. I guess I could see... I can see his paintings attracting attention... because they're so—harsh."

"Yeah."

"An' uh... And the themes are so in-your-face."

"Right."

"And... It seemed to me like nearly every painting was a self-portrait."

Poteet gives a slight chuckle and responds, "Yeah."

"Just drawn about whatever crazy thing he was thinking at the time."

"Ya know, that's one of the things I've always said an' had arguments with other artists about—especially modern art..."

"Which is?"

"A lot of the time... All you're doin' is lookin' at somebody else's madness. Ya know... I... When I see one of these crazy paintings, like a Basquiat..."

"Yeah?"

"...an' then see all this art-speak written about it. I'm goin', 'That... That's total bullshit.' Ya know. That's not what that is. It's just... That son of a bitch is crazy."

Elliott and Poteet laugh.

Still laughing, Elliott says, "I guess we should just accept it and go on."

Poteet nods. "I think that's what I'm sayin'."

Elliott picks up his satchel and says, "Okay. It's time to go."

CHAPTER 29

Jean-Michel

The next afternoon at three-thirty, Elliott again shows up at the double doors. After a short discussion of the previous night's dinner in town and some crazy entertainment on the square, Elliott sits, and Poteet gets back to his latest painting.

Elliott says, "So... Last night after I got back to the room... You know... Yesterday, you mentioned the Basquiat movie."

"Uh-huh."

"So, I thought, 'I have a little time. I'll see if I can find it.' So... Using my iPad, I looked on the Internet and found a trailer for it. I thought, 'Great,' and started watching. After about an hour or so, I thought..." Elliott laughs as he says, "Well, David Bowie's not in this."

Poteet chuckles and turns around to ask, "Was it a different movie?"

"Yeah. It was a documentary."

"Okay."

"But it was still cool."

"I'll bet the movie's better."

"Probably, as far as entertainment's concerned... But I think the story's a little bit different. Uh... The trailer seemed to indicate some differences. And *this one* had a lot of actual footage of Jean-Michel."

"Huh..."

"Yeah. He was... You know, somebody had a home video camera, and it was footage of him. An' this was, I think, probably just a few months before he died."

"Hmm."

"And uh... So... I learned a lot."

"I'm sure."

"But it brought up some questions for me, like..." Elliott looks away and then says, "Uh... He... He was somewhat like Andy Warhol, I think, in that... He was a personality."

"Hmm..."

"At least... According to this documentary, he was."

"Okay."

"It seemed like he was a personality—first—even more than being a painter."

Poteet squints and slowly nods.

"And... He was about getting famous—mostly. And then, kind of figured out how to do it with graffiti. And then, uh... So... When I look at his art, it's like, 'Huh? I don' know.'"

Chuckling, Poteet says, "I know what ya mean."

"What's there to like about it?"

"I know. That's what I've always said. It's like... It's what I mean about artists like him bein' a big hoax."

"So, you... I think you indicated yesterday that Basquiat probably falls into that category."

"He does—definitely."

"Hmm."

"Because... I mean, there were a lot of people who, uh... stood to make a ton of money by him becomin' famous, ya know. I mean millions an' millions an' millions of dollars."

"Yeah. Well, the point they were making about that... I think they were saying that the art world was ready for someone like Jean-Michel to come along."

"Maybe..."

"Because"—Elliott chuckles—"they showed some of the paintings that were going up in these art galleries at the time. And one was just..." He shakes his head. "The whole thing was white."

"Yeah," Poteet responds and chuckles.

"It was completely white."

"Yeah."

"And they put it up on the wall as a great work of art."

"Yeah."

"So, you're going, 'Hmm. What's that about?'"

"There was a Broadway play about that," Poteet says.

Elliott chuckles as he asks, "Oh, really?"

"Yeah. It was called *Art.* It's about whether a completely white canvas is art."

Elliott laughs and says, "Seems like a reasonable question."

Poteet says emphatically, "No."

Elliott laughs harder."

"It ain't. But yeah... They got a lot of buzz outa doin' that. An' yes, I am familiar with that story."

"But... I think Jean-Michel was the opposite of that," Elliott says. "In fact..."

"Yeah?"

"He... He was going to get your attention, whether you liked it or not. Uh... His paintings *do* get your attention."

"Yeah. An' he didn' care anything about what he painted on or what kind of paint he used. He jus'..."

"Yeah. Oh yeah, that's right."

"...just crazy shit," Poteet says.

"Yeah. He painted on glass, a door he'd found out on the street, or anything. ...particularly when he didn't have any money. But... He kind of became a character. And... Then, he was accepted by the New York City art people..."

"Yeah."

"...because he lived out on the street."

"Yeah. An' he became a drug addict."

Elliott nods and sighs. "They covered that. He became a drug addict. And then, once he started making money, his story seemed a lot like most of the stars of that time."

Poteet sighs and says, "Yeah. It did."

"And then... Not very long after he had his big successes, his career started winding down. And I guess, he felt like he was a failure—like it had come quickly and then gone."

"I think that's right."

"And he didn't know how to get it back."

"Ya know... He died at a young age too."

"In this documentary they left the impression that he died of a drug overdose."

"I think he did, but he also had AIDS."

"I mean... The way he looked, I can believe that."

"Yeah, he did," Poteet reiterates.

"And I mean... His face was all covered with sores. He looked pretty bad. Because, he'd been on drugs, and then he'd gone to some program for help. And he was clean for a while. And then... He got back on drugs. And soon after that, they found him dead."

"Mm-hmm."

"...in his apartment."

"Let's see. Warhol died in... What was it?" Poteet asks. "...'85?"

Elliott sighs.

Poteet says, "I think it was '85."

"I actually looked that up," Elliott responds.

"Okay..."

Elliott turns some pages in his notebook and says, "'87. It was in '87."

"Okay."

"Warhol died in '87. Uh... And Basquiat died in '88."

"Oh, okay."

"So... Basquiat was born in 1960. So, he would've been twenty-seven, twenty-eight years old when he died."

"That sounds right."

"They said that Warhol and Basquiat did a project together at some point. Andy would paint—whatever he would paint. And then, Basquiat would come along and paint over some of it."

"Yeah?"

Elliott chuckles. "But they also said... At the showing, they didn't sell one painting."

Poteet laughs and then Elliott laughs.

"Yeah..." Poteet says, "Can you imagine what one of those would go for today."

Elliott says with enthusiasm, "Well yeah..." He chuckles. "They'd be through the roof. And I'd be interested to know how many there are and what they've been selling for."

"Yeah. I'd like to know too."

"They showed some of them in the documentary."

"Huh."

"Yeah. And they had some movie footage of them actually working together on one."

"I'd like to see that."

"So... At the end, Jean-Michel seemed to feel like he'd been used by the art dealers and everyone else who'd made money because of him."

"An' yeah. That's what I've been tryin' to say."

"Here's a young guy. They can build up his art, get some buzz, get some attention..."

"Yeah."

"They can say it's great. They can say it's different."

"...which it was."

"So... Everybody's making money. Jean-Michel's feeling

good about himself. But... At some point, it goes away. But it's like that in the movie business too. How many 'stars'"—he uses air quotes—"have short-lived careers?"

"Sure." Poteet adds, "Ya know, I don' know if he ever bought into what they said about 'im. I'm not sure that he thought he was all that great, ya know."

"Really?" Elliott asks. "So... You think he had doubts about his own work?"

"Yeah, I do. 'Cause he wadn'... I mean, he wadn' that good. He was nuts."

Elliott laughs and says, "Yeah."

"So no, I don't think he... But... Uh... About how he died an' all... I tol' ya what Harold said about Andy—about bein' a big heroin dealer."

"Yeah."

"Well... I'm sure that's where Basquiat got his stuff too." Poteet shakes his head. "An'... Ya know... Andy never touched it himself." He whispers, "But yeah... Yeah..."

After a moment of quiet reflection, Elliott continues, "Well, they had some video of Andy and Basquiat. I mean... They looked like really close buddies."

"Mm-hmm."

"Uh... I mean... They looked like closer buddies than you might think jus' colleagues would be."

"Yeah. Well... Andy could see he was gonna make some money—a lot a money, ya know, from Jean-Michel. An' he did. I'm sure he did. An' he needed to keep 'im close. That's what I'd say."

"Well... Okay... But... Regarding Basquiat's style and technique, he's uh... unconventional, at the very least. And let's just say that you don't like it."

"No. I mean, it's... Ya know... An' I've had this argument with a lot of artists. An', what you're lookin' at really—to me. It's just someone else's madness, ya know? If you think that's cool? Okay. I don't. It's just not my..." He shakes his head. "But... I mean... There's a lot of 'em out there like that. An' there has been since, ya know, forever. It seems like the crazier that shit is"—Poteet chuckles—"the more people seem to like it. But, ya know, I've seen some really great art from some great young artists. As a matter of fact, one of 'em... I can't remember who the artist was. It was at the Fort Worth Modern. An' I really loved the painting. It was... It was a huge painting." He points at his studio wall. "It was about the size of that wall over there. An'... Man... When I first saw it, I was real impressed with it. An' that's the type of thing..." Poteet shakes his head and then nods. "Yeah, I know what it took to do it."

"I see."

Poteet continues, "You look at it, an' you know it took a lot of imagination. ...totally non-representational. I mean, there's nothin' in it, ya know, that would hint of an image or somethin'. But... So... Yeah... It was beautiful. It really was. An' Basquiat..." Poteet shakes his head. "He couldn't do that. He couldn't even come close. He couldn'. He wouldn' even know where to start. But no... It's a racket. Ya know, this... It's a... It's a real racket."

"Yeah. I think you're talking about the branding thing..."

"Yeah."

"And making money off of that."

"Yeah."

"But... I mean, Andy was always very nice to me. He jus', ya know. But... When it came down to it, I didn' really want anything to do with 'im."

"I think I get that."

As he watches Poteet tidy up his painting table, Elliott is thinking about how he would handle Andy Warhol in a film. Would he include him, or should he ignore him completely? Would he open up that can of worms, or would he try to sweep it all under the rug? As he reflected for a moment, he didn't see how he could sweep it under the rug. In fact, it seemed like he might be revealing new information on a cultural icon and that he had a responsibility to do that. He nods slightly and reaches for his recorder as he prepares to leave for the airport.

Elliott takes his leave from Poteet and heads out. In the waiting limo, he pulls out his phone and goes to his text messages. He shakes his head and knows there are difficult times waiting. There are company issues he must address right away.

CHAPTER 30

Gunfight in Hell's Kitchen

After a warm handshape and an exchange of smiles, Elliott uses his fingers to count. "...finicky actors... nervous investors... too many lawyers." He shakes his head. "Believe me. I'm glad to be back in Santa Fe. It's been a rough couple of weeks."

"My weeks don't change very much."

Elliott grins and says, "I know, and I envy that."

Poteet chuckles to himself as he turns to his painting table.

As Elliott quietly settles in, Poteet squeezes various colors of paint onto a clean sheet of white paper.

When Elliott has his recorder set up, he looks over the top of his glasses and says, "With uh..." He smiles. "...New York City."

Without reacting, Poteet squeezes more paint onto his palette.

"Uh..." Elliott looks away and touches his lips. He says, "Tell me more about New York City."

Poteet turns to Elliott with a loaded painting knife. He asks, "Did I tell you about the gun fight I had there?"

Shaking his head, Elliott answers, "No."

Poteet chuckles. "Yeah. When I was gettin' ready to go to New York, my buddy tol' me. He said, 'Look, that's a dangerous place up there.' An' I said, 'Yeah. I know.' So, he gave me a pistol. It was a little twenty-five automatic. He said, 'You carry that with you.' He said, 'I... I don't feel real comfortable with you bein' up there with nothin'.'" Poteet looks up at Elliott and says, "I also knew about the gun laws in New York City... If they catch you with an illegal handgun, you spend a year in the penitentiary—no trial, no nothin'. You're gone." He asks Elliott. "Did you know that?"

"I do. I'm from there, you know."

"That's true. So... But one night... I had a night class an'... Well... Back up a little bit. Like, a week before... We lived in this ol' walk-up. It was a five-story—in Hell's Kitchen. An' uh... The week before... When everybody was out of the buildin', somebody broke in an' stole every damn thing I had. Uh... He even took the sheets off my bed, an' I was sick about it, ya know. I lost a couple of pieces of jewelry, an'... I didn' really have any money, but..."

"That was a tough break."

"It was," Poteet says and turns to his painting. "So... The very next week, I'm comin' home from class at night. I'm walkin' up the stairs to get to my room, an' this black guy come runnin' by me on the stairs. An' uh... I knew he didn' belong in the buildin', 'cause I knew all the people who lived there. So, I yelled at 'im to stop. I said, 'Where do you think you're goin'?' He said, 'I'm goin' to the roof,' an' he jus' kep' runnin'. So I run after 'im. An' uh..."

"So, you ran after him?"

"I did." Poteet chuckles, turns away from his painting to face Elliott. "I pulled my pistol out, an' he did run up to the roof. Then, he ran to the edge of the buildin'. There was another buildin' a floor below us, an' he jumped. An' uh... I told 'im. I said, 'If you don't stop, I'm gonna blow your fuckin' head off. An'... An' I saw 'im. He pulled out somethin' an' I saw it glint, ya know. An' I thought it was a gun. So, I go, bam,

bam, bam, bam. But a twenty-five automatic... You can't hit nothin' with it. So... Damn bullets were flyin' everywhere."

Elliott shakes his head.

Poteet chuckles and continues, "An' he started screamin', 'Don't! Don't! Don't shoot me!'"

Elliott chuckles.

"An' I said, 'Well, you stay right where you are or I'm gonna blow your damn head off.' An' uh... Boy, I mean I had no more done that than these helicopters... An' then all of a sudden, all these cops jus' come runnin' up on the roof. So, I took that pistol, laid it down on the ground, an' I pointed, 'He's over there.'" Poteet laughs. "An' so, they run over there, pulled their guns, an' said the same thing I did. Said, 'You move, we're gonna blow your fuckin' head off.' An' uh... So... This one cop come over to me an' he said, uh... He looked down an' he said, 'Is that your gun or is that his gun?' I said, 'No, that's mine.' He said, 'Is that registered to you in New York City?' An' I said, 'No, sir.' He said, 'Where, then?' I told 'im I was from Oklahoma. He said, 'Is it registered to you in Oklahoma?' I said, 'Yeah.' Which, it wadn'. An' he said, 'Well, you do know what the gun laws are in New York City, don't you?' I played dumb. I said, 'No, I don't know what they are.' He says, 'A year in the penitentiary—automatic, no trial, no nothin'. You're gone.' I said, 'Well, I didn't know that, an'...' He said, 'Look... I appreciate what you did.' He said, 'We were already in pursuit of this guy. He's killed two people—down on the street.'"

"Wow," Elliott says as his mouth drops open.

"Yeah. He'd stabbed... He killed a cab driver. An' then he told me there was a couple walkin' down the street, an' this guy stabbed the man in the neck. An' he said, 'We were after 'im. So, when we heard these gunshots...' An' uh..." Poteet chuckles. "He said, 'I'll tell you what. You forget about that gun.' I said, 'Well, I want it back.' He said, 'No, you're not gettin' it back.' An' he said, 'Just shut up about the gun.' An' uh... So, I set around a minute an' then said, 'Lemme have my gun back.'" Poteet snickers. "An' I just kep' on an' kep' on. He said, 'If you don't shut up...'"

Elliott begins to chuckle.

Poteet begins to laugh and says, "An' so... There was another cop there, an' he got tired of listenin' to me, I guess. So, he walked over an' he said, 'Okay, you're under arrest.' An' I said, 'What for?' An' this other cop said, 'Jus'... Leave 'im alone.' He said, 'I'll take care of it.' So... He said, 'You see there? Now shut up.' An' I said, 'Well, dammit... I want my gun back.' An' it was really cold. I had on a big coat. So, he said, 'All right, let's go downstairs.' So... We go downstairs to the street, an' there're cop cars everywhere, ya know. An' he said, 'You stand right there, an' don't say anything.' I said, 'Okay.' So... Ya know, they took my statement an' all that. An' this cop walked over to me, an' he just shoved that gun down into the pocket of that big coat. He said, 'Now, get your ass outta here, an' don't ever get caught with that gun again.'"

Elliott chuckles.

"I said, 'Yes, sir. Thank you, sir.'" Poteet and Elliott laugh.

When the laughing subsides, Elliott says, "I can't believe you wouldn't just let that go."

"Yeah. But... I jus' kep' on pressin' for it, ya know. An'... I got it back too."

Quietly, Elliott mutters, "Yeah, you did. You sure did." He looks at Poteet. "But you took a pretty big risk."

Poteet chuckles and says, "An' it was funny, ya know... Like in New York, there're these little communities inside of communities. An'... That little place there in Hell's Kitchen where I lived... I knew some of the merchants around there. But, right near us was a little store—a corner store. An', they put the fruit out on the sidewalk in these little bins an' stuff. So, the next day, I'm gettin' ready to go to class... I happen to walk around the corner, an' this merchant's standin' there. An' he said, 'You're that crazy kid from Oklahoma, aren't ya?'"

Elliott chuckles.

"I said, 'Yeah, I guess so.' An' he jus' threw me an apple."

They both laugh.

Elliott says, "He'd heard..."

"Yeah, everybody already knew about it."

"I'll admit," Elliott says, "I never would have done that—like, get in a gunfight."

Poteet chuckles.

"But... Who doesn't like some action in their movies—regardless of the genre? I mean... You're watching a flick about a Native American painter... And then, all of a sudden... This damn painter's chasing a perp up some stairs to the roof, shots are fired, the cops show up... You got lights and sirens... You got helicopters... Then, you got this idiot painter arguin' with the cops about getting his illegal gun back." Elliott shakes his head and takes his glasses off to rub his face. He repositions his glasses and massages his lips slowly. He nods and mumbles, "Hmm... quite a scene."

With a freshly loaded knife, Poteet moves to his painting.

After a few moments of silence, Elliott says, "...back to Andy Warhol for a moment."

"Okay."

"...and The Factory..."

"Yeah."

"...and the New York City party scene."

"Right." Poteet looks away and then back at Elliott to say, "I knew it was there. I saw plenty of it, but it just didn' fit my personality. And I think I told you that." Poteet turns back to his table.

"You did, and I think you should be grateful. A lot of those people didn't survive."

"That's right. They didn'."

"I remember New York City in the late seventies and early

eighties. It was a rough place."

"It was. It sure was when I was up there. Ya know... At that time, Times Square was... I mean, it was sleazy—really sleazy."

"Yeah. I remember, and they showed some of that."

"It was just like one peep show after another. Crime was horrible. Where I had to catch the subway... It was there on 42nd Street, ya know—an' always after midnight. They finally had to close it down, there was so much crime."

Elliott says quietly, "Yeah, I remember."

"An' uh, that's... An' then after I left, Rudy Giuliani became the mayor, an' he cleaned all of it up. I mean... He made it look like Disneyland, ya know."

"Yeah."

"It really did. But boy, it was sure sleazy before."

"In the documentary, they talked about this group they called the Five Hundred. It was five hundred people who would just be out all night—partying."

"Hmm."

"And Jean-Michel got in with that group."

"Well, that sounds right. Ya know... Like they say, 'Vegas never sleeps. Well, New York dudn' either.'"

Elliott chuckles.

Looking up from mixing his paint, Poteet adds, "I remember... We used to get off work at two o'clock on Saturday nights, an'... We'd go down to Sardi's, an' we'd sit down there 'til four or five in the mornin'—drinkin', ya know."

"But even so, you had a goal."

"I did."

"And you worked hard for that."

"I had to."

"And I think that's a major theme of your life."

"Is what?"

"...that you worked hard."

Poteet grabs a tube of paint and says, "I had to. But,

thinkin' about New York an' those times, AIDS was a big problem for a lot of the people I knew. It was a big-time issue when I was there."

"I'm sure."

"This one guy I worked with, he actually, uh... He was an actor an' he became a priest."

"...a priest? Did he get AIDS?"

"No. But, what I wanted to tell ya..."

"Yeah?"

"After I left, he stayed up there, an' that's when he became a priest. Well, I talked to 'im... I don' know—probably ten years ago—or so."

"Okay?"

"But what happened was... A priest from New York, another guy, came into the gallery here in Santa Fe, an' he bought one of my crucifixion prints. An' uh... I said, 'Uh... I'm sure you don't know this person.' But I said, 'Do you happen to know a guy named Paul Farin? I think he's a priest.' He said, 'Yes, of course I do,' He said, 'Yeah, I know Paul. I know 'im pretty well.' An' I said, 'Where is he?' So, he gave me the information. I called Paul an' talked to 'im. An' I said, 'Do you ever see any of the guys that we used to know up there?' An' he said, 'They're all dead.' He said, 'They all died of AIDS.'"

Elliott nods.

"'Cause... Ya know, back then..."

"If you got it... Yeah."

"...there was nothin' you could do. If you got it, you were dead."

They were both silent for a moment before Elliott adds, "Yeah. That's tough. I'm glad they've made progress there." He sits back and folds his arms and says, "I lost some friends that way too."

Poteet turns to his palette and begins mixing with his knife.

Elliott picks up his notebook and looks for the next question. He says, "I've got a topic here, and it's just one word."

"What is it?"

"Women."

They both chuckle.

Elliott wonders if Poteet will hold back, but he actually expects to find a treasure trove of stories here. He wonders how much of it he'll be able to use and not get an 'R' rating.

CHAPTER 31

All the Women

Elliott grins and says, "After listening to you for all this time...
It seems like there was always a woman around."

"Uh-huh. Yeah. Seems like that was always the case. No
matter where I was, there were always women."

"And I'm sure you didn't have to try very hard."

"Well, no. Not really. I mean..."

"Women flocked to you for some reason," Elliott says with
an attitude.

"Yeah, I guess. ...for some reason."

"Well, you're a good-looking guy."

Poteet shrugs.

"Seems like it might have been more than that but looks
go a long way. That's for sure."

"Well, I mean... Especially when I was younger, I was... But
I never really thought about it that way. I never did, ya know."

"But then the one you mentioned a couple of months ago,
with"—Elliott chuckles—"the younger prostitute..."

Poteet chuckles.

"...uh, loaning you money..."

Poteet laughs.

"...so you could pay 'er."

Elliott laughs.

"That's true. That really happened. She really did that." Poteet chuckles and shakes his head. "I don't think I'll ever forget..."

"And then... The next day or soon after, she's telling you, 'You don't need to go to work. I'll take care of you.'"

"Right." Poteet chuckles again and adds, "Here's another one, an' I don' think I'll ever forget *it* either."

Elliott smiles and says, "Okay?"

"I was at this club in Dallas, an' this couple come in. An' this was the prettiest girl I... I think I'd ever seen."

"...the prettiest one?"

Poteet glances up and nods. "Yeah. She was like... She really was. An' I was like, 'Man.' An' I kept lookin' at her durin' the night. An'... She got up to go... I don't know whether she went to the restroom, or what. But when she was comin' back, I stopped 'er. An' I said, 'I jus' gotta tell you.' Ya know, I said, 'I think you're the prettiest woman I've ever seen, an' I would *love* to get to know you.' An'... We kept talkin' there for a minute. An' she left her date at the table, an' we left together. I look back on it today, I think, 'How the...' Yeah. Her sister was a Dallas Cowboy's cheerleader, an' this girl was prettier than her sister—to me."

Elliott starts laughing, and then Poteet joins in.

Elliott says, "She must've thought you were pretty nice lookin' too."

Still chuckling, Poteet says, "But I just couldn't believe... She jus'... Yeah."

"Wow."

"Sometimes you just gotta ask," Poteet says and laughs.

"You must've been somethin' else when it came to your looks."

"Well... I guess I was a pretty cute kid, ya know."

"I know you were, but it must have been more than that—

to have all these women lose their good sense..."

Poteet chuckles again.

"Well, it's your personality too. I know you well enough now to understand that. And I don't know if I'd call your story 'romantic.'" Elliott uses air quotes. "But I think it *is* the good-lookin', bad-boy syndrome, you know." He shakes his head. "For some reason, women go crazy for that."

Poteet sets his painting knife down on his table and says, "I probably shouldn't tell you this."

Elliott grins and says, "Well, of course, you have to now."

Poteet smiles and continues, "But... I had on both sides of my family—on my dad's side an' my mother's side. I had these cousins. An' both of 'em were really..." He shakes his head. "...really pretty. An' I ended up in a relationship with both of 'em."

Elliott chuckles and utters, "Wow."

"An' one of 'em... She said when we were gettin' together..." Poteet chuckles. "She said, '*Everything* is wrong with this.'"

Elliott snickers and says, "Oh really?"

"An' I said, 'Yeah. I know.'"

"At least, y'all agreed that it was wrong."

"Yeah. But we did it anyway. An' I didn't intend for either one of those relationships to happen. But the other one on the other side, she was a... That's when I was goin' to school in New York, an' she lived in Connecticut—up around, New London."

"Did she grow up in Southeastern Oklahoma too?"

"No. She grew up in Tulsa."

"...but then moved to Connecticut?"

"Yeah. She got married an' moved there."

"Okay."

"An' she... She had just gotten divorced when I was goin' to school up there. An' she was a... She was like an anchor for a TV station."

"Hmm."

"An' uh... So, I called 'er, an' she said, 'Well, come on up, ya know, an' spend the weekend.' I decided to, an' I could catch a train an' go right there. She'd pick me up, an' I'd spend the weekend, an' this went on for two or three weekends."

Elliott laughs in anticipation, and then Poteet laughs.

"She said, 'I'd like to take you around to all my girlfriends.' She said, 'Because, ya know, they'd... They'd like lookin' at ya.'"

Elliott shakes his head.

"So... So, they..."

"So that's what you did? I mean... You'd go up there and hang out with her girlfriends?"

"It wadn' quite like that. I hung out with her mostly. We'd go around, ya know...different places."

"Yeah."

"But it's a cold-ass place up there. Man, she lived right on the water too, ya know. An' this was durin' the wintertime."

Elliott chuckles.

"I sure remember how damn cold it was," Poteet says and turns toward his palette. "An' she started tellin' me about this group of people up there that were into satanic worship."

Elliott looks over the top of his glasses at Poteet.

"An' uh... She did. She actually had the tape, the audio tape of an encounter with 'em. Her an' this other reporter snuck up on 'em to do some filmin'. An' she tol' me that, uh... They went through the woods, ya know. An' then, she said they heard these people. They got up pretty close. An' she said, 'I know they didn't see us or hear us.' But she said those satanic worshipers just stopped everything they were doin', turned towards 'em, an' started comin' at 'em. So, her an' this reporter took off runnin'."

Elliott throws up his hands and says, "I want to hear the rest of this. But I wanted to stop and say that making this scene jump off the screen won't take a lot of creative input." He chuckles. "Looks like we might be hitting all the hot buttons with this story." Sitting up and with both hands on top of his head, he says, "Please continue."

"I'm jus' tellin' ya. I mean, it was on tape, an' I listened to it." He turns his attention to the sheet of paper that serves as his palette and says, "An' uh... She said, 'Man...'" He stops mixing and looks up. "She said, 'It scared the hell out of us.'" He starts mixing again. "An' I kept tellin' 'er, I said, 'Let's go back. I wanna see this. She said, 'No, I'm not gonna do it.'"

Elliott chuckles.

"She said, 'I ain't doin' it.' An' I kept on, an' kept on, an' kept on. She finally said, 'Okay.' She said, 'But this ain't playin' around. This is serious shit.' I said, 'Well, let's do it.' She said, 'Okay. When you come back up here next weekend, we'll do it.' An' I said, 'Okay.' So... Monday mornin', the very next day, I show up at the Art Students League in one of my classes. I remember... It was my life drawing class. An' I knew pretty much everybody—same group of us all the time, ya know. But there was this one girl I hadn' seen before, which wasn't *that* unusual—students could come in durin' the year, ya know. But she was... This girl was lookin' at me. ...starin' at me the whole time. She wadn' very good lookin', so I wadn' payin' much attention. So... At our regular time, we took a break. Every hour on the hour, we'd get five-minutes, an' we'd usually step out in the hall or out on the street—smoke a cigarette or whatever. An' uh... So, when I come back in... On my chair, where I was sittin', was this pentagram. Ya know... I mean, this satanic symbol was layin' in my chair. An' I'm thinkin', 'What the hell is that?' An' so, I look up, an' this girl—the one that was new. She's over there laughin' at me. Yeah. She's just laughin', 'cause she sees that I see this thing."

"Wow."

"An' uh... It pissed me off. So, I crumpled it up an' threw it at 'er. An' she just laughed an' walked out of the class. I never saw 'er again. Yeah. An' I told Sandra, my cousin. She said, 'I'm tellin' ya.' She said, 'There's somethin' to this shit.' An' so she said, 'I ain't doin' it.' She said, 'Nope. No way.' So, we never did go back out there."

"Under the heading of 'Supernatural,' that's a great story, Poteet. It's another unique one. Somebody showing up in class... The pentagram thing... I don't remember ever seeing a storyline like that before."

Staring at Elliott, Poteet says, "Yeah. It's weird—really weird. But... It happened jus' like that."

"So, how did this girl connect you to your cousin and what she had done with that reporter? I don't see the connection to you?"

"Exactly."

"You weren't out there..."

"Right. I wadn'."

"You and your cousin had only talked about it."

Poteet nods. "That's right. An' New York City's a pretty good distance from New London, Connecticut."

"And for that girl to just show up there that one day."

"Yeah... weird."

"...only time she ever came to your class."

"...the only time."

"And she picked you out."

"Yeah, she did. She picked me."

"The right director could give everybody goose bumps with that one."

Poteet chuckles. "But I've had other strange things like that happen to me. Have I told you about the fortune-teller in Detroit?"

Elliott chuckles. "No. But I'm interested."

"I'll tell ya sometime. But... After that adventure with my cousin, I started datin' this girl who was an actress."

"What about the fortune-teller?"

"Like I said. ...some other time."

Elliott rolls his eyes.

"But anyway... I ended up marryin' the actress."

"...in New York?"

"Yeah. We met in New York City, an' she wanted to go to Hollywood. An' I told 'er... I said, 'Well, that's fine with me, I can paint anywhere.' So, we actually decided... Uh... Rather than head to California, we went to Idabel."

"Hmm..." Elliott holds out his hands like he's balancing something. He smiles and looks at Poteet. He tilts one way and says, "California..." He tilts the other way. "Idabel, Oklahoma..."

Poteet smiles back. "Sure. I get it. Why would anyone go to Idabel? But... Harold had an ol' barn that he'd converted into a studio down there. An' then he found a little one-bedroom house that they moved in next to it an' turned it into his livin' quarters."

"Sounds nice."

"It was pretty cool—the way Harold did it an' all. Like for his studio... They'd torn down the bank there in Idabel. An' Harold bein' Harold... He went up there an' talked 'em into givin' him the teller's cages—those ol' teller cages. ...remember those?"

"Sure."

"An' he set those up as a bar in the studio. Yeah. It was really cool lookin'."

"I'll bet."

"An' he had a huge... This was just in the barn. He had a huge crystal chandelier hangin' in there. Yeah. I mean, it was the perfect touch."

"So, is that where you painted?"

"Yeah, an' it was great. A lot of famous people had come to visit 'im there. When they'd come, he'd have 'em sign the wall. Ya know. I remember Sal Mineo, Tom Jones... There were a lot of others." Poteet shakes his head. "How he got those people to come down there, I'll never know. But..."

"So, when these friends of his came, did he paint their portraits?"

"Mmm... some of 'em. Yeah. But he didn' paint everybody. Some were just friends who wanted a road trip, I guess. But... He'd do a portrait of ya at the drop a hat. An' uh... I appreciated him lettin' me use his studio there. I was married an' needed to make some money."

"Sure. And it sounds like you were trying to make it as an artist, and that had to have helped."

Poteet nods, takes a deep breath, and says, "It did, an' I had an idea. The company I worked for in New York City, ya know—the one where I was copyin' the masters..."

"Yeah."

"Well... I knew one of their big outlets was in Dallas. So... I drove over there, an' I talked to the people who sold those paintings. An' uh... They had 'em all over the walls. An' so, I told this woman, I said, 'Ya know, I can do these paintings for you cheaper than what you're buyin' 'em for.' An' she said, 'You can do that painting right there?' An' I said, 'Ma'am, I did that painting.'"

Elliott chuckles.

"She said, 'Really!' An' I said, 'Yep.' An' so, they jus'... They gave me a lot of work. An' I was tryin' to build up some money to go to L.A., ya know. An' so, this girl I was married to... She goes over to Dallas an' signs with the Kim Dawson Agency, an' starts doin' modelin' for 'em. An' uh... We... We never made it to L.A. We ended up gettin' divorced in Dallas."

"So... Did your wife get caught up with her job and career there in Dallas?"

"Yeah, she did."

"I'm sorry about your marriage. But from my point of

view, this just gets juicier and juicier. Now, we've got an actress-slash-model—good looking I'm sure..." Elliott can't help but reveal how pumped he is.

CHAPTER 32

Checking the "Genius" Box

Elliott continues, "...flashing herself around in Dallas, Texas, the jet-setting home of J. R. Ewing." He nods. "Yeah. I like it."

"An', by the way, since you mentioned J. R. Ewing..." Poteet indicates.

"Yeah. What about him?"

"Larry Hagman was a good friend of mine."

"Huh."

"Yeah. He got interested in my OU project, an' we hit it off. We became good friends."

"That project must have been a big deal—for you to get his attention." The reference to the OU project tweaked Elliott's interest, and he hoped this conversation would lead to more information about the project. But, he decided not to push it for now.

"Uh... I guess."

"Hmm."

"But yeah... About my wife..."

"Right."

"What really did it for our marriage... She wanted me to come over to Dallas an'... An' to paint over there, an'... I was reluctant to. I kept sayin', 'Well, ya know, I've got this great studio'—Harold Stevenson's studio. An' so... Finally, I did move over to Dallas, an' uh... I didn' have a studio. I wadn' makin' any money, an' it wadn' workin' for either of us. So... We got divorced there, an' uh... I didn'... I didn't know what the shit I was gonna do."

Elliott nods. "Sounds like a tough time—for you."

"So, while I was wonderin' 'bout that, this friend of mine... This *Senator* friend from Idabel... He called, an' he said, 'What are you doin' anyway?' An' I said, 'I ain't doin' nothin'. I jus' got divorced.' An' he said, 'Why don't you come on up here. ...jus' stay a couple weeks with me.'"

"...in Oklahoma?"

"Yeah. ...in Oklahoma City. So... I was gonna go up there to stay, ya know, just a couple a weeks, like he said." He smiles. "I ended up stayin' two years."

Elliott chuckles and repeats, "...two years."

"An' it was just one big party." Poteet chuckles as he says, "I mean... This friend had just retired from bein' a State Senator, ya know. He became a lobbyist, an' uh... So, the house we lived in... It was a really nice place—right north of the Capitol up there on Lincoln Avenue, an' uh... But it was just a steady stream of people—in an' out of there all day, ya know, an' up into the night. An' it jus'..."

"And you lived there?"

"Mm-hmm."

"So, you participated in most of the parties."

"Oh, yeah. I was there to party. I mean, we were out *every* night."

"...politics, backroom deals, sex, drugs, rock-n-roll."

Poteet nods.

"And this was for *two* years," Elliott repeats to be clear.

"It was."

"So, tell me... What boxes don't you check?"

"I never thought of myself as checkin' boxes."

Elliott chuckles. "So, during this two-year period—the party period..."

"Yeah."

"Did you have a sense that you were going in the wrong direction?"

"Oh yeah. ...for sure."

"If I wasn't sitting in your studio right now in Santa Fe, New Mexico... I would swear that this guy you're describing, this guy named Poteet Victory, would not... could not"—he looks at Poteet—"ever have a career as an artist—much less a successful one."

Poteet nods and smiles.

They both turn at the knock on the double doors. Terry peeks in and says, "I heard what you jus' said, Elliott, an' I agree—totally."

Elliott chuckles and says, "Come on in."

She steps in and says, "Elliott, we're gonna take ya to dinner tonight. We wanna take ya to Tomasita's. It's Mexican food, an' it's really good, but ya gotta get there early. They get real busy."

"Sounds good."

Poteet shrugs and says, "You can bring your recorder. We can keep talkin'."

Terry moves to her spot across the room by the fireplace.

When she's seated, Poteet looks at Elliott and says, "At a point, I knew I had to do somethin' else." He chuckles. "An' I... I just fell back on where I knew I could make some money."

"...copying the masters in Dallas?"

"No—in the pipeline business."

Elliott and Terry laugh. Elliott shakes his head. "I still don't see how you became an artist in Santa Fe."

"I know whacha mean," Terry says, still laughing.

"Well, I had some connections in the pipeline business, but I was thinkin'... Maybe I should learn a new skill this time."

"Seems like you already knew how to paint," Elliott notes sarcastically.

Terry chuckles.

"I guess I didn't have confidence enough to follow through on that. I don' know. An' uh... I wanted to make decent money. So... There was a school down in Houston, uh, San Jacinto College. An' it's the only place in the United States where they taught a course on nondestructive testin' of welds. Ya know, the welds on a pipeline?"

"I'm sure that's important."

"It is. An' you gotta be certified to do it."

Elliott nods.

"An' you can get certified there. An' that's why I went. I wanted to make some money."

"Okay. I get it."

"An' uh..." Poteet stands at his painting table to continue, "The course was only one semester, an' they teach you how to handle radioactive isotopes. An' uh... You learn to x-ray welds. Those are at the joints on pipelines."

"So, you did that? You worked with radioactive isotopes?"

"Well, I..." Poteet chuckles. "I went down there to that school, ya know. But..."

Elliott sits back.

"First of all, it's a *hell* of a course. I mean, it's *hard*. An' I... You had to know a lot of trigonometry an' stuff. An' I'd never studied trigonometry. So... I get down there, an' I'm a week late anyway to enroll. So... This instructor... He told me, he said, 'I hate to tell you this, but...' He said, 'I don't think you're gonna be able to catch up.' He said, 'This... This is a short course, an' one week could make all the difference.' An' uh... An' he said, 'Ya know, it's really hard. You gotta know trigonometry.' He said, '...you know any of that?' An' I said, 'No, I don't. ...never had it.'"

Elliott says, "He knew you couldn't make it, based on his

experience with other students."

"Yeah. I'm sure that's true. But... I said, 'Well... I've gotta do this. I don' have anywhere else to go. I jus' gotta do it.' An' he said, 'Well... Okay.' An' then I got a job bartendin' at night. But... I got into this thing an' learned it on my own—the trigonometry part of it. An' uh..."

"You learned trigonometry on your own?"

Poteet nods and confirms, "I did."

"I'm impressed."

"Well, anyway... We were tested every week. An' every time... It was like in the army. I was top in class. An' we... Our final exam... We took this test. He called me aside, an' he said, 'You scored higher on this test than anybody ever has.'"

"So..." Elliott remarks. "Now we're checking the 'Genius' box."

Poteet smiles and says, "But... This instructor... He said, 'Ya know, we get so many people through here.' He said, 'I don' tell people this.' He said, '*You* could make a ton of money at it.' He said, 'No. If I was you. I'd buy my own truck.'" He looks at Elliott. "Ya know... You get a pickup an' on the back of it... It's like is a big camper. But inside that camper is where you develop the film. An' he said, 'Uh, you could do this.' An' I said, 'Well, what kind of money is in it?' He said, 'Well, I don' know. It depends on the size of the pipe.' But he was sayin', 'We laid this six-inch pipeline through Houston down there.' An' he said, 'We got ninety bucks a shot.'"

Elliott nods and says, "Okay."

"An' this was thirty somethin' years ago. An' I said, 'Well, how many joints are y'all layin' a day?' An' he said, 'Ninety to a hundred.'"

Elliott's eyebrows tick up, and he asks, "So... Is that like ninety to a hundred times ninety dollars?"

"Yeah."

"And that's every day?"

"Yeah. An' that was thirty years ago."

"Yeah. Wow. That was good money."

"Yeah. An' that's what I've been tryin' to tell ya."

"Okay. I see."

"An' I think I could've done it. But... That's when M. L., my buddy up there in Oklahoma City... He called me."

Elliott smiles and shakes his head. "I'm guessin' this is where things go sideways."

Poteet chuckles. "I think you're seeing how things usually go for me."

"It's not that hard."

"But anyway... What we had done was... We knew this guy that was doin' parkin' lots—like layin' asphalt..."

"Yeah?" Elliott says and chuckles.

"An' so... He was hirin' contractors, an' he thought we could probably do this for 'im.' An' so... We got this machine that would do the striping. He'd put down the asphalt, an' we'd paint the stripes. But... After a while, we kind of got out of that. An' when I left Oklahoma City, my friend was gonna sell the equipment. An' when he did, we'd split the money, ya know. So, I get a phone call, while I was in this class—down there. An' uh... I had to go over to the administration buildin' to even take the call. An' it was him."

Elliott begins laughing softly.

"An' I said, 'What's the deal?' He said, 'Well, I... Uh, uh, uh...' I said, 'Spit it out.' He said, 'Uh, I gotta tell ya, we sold the equipment.' I said, 'Well, good.'"

Elliott begins chuckling.

"He said, 'But I invested it for us somewhere else.' An' I said, 'Oh yeah? What?' An' he said, 'Well, we own La Bare's.'"

Elliott asks, "What's La Bare's?"

"...a male strip club."

Poteet and Elliott roar. Terry joins in.

Elliott and Poteet both sigh to end the laughter.

Looking at Elliott and shaking her head, Terry asks, "Can ya believe it?"

Grinning, Elliott responds, "Yes *and* no."

They crack up again.

As Elliott is wiping away the tears but still chuckling, he asks, "So... How long did you own a male strip club?"

"Oh, not long. Probably... I don' know... four or five months."

"I think we've just checked another box."

Poteet and Terry laugh.

"'Cause, when we first opened it... Man, I mean, we just had all this business, ya know, an' then the novelty kind of wore off."

Elliott chuckles.

"But I'd had some experience with male strippers. It was when I was workin' down in Houston as a bartender. An' uh... So, down there... On Sundays, they turned that place into a male strip club, ya know. An' all the women would come in there... So, I got to know these dancers pretty well. An' uh... So, when we started this thing in Oklahoma, there was a group of local guys that were the dancers. So, the first meeting we had with 'em, one of the dancers was bein' a total asshole. An' my partner is up in front of 'em tryin' to talk, an' this guy keeps interruptin' 'im—blah, blah, blah. An' uh... Finally, I jus' got tired of it. An' I tol' 'im, I said, 'Why don't you just shut your damn mouth an' let 'im finish what he's sayin'?' An' uh... So, he jumps up an' says, 'Well, who the hell are you?' An' I said... 'I'm the guy that's here to whip your ass.'"

Elliott and Terry laugh.

"An' uh... Boy, all the dancers jump up. Yeah. An' they walk out. All the dancers walked out of that meeting, an' M.L. said, 'Boy, you did it this time.'"

Elliott chuckles.

"I said, 'Don't worry 'bout it, I'll take care of it.' An' he said,

'What the hell are you talkin' about?'"

Terry smiles, enjoying the laughter.

"So, I get on the phone, an' I call these dancers down in Houston. An' they're a real professional group, ya know. An' I told this one guy, sort of the head of it. I tol' 'im what happened. He said, 'Don't worry 'bout it.' He said, 'We'll be on the plane tomorrow.' An' they did. They come up there, an' they stayed. An' we really got this thing rollin'."

"Huh."

"Then the guys from Oklahoma City started comin' back, sayin', 'Well, we'd like to work here.' So... Yeah... But boy, M. L. was just..." Poteet laughs as he says, "He jus' could not believe I'd run all the dancers off."

Elliott and Terry laugh again.

Elliott mutters, "Wow."

Still chuckling, Poteet says, "Yeah."

"So, you just had women flooding into this place every night..."

"We did, at least for a while."

"Again, I think you've got me salivating to produce this scene. I can see it. The Native American painter operates a male strip club and gets in a fight with all the strippers." Elliott chuckles and adds, "We're breaking new ground here."

"We didn't actually fight."

Elliott snickers. "I know. But I'd produce it like you did."

Poteet, Terry, and Elliott all laugh.

Poteet shakes his head. "An' women are worse than men in a strip club."

Elliott chuckles.

"Oh yeah. They are. I mean, we had to keep a close reign on 'em. 'Cause..."

Elliott continues chuckling.

"They'd try to take their clothes off. Yeah. An' all kinds of crap like that. It was every night, too. An' I just got sick of it. I got to where I jus' hated goin' in. I really did. But it wadn' all bad. I used that time to get my college degree. I finished up there at UCO in Edmond."

"Oh? I guess that's a college near Oklahoma City?"

"Yeah, it is. It's the University of Central Oklahoma on the north side of the, uh, Oklahoma City metro area."

"Okay."

I really didn' have a lot to do durin' the day. The club thing was mostly at night. So, I thought, 'I'll go get my degree.' An' that's what I did."

"Hmm. That's impressive. It really is. I don't think too many would have made the effort to finish their degree in a similar situation."

"...made sense to me."

"So now... I guess we've got a new title: 'Poteet Goes to College.'"

Poteet chuckles. "Yeah. An' I got one B. An' that's 'cause the instructor was jealous. 'Cause I could paint better than she could."

"I don't doubt that."

"Yeah... So... But yeah..."

"Because you'd already been to art school in New York City."

"Mm-hmm."

"I mean, how could she think you wouldn't be better than her?"

"That's what I thought. But anyway... I graduated. An' I was wonderin'... Thinkin' 'bout myself, 'What are you gonna do with your life?'"

Elliott nods.

Terry says, "So... At that time, they sold La Bare's, and he started sellin' insurance."

"Right," Poteet responds.

"An' that's where number four comes in."

Elliott looks at Terry and asks, "Do you mean his fourth wife?"

"Yeah."

Poteet smiles and says, "But, on the insurance... Me an' this other guy... We worked as partners, an' we went to work for United Funeral Directors."

Elliott raises his hand and asks, "United Funeral Directors...? Really?"

"Yeah. It's what we did."

Chuckling, Elliott says, "This is bizarre." He shakes his head. "I must admit, something that begins with 'United Funeral Directors' doesn't get me all that excited."

"Right. I get that. But... This company was out of Wichita Falls—somewhat local. An' what we did was, uh... We sold burial insurance."

"Whoa! ...how exciting."

Without even changing his expression, Poteet continues, "So... We'd go into a little town, an' we'd hook up with the local funeral director, an' we'd offer to pay 'em a small percentage. They'd say, 'Yeah. You can tell 'em you're with so an' so funeral home. So, that's what we did. An' uh... Shit, I was makin' a lot of money."

"Well, that part sounds good."

"Yeah. An' uh... After about a year, we got called into the home office. An' this guy said, 'Well, it's good news an' bad news.'"

"...so typical."

Terry chuckles.

"I said, 'So, what is it?' He said, 'The good news is, uh... You sold more than anybody we've ever had.'"

Elliott laughs.

"An' he said, 'The bad news is... You sold us out of business.'"

Elliott shakes his head, laughing.

"You sold up all our reserves. We can't sell anymore.'" Poteet looks at Elliott and says, "No shit. He said that." Poteet chuckles. "I went to another company, an' said, 'Ya know, I want blah, blah, blah.' An' they said, 'Well, what's your background?' An' I said, 'Read this.'" Poteet nods. "'Oh, you're hired.'"

Chuckling, Elliott says, "Yeah... You were good at sales."

"I sold clothes, an' uh..."

"Right. For that store in Idabel."

"I sold shoes. I sold insurance. I sold those T-shirts. I try to sell paintings in here every day."

Elliott nods. "Yeah. And I'm still thinking about a painting for myself."

"Like I said, 'We can help you with that.'"

Terry sits forward. "Ya know, I've had several people look at that one downstairs with the red roses."

Elliott smiles. "You don't expect for me to fall for that, do you."

"I know what you mean, but I'm not kiddin'. We've had several look at that one. I don't think it's gonna last much longer, Elliott."

He tilts his head in acknowledgement.

"I didn' ever think sellin' was hard. The main thing about sellin' is to gain somebody's confidence, ya know. They've gotta like you. If they like you... You've pretty much got it sold, if they've got any money." Poteet glances at the time on his computer and says, "You ready...?" He looks at Terry, and she begins to stand.

Elliott says, "Sure," and reaches for his recorder.

CHAPTER 33

Everything but Art

"Look at 'im," Terry says from the back seat of her Escalade. She sees Honey Badger looking out the front door of the gallery and adds, "He looks so sad."

Navigating down the narrow driveway out of the parking lot, Poteet reassuringly says, "He'll be okay. We should be back to get 'im in an hour or so."

Elliott smiles and says, "I'd say that Honey Badger's got it made."

Poteet chuckles.

Terry turns for a better look at the gallery and says, "He's not too happy about it right now. He's wonderin' where his Mama an' his Papa are goin', an' why he's not goin' with 'em."

As they pull out onto Canyon Road, Poteet says, "We're goin' to the Railyard District. There're a lot of galleries in that area now. We thought about movin' over there at one time but decided to stay where we are."

"I guess they call it the 'Railyard District' because it's where the train station was at one time."

"Yeah. An' in fact, it still is. There's a train that runs every day between Santa Fe an' Albuquerque."

"It makes that run several times a day," Terry says. "I have no idea how many people take it. I've never done it myself. I wouldn' know how I'd get around in Albuquerque without my car."

"Thus... the dilemma with mass transit," Elliott points out.

Terry responds, "True."

She and Elliott remain quiet as they watch Poteet deal with the narrow streets of Santa Fe at rush hour. As they pull into the parking lot of Tomasita's, Elliott looks over and says, "Well, there's the train right there."

"Yep," Terry says and nods. "You get on it right here. I may have to ride it someday."

Elliott looks around and notes, "To be this early, the parking lot's really full."

"That's what I was sayin'. You gotta come early or plan to wait."

As they walk in, Elliott detects the aroma of freshly prepared Mexican food.

Poteet tells the hostess, "How 'bout outside today?"

She nods, grabs some menus, and heads into the restaurant—leading the group. They're soon through another door and back outside. She seats them at a table in the shade. Bright mountain sun lights up the surrounding area.

Elliott says, "What a nice day." He looks around the patio area and smiles. He moves forward and looks at Poteet. He says, "I'm so glad you asked to be outside."

"Oh, yeah. Early summer is great out here."

Terry says, "I've had a few days of sittin' out by my pool already."

Elliott smiles and nods.

Terry bends forward and says, "They've got a drink here called a swirl. That's what I always get."

"Their margaritas are good too," Poteet mentions.

Someone comes and sets down a basket of chips and a bowl of salsa. A waiter then quickly appears and asks, "Can I get anything for anyone from the bar?"

Terry looks up with a sparkle in her eye. She says, "I want one of your swirls."

Poteet says, "I'll have a margarita."

"...margarita for me too," Elliott adds.

The waiter nods. Before he can get away, Poteet says, "Bring a bowl of queso for the table."

"Yes sir, Mr. Victory."

Terry looks at Elliott and says, "We come here a lot."

Elliott starts messing with his recorder, and then he strategically sets it on the table. Looking around, he asks, "Is this okay?"

Poteet nods.

Elliott looks at Poteet and then Terry. "So, where were we?"

Terry says, "I was tryin' to sell you a painting, I think."

Elliott chuckles. "I've got to convince my wife's decorator..."

Smiling, Terry says, "I think I've heard that excuse before." Almost singing the words, she says, "You're gonna miss it. Somebody else is gonna get it."

Elliott smiles, looks at Terry, and says, "I know." After a moment, he looks at Poteet. And with a slight chuckle, he says, "I think you were telling me about selling burial insurance."

"That didn' last long."

Terry chuckles.

Poteet says, "Then, somethin' else came up."

"Oh?"

"Well, I told you about my friend who was the lobbyist."

"Oh—that guy you stayed with for two years?"

"Yeah."

Chuckling, Elliott says, "...where you partied night and day the whole time."

"Yeah, that guy. Well... He got into trouble."

"Hmm."

Poteet dips a chip in the salsa and says, "Yeah. He was on the front page of every newspaper in Oklahoma for I don' know how long... about him an' some other lobbyists takin' these congressmen on a ski trip somewhere. They had these pictures of him comin' off the plane an' all this. So... It kind of ruined his reputation. But... He knew this guy that was in the seismic business, ya know. An' so this guy... He told M.L. He said, 'If you'll come up here, I'll get you hooked up with one of these companies.' An' uh... So, M.L. said, 'I'm gonna bring Poteet with me.' He said, 'Bring 'im on up here. We'll get 'im a job.'"

Elliott nods and dips a chip in the salsa.

"So, we made the trip, an' I went over to see the guy about a job. When I pulled up there at the office, him an' this other guy come out. An' boy, they were arguin'. An' I thought, 'There's gonna be a fight out here.' An' uh... This boss... I mean, he really got on this guy, ya know. An' as soon as that guy walked off... He looked at me, an' he said, 'What're you here for?' An' I said, 'Well, I'm here for the job.' He said, 'Come on in.' So, we went in an' I said, 'I saw what happened out there.' He said, 'Yeah.' I said, 'I think I can work for you.' An' so... He gave me the job."

"What did you do?"

"I had to be able to lay out land descriptions an' stuff like that, which I didn' know how to do. An' then... Not only did I have to go to the courthouse an' figure out who owned the land, but I had to, ya know, contact the landowners. To do it, I had to go through tax records. An' then, I had to go through other records, like abstracts an' stuff, to figure it out. Then, there were other questions... Well, did they actually own the mineral rights? I mean, it was a pretty complicated job."

"I'm sure it was. I know people who do that."

"An' I... I learned how. I didn' ask him or anybody else, but

I learned how to do it."

The waiter shows up with two margaritas and a swirl. He sets them down, and the three smile at each other. Someone from the wait staff reaches over to move the recorder. Someone else sets down a bowl of hot queso.

Elliott rearranges the basket and the bowls to get his recorder back in a good spot. He then lifts his glass. The others follow. He says, "To a beautiful day in Santa Fe."

Poteet and Terry smile. Poteet says, "Cheers," and Terry says, "...to Santa Fe." They touch glasses and take a drink.

Elliott nods and says, "That's good."

"Mine is too," Terry says.

All three chuckle.

Poteet sets his glass down, looks at Elliott, and says, "On that job I had... I was an independent contractor."

Elliott nods. Looking at the queso, he says, "That looks good."

Terry says, "Oh yeah. Everything's good here."

Elliott turns to look at Poteet and says, "Sorry."

Poteet chuckles and continues, "So... They had their own guys who did this. But those guys would jus' sit in the coffee shop all day. But not me, man. When I'd get up in the mornin'... Ya know, I was out there. An' that's why those guys hated me. 'Cause I'd get twice as much done as they would—course, I was gettin' paid three times the amount of money too. Because my boss... He said, 'We can put you on a salary.' An' I said, 'Nope. ...don't wanna do that. I'll jus' do it by the mile.'"

"Oh... by the mile."

"They paid me a lot of money. It was... We're goin' back—what, 35 years. An' I was makin' ten, twelve thousand a month. Ya know, that's pretty good."

"That was a *lot* of money."

"Yeah."

Sitting back, Elliott says, "I can tell you this. And I saw it quoted recently—for the year 2000... If you made fifty-five thousand dollars a year, you were in the top ten percent of income earners."

"Hmm. An' that was in 2000?"

"Yeah. Imagine what it was in 1980."

"I'm sure it was a lot less than that."

"And you made a lot more that fifty-five thousand dollars."

"A lot more..."

"So... If you were making a hundred-twenty grand or more a year, you were probably in the top two or three percent— maybe four. That was a *lot* of money."

"An' I liked the work, ya know. I did courthouse research. I talked to the landowners. An' there was somethin' else I had to do too. I mean, this happened all the time... Every town we went into, we got sued. 'Cause they knew that it was an oil company."

"Uh-huh," Elliott responds as he reaches for another chip.

Poteet chuckles. "An' I'd usually have to go to court, ya know. An' uh... My boss was like, 'Don't worry 'bout it.' He said, '...happens all the time.'"

Elliott chuckles, and Terry continues to work on her swirl.

"I testified this one time. A family was suin' us, ya know. An' their attorney had put this woman up on the stand, an' uh... She said... An' she was talkin' 'bout me. The lawyer there... He asked, 'What did he tell you?' She said, 'Somethin', blah, blah, blah.' An' then he asked, 'Well, how did you... How did you feel about their representative?' An' she said"—Poteet imitates a female voice—"'Oh, he was so charming.'"

Elliott breaks out in a full laugh.

"She said..." Again, in a female voice, Poteet says, 'I jus' loved 'im.'" Then, back to his own voice, "An' I could tell that this lawyer was jus' goin' crazy..." Poteet laughs.

Elliott continues laughing.

Poteet says, "That was so funny."

"Oh, man."

"Yeah. We still ended up havin' to pay 'em, of course."

"So, I guess the seismic company always lost?"

"Oh yeah, we always lost."

Elliott observes, "...the cost of doing business, I guess."

"It was. They weren't ever really huge settlements or anything like that, but... It would be a few thousand dollars. An'..."

Elliott starts chuckling again and repeats under his breath, "The representative was charming."

Poteet says, "Yeah."

Elliott takes a drink and looks at Terry. He shakes his head, and says, "Seems like we're talking about Poteet doing everything but paint."

Terry smiles and giggles. She gives a wave of her hand and says, "I know. It's a wonder he ever painted a thing after art school."

Elliott nods, looks at Poteet and says, "Well, you can go on, I guess. I'm still wondering how you ever made it out here."

"Okay..." Poteet pauses for a moment, then continues, "But, I'd worked for this guy for—I don' know, five or six months. So... We all had a party one night an' everybody was drinkin'. An' he tol' me... He said, 'Ya know...' He said, 'I gotta tell ya. When you came into my office that day...' He said, 'I knew you didn' know a damn thing.'"

Elliott and Terry chuckle.

"But he said, 'I saw somebody that really wanted the job. An' you seemed like you were smart enough to do it.' An' he said, 'So, I jus' gave you the chance.' An' he said, 'You did it too.'"

Elliott nods.

"Yeah, I did. But it was... Uh... Yeah, that was... But that last year that I worked... Yeah. Out of three hundred sixty-five days, I spent three hundred thirty-somethin' in hotels an' motels."

"I'm not real smart, but I think that's most of the time."

"Yes, it is—nearly all the time. An' when I was workin' on that job... I think that was the same... Yeah... Yeah, it was. ...the same year that my brother-in-law was up there workin'. An' that's before he was married to my sister. We were stayin' over close to Detroit, an' we got a weekend off for some reason. So, he said, 'Let's go to the racetrack.' He said, 'Ya know, I've got a good friend down there. He's the blacksmith at the track.'"

Terry reaches for a chip and says, "I've heard this one."

"An' that's when I got in on that fixed horse race."

Elliott asks slowly, "...a fixed horse race?"

"Yeah," Terry answers.

"So, there really are such things?" Elliott asks as he takes a drink.

"There was that day," Poteet replies.

Elliott chuckles. "And your brother-in-law knew about it?"

"No—not when we were goin' down there."

"Really."

"Mm-hmm."

"But..." Elliott asks, "His friend bein' a blacksmith... I guess that's relevant?"

"It is. Because... As the track blacksmith, he had to check the racin' plates on every horse before each race."

"...racing plates?"

"...horseshoes."

"Oh."

"An' uh... Yeah. But he... An' it jus' so happened that this blacksmith was a real good friend with the top jockey there. An' this little ol' jockey... He was from Arkansas, ya know—crazy little bastard. An' uh... He come in on his horse. He leaned down, an' tol' the blacksmith how to bet. He said, 'This jockey's been hurt, an'... It's his first race back, an' we're gonna let 'im win.'"

Elliott's face shows his surprise.

"An' they did. An' uh... We couldn' believe it. When they come around there to the home stretch..."

Elliott starts chuckling.

Poteet smiles and raises his voice. "These jockeys were jus' pullin' back on their horses. Yeah. I mean, really... I'm thinkin', 'Come on...'"

"So, it seemed a little obvious."

"More than a little..."

Elliott and Poteet laugh.

As he's gaining his composure, Poteet says, "Yeah. That little bastard... He got us into a hell of a fight."

"Really?" Elliott asks and chuckles. "What might make me think you could go somewhere and *not* get into a fight?"

Terry grins as the waiter shows up again.

He asks, "Are you ready to order?"

Poteet looks up and answers, "I don't think so."

"How 'bout another round?"

Poteet looks at Elliott who nods. Poteet answers, "Sure." He chuckles and continues, "But... It wadn' my fault. An'... Oh man... Yeah... I think it was that night. Uh... We had gone to this place where all the people from the track hung out. It was a restaurant/dance hall kind of place, ya know. An' uh... We were out there on the dance floor an' this little jockey was dancin' with this girl." He holds out his hand to about five feet above the floor. "An' he was only about that tall, ya know. An' uh..." Chuckling, Poteet says, "So... While he's out there dancin', this bigger guy... He come up there, an' uh... He jus' pushed that jockey out of the way an' started dancin' with his girl. An' I remember... This jockey's name was Lonnie Ray, an'... So, Lonnie come back around an' just jumped up an' hit this guy right in the nose. Shit. Blood went everywhere. An' uh... An' then... This big guy was gonna do somethin' to Lonnie, so me an' Rowland couldn't let 'em do that."

Elliott smiles and says, "Of course not..."

Conversation stops as fresh drinks are set in front of everyone and empty glasses taken away.

Poteet dips a chip in the salsa, takes a bite, and continues, "So..." He chuckles. "An' I remember... This one guy in there... He was about six-four, six-five. So, Rowland started to get up. An' this guy..."

"Yeah?"

"...took a swing at 'im, an' Rowland jus' kept standin' up. An' he hit Rowland right in the chest, thinkin' he was gonna hit 'im in the head."

Elliott chuckles and says, "Oh. So, Rowland's a big guy."

"Yeah."

"Okay."

"So... Rowland jus' goes, 'wham'"—Poteet demonstrates, swinging his fist over his head—"an' his fist comes right down on top of 'im. ...flattened his ass."

Elliott grimaces and says, "Oh..."

"An' then, the whole damn place started fightin'. I mean everybody was fightin', an' uh... An', we were kind of the outsiders, ya know. An'... This one guy... I was fightin' him, an' I'm tryin' to watch, 'cause I didn' want any surprises. An' I see this one guy come runnin' towards me with his hand drawed back"—Poteet pulls his hand back in a fist—"like that, an' I knew he was comin' for me. So, this guy I was fightin'... I jus' reached out an' grabbed 'im like this." Poteet grabs the front of his own shirt. "I turned 'im around. An' that guy hit 'im." Poteet smashes his fist into his other hand.

Terry laughs.

Elliott chuckles and says, "Really?"

"No shit."

"That's like you see in the movies."

"Yeah. ...knocked 'im completely loose from me."

Elliott shakes his head.

Poteet chuckles and says, "Yeah."

"Wow."

Still chuckling, Poteet says, "I don' know how we got out of that damn place, but... We did. Yeah... That was..."

"Well, sounds like you might've needed Wayland that night."

"Yeah. I wish Wayland *had* a been there. I could *always* use Wayland in a fight. But yeah... We did. We got out of there without too much damage."

Elliott shakes his head.

Poteet says, "But bein' away like that, ya know, that right-of-way job... It destroyed my marriage."

Terry moves forward to say, "An' Elliott, that was number four."

Elliott begins to do the mental gymnastics to remember numbers one, two, and three. And he can't quite do it.

CHAPTER 34

Getting to Santa Fe

Elliott smiles and says, "I haven't quite got all the dates and times down, but I know you're number five."

"I am. But... I came along several years later."

Elliott turns to Poteet. "Just to recap... You were making money at that time."

"I was."

"And... I guess, you were sending it home."

"I was."

Terry reaches out and touches Poteet's hand. "Tell 'im the story about the lady you met in Michigan."

Poteet smiles back and says, "Okay."

Terry looks at Elliott. "Do you wanna hear this?"

"Sure," he says as he reaches for a chip.

"I mean, it's interesting. It really is."

Elliott grabs his margarita and sits back.

After a moment, Poteet begins, "Her name was, uh... Her name was Virginia Dragus. I'll never forget 'er. But she was in Detroit, an' I was workin' a different part of Michigan. My boss called me, an' he said, uh, 'I need for you to do me a favor.' He said, 'I need for you to go over to Detroit an' meet with this woman over there.' An' I said, 'Well... That's not my territory.

289

You've got people over there.' An' he said, 'Yeah, I know we've got people, but she's already run everybody else off. She says she won't talk to anybody.' An' he said, 'We've really got to get across her land.'"

Poteet turns to Elliott to explain, "'Cause... When you're doin' a seismic test, ya know, you're testin' from here to there in a straight line. An'... So, every landowner down through there has to give you permission. An'... If one of 'em's missin', it's gonna screw up your whole project."

"I think I understand."

"So, I drove over..."

"What was her name again—this woman that you mentioned?" Elliott asks.

"Virginia Dragus, ...D-R-A-G-U-S. An' uh... So... I drove over to Detroit. An' boy, it was snowin' like hell. An' uh... I finally found her house—a really nice house in a nice neighborhood. So, I get out an' go up to the door... knocked on the door... rang the doorbell... nothin', ya know. An' I kept doin' that. Nothin'. So, I think, 'Well, maybe she's not here.' So, I was walkin' back to my pickup to write 'er a note. When I got about halfway there, she opened the door. She said, 'I told you. We're not... I don't want any of you damn oil men around here. I don't want you on my property an' blah, blah, blah.' An' I said, 'Well, if you'd jus' listen for a second.' She said, 'No. I told you. I don' want you damn oil men on my property.' I said, 'To tell you the truth, ma'am, I really don't give a damn.' I said, 'They sent me over here 'cause you were rude to everybody else.' An' uh... So, I started to walk back to the pickup, an' she said, 'Hey.' An' uh... I said, 'Yeah?' She said, uh, 'Come here a minute.' So, I walked back over there, an' she tol' me. She said, uh... An' this is paraphrasing what she said. But she said, 'God told me to tell you something.'"

Elliott chuckles.

"An' I said, 'Oh, yeah? What was that?' She said, 'Well...

Come on inside.' She said '...like to have a cup of coffee?' An' I said, 'Yeah... Sure...' So, we go in an' sit down—at the kitchen table. An' uh... She says, 'You don't know who I am. But I'm the number one psychic in all of Detroit.'"

Elliott interrupts, "This must be the other mystical experience you had—the one you wouldn't tell me about earlier."

"It is."

"...just wanted to make sure."

"Right. So... Ms. Dragus... She said, 'All of the politicians an' everybody... They come to me.' An' she said, 'I was born with a gift, ya know.' An' uh... She said, 'God told me to tell you somethin'.' An'... I said, 'Okay, what is it?' She said, 'Well, get your pad.' She said, 'You need to write this down.' An' I said, 'Okay. I'll write it down.'"

Terry smiles.

Chuckling, Poteet continues, "She asked, 'You like your job, don't you?' I said, 'Yeah, I do. I like my job.' I said, 'I make quite a bit of money doin' it.' She said, 'Well, you won't even have this job in thirty days.' An' I said, 'What are you...? Are they gonna fire me?' She said, 'Nope, you're gonna quit.' An' I said, 'Oh, I'm not quittin'.' An' she said, 'You're gonna quit this job, an' you're gonna move someplace new. It's gonna be out west somewhere.' An' she said, 'I can't see where it is.' But she said, '...probably be a good idea if you learned how to speak Spanish.'"

Elliott and Terry chuckle.

Poteet looks over at Elliott and says, "I wadn' even... Santa Fe wadn' even on my radar." He takes a drink of his margarita and then continues, "An' uh... I said, 'Well, alright, I'm writin' this stuff down.' Then... She said, uh... She said, 'Ya know, you would've been a great general in the Army.' An' I said, 'Well, that's just where you went off track.'"

Elliott and Terry laugh.

"I said, 'I was in the Army.' An' I said, 'I was terrible.'"

They continue laughing.

"She said, 'Yeah. But it was because it wadn' your idea. Was it?' An' I said, 'No. An' I guess you're right.' She said, 'You would've been a great general.' An' then, she said, 'Where you're goin'...' She said, 'I can't see what you're gonna do, but I think it's gonna have somethin' to do with art.'"

Elliott looks at Poteet over the top of his glasses.

Poteet dips another chip in the queso. "That's what she said. An' uh... I went, 'Wow! Really?'" He eats the chip. "An' she said, 'You're gonna make a ton of money.' She said, 'You're gonna make more money than you thought you could ever make.' She said, 'You're gonna have to work for it, an' it's gonna take you a while. But you will.' An' uh... Ya know, we talked for a long time. Then she said, 'There's one other thing I want to warn you about.' She said, 'When you get to where you're goin'...' She said, 'There's two women that I can see... An' you should watch out for 'em.' An' she said, 'One will be named Rose. An' the other one will be named...' She looked down an' shook her head. She said, 'Her name will start with an "S."' An'... She said, 'Jus' remember that.'"

Elliott chuckles quietly.

"I said, 'Okay.' So... When we got through with all that, she said, 'Do you want me to sign your papers?' An' I said, 'Would you, please?' She said, 'Yeah.' An' she signed 'em." Poteet smiles, looks at Elliott, and says, "She damn sure did."

"It's that salesman in you."

Poteet takes another drink of his margarita. "An' uh..." He explains, "Within a month, I'd quit my job, an' I was in Santa Fe, New Mexico." He chuckles. "An' sure enough, I uh... I started datin' this girl out there. Her name was Sylvia, an' she was a nut. An' uh..."

Elliott shakes his head.

Poteet looks over at Terry. "I guess I should go ahead an'

tell 'im the rest of the story."

Terry snickers. "Yeah, I think you should."

"...might as well," Elliott says.

Poteet says, "Okay."

Elliott sets his glass down and says, "Let's hear it. I love that mystical, supernatural stuff. Every film needs some of it."

Poteet chuckles. "...you ready to hear 'bout Sylvia?"

"Sure. ...the nut?"

"Right," Poteet says and takes a drink. "Uh... Well, I dated 'er for a while, an' then I broke up with 'er. An' she got all pissed off, ya know. So, I started datin' somebody else."

"Sounds like I've heard this before."

Poteet chuckles. "So, this new girl I was datin', ya know... We'd gone somewhere an' had come back to my apartment. An' uh... So, we were in bed, an' the room was dark. I happened to look up, an' I see somebody standin' at the foot of my bed. So, I jus' naturally jumped up an'... An' when I grabbed this person, I knew it was a woman. An' it was her— Sylvia. An' boy, she was kickin' an' screamin'. An' she said, 'I should've killed you, you son of a bitch, when I had the chance.'"

Elliott sits forward with his eyes wide open and says, "She *was* a nut."

"So... What she had done is... She had stolen my keys at some point an' had one made. So, she came in an' hid in the closet. I don' know how long she'd been in there. But... Like I say, she was kickin' an' tryin' to hit me an' scratch me. An' I'd never done this to a woman before. But I was so mad at 'er. When I got 'er to the front door, I went POW"—demonstrating with his fist—"an' I hit 'er."

"Ooooo..."

"...an' jus' knocked 'er right down the hallway, an' uh... About, I don' know... Fifteen, twenty minutes later"—Poteet knocks on the table three times—"police. So, I open the door, an' this cop says, 'There's a woman out here that says you hit 'er.' An' I said, 'I damn sure did. An' if she comes back, I'm gonna break her damn neck.'"

Elliott and Terry start to chuckle.

"An' he said, 'Well... Tell me what happened.' So, he come in, an' I tol' 'im my story. An' he said, 'Boy, you be down at that courthouse tomorrow at nine, an' you get you a restrainin' order.' He said, 'I won't do anything to you.' He said, 'She broke into your house an'...' But he said, 'I've seen this before.' An' he said, 'It never gets any better. It jus' gets worse.' So... I did. I did what he said. An'... When I got the restrainin' order, it was like for six months or somethin'. An' I wadn't payin' any attention to it. But... At twelve o'clock midnight... When that thing had expired, she was right back at my door."

"Oh my gosh."

"Yeah. So, I had to go get another one the next day— another restrainin' order."

Elliott shakes his head. "...even after six months."

"Uh-huh."

"...it was still on her mind."

"Yeah."

"I can't believe it. It's crazy."

"Yeah, it was. An', I mean, she had it down to the minute too, but..."

"Damn," Elliott says, still shaking his head.

"What seemed so strange to me was... That woman... Virginia Dragus... She had told me all this."

"Yeah. Sylvia was that woman—the one starting with an 'S.'"

"She was."

"What about Rose?" Terry asks.

"That... I don' know. I didn't run into a Rose."

"Maybe it's the roses in your paintings," Terry suggests.

"Could be. I don' know."

"I like that story about Virginia Dragus. It's a lot like those other stories. It's unexpected. It's something unexplainable... something supernatural... something other-worldly," Elliott says as he reaches for another chip. He holds the chip and says, "Okay. I'm trying to get your wives straight, Poteet." He points back and forth to Poteet and Terry. "I think one of you said that wife number four lived in Oklahoma."

"Uh-huh," Poteet replies.

"Um... And you weren't married very long before you took off on this right-of-way job."

"Mm-hmm. Right."

"Had you planned to go away like that before you got married?"

"No. I was actually, uh... That's when I was sellin' burial insurance, ya know."

"Okay."

"An' uh... No. I wadn' plannin' to be gone like that."

"And you were doing well with burial insurance."

"I was. But... I got bored with that. It was like... Shit, I don't wanna do *this* my whole life."

"Mm-Hmm."

"An' ya know. Those long-distance marriages usually don't work out too well."

"I've had some of that, but not a lot."

"...especially if you hadn't been together very long."

The waiter returns and asks, "Are you ready to order?"

"I haven't even looked at the menu," Elliott confesses.

Terry says, "The burritos are really good—an' they're big."

Elliott looks up at the waiter and says, "I'll have a burrito."

Terry says, "Same for me."

"Me too," Poteet says to complete the order.

The waiter nods and turns.

Poteet continues, "So, when I got served with the papers

for divorce number four... That's when I tol' myself, 'This will never happen again.' An' I'm gonna go do what *I* wanna do. Ya know, I'd already been to New York. An' I thought... I know about Santa Fe." He turns to look at Elliott. "I'd never been here. But I thought, 'Yeah.' I know there are a lot of Indians here. An' so... Like Virginia Dragus had tol' me... She said, 'You're gonna go out west.' An' that's what I did."

Terry interrupts, "But number four left 'im on the courthouse steps..."

Poteet nods and confirms, "Yeah, she did."

"She even left 'im without a vehicle. An' he had a Corvette, a Cougar, an' a... somethin' else."

"...a Chevy SUV."

"Yeah. An' she got 'em all," Terry explains.

"Yeah. She did. My friend had to come pick me up at the courthouse."

Elliott squints and cocks his head. "Like... How... How could she just take *everything*?"

Poteet takes a drink and answers, "There had to be somethin' else goin' on."

Elliott adjusts his glasses.

As she's dipping a chip into the queso, Terry says, "She was probably seein' the judge on the side, if you know what I mean."

"I don't doubt it," Poteet says.

Elliott grabs his glass but just holds it. He says, "Oh... So, he might've been getting some"—he uses air quotes—"special consideration."

"Exactly!" Terry says.

"It was bullshit. There had to be more to it. 'Cause the Judge tol' me... An' he knew it wadn' fair. He said, 'Well, you have the means to replace this. She dudn'.'"

After a moment, Elliott replies, "I think that's unusual."

Energized, Poteet sits up. "An' my lawyer was goin' nuts

about it, ya know. He said, 'You can't...' An' he said, 'This is unfair, an' you can't do this, an' blah, blah, blah.' But no... I got screwed. So, I... Yeah... I had to call a friend to come pick me up at the courthouse, an' he jus' laughed his ass off," Poteet says and chuckles.

"I guess you didn't think it was that funny at the time."

"No, I didn'. But anyway, I had to go back up to Pennsylvania. I'd been workin' on this job, an' I had to finish it up."

"So, how did you get back there?"

"I don' really remember. I must've had enough money to buy a plane ticket. But there was a guy up there, an' he had this ol' car. An' uh... I bought it from 'im for nothin'. An' then, when I finished that job... I thought, 'This is it. I'm gone. I'm leavin'. An' yeah, I drove it to Santa Fe."

"Finally!" Elliott proclaims as he lifts his glass.

Poteet and Terry do too. They clink glasses and take a drink.

"Poteet finally made it to Santa Fe," Elliott says and sets his margarita glass down.

They laugh.

Elliott looks over at Poteet. "You're here. I knew you were going to make it somehow. But..."

"With that ol' car, I didn' know..."

"Why is that?" Elliott asks.

"It had a busted block."

Elliott chuckles. "Hmm—a busted block."

Poteet's face goes cold, and he says, "I look back an' think... Ya know, the eighties for me were—other than New York— were pretty much of a bust. They really were a waste of my time."

Elliott nods.

"An' I've thought about this." He stares at his drink in silence and then says, "Whatever you do in life, there's gonna be pain—especially with the things you love to do. Just accept it. There's gonna be pain, like in rodeoin', boxin', other things... You can either take it, walk through it, or you can't, ya know. To me, that's kind of a metaphor for life. I mean... When you get knocked down or get hurt... Well, what are you gonna do? Sit in a corner an' cry?" He answers his own question emphatically, "No!" He looks back at his glass as he turns it slowly. He continues, "So... I'd been knocked down by the divorce, an' I had to get up an' move on."

"You did."

Poteet gets the waiter's attention who then walks over. Poteet points at the table and says, "We need water." He looks at Elliott and asks, "Do you want a glass of water?"

"Sure."

"But it worked out for me. An' uh..." Poteet nods. "I had those times when I had to throw myself out there an' trust the universe."

"Like Hawaii?"

"Yeah. An' you can see how that worked out."

"It worked out well."

"An' so, I did the same thing in New York, which also worked out. 'Cause that was a really good experience for me. I got really, really, really good training at the Art Students League. I had some great instructors there. An' that pretty much set the tone for what I was gonna do. I mean... An' then... Comin' to Santa Fe was another one of those things. I didn' know anybody out here... didn' have a job. I was goin' through a divorce, an' I didn' have any money. An' I thought, 'What the hell...'"

"...a step of faith."

"So, I got out here. I was goin' through the classifieds, an' I saw an ad. It was for Vanessie restaurant, which is a very nice place. An' uh... They needed a bartender. It said to come down on Saturday mornin' to fill out an application. So, I did. I went down there, an' there were *ninety* people—ninety people applyin' for that job. Yeah. So, I filled it out, ya know, an' I put my resume with it. Well... I got the job, an' I worked there for three years."

"Sounds like you were very fortunate to get the job."

The waiter sets three glasses on the table.

"I remember... Sometimes I had to close, ya know. An' it usually wadn' so bad durin' the week. But sometimes on Saturday night... We didn' close 'til two. An'... I'd turn on the lights."

"Yeah. I've been there many times."

"...real bright."

Terry chuckles.

"Still, sometimes they wouldn't get up."

"...been there, done that," Elliott says as he chuckles.

"So finally, I got to where... If they wouldn't leave, I'd turn 'em all *off*. It'd jus' be completely dark."

Elliott and Terry laugh.

"That'd get 'em out of there, usually."

Poteet joins in the laughter. After a moment he takes a drink of his water and says, "Yeah, you gotta do somethin' to get their asses outta there."

Terry smiles and says, "Funny."

"But, workin' at Vanessie was so good for me, because... *Everybody* came in there. So, I got to meet... Hell, I knew the Mayor, people from the Governor's office, art collectors... An' I got to meet the owners of some of the galleries."

CHAPTER 35

Down to His Last Fifty Bucks

"An' so, the owner of Vanessie... He'd seen my paintings, an' he said, 'Ya know, you should bring some of your work down here an' hang it.' An' I said, 'Okay.' So, every time I'd do that, it'd sell."

"That had to have been very reinforcing."

"It was. But I had another situation I had to address. An' this is somethin' you need to know. It might change your opinion of who you think I am."

Elliott sits up and says, "You've got my full attention now." He looks at Terry for a hint.

She shrugs and turns to stare at Poteet herself.

"There was a time in my life..." Poteet says and then pauses. "...an' that's when I got out here, that uh... My drinkin' got out of control. An'... Thank God, I realized it."

Terry nods and sits back.

Elliott asks, "So, what did you do?"

"I quit drinkin'. An'..."

"...just on your own?"

"No. I went to AA."

"Okay—the twelve-step program thing?"

"Yeah. An' uh... There was an Indian guy that became my

sponsor. An' uh... He was a big help to me. 'Cause... Boy, he was a strict disciplinarian, an' he tol' me... He said, 'I don' have time to fool with people.' He said, ya know, 'When I tell you to do somethin', you're gonna do it.' An' he said, 'Now... If you don't, then I'm out.' An' uh... I tol' 'im, I said, 'Well, I'll do it. Whatever you tell me to do.' An' ah... So, one of the things that he made me do... First, I had to, uh... He said, 'Every mornin'... When you get up, I want you to write.' An' he said, 'I want you to go back—as far back as you can remember. I want you to write all about your mother. An' then, I want you to go back an' write all about your dad.' So, I did. I kep' all the notebooks an' stuff. But I did what he said. An' I started seein' a lot by doin' that. He said, 'Well, I knew you would.' 'Cause I'd write somethin' down, an' I'd go, 'Holy shit. That's *exactly* what my dad did.' Ya know. I started seein' those things."

"It was good therapy," Elliott observes.

"From what he's told me, I think it was," Terry adds.

"It definitely was. I mean... I had a lot of resentment an' anger about it all. But once I could look at it, then it was gone. I think it was really helpful an' beneficial for me to do that."

"I didn't know that was part of the twelve-step program."

"It was for me. But... What I wouldn't do... I wouldn't date anybody that drank. I wouldn't do that. I jus'..."

"Was it hard to find women who didn't drink?"

"You'd be surprised. 'Cause a lot of the time... I mean, some of the women I'd date, I'd say, 'I don't drink, an' I can't... Ya know, I'm not gonna be involved with somebody that does.'"

Elliott nods.

"An' uh... Ya know, I had several of 'em go, 'Okay, it's fine with me. I don't have to drink.'"

"I see. And then, they'd just quit, at least around you."

"Yeah. They jus' wouldn't drink..."

"That makes sense."

"I didn' want it brought into my house, ya know."

"Sure."

"Because, if somebody drank all the time, I jus'... I wadn' gonna have anything to do with 'em. So... No, that wadn' a problem."

"I see... Well, with the twelve-step program, I understand there's a faith component..."

"Absolutely."

Terry nods and says, "That's a big part of it."

"Right. Which was easy for me, 'cause I already had it, ya know. It wadn' a... I didn' have to learn that."

"Okay."

"No... The faith part was easy." Poteet chuckles. "Yeah... But if you work those twelve steps... An' uh... Ya know... There's one step there where you have to go make amends to everybody that you've ever wronged. An' you think, 'Shit!'"

Poteet and Terry chuckle. Elliott looks stunned.

"You think... 'I can't do this. Damn.'"

Poteet and Terry laugh.

"I didn't know you had to do that," Elliott says. "So, it's everybody you can think of that you've ever wronged? Really?"

"Yeah. Yep. Yes, sir. An'..."

"For some people that'd be a pretty long list," Elliott says, nods, and points to himself.

Terry nods and points to herself.

"An' uh... I tol' my sponsor... I said, 'Well, they may not wanna hear from me.' He said, '...dudn' make any difference. You do what you gotta do. An' they can either accept it or not. But you've done what you're supposed to do.'" Poteet nods. "An'... I did it. Some didn' like hearin' from me. An' then, there were others that thought, ya know, 'That's really a big thing for you to do, especially'"—he pauses and then adds—"'to admit you were wrong.'"

Elliott breathes a deep sigh.

"An' it's humbling."

"I'm sure it is," Terry says.

"But it's good for ya. You think you're gonna die. Or, you wish they'd die or somethin'."

Elliott and Terry laugh. Poteet joins in with a chuckle.

"But it's... I mean, once you get through with that, though... Boy, I'll tell ya, it's a big, big relief—a *huge* relief."

"I'm sure," Elliott responds, nodding.

"'Cause a lot of people... They become alcoholics just out of guilt. A lot of times they don't even know what it is. 'Cause you can ask an alcoholic, 'Why do you drink?' He'll say, 'I don' know. I don' know. I just do.'" Poteet nods. "Like my dad... I mean, he never even tried to sober up. But... Uh... If he'd done this..."

"Yeah?"

Poteet looks down at the glass of ice water he's holding. He says, "It would've worked. I think it would've worked on him too."

Elliott takes a deep breath. "I can tell it makes you sad to think about your dad like that."

Poteet sighs and says, "Probably... It probably does."

Terry turns to notice a hot plate being delivered to her. Two others follow.

Elliott says, "*That's* a large burrito."

"It's like I told ya," Terry says. "But it's good."

They all grab silverware and begin tackling their burritos.

Elliott takes a large bite and quickly reaches for water. He says, "Oo... That's hot!"

"Sorry. I should've warned ya," Terry says.

"But it's really good. I'll just take it a little slower," Elliott says as he cuts a smaller bite and lets it set for a moment to cool.

Poteet takes a bite carefully and then says, "But... Did you know that AA has the highest... Uh... The highest rate of success of any program?"

"No."

"An'... Do you know what that rate of success is?"

"I don't."

"...five percent. It's five percent. That's it."

"Damn."

"Yeah, I know... When I read that, I was like, 'No shit.' Because... Most people can't make it. They can't stay with it. I mean, they jus' don't."

"That's sad," Elliott responds.

"It is. Yeah. An' I tried to help others. I sponsored people. An' uh... Some of 'em would hang in there a month or two, an' others would hang in for a year or more. An'..."

"So, when they'd fall off the wagon, they'd fall completely off, I guess."

"Yeah. They would."

"And not like you..."

"Right. I was able to control it." He takes a deep breath. "Thank goodness. Yeah..." He nods. "But, when I was goin' through it, I heard some horrible stories. Because you... You have to get up an' tell your story, ya know. An' I heard some doozies." He shakes his head and utters, "Whoo!"

"I'll bet."

"I'll tell you the one that shocked me the most."

"Okay."

"I think I know..." Terry says and smiles as she turns her attention back to her food.

"This boy who was talkin', ya know... He was from a rich family in Texas, an' he'd black out. He'd get drunk, an' black out."

Elliott says, "I've been close to that, I'm afraid."

"He said, 'Hell, I'd get drunk an' black out an' be blacked out for several days or a week.'"

"...several days! Or even a week?"

"Oh yeah."

"I mean, that *is* a problem."

Terry looks at Poteet and says, "Your burrito's gettin' cold."

"That's okay," Poteet replies. "But... It *was* a big problem. An' uh..." The guy talkin' to us said, 'I'd usually end up in jail. An'... When I'd sober up... Well...' He said, 'I'd call the lawyer. The lawyer'd call Daddy. Ya know, they'd bail me out.' I mean, he... His family was well known an' all this stuff. An' he was married. He said he'd call his wife, an' she'd come get 'im or somethin'. An' he said this rocked on for several years. An'... He said he woke up one day in jail, an' uh... He said... He told the jailer... said, uh, 'I want you to call my wife an' tell 'er to come down here an' get me.' The jailer said, '...can't do that.' He said, 'Whadaya mean, you can't do that?' He said, 'Call my wife an' tell 'er to come down here.' He said, 'I can't do it.' He said, 'Why can't you do it?' He said, "Cause you killed her last night.'"

Elliott sets his fork down and says, "Whoa!"

"Yeah... Yeah... Now, that's a true story. An' uh... This old boy'd been tellin' it to lots of AA groups. An', he'd been sober for several years. But... That was his story, an' people needed to hear it. That's... There're some..." Poteet shakes his head.

"Oh, that's awful," Elliott says quietly.

"Yeah, I know. When I heard that story, I was like... Like it did you... It jus' put chills on me."

"Yeah."

Poteet continues, "He didn' know. *He did not know.* 'Cause he'd been blacked out, ya know, for days. He didn' know what he'd done."

"I'm surprised he wasn't still in jail," Terry points out.

"I know," Poteet agrees.

"I was wondering too about that," Elliott questions.

Poteet grabs his fork and begins diving into his burrito.

After a moment, Elliott notes, "I think I could make a movie out of *that* story. Yeah. I know I could." He nods. "I've got to remember that one."

Poteet finishes his bite, takes a drink of water, and continues, "I jus' knew that I was on the wrong track." Holding his knife in one hand and his fork in the other, he says, "An' it bothered me, because I knew my dad was an alcoholic. An' then... So, I thought, ya know... I'm not gonna do that. I'm gonna take some steps to straighten it out.'" He begins cutting another bite but looks up to say, "An' yeah, it was a big help to me. It was. An' I didn' drink anything for seventeen years."

"I can see how that probably made a big difference for you."

"It did. I know it did. An' I didn' backslide either. Nope. Once I made that decision, uh... Nope. I didn' fall... I didn'. An' then, ya know, as time went on, I realized that... *That* demon had been exercised. It was gone, an' I didn' have to... I didn' have to deal with it anymore."

"So, you're okay with social drinking—like this." Elliott points to the drink glasses.

"I am. An' I didn't smoke pot or do any drugs durin' that time either. I didn' touch a thing."

"That takes a lot of discipline."

Poteet continues to eat but manages to say, "But... I did buy some pot a couple of years ago. An' it lasted a long time, but uh... Ya know... I ran out, an' Terry asked me... She said, 'Are you gonna get some more of that?' An' I said, 'I don't think so.'"

"You didn't want any more pot?"

"Huh-uh. I didn' want it anymore. I jus' didn'. An' she's like, 'What?' I said, 'No, I don't want it.'" Poteet looks at Elliott and says, "An' I don't.'"

Elliott chuckles.

"I don't like bein', uh... not bein' fully in charge of my faculties, ya know. That's somethin' that concerns me, even with pot. Maybe it's my age. I mean, shit... Through the years... Hell, I've done it all. All of it. The only thing I never did, I never would take anything intravenously..."

"Oh yeah?"

"Right. Yeah, I'd never do that, 'cause I knew better. But... When I was in college, a lot of my friends were doin' it."

"Shootin' up?"

"Oh yeah."

"Really?"

"Yeah. An' uh... Askin' me if I wanted to do it. But I knew that... If I never did it that first time, I'd never have anything to worry about. An' by God, I never did."

"Huh."

"I did LSD. I did mushrooms, mescaline, peyote, you name it, ya know. But... No, I didn'..."

"Cocaine?"

"Oh, yeah."

"Plenty of cocaine?"

"Well, not... Naw. If somebody had it or somethin', ya know. Cocaine to me was like, 'It cost *how much*?'"

Elliott nods and says, "Yeah, it's expensive."

Poteet says, "But... I never was a big druggie."

"Okay... But, back to AA and your drinking problem."

"Okay."

"Your situation was a little bit different from most, because you had relocated to Santa Fe."

"Yeah."

"And so, you didn't have a lot of the friends... You didn't have the influences..."

"That's right."

"Uh. ...from before."

"You do have to change your friends. My sponsor tol' me

that. He said, 'All these ol' drinkin' buddies... They're not your friends.' I mean... An'... Sure enough, I found out that they weren't. Ya know. You're codependents. An' you have to get away from that—totally. But you're right about movin' out here, 'cause I didn' know anybody. So... It was kind of..."

"It was a good time to be making that change."

"Right. I was jus' startin' out, an' I didn' have any of those distractions. So, I put my nose to the grindstone an' stuck with it. An' it paid off."

"Along with being sober, you've mentioned several times how hard you had to work."

"I did work hard. I had to. An' I don' know any other way to live—really. I mean... I've always worked hard. An' yeah... The twelve-step program was important to me in a lot of ways. It certainly strengthened me spiritually. An' then... I quit the bartendin' job, so I could jus' work on painting."

"That must have been exciting."

"It was. But that's when I got down to my last fifty bucks."

"Oh. I thought you might have been further along in your career by then."

"Yeah. But..."

"Did you tell 'im about prayin'?" Terry asks.

Elliott looks over at Poteet.

"Uh... I don' think so."

Elliott cocks his head and asks, "Praying?"

"Yeah. Well... I'd been stressin' out. I was always workin' without a net, ya know. There wadn' anybody gonna save me. An' I wadn' gonna call anybody. Who the hell would I call?" Poteet stops to take a drink of water. "So... But I was stressin' out about it, an' I was out there tryin' to hang on. It was a two-story place, an' I was upstairs paintin'. An' I finally jus' said, 'I can't deal with this. I can't be worryin' about this all the time.' So, I did. I went downstairs an' got on my knees. An' I said, 'Listen, if this is not what you want me to do, get me out of it.

But if it is what you...' I said, 'If I'm supposed to be here, then open the doors.' An'... After I got through prayin', it felt like a big weight had been taken off my shoulders. I went back upstairs an' started paintin' again. An' I felt pretty good about it."

"I see."

"So... The next mornin', this guy knocks on my door—an' I'm out here by the racetrack. I don' know how the hell he found me. An' uh... He introduced himself. He said, 'Somebody told me I should look at your paintings.' An' I said, 'Well, please come in.' So, he come in. An' when he left, he'd bought a painting for $3,500. An' I thought, 'Well great. Ya know.'"

Elliott begins to nod and says, "That's amazing."

Under his breath, Poteet says, "I appreciate that, Jesus.'"

Elliott chuckles.

"An' uh... Yeah. An' then, the next day, the same thing happened. This woman shows up, an'... She said, 'I'd like to look at your paintings.' I said, 'Yeah, sure.' She bought one for $3,500. An' then after that happened, I thought, 'Well, if you're lookin' for a sign, there it is.'"

"I'll admit," Elliott says, "I'm a Presbyterian, and things like that don't happen to Presbyterians."

Poteet chuckles and continues, "An' then I... But... My career took off, an' I was never broke again."

"So... You were ready to give up on your dream, if that's..."

"If that's what God wanted... Yeah."

Elliott nods.

"But it's funny. Because... I mean, you get down on your knees, you pray about it, you're ready to make a commitment... Then, out of nowhere..."

Elliott chuckles again and then says, "You got an answer."

"Yeah. I did."

"...maybe not what you thought it was going to be."

"I don' know."

"But I think that's..." Elliott nods slowly. "I'm saying... I think that your story is amazingly inspirational." He pauses. After a moment, he adds, "It really is. To somebody who's struggling with their business, their art, a *lot* of things..."

"Yeah. I would say, 'Have faith.' Ya know. 'Have faith.'"

Elliott becomes more animated and says, "Even at a later time in life..."

"Right."

"Even when you don't think it can happen. Even when you think life has passed you by."

"Yeah. I got a slow start. I mean... I came out here. An' there were so many younger artists startin' out."

"Yeah. And you were like forty years old at the time, or something."

"I was. An' I'm tellin' ya. I was too old to be startin' a career in Santa Fe as an artist."

"You can say that, but you weren't. Your story's inspirational. I've been giving you a hard time about taking so long to get out here. But... That you didn't start your art career until you were forty... That makes it even better. Like me, everybody would be wondering how you ever became a successful artist."

Poteet chuckles and says, "It was close. It could've gone either way."

"It could've. That's clear. But you can be an example for people."

"I don' know 'bout bein' an example..."

"I would never say you lived a perfect life."

"...far from it."

"...or that you didn't make some bad choices along the way, because you did."

"Yeah. ...plenty of bad choices."

"You had little or no adult supervision when you were young. You were forced to make most of your own life decisions."

"I was."

"And a lot of that was trial and error. It had to be."

"It was. I had to learn from my mistakes."

"Among other things, you became an alcoholic."

"I did."

"And no one would suggest that that was a good idea."

"It wasn't. I had to work very hard to overcome that."

"You did. But... In addition to the alcohol, you did a lot of drugs along the way."

"I did."

"And they could have destroyed you, like they have so many others."

"That's true, an' I'd say it was a close call—probably closer than I realize. I was lucky to have survived."

"And I've told you that."

"Right."

"But... To me, that's what makes you worthy of review and study. That's what makes you interesting. It's why people should learn about your life. I think you offer people some hope."

"I guess."

"You made more than your share of mistakes, because of where you started."

"I hadn' really thought of it like that, but yeah..."

"And you overcame all of those obstacles. It's proof that it can be done. And that's a big deal." Elliott holds out his hands and looks around. "And here you are—living the good life in Santa Fe, New Mexico."

Terry smiles and responds, "It *is* a good life."

"Like I say, it's inspirational."

"But... When it came to my career... Gettin' back to when I was outta money."

Elliott chuckles quietly and shakes his head.

"I jus' trusted God at that point, ya know. An' I thought, 'I can't continue to do this.' An' sure enough..." He chuckles. "When I got down to my last fifty bucks, I thought, 'Man, you screwed up. You should've stayed bartendin'.'"

Elliott and Terry laugh.

Poteet says, "A lot of people don't think, ya know, that prayer works. Well, I can tell you... It does."

Elliott sits up—his smile fading. His expression turns to a look of concern. He says, "Poteet, we've got to talk about something."

Poteet looks at Terry and says, "I get the feelin' that Elliott's already changed his mind about me bein' inspirational."

Elliott shakes his head and replies, "...not really that. But there is an issue."

CHAPTER 36

"They Kicked Me Off Campus."

Elliott looks away for a moment. He then says, "I'm sorry, but I'm not looking for a story about religion."

Terry furrows her brow, sits back, and watches.

"I get that," Poteet replies.

"Those aren't the kind of movies we make. We leave that to the Billy Grahams and the Jerry Falwells of this world. Like I say, I'm a Presbyterian, and I'm not trying to *save* anyone with my films."

"An' I'm not a preacher either," Poteet responds.

"But I am surprised at the depth of your beliefs, given your background and all. I've tried to understand it, and I've tried to see it from your point of view. But... It could be a problem."

Poteet sits quietly for a moment, staring away. He looks back to respond, "Like I say... Since I was a little kid, I've known about God. I've had a connection to God." He pauses. "But... When I was tryin' to quit drinkin', I prayed. I prayed a lot. I had to. I had to have help."

Elliott nods and says, "That's fair."

"So... If you wanna know about me, you gotta know 'bout that part too. I don' talk much about it, but it's an important part of who I am."

"It is," Terry says and nods.

"Sure. And I need to know it all. I need to know what came together for you—to help you overcome the obstacles and then allow you to become successful."

"Well... There was that. An' then... About that same time, I made some decisions about how I wanted to paint. That was important too."

"Great. Let's talk about that."

Terry's smile returns. She leans forward to ask, "Y'all want some sopapillas?"

Poteet answers, "Sure. Let's get some." He then continues, "Okay. Well, it changed after bein' out here for a while. I got to where I wanted to do my art where it didn' look like other people's, ya know. It's okay when you first start out. You kind of... You pick somebody whose work you really like, an' you sort of emulate what they do. An' then... At some point you break away, an' uh... You wanna get your own voice, ya know. So basically, that's what I did. I pretty much abandoned the brushes an' started paintin' with a knife."

The waiter comes to clean the table.

Elliott nods. "I've been watching you paint. I guess I didn't realize how significant using a knife was for you."

"Right. It was a career decision for me. An' I think a good one."

"Obviously... And I understand artistic identity. Ya know... With film... A lot of the young directors try to have a style that's recognizable. Sometimes... And I might say often, in my opinion." He nods. "*That* can turn out badly. If a director is too creative, he can detract from the action of the scene. I'm more of a traditionalist. I want the scene to speak for itself. I want the actors to be real. I want the audience to be completely drawn in. I don't like distractions that remind you that you're just watching a movie."

"I jus' know..." Poteet says. "That to make a name as a

painter, you need a recognizable style. An' I wanted to do that."

"Right. And you needed to do that."

The waiter, who had been standing at the table for several seconds, breaks in and asks, "Can I get you anything else?"

Terry perks up to say, "Yes. We would like an order of sopapillas, please."

"Anything more to drink?"

"How about some more water?" Poteet requests.

"Yes sir, Mr. Victory." The waiter bows slightly and reaches for a pitcher. The group watches as water is being poured all around.

Poteet continues, "An' uh... But the gallery I always wanted to be in was downtown, an' uh... I had a sold-out show at the gallery where I was at, an' it got their attention. They came to me an' said, 'We want you to show with us.' An' that... That kicked me up to a new level. But... I never dreamed... I jus' wanted to get in a gallery where I could sell enough to paint every day. I never knew it was gonna really take off."

"Yeah. I understand that. I think... For you, a subsistence living would've been okay."

"It would've been."

"But you needed to paint."

"I did. ...every day. An'... Ya know, I'm hard-headed as hell."

Elliott smiles.

Poteet takes a drink of water and says, "If I get an idea, I don't like givin' up. An' I'll usually stay with it. So... An' I kind of think that's the secret to most everything—not to give up. Stay with it. Because... I've known a lot of people... If they'd stayed with their original idea, ya know..."

"Yeah?" Elliott responds quietly.

"...but they didn'."

"I understand. And I've got some regrets of my own, in that regard."

"But, especially as an artist tryin' to make it... I mean, you don' know where you're really headed. But then, things can start to happen for ya, an' you can achieve success beyond your wildest dreams." Poteet chuckles as he says, "It's been great for me, but I wouldn't suggest anyone get into this for the money part. That's..." He shakes his head. "'Cause, when I was first startin' out... Man, there were some bleak times."

The sopapillas show up with a bottle of honey. Fresh plates are handed out. The smell of freshly-fried bread and sugar puts a smile on everyone's face.

Poteet reaches for a sopapilla and the bottle of honey. He moves quickly to his obvious routine. Terry gets her sopapilla and receives the honey from Poteet. Elliott follows the lead of the other two. And they're soon eating quietly.

When she's finished, Terry says, "I shouldn' of eaten that, but it was *so* good."

Finishing his last bite, Elliott nods and says, "That *was* good. The whole meal was good. This was a good choice."

"Yeah, we like to come here. It's one of our favorites."

After a quiet moment, Elliott says, "I've been thinking about what I said." He looks at Poteet.

Poteet responds by staring back.

"...about not wanting to make a 'religious' film."

"Right."

"But it's hard to avoid showing you that way. And we *should* show that part of you. I feel like I left the wrong impression about that."

"I don' know what you wanna show. But it's the only thing that got me through a really tough time. Because... Yeah... Like I say, I was always workin' without a net. You either make it, or you don't. Relyin' on God an' bein' calm about it. Not bein' worried... Lettin' it unfold before you..." He pauses before finishing his point. He then adds, "An' it always did."

"You discovered a comfortable way of living and working."

"I did. An' then... At one point, I started havin' some success. They were sellin' my paintings, an' I was makin' more money than I ever expected."

"How great was that?"

"It was extremely rewarding."

Elliott nods and then changes direction. "I think it was about this time in your life that you got hooked up with the University of Oklahoma."

"It was."

"You've been hesitant to talk to me about that."

Poteet nods slowly.

"Are we ever going to be able to talk about it?"

Poteet shrugs and looks at Elliott. "I guess we can."

"So, this was about the Trail of Tears?"

"It was. I was meeting with people at that time about our history."

"I see."

Poteet chuckles and says, "Well... I remember one meeting where we were sittin' around this table, an' I said, 'I know what I see about this.' I said, 'But I want each one of you to tell me what you see.'" He looks at Elliott. "I wanted to know..." After a pause, he says, "I *really* wanted to know. An' I said, 'If you can say it in one sentence, say it in one sentence. If you can say it in one word...' An' so, they all pretty much said the same thing. I finally got to this one historian, an' she said, 'Well, I'll tell you what it meant.' An' I said, 'What?' She said, 'Death.' An' I said, 'That's exactly what I saw.'"

Almost overwhelmed with the statement and thinking that he is onto something regarding Poteet's Native American background, Elliott responds, "That's powerful... very powerful."

Totally focused, Poteet continues, "That was the covenant. It was a covenant of death—with the American Indians. So, I started thinkin', 'Where's the memorial?' An' what I came to discover... There wadn' a memorial. 'Cause I kept talkin' to people... An' the reason there wadn'... It was because it was a big black eye on the American government." Poteet's face remains stern as he adds, "They've never apologized—ever. And... I jus' started thinkin', 'Ya know, someone should do a memorial.' An' I thought, 'Well... What about you? This is your background, an' you're buildin' a reputation as an artist.' So, I jus' kept researchin' it. An' the more I found out, the more I wanted to do it. I felt like it needed to be done, an' it did. Because it wadn' the Indians, ya know. They didn' start this crap." Poteet pauses and then adds, "They didn'." He says again, "They *didn't*. When the white man first came here, they were welcomed, ya know—with open arms. An' then... As time went on, the white man was tryin' to take over the Indian lands, an' that's what started the whole thing. An' soon, the white men were fightin' *every* Indian."

Elliott sighs and nods.

"Before the white man arrived in North America, there were an estimated twenty-nine million Indians. By 1890, there were less than two hundred fifty thousand."

Elliott stares blankly at Poteet and asks for clarification, "Twenty-nine million?"

"Uh-huh."

"Is that right?"

"There's different accounts of that. I've read different things. Some would say, ya know, nineteen million or whatever, but... An' so, I started callin' it..."

Elliott interrupts, "...at the very least, there were *many* millions in North America before the Europeans came."

"Yes. *Many* millions."

"...and less than *two hundred fifty thousand* by 1890."

"Yeah."

Elliott breathes deeply and says, "I didn't know that."

"...my point exactly."

"I see."

"Yeah. An' there were some tribes that were wiped out completely." With cold eyes, Poteet continues, "*Completely.* Every one of 'em was killed. An' so, I started callin' it the 'American Holocaust.' An' people were sayin'"—he changes to a weak, high-pitched voice that mimicks his critics—"You can't say that. You can't say that."

Elliott turns away to stare blankly.

"An' then, a friend called me an' said, 'Turn on your TV. Steven Spielberg's on there talkin' about the American Indians. An' he's callin' it the American Holocaust. An' I thought, 'Well, *thank you,*' ya know. 'Cause, here's a Jewish guy, an' *he's* callin' it a holocaust, an' so..." Poteet's eyes focus. "An' it *was...* It was a *holocaust.*"

"Was that the first time you heard someone else use the phrase, 'American holocaust'?"

"Yeah. An' I'd used it, 'cause it was the biggest mass killing America has ever seen. It *was* an Indian Holocaust."

"Yeah," Elliott says and nods slightly. "I think you'd have to say that it was."

"It was a *tragedy.* An' it's a tragedy that people don't know about it."

"It is. And I have to confess. I should know more."

"You're far from the only one. So... My focus became educating people."

"And that's how you got hooked up with the University of Oklahoma."

"It is. Because... I'm sure there's kids in Oklahoma who've never heard of the Trail of Tears. If you get outside Oklahoma, I'm tellin' ya, none of 'em has. Nobody has. An' the only thing, like a memorial, I'd ever seen at that time on the Trail of Tears... Uh... It was a painting." Poteet holds his hands about four feet apart. "...'bout this size. Okay? The painting was of a wagon. ...kids on the ground. ...walkin' along with it. Ya know, they had some horses an' cows..." He looks at Elliott and says, "*Bullshit.* That wadn' the Trail of Tears. No. The Trail of Tears was *murder.*" He nods slightly and adds, "It was *genocide.*" He pauses, then continues, "Yeah, when I first got into this, I started sayin', 'Maybe I could get a government grant or somethin' like that.' No... No way. Nobody would even talk to me about it."

"...to do a memorial?"

"Right."

"So, you experienced the bias firsthand."

"I did. Yeah."

Elliott breathes deeply and strokes his beard.

"An' so, I thought, 'Well, okay... Don't help me then. I'll just do it my own damn self.'"

"So, what did you do?"

"It meant that I had to raise money for this memorial—myself."

"Okay. So, I assume that's what you did."

"Yeah."

"How?"

"...with fundraisers."

"...fundraisers?"

"Yeah. Like the first one I did was right here in Santa Fe—at a gallery. It was the gallery I was showin' in at the time."

"Okay."

"An' that's when I met Bear Heart. An' I remember what he said that night. He told me, 'If you're tryin' to do somethin' good, there's gonna be forces workin' against you.' An' he was right. There was *always* a force workin' against me." Poteet folds his arms and closes his eyes for a moment with his jaw cocked to one side. He shakes his head before adding, "Those forces workin' against me still continue *to this day.*"

"And so, who was Bear Heart?"

"...a big-time medicine man."

"And... This Bear Heart told you that there would be forces working against you?"

"Yeah."

"What tribe was Bear Heart?"

"He was Muscogee (Creek)."

"Even being of a different tribe, he was willing to help you?"

"Oh yeah..."

"I've read where some old rivalries still exist."

"They do, but that didn't matter to Bear Heart. He truly was a man of the spirit. Ya know, he was a man of the earth. He carried an ancient Indian wisdom in his being." Poteet pauses to take a drink of water. "He carried the ancient arts of Indian healing in his mind. An' uh... His wisdom an' knowledge were sought after—'til the day he died. I wish I had stayed closer to 'im."

"I see."

"Yeah. An' Bear Heart actually became a sort of cult hero with some people."

"Like who...?"

"It was... It was people in the New Age movement— primarily."

"Really?"

"Yeah. An' he wrote a book that became quite popular among that crowd. The name of it was *The Wind Is My Mother*."

"Maybe I should get that."

"You probably should. It's a good book." Poteet then points in the general direction of Elliott. "Something else you might wanna know... Bear Heart came to me in a dream on the one-year anniversary of his death."

"Really?"

"It's true. I woke Terry that night to tell 'er about it. So, the next day we tried to call 'im."

"You said that he had died."

"That's right. He had, but I didn' know. We found out that he'd died the year before—one year *to the day*."

"Hmm. That's pretty strange."

"I had tried to stay in touch with 'im over the years. But he gradually lost his hearing, an' you couldn' talk to 'im on the phone anymore."

"Sounds like an interesting man."

"He was. He had a special connection to the earth, to God, an' to the universe. You might want to Google 'im."

"I'll do that."

"You can search for 'Bear Heart Williams.'"

"Okay," Elliott says and glances at his recorder.

"An' I remember that first night when I met 'im. When I got to the podium to speak... That's when he walked right up to me. It was at a fundraiser, ya know. An' that was even before our speakers got up to talk. Somehow, he knew. He thought, 'This is a person I need to help.' An' he did. He helped me a lot."

"So, what'd he do?"

"Well, to start with... He performed a ceremony that night, an' he gave me this Indian name. He told everybody. He said, 'His name means, "Does not hide the truth." That's his name.' He said, 'This needs to come out. What he's sayin' needs to be brought to everybody's attention. You need to listen.'"

"I'm sure that was a big deal for you."

"It was. It made me feel like I was on the right track for one thing. An' it gave me great confidence."

"Did he continue to help?"

"Yeah. He would come to my fundraisers whenever I asked."

"And he would speak or..."

"Yeah. But he was... Boy he would..." Poteet shakes his head. "He was a moving speaker. When he got through talkin'," there usually wadn' a dry eye in the house. An' he would say, 'I love everybody. I love *everybody*.' He said, 'But you've gotta understand.' He said, 'There's no... There's no hate here. *None*.'"

"Sounds like you and he were effective."

"We were. But we always had plans for more than just a monument. We were fundraising for education too—which was a big part of it. An' we'd talk about that. We were gonna have people go to schools an' take images of the painting to show the kids. This was gonna be our way of teachin' kids about the Trail of Tears."

"...sounds like an aggressive plan."

"It was." Poteet strokes his forehead and then continues, "You know, I worked with a professor at the University of Oklahoma to design the curriculum, an' I thought it was good."

"I'll bet it was."

"Yeah. An' I knew a person who was the head of the schools in Texas, an' she looked at it. She said, 'This is very good.' But... We never got that far. We ran out a money. But it still could be done. I don't know why it couldn'."

Elliott holds his index finger on his chin, and asks, "So, this memorial you were creating..."

"Yeah."

"It was a painting?"

"Yeah."

Elliott nods.

Poteet smiles and adds, "...a helluva big one."

"Oh yeah?"

"Yeah. It was as long as a basketball court an' sixteen feet high."

"Oh shit!" Elliott says as his face lights up. "That's huge." He chuckles. "I've never seen a painting that big."

"There may not be one—at least, not in the United States."

"So, your painting's at the University of Oklahoma now?"

"No. They kicked me off campus, before I could finish."

"They kicked you off campus?"

"Yeah."

"So, why did they do that?"

"Among other things, the mural became controversial. I regularly had protestors."

"...protestors?"

"Yeah. "An' some people at the university didn' like that. They thought it was bad PR for 'em. They were bein' asked questions, an' they didn' have answers."

"Like what questions...?"

"...like, why they'd want people to think about what happened to the Indians."

"Hmm. I see."

"Yeah. An' that's why I'm still a little angry." Poteet repositions his water glass and says, "There's more to it, but OU should've let me finish."

Elliott looks at Poteet and nods. "I can understand why you might feel that way."

"Yeah. There were to be three panels. The one I didn' finish was the one showin' the rebirth of the tribes an' their successes." He shakes his head slightly and looks down before looking back at Elliott. "I'd still like to finish that one." He nods. "It needs to be done. An' I've been tryin' to get over it ever since."

"I see."

Poteet looks at Terry and asks, "...you ready?"

"Yeah. I'm sure they need the table."

He glances at Elliott, who scoots his chair back.

They stand and walk through the crowed restaurant on the way to the front door. The waiting room is full, and there are more people outside.

"I told you it was popular," Terry says. "There's probably an hour wait to get in there now."

"...glad we came early."

CHAPTER 37

The Medicine Man

As they walk through the parking lot, Elliott feels like the last piece of a thousand-piece jigsaw puzzle has just dropped into place. Once in the Escalade, he asks, "Could you possibly do a session with me tonight? I know that's not what we typically do, but I feel like we're rolling here." As they make the turn onto South Guadalupe Street, Elliott is excited about finally getting some answers about Poteet's project at the University of Oklahoma.

Poteet shrugs. He then says, "Where do ya wanna do it?"

"...my hotel?"

"Sure. We can go there, an' Terry can take the car." After a moment, Poteet asks, "Or, do ya want Terry to be there too?"

"I always like havin' Terry."

She leans forward from the back seat and says, "I jus' need to get Honey an' take 'im home first."

Elliott nods and says, "That's no problem."

Within minutes, they've stopped on San Francisco Street in front of the La Fonda Hotel. They all pile out, and Terry climbs back into the driver's seat. She says, "See y'all in a few minutes." Before hearing a response, she closes the door and is off.

Elliott leads the way into the hotel with satchel in hand. The aroma of the Mexican spices emanating from the kitchen isn't quite as seductive as it might have been two hours earlier. Elliott spots an out-of-the-way corner of the large lobby and begins putting two comfortable chairs around a coffee table. Poteet pushes over the third.

Still standing, Elliott says, "This should do." He then sets his recorder on the table in the middle of the arrangement and says, "Do you mind if we start?"

Poteet shakes his head slowly and asks, "Whadaya wanna know?"

Elliott sits and says, "I think there were times when you thought life had passed you by."

Poteet also sits. "Yeah... for sure. I got a slow start. I mean, when I first got out here, there were so many younger artists. But... I kep' workin'."

"Uh-huh."

"An' it paid off. Ya know... That restaurant where I started... I even..." He chuckles. "I heard it was for sale. So... I started checkin' into it. I even considered buyin' it. An' I'm thinkin'... Ya know... 'You started out workin' there as a bartender. Now you're thinkin' about buyin' the son of a bitch.'" He chuckles. "The same thing, ya know, about the gallery where I started... An' now, I own it."

Elliott laughs and says, "I mean, yeah... That's a great success story."

"An' then, there was the ranch I bought."

"And that's down by Idabel?"

Poteet nods and explains, "At the time, I risked pretty much everything I had—not knowin' how it would turn out. My attorney said, 'This is... I don' know, man.' He said, 'That's a big risk—what you're thinkin' 'bout doin'.' But I took the chance."

Elliott nods.

"My brother-in-law an' sister owned it."

"Okay."

"An' he was in trouble with the feds."

Elliott raises his eyebrows and stares at Poteet.

"So... He called me, an' he said, 'If you don't buy it, we're gonna lose everything.' An'..."

"So, you stepped in."

"I did. I thought, 'I'm single. I've got enough money to start the process.' An' uh... I thought, 'Well...'" He shrugs. "'This is somethin' I gotta do.' So, I took the chance, an' it paid off. I mean... I made over a million dollars on the damn thing after it was all said an' done. So..."

"It worked out well," Elliott notes the obvious.

"It did. An' you can probably tell by now. I ain't one to run away from a gamble."

Poteet and Elliott chuckle.

"And the ranch is probably not one of those situations you considered a step of faith," Elliott suggests.

"No. I didn' consider it that at all. At the time, I was workin'. I was stable. I had friends. But, lookin' back on it..." Poteet pauses, scratches the side of his face, and shakes his head. "I don' know if I'd do it again. But... Like I said, I was single... no children, an'... Here's my sister an' brother-in-law with their family an' everything. I don' know how I'd a felt, if I hadn' done it, ya know. An' they'd lost everything."

"Sounds like you took a risk to help your family."

"I did. Yeah, I did."

"So, getting back to what we were talking about earlier..."

"...the mural?"

"Right." Elliott pauses delicately and then proceeds ahead, "Can you tell me what motivated you to take on a project like that?"

Poteet nods and speaks slowly. "Yeah. I thought about my family—my dad an' his family. I had cousins an' we'd talk about our Indian ancestors—especially the ones we knew. We'd talk about what our great grandfather saw sometimes." Poteet looks away. After a moment, he adds, "I thought about some of the kids I went to school with too, ya know."

"Seems like you were bothered by some of those memories."

Poteet takes a deep breath and says, "I was. I was bothered by a lot of things." He looks directly at Elliott and continues, "Did you know that...? It was... There are certain parts of the country where Indians couldn't vote until 1957." He pauses and adds, "I'll bet you didn' know that."

"I didn't."

"But it's the truth."

"Well, they'd be the last group to be allowed to vote then, I guess."

"Yeah, they were."

"That's another sad fact. Sounds like another reason to not want to be known as an Indian."

"Right. If you were a quarter or more Indian, you became a ward of the state. An' so... A lot of 'em didn' want to be a ward of anybody."

"I get that, and it makes sense."

"Back then... I mean, you were kind of shunned if you were Indian. Most wouldn' tell ya if they were." Poteet gives a single chuckle. "'Cause, it was embarrassing."

"Yeah."

"But... It didn' embarrass me."

"Really?"

"I wadn' embarrassed by it at all."

"Yeah? Well... I've had friends for decades..." Elliott says. "Now, they tell me they're Indian."

Poteet chuckles.

"Now, you wanna be..."

"Oh yeah, now everybody's part Indian," Poteet says as

they both laugh.

"It's funny how that's worked out."

"It is. But our family never backed away from our Indian heritage. We didn'."

"I'm not very clear on how much family you have."

Poteet nods. "Well, I have my sister. An' I had other family around, they jus' didn' have much to do with me."

"That's what I thought."

"But I had one cousin... She an' I became good friends. We were in school at OU at the same time, an' we got to know each other there. An' uh... Her name was Elizabeth McAlister, an' she became a judge in Guthrie, Oklahoma. We stayed in touch. An' I remember... It was in 1999. I was gettin' ready to move some of my things to OU to do the mural. I saw 'er, an' she said that she had done a lot of work for the Indian tribes. As a matter of fact, she'd even done work for 'em out here. I called her Beth, an' she was the one that talked me into addin' Victory to my name."

"Yeah. You mentioned her."

"So... Back in the nineties... Uh... When I started gettin' really popular, I just decided to change my name legally. So... Yeah... If somebody out here would call me Robert, they wouldn' know who the hell you were talkin' about."

Elliott smiles as Poteet laughs.

Elliott stands as Terry approaches. He says, "That was quick."

"Oh yeah. The gallery's not more than three or four blocks away. I ran Honey to the house, an' the valet here parked my car."

Elliott helps Terry get comfortably seated.

Elliott then sits, and Poteet continues, "My grandfather was Robert Erie, an' my dad was Robert Edward. An' then, I was Robert Lee. Because my mother's middle name was Lee, ya know—Dorothy Lee Davis."

"Okay."

Poteet shrugs. "So, that's the deal on my name."

A waitress appears and asks, "Can I get anyone anything?"

Terry looks at Elliott. "How 'bout an after-dinner drink?"

He shrugs and says, "Why not?"

Terry looks at the waitress and says, "I'll have a Baileys on the rocks."

Elliott says, "I'll have the same."

Poteet says, "Bring me a shot a tequila an' a Modelo." He looks at the waitress. "...Patron?"

She nods and says, "You got it," and disappears.

Poteet turns to Elliott and says, "But, here's somethin' else about my family. An' you already know some of it."

"Okay."

"It's about my grandmother, who was the Cherokee. An' uh... She wrote that article back in the sixties for *True West* magazine."

Terry turns to Elliott and says, "Remember, that's the article Judy read."

"Right. And we all talked about that. So... Your grandmother's name was Willie, I think."

"Yeah."

"And... She was not on the rolls."

"No."

"Because her father didn't sign up."

"Right. He wouldn' do it."

"But..." Elliott says and shrugs. "Because of the way Willie's father saw his parents being slaughtered... I find that totally understandable."

"Of course..."

"So... All of Willie's father's descendants are not on the rolls."

"They're not. Over the years, some of us have talked about tryin' to straighten that out, but..." Poteet sits back and interlocks his fingers. He says, "My great-grandfather's name was J.C. Victory. His cousin's name was C.C. Victory, an' C.C. was Vice-Principle Chief of the Cherokees for twenty-two years."

"You mentioned that."

"An' my cousin Beth..."

"...the one who suggested adding Victory to your name?"

"Yeah. Well... She tol' me that she had met C.C. She said that when she told 'im who she was. He said, 'Oh, darlin', I know who you are. Of course, I do.' An' then, he told 'er that he went to J.C. many times, an' uh, he told J.C., 'You need to sign up for this.' An' J.C.... He said, 'I'm not havin' anything to do with the white man. Nope.'"

"So, she's not on the rolls either."

"None of us are."

"Does that bother you?"

Poteet nods and replies, "Sometimes..." He sits up. "But. What really bothers me is that these kids are growin' up never knowin' what our true history is. An' they ain't ever gonna know unless somebody, ya know, like me or... I don' know."

Barely perceptible, Elliott responds, "Yeah."

"Look..." Poteet holds up both hands for emphasis. "Everybody in this country needs to know what actually happened to the Indians."

Elliott points at Poteet and says, "That's your passion. It's obvious, and that's why you decided to do that mural."

"An' it's still a passion, I guess. It's jus' that... Now, I have an equal amount of frustration."

"I understand. So... Regarding the mural..."

"Yeah?"

"You mentioned a medicine man who helped you with that."

"Yeah?"

"His name was, Bear..." Elliott sits forward and squints.

"...Bear Heart, I think."

"Right," Terry says.

"He helped you, and he gave you a new name."

"Mm-hmm."

"That's very powerful."

"It was. It was a lot to live up to."

"I can imagine. And he held a ceremony to give you that name."

"He did."

The waitress appears with drinks for all three, and she sets them on the table.

Terry leans forward to say, "The name was 'Does Not Hide the Truth,' but it was actually pronounced in Creek."

"Right," Poteet says and then adds, "When Bear Heart held that ceremony, he said the name in the Creek language."

"Do you know how to say it?" Elliott asks.

Poteet quickly responds, "Nope."

"I do... I think," Terry answers. She holds up her index finger and looks down at her purse. She reaches inside and digs out a sheet of paper. She says, "Okay. This is it."

"Let's hear it," Elliott says.

Terry smiles. "I called the Creek tribal offices, an' this is the way I understood this woman to say it."

Elliott and Poteet sit forward and watch Terry.

She intently stares at the sheet of paper and carefully pronounces, "Footztya ee-hecko."

Elliott requests, "Say it again."

Terry carefully pronounces, "Footztya ee-hecko."

"Again."

"Footztya ee-hecko."

Terry and Elliott laugh. Poteet smiles.

"That was good," Elliott says. "At least, you were consistent with it."

"Well... That's the way I understood 'er to say it. I had 'er say it multiple times for me, an' then I just wrote it down, ya know—like I would pronounce it."

Elliott nods and says, "Sure."

"Because... Look at this." She shows Elliott her notes. "Here's how they spell it, 'S-C-B-B...'" Terry chuckles and looks at Elliott.

He says, "That doesn't look like anything to me."

"But it's how she tol' me they spell it."

Elliott smiles and says, "There aren't any vowels."

"Right. So, I just had her pronounce it for me."

"Thank goodness you did."

Poteet speaks up to say, "But he also adopted me as his grandson."

Elliott turns and looks at Poteet over the top of his glasses. He responds, "What?"

"Yeah. He adopted me as his grandson."

Elliott breathes deeply.

"He performed another ceremony where he adopted me as his grandson."

Still looking over the top of his glasses, Elliott nods and says, "In addition to the name he gave you, that was another significant honor."

"It was. An' that's how I thought about it. It *was* a great honor."

"Yes, it was," Terry echoes.

They all reach for their glasses and take a drink.

Poteet sets his down and says, "...Okemah, Oklahoma."

Elliott and Terry look at each other and then at Poteet.

"I was tryin' to think... But that's where he's from."

"Bear Heart?" Elliott asks.

"Yeah. An' that's where he became a medicine man. It was Okemah. An', ya know... Bear Heart was a pretty famous guy. I mean, uh... He was great support for me, ya know... He talked about the courage it took for someone to come forward an' do this. ...an' the sacrifice I was makin'. I mean... When he got through speakin' about it... Well, people were writin' checks."

"So... How do you become a medicine man?" Elliott asks.

Poteet nods slowly. "Well, uh... He told me that he was chosen."

Elliott nods.

"...that he had two different medicine men choose him to be their protégée when he was young. An' both medicine men, unbeknownst to the other, chose him."

Elliott reaches for his glass of Baileys and takes a drink.

"An' then they jus' started trainin' 'im, ya know—doin' whatever they do."

"Huh."

"But... He tells this one story... He said that one of the medicine men came an' got 'im one day. He said, 'Come go with me.' An' so, they went out. An' this was in Oklahoma. ...someplace out in the country, ya know. An' uh... This medicine man told 'im... He said, 'Now, Bear Heart, I'm gonna go across over here.' An' he said, 'When I get to this other side...' He said, 'I want you to walk a straight line to me.' An' he said, 'No matter what happens...' He said, 'Don't quit singin' your medicine songs.' He said, 'No matter what you see or what happens, you continue to sing those medicine songs. It's *very* important. It's your life.' An' so, Bear Heart told 'im, 'Okay.' He didn' know what was gonna happen. So anyway... The guy gets over there, an' uh... He tells Bear Heart, 'Okay, start singin' your songs an' walk to me.' An' so, Bear Heart said he was walkin', an' he walked right into a pile of rattlesnakes. They were all around 'im. An' he said he jus'... He remembered. He said he jus' kept singin' his medicine songs an' walked right through 'em. An' he got to the other side, an' uh... The medicine man said... He said, 'You did good.' He said... He told Bear Heart... He said, 'You had 'em enchanted an' hypnotized with your song.' An' he said, 'Do you remember...?' Did you see the great big one?' An' Bear Heart said, 'Yeah, I saw 'im.' An' he told 'im... He said, 'That's the grandfather.' An' he said, 'You've got 'em hypnotized. Now, you have to go back in there.'"

Elliott's mouth gapes open, and he says, "Go back?"

"Yeah."

"You're kidding."

"Nope." Poteet takes a drink of his Modelo and continues, "An' he said... That medicine man told 'im... He said, 'You have to walk up to the big one, an' you tap 'im four times on the head.' An' he said, 'Continue to sing your songs.' He said, 'Once you tap 'im four times on the head, then you're gonna release 'im from bein' hypnotized.' An' so, Bear Heart said he did that. He walked back in there, an' saw that big rattlesnake. So, he walked over to 'im an' tapped 'im four times on the head. He said that big rattlesnake jus' slumped down an' took off."

Looking stunned, Elliott shakes his head.

Poteet laughs and says, "Yeah. No shit."

"Wow! So, the older medicine man was obviously guiding him right into that..."

"He was."

"...that den of rattlesnakes."

"He was. Yeah. ...right into it."

Elliott cocks his head and says, "At that point, I think I might have questioned how badly I wanted to be a medicine man."

Terry and Elliott chuckle.

Poteet continues, "Yeah. But... He, uh... I mean, he was one of the... I mean, he was a *good* person. He believed in being a *good* person, ya know, to everybody."

Elliott looks down and strokes his beard again. He looks up and says, "That's another great story." He shakes his head. "...a unique story. I've never seen or heard anything like that." He grabs fingers to count. "It's got the mystical Indian part. It could be set in a beautiful outdoor location. Like I say, it's got the mystical part of the Indian chants and songs. The drama of the rattlesnakes would be spellbinding. Then, you have the great ending to the piece, where the snake gets tapped on the head and slithers away." Elliott cocks his head. "It would be fun to do." He smiles.

Poteet nods and says, "I'm sure *I've* never seen a story like that anywhere."

Elliott takes a deep breath before saying, "I'll have to admit. I've started to get a little excited about doing this, Poteet. However, I've got a board. I've got partners, and I can't get ahead of myself. But I can tell you this... The creative juices are flowing for me, and it feels good. I can visualize these scenes, and I'm ready to capture 'em on film."

Poteet chuckles.

Elliott looks at Poteet. "I can see such a great variety of scenes and settings with your story—from the glitz of New York City, to your mom's beer joint/café, to the beautiful blue Pacific ocean of Maui, to the backwoods of eastern Oklahoma." He closes his eyes and nods. "And, in my opinion... It's that breadth of variety that really brings richness to a film."

Poteet smiles and sits back.

Elliott sighs and continues, "Sorry. That story about Bear Heart really triggered my imagination."

"Sure. I get it. It does that to me too."

Elliott lifts his glass and says, "And maybe it's the margaritas talkin' now."

Terry says, "...could be."

Terry follows Elliott's lead and lifts her glass. Poteet lifts his and says, "Cheers."

All three laugh.

After a moment, Poteet says, "But... Talkin' 'bout Bear Heart... He... Ya know... Especially with nature, the animals an' all that, he was so connected."

Elliott sits up and begins using his hands and emphasizing every word. "And that's part of the drama. That's what draws you in. That's the magic." He grins and shakes his head. "But... There I go again."

Poteet and Terry chuckle.

Poteet says, "But... He had these little things he'd tell you to do. He... He tol' me one time. He said, 'If you ever buy a ring, ya know... Or, if you've got anything with a stone, don't bring it right away into your house.' He said, 'You keep it outside. You dig a hole, an' you bury it. An' you leave it in there for one day. After that, you can bring it in,' He said, 'Because anything bad that would've attached to it, the earth will take it out.'"

"So... There might be something bad attached to a stone?" Elliott asks. "An evil spirit? ...or something else?"

"Yeah. An'... I mean, I've done that," Poteet explains.

"You've done that?"

"Oh yeah, I've done it."

"Huh."

"If Bear Heart ever said that's what I should do... It's like, 'Okay, buddy.'"

"Wow."

"An' I'd do it."

"He would," Terry says as she nods

"Well, I *haven't* done that. Maybe that explains a few things."

They laugh.

"Yeah, maybe it does," Poteet adds.

Elliott and Terry chuckle.

"But... He also talked about sweat lodges an' some other things."

"Oh yeah?"

"On sweat lodges, he always said, 'Unless you know what you're doin', they can be dangerous.' An' uh... Another thing he tol' me... He said, 'You take a lot of herbs an' stuff, don't you?' An' I said, 'Yeah.' An' he said, 'Don't do that.' He said, 'Herbs are very, very potent, an'...' He said, ya know, 'When you start mixin' all these herbs together, you... You don' realize...' He said, 'They can be very harmful.' So..."

"That's probably good advice," Elliott notes.

"Right."

"I wonder if that counts for, like herbal teas or uh..."

"I think... Yeah, I think so. I think that's what he was gettin' at. Yeah, because... I mean, herbs are very important in these Indian ceremonies. An' uh... I know that every time I'd go see 'im, I'd take 'im tobacco. Because that's... That's used in ceremonies too. He didn' use it... Ya know, he didn' smoke or anything like that. But I'd go buy, like a sack of tobacco... Like they used for rollin' cigarettes a long time ago. An' I'd take those to 'im every time I'd see 'im. He'd always really thank me. Yeah. Bear Heart was great. An' I remember... We had a meeting in Houston... An' there was a group of Coushatta Indians from Alabama that come up to dance at this thing. They jus' worshiped Bear Heart, ya know. I mean, they... You wouldn't believe how they treated 'im. It was an honor for me to be there with 'im."

"To me, that says a lot about him and the significance of his support for your project."

"It does. But... I talked to a lot of the Chiefs an' elders. Every one of 'em said, 'Yeah, you need to do this. It needs to be done. No one's ever done it. You need to do it.' So... I go... 'Okay, I'll do it.'"

"And the meetings..."

"Right. I had several, with everybody I could think of." Poteet sits back. "'Cause, I told all the Chiefs there... I said, 'Look, I'm not here to ask you for money. I'm here to ask for your blessing.' An' they went, 'Okay, you got it.' Ya know... Of course, most of 'em chipped in a little money. ...not much, but some. All five of the so-called 'Civilized Tribes' supported me."

"You say, 'so-called...?'"

"Yeah. I don' like callin' 'em 'civilized' tribes."

"Because...?"

Poteet looks at Elliott. "So... What are the others? ...uncivilized?"

"I see." Elliott takes a drink and says, "I guess, that's what you'd have to think."

"Right. But anyway... A lot of the tribes supported me. Yeah, they were all for it. An' they told me... They said, 'Ya know, you're gonna catch hell from both sides. Jus' get ready for it. An' they said, 'Some of the Indians, they just wanna leave it alone... jus' let sleepin' dogs lie, ya know.' An' then, the whites are gonna say, 'Well, you're blowin' this all out of proportion. You're makin' up stories.' They're gonna say, 'It wadn' like that.'" Poteet sits forward and gets louder. "Yeah, it *was* like that. Yeah, it *damn sure* was like that. That's *exactly* what it was." He sits back to continue. "An', ya know... There were tribes from New York to California that were all brought into Oklahoma territory—even from up into Canada. An' I wanted to include all of 'em."

"Of course..." Elliott says.

Terry sits forward and looks at Poteet. She says, "Ya know... An' I know this is true. If Bear Heart was still alive, he'd be encouragin' you to get this thing done."

"Yeah, he would. He'd be all about that," Poteet says and looks at Elliott. "But... I've gotta tell ya this." He smiles. "It's another story."

As Elliott grins at the thought of Poteet launching into another tale, he reflects on the mural project and all of its related elements. Of course, there was the painting itself and its rejection by the university—a narrative already teed up and ready to be hit out of the park. But... Then, there's Bear Heart— the man himself and then *his* stories. It was all amazing and about as Native American as you could get.

CHAPTER 38

The Mural

Elliott turns his attention back to Poteet and says, "Okay. Let's hear the story."

"It's about Bear Heart."

Elliott chuckles and responds truthfully, "That's perfect."

"I was in California, an' I was over at my friend's house. He uh... He owned the gallery where I showed, an' he was always hangin' out with all these New Age people, ya know."

"You mentioned something early on about Bear Heart and New Age..."

Poteet drinks his shot of tequila and continues, "So... There was a group a guys there that night, an' uh... I wadn' really eaves droppin' on 'em. I mean, I was jus' close enough to hear what they were talkin' about. An' it was Bear Heart. So, I listened. An' they said they wanted to go find 'im, so they could talk to 'im. So, I walked up, an' I said, 'Well, I can tell you where he's at.' They said, 'Where?' An' I said, 'Well, he's out in Albuquerque.' They said, 'How do you know that?' An' I said, "Cause I know 'im.' 'Well, how do you know 'im?' An' I said, 'Well, I'm his adopted grandson.'"

Elliott and Terry chuckle.

"An' they went, 'Oh bullshit.'"

Elliott and Terry laugh.

"They really said that. Ya know, they didn' believe me at all."

Elliott says, "I'm sure. Yeah."

Poteet chuckles. "So... A few months later, my friend tol' me... He said, 'Ya know, those guys went out there an' found Bear Heart an' talked to 'im.' An' this guy come back, an' he said, 'When you see Poteet, you tell 'im that I'm really sorry.'"

Elliott and Terry laugh.

"'An' I offer my apologies.' 'Cause... He said what happened was... He said when they got to Bear Heart's house an' walked in... He said, 'One of the first things I asked 'im...' I said, 'Do you know Poteet Victory?' An' he said, 'Of course I do. He's my grandson.'"

They laugh again.

"He couldn' believe it," Poteet says and joins in the laughter. "Well... Like I said, they were into all this New Age shit. An', ya know... He was popular with that group because of his book."

"Huh."

"So, they found 'im."

"They did, and you were vindicated."

"I was."

All three chuckle.

Terry says, "After that dream he had, I told Poteet I wanted to go meet Bear Heart."

"Right. A year after his death..." Elliott notes.

"So anyway... Terry Googled 'im an' discovered that he had died, an' that's how I found out."

"Don't you hate to learn of someone's death that way—someone you've been really close to?" Elliott asks.

"Yeah. ...very much so. I hated to find out about Bear Heart like that. I'd have gone to the funeral if I'd known."

"Of course..."

"He was a great friend, an' I respected him as much as anyone I've ever known. Needless to say, it was a disappointment for Terry an' me when we couldn't go see 'im."

After a moment of silence, Elliott says, "So... Tell me more about the mural."

"Well, once I made my mind up to do it, I got right to work. I knew it was gonna take a lot of money, 'cause I was gonna have to spend all my time workin' on it."

"Mm-hmm."

"So... I started doin' fund raisers, like where I met Bear Heart. Ya know... I figured it was gonna cost over a million dollars to do it...to do it right."

"...and take how long?"

"I figured it'd take me a couple of years."

Elliott scratches his head and says, "...two years?"

"Uh-huh. An' uh... It did. I could've done it faster, ya know. But I'd be workin' on it, an' my business manager would call an' say, 'Hey, we're runnin' really low on money. We gotta do somethin'.' So, I'd put on a different hat an' go out an' talk to different companies an' things. An' uh... So... I thought, 'Man, I gotta have a big sponsor—somebody that can really step in here an' take the lead on this thing.'"

Elliott nods and says, "...makes sense."

"So, I tol' myself, 'If you jus' keep talkin', you're gonna run into that person.'"

"And the one person was...?" Elliott asks.

"My cousin..."

"Oh?"

"A lot of people had tol' me, 'You need to get Williams Corporation on board.'" Poteet explains, "They're Oklahoma based, an' they have a history of sponsorin' things."

Elliott nods as he takes another drink.

"An' uh... Well... I called an' tried to set up appointments— no dice... sent emails, sent letters—nothin'. An' so, that's when

I finally said, 'Fuck it.' So, I called my cousin, an' I said, 'Do you know anybody at Williams Corporation?' He said, 'Oh, hell yes.' He said, 'Me an' ol' Keith Bailey... We were roommates, an' I got 'im his first job down there in Houston.' An' he said, 'We're still great friends.' An' he said, ya know, 'I jus' got back from Vietnam.' He said, 'I bought 'im a present over there.' He said, 'Why don' you to take it to 'im.' I said, 'Well hell, they won't even lemme in the buildin'.' He said, 'Lemme make a phone call.' So... In a couple days, I get a call from Williams. ...said, 'You got an appointment over here.' An' it was this lady. She was the head of... I don' know... somethin'. I forget what her title was. But anyway, she was like public relations an' all that."

"I hadn' heard this," Terry says and sits forward.

"But anyway... She said, 'You've got an appointment next Tuesday at ten o'clock.' I said, 'Okay great. I'll be there.' So, I went, an' I met with... I didn' meet with Keith that day." He chuckles. "An' when I walked into her office... She's settin' behind her desk like this." Poteet scowls and crosses his arms real tight.

Elliott snickers.

"'Cause I'd gone over her head, ya know. She was pissed off."

"Uh-huh."

"So... I introduced myself, sat down, an' started talkin' about it. An' I thought, 'Well, ya know, I've got one shot at this.' So, I jus' kept talkin'...kept talkin'."

"...just to her?"

"Yeah. An' we ended up talkin' for almost two hours. An'... But I could tell as this went on, she started to loosen up a little bit. So... After I got through with my presentation, she said, 'Okay. Well... We'll get back in touch with you.' An' I said, 'Okay.' Then, I came back to Santa Fe."

Terry says, "I'd have been so nervous..."

"I *was* nervous," Poteet says and shrugs. "But I'd done everything I could do."

"I'd love to have seen what you painted while that was goin' on," Terry says.

"But anyway, she called me on Christmas Eve."

Terry shakes her head and whispers, "...Christmas Eve."

"This lady... She said, 'I've run this by the Board, an' ya know, blah, blah, blah... We all think it's a great idea.' But I was waitin' for the other shoe to drop, ya know."

"Yeah," Elliott says.

"I was waitin' to hear the word, '*But...*'"

"Of course..."

"Instead, she said, 'So...' She said, 'I'm sendin' you a check today for three hundred thousand dollars.' An' she said, 'We will be your lead sponsor on this an' help you,'" an' all that. So... An' I..." Poteet laughs.

Elliott half-sings, "Merry Christmas," in a high-pitched voice.

"Yeah. She tol' me... She said, 'You... You thought I was gonna tell ya we couldn' do it.'"

Elliott laughs.

"I said, 'I damn sure did.' She said, 'You didn't think I'd do that to you on Christmas Eve, did ya?' I said, 'Yeah, I figured you would.'" He looks back at Elliott. "But that's how it got started. An' they did help me."

"I'm sure that made a big difference."

"It did. An' I'd told 'er when we talked. I said, 'I wanna make this an educational type of thing too, ya know. Where we take, not the mural itself... But we can do replicas to take to schools to set up an' tell 'em what happened.'"

"I'll bet she liked that," Terry chimes in to say.

"She did. An' uh... But that educational part was so needed...still is for that matter. But... We found out that in America this is only taught, like for two hours on average—in school. That's all a kid will ever hear about it—not two semester hours, just *two hours*. In Europe, they teach it for over *forty hours*."

"Really?" Elliott asks.

"Yep. Really."

"It's amazin' how many people don' know about the Trail of Tears," Terry says.

"They jus' don' know," Poteet echoes. "An' so, I was serious about the educational part. It was needed, an' we spent a lot of money developin' that curriculum."

"That's your passion."

"But there was still another piece to the mural project I had to figure out."

"What was that?"

"It was about hangin' 'em."

"...because of their size?"

"Yeah. So... Before I started, I uh... I went an' talked to the guy that did the big murals at the Cowboy Hall of Fame in Oklahoma City. His name was Wilson Hurley."

"Okay."

"At that time, Wilson lived in Albuquerque. So, I... Uh... I went down there an' talked to 'im. An' he actually gave me some good advice. An' uh... He showed me how he did it. Ya know, they paid Wilson five million dollars to do 'em. But it was interesting—the way they had to be installed."

"Huh. I'm curious."

Holding his glass of beer, Poteet moves slightly closer to Elliott and says, "What he did was... He said he went over to Europe, an' he went to all these museums—lookin' at these ol' paintings. An' he said... He noticed that anything that was over ten feet wide was saggin'. Over time, ya know, it jus' sags down, because it's on material. The frames would still be okay, but the material itself would sag down."

"I see."

"So... He said they came up with a way to overcome that with a large, honeycombed piece of plastic. On the front side of this honeycombed piece, they put a plastic sheet that they glued to the honeycomb. All of that together was still pretty light. An' then, the painting had to be glued to the plastic sheet. An' so... The way... He showed me how they attached the painting. They had, uh, this guy in a harness on a crane. An' they lowered 'im down. 'Cause you couldn' walk on the painting."

"Oh! So, this guy was hanging down over it—from a crane."

"Yeah. While he was hangin' over it, he'd start gluin' the painting down, an' then they'd move 'im across, ya know. An' eventually they got it all glued down. He told me. He said, 'The first one we did...' He said, 'When we got it on there, it was crooked.'"

Terry thinks that's hilarious, and Elliott blurts out, "Damn."

"Yeah. An' he said 'But... He had used a glue that would... When you put the heat to it, it would release.' So... They finally got it square on there."

"Wow," Elliott responds.

"Yeah. An' so, that's the way I'd have to do it too."

"I hope you have that chance."

Poteet takes a deep breath and says, "...gettin' less likely all the time."

After a moment, Elliott responds, "All this helps me understand the significance of your mural."

Poteet reaches for his glass.

"It'd be hard to do," Terry shares. "An' part of it is just how good we have it out here in Santa Fe. Poteet loves his studio. We have our collectors who come out. We love to see 'em, ya know. Sometimes they commission Poteet to paint somthin' special for 'em."

"I really enjoy those projects."

"We have new people drop in all the time. We sell everything he paints. Of course, the new people... They love to look at the abbreviated portraits, ya know."

"...like Marilyn Monroe?"

"Yeah. Everyone loves that one, but they like the other ones too. It's like a game with 'em. They like to outguess each other on who's who, ya know. It's fun to watch."

"I'll bet." Elliott nods. "I get that. But still..."

"Some things just aren't as easy as they used to be," Poteet says. "An' I'm talkin' 'bout the mural."

Elliott nods.

Terry adds, "But in a lot of ways I agree with you 'bout finishin' the mural. I know Poteet does too."

"Ya know," Poteet says and sets his glass down. "I had a lot of support for that mural. All the Chiefs I talked to were behind it. I had to raise money, but that was comin' in okay. An' I was always thinkin' about what the Indians had gone through."

"You had a heavy heart," Elliott affirms.

"I did." Poteet takes a deep breath. "But even so... I was strugglin' with the message I wanted to convey. I really was."

"I can believe that."

"But then I had to decide," Poteet says and sighs. He explains, "It was the Holocaust—the American Holocaust."

Elliott nods slowly. "You mentioned that you got a lot of pushback on those words."

"I did. I'd say it that way in an interview or just in a conversation, an' some people didn' like it. So... I got a lot of criticism for that—a *lot* of criticism."

"...until Spielberg used that phrase."

"Right. That's right. But... What I'd do... I'd work on small pieces—tryin' to get ideas, ya know. I'll bet I did a thousand drawings."

"Hmm."

"When I first got to OU, I would jus' sit down an' draw all day long—jus' this idea an' that idea an' this idea. An' finally... Uh... I came up with 'em."

"I'd love to see what the mural looks like."

"We have some photos," Terry says and stands. "They're in my car. Maybe I can get the valet to help me get to 'em," she says as she's walking away.

Elliott makes a gesture in Terry's direction like he's wanting to stop her, but he then turns back to Poteet. "You've mentioned the third panel several times—the one you'd like to finish."

"Right."

"Can you explain the idea behind it?"

Poteet grabs his drink glass and sits back. He looks away for a few seconds before saying, "Not really."

Elliott chuckles.

Poteet sits forward and says, "Well... Picture this. Down at the bottom you have the children."

Elliott nods.

"An' there's a woman in the center, ya know. She's a judge, an' she's Indian. There's a lot more to it. It's the inspirational one."

"Did you keep your sketches?" Elliott asks.

"Most of 'em."

"Good."

"I've still got my sketchbooks, where uh..."

"I think you'll be glad you've hung on to those."

"Ya know, I put a lot into 'em. I couldn't see throwin' 'em away."

"Right. And you were how old when you did this?"

"I was fifty-three when I started."

"It was a lot to take on, even at that age."

"It was, an' I'd never done anything that big. Uh... Ya

know... David Boren, the President of OU at the time... He asked me. He said, '...you ever done anything this big?' An' I said, 'No.'"

Elliott chuckles.

"I said, 'I haven't, but I can do it, though.' An' I guess I convinced 'im. So... Yeah. But... When I was first gettin' started, there was another thing I did. I went over an' talked to the art department an' told 'em 'bout my project. The head of the department... He said, 'Great.' I said, 'I need some help.' An' so he set it up where, uh... If somebody would work over there with me, he'd give 'em three semester hours. So... I started out with three assistants an' ended up with jus' one— me an' this grad student. We did the whole thing. An'... He tol' me he was from China—where they discovered all those terra cotta soldiers."

"Huh."

"...you ever see those things?"

"I think I've seen pictures."

"...where they excavated, like fifteen hundred of these life-sized..."

"Yeah. It seems to me that it's some really great historical art."

"It is. An' we used to talk about it. But that's where he was from. Right there... Right there in that town...'"

"...interesting. But I'm also curious about your day—when you were there painting."

"Oh, I'd get up every mornin'... I'd usually be at work by 8:00, 8:30, ya know...go to lunch, come back...knock off about 5:00."

"...just pretty much what you do now."

"Pretty much, exactly what I do now. I... Uh... There was a lot I could do on my own, but that Chinese grad student... Yeah, he'd show up in the afternoons when he got out of class. An' he was there every day. He was a damn good worker, an'

I didn' ever pay 'im a thing."

"That was a good deal for you."

"It was."

"So, where'd you live?"

"They supplied, uh... It's like, what out here we call casitas."

"Yeah."

"They were small duplexes. An' so, they gave me one of those to live in."

"Sounds like it was a good set up."

"An' then, I could go... I ate for free at the cafeteria."

"Wow. You didn't have many expenses."

"I didn't."

"It was a pretty good deal."

"Yeah... An' I tried to do it the right way. When I was gettin' started on the second panel, I hired a model to do these poses. I built this thing—kind of like a saddle rack. An' I got a model in there. ...this male model, an' I had a photographer there. An'... He couldn't... It jus' didn' look right to me. An' so... I let the model go, an' I tol' the photographer, 'I'll do it.' So... I got up there, an' he shot it. An' I thought, 'That's... That's it. That's the pose I want.'"

"Hmm."

They both look up to see Terry returning with photos in hand. She says, "I got 'em. The car was jus' right there." She points vaguely toward the parking garage. She hands the photos to Elliott who inspects them closely.

Terry and Poteet remain quiet.

Elliott eventually sets the photos on the coffee table.

Poteet points. "So... Yeah... The guy on the horse... In the middle panel... Yeah, that's..."

"That's you."

"That's me. Nobody knows it. You can't see the face."

"Sure."

"Ya know, I modeled for Stevenson. An' he was real particular. I mean, you had to be jus'... Ya know... It had to be jus' right for him."

Elliott nods as he continues to look.

Poteet points at the other photo and says, "Ya know, my first panel was more like mythology."

Elliott looks back and forth between the photos and tells Poteet, "From what I'm looking at in this first panel, I can't tell what you're trying to show."

Poteet nods and says, "I need to explain. It's what I started to see as I was researchin' the history of the tribes. They all have a creation myth. An' I wanted that first panel to have a mystical look to represent that."

"Are they mostly similar?"

"The...?"

"...the creation myths of the different tribes?" Elliott clarifies.

"Oh, yeah. They're similar. But still, they're all a little different. Uh... The only tribe that dudn' have a creation story is the Cherokee. Because, they say they came from the east on floating islands."

"Huh."

"But on the first panel, I've got this white abstract figure comin' down out of the sky."

Elliott looks down at the photo.

"He's holdin' an egg—a transparent egg. An' inside that egg is the first Indian. It's an embryo of the first Indian, ya know. 'Cause it... I mean it's... Like I say, it's a common theme."

"Huh."

Poteet smiles and adds, "It's a beautiful painting." He shakes his head. "I love it."

Elliott picks up the other photo and studies it. He says, "This one has a group of Indians down here." He points.

"They're reaching out. It looks to me like they're in distress."

"They are...very much so."

"Then, you have this horse and rider at a larger scale, almost like they're coming down out of the clouds."

"Right. They dominate the painting, an' that was very much my intention."

"And the rider... That would be you."

"Yeah."

All three chuckle.

"But you're not supposed to know that."

The chuckling continues.

"Anyway..." Elliott eventually asks rhetorically, "It looks like the rider and the Indians are trying to connect?"

"...in a way."

"It sort of reminds me of Michelangelo's painting in the Sistine Chapel where God and Man are reaching toward each other."

Poteet smiles and looks at Elliott. "It's hard to know for sure where the inspiration for these things comes from."

Elliott and Terry chuckle again.

Poteet points. "But the Indian on the horse..."

"Yeah."

"He's uh... He represents the American government."

"Huh."

"But, in the actual mural—the big painting..."

"Yeah."

"He's wearin' an old, tattered Union soldier's uniform."

"Oh, okay. Which more clearly represents the U.S. government, I guess."

"Right. That was what I was goin' for. Yeah. An' it's a more provocative image, I believe. An' the horse, ya know... it's symbolic of the first horse of the apocalypse."

"Huh."

"Death rode the pale horse. An' this is a pale horse. You

can see it's pale in color."

Elliott draws back and raises his eyebrows.

"...an' hell followed after 'im. But you see in his hand he's got this Arc of the Covenant."

Elliott looks more closely and points. "So, that's what *that* is."

"Yeah. An' uh... In the background... These are like the wheels of progress."

"Hmm."

"An' that's important. It was progress that drove a lot of this. Like the railroads... Like the ability to communicate... Like guns... An' then, better guns..."

Elliott nods.

"In my opinion, you can't really tell this story without mentioning the wheels of progress." Poteet leans over toward Elliott to point at the photo. "See this. It's the 'Tree of Life' that's dyin', an' uh..."

"It's a very bleak setting."

Poteet nods and replies, "Yes, it is. You can see that it's a cold an' snowy landscape. The Indian people are trudging through the blizzard." He points again. "An' over here, this skeleton's beckoning them to 'Come on'."

"I see," Elliott says. He looks more closely at the photo. "You mentioned the Ark of the Covenant."

"Yeah."

"I think of Moses and the Israelites when I hear that."

"Me too," Terry says and sits forward.

"Well... This is different. This is the covenant the U.S. Government made with the Indians."

"Okay?"

"An' that covenant was: Death."

Poteet and Terry remain still as Elliott continues to study the photo.

He asks, "So... I know these are big, but... How big is each one?"

"This panel, the middle one, is twenty-four feet by sixteen feet. The first one is sixteen by sixteen. An' then, the third one was to be sixteen by sixteen. I wanted to tell the story of the birth, the death, an' the rebirth."

"So, the third panel is the 'rebirth.'"

"Yes. It's what I was talkin' about earlier with the female judge an' the kids around 'er."

"I like what that says. I guess, that's about the future."

"It's actually what's already happening."

"Yeah. The tribes are doing very well now, it seems."

"Many of 'em..."

Elliott crosses his arms and strokes his beard. He says, "I can see why..." He nods at the photos. "I can see why this was controversial."

"Sure," Poteet says. "An' I get it. But I couldn't tell a story that wadn' true."

"So... Let's fast forward."

"Okay."

"Based on what I've seen here... It makes me wonder. What do you think is owed the Indians now?"

Poteet sits silently for a moment and then says, "I jus' think that... Ya know, I'm not talkin' about reparations or anything like that."

Elliott relaxes his arms.

"Uh... No, it's jus'..." Poteet looks away for a moment. He looks back and continues, "Um... It's like with these reservations an' everything. I mean, they've destroyed these people's dignity, ya know... There should be a lot more help for 'em. Why are they livin' in such squalor? It's terrible."

Elliott sighs and leans forward. "I've been on some sets where I've seen what you're talkin' about, and I agree with you."

"Yeah. Some of 'em are pretty bad. But... My deal..." Poteet shakes his head. "Ya know, I jus' think that this should be taught in our schools. That's all. Why *isn't* it taught in our schools?"

Elliott takes a deep breath and reaches for his glass. He drinks the last bit of Baileys.

Poteet looks at Terry and nods.

Terry reaches for the photos on the table.

Elliott detects the signal. He smiles and says, "It's been a good day."

"So..." Poteet asks, "Are you comin' back tomorrow?"

"I plan to, unless there's an emergency of some kind— somewhere."

They all stand. Terry gives Elliott a hug, and the men exchange a warm handshake.

As Elliott watches the couple walk out, he thinks about that third panel and the injustice Poteet suffered at the hands of the university. What they did was wrong.

He feels the sense of a cause building in his soul.

CHAPTER 39

Support, Blessings, & Honors

The next day was another beautiful day in Santa Fe. The sky was clear, and the sun was bright. It was one of those days when you need a jacket when you're in the shade, and a jacket is too heavy when you're in the sun. Elliott blissfully walks the few blocks from his hotel to the gallery. He removes his jacket as he approaches.

Wearing a big smile, Terry is standing at the door to greet her guest as he walks in. She says, "Hi, Elliott," and they hug.

Elliott detects the clean smell of her hair and the familiar fragrance of her perfume.

As they back away from each other, he says, "I had a great time last night, Terry. Thanks for making it happen."

She smiles and says, "We've got some great restaurants here in Santa Fe. That's one of the main reasons people like to come here."

Elliott nods. "I've decided to stay another night. I feel like we're on a roll, and I want to keep it going."

"Great."

Elliott points at his satchel and smiles. "I got a great recording last night."

"I jus' remember laughin' a lot."

Elliott chuckles. "Yes, we did. But it was a breakthrough for me on the mural. He hadn't really told me much about that before."

"It's a touchy subject with 'im."

"I know," Elliott says and takes a slight step back. He asks, "Do you have those photos we were looking at last night?"

Terry turns away for a moment. She then quickly walks to her office and heads for her purse.

Elliott follows.

She pulls out the photos and glances at them before offering them to Elliott.

He takes the photos and says, "I had a few more questions about these for Poteet."

She nods and says, "Well, there ya go."

He bows slightly and says, "Thank you."

"Sure. I want you to ask all the questions you can think of."

Elliott points in the direction of the studio and says, "I guess Poteet's up there."

"He is, an' he's lookin' for ya."

Elliott turns and heads for the stairs.

Terry says after him, "I'll be up in a little bit."

He turns and responds, "Great."

At the double doors, Elliott says quietly, "Knock, knock." As he pushes through, the familiar smell of paint is in the air.

"Come on in," Poteet says as he turns and smiles.

Elliott puts his satchel down and begins digging inside. He pulls out his recorder, turns it on, and sets it on Poteet's worktable.

With a loaded knife, Poteet turns to his painting.

After sitting down, Elliott says, "I've been thinking about a few things."

"Okay."

"Looking at those photos last night brought up some questions for me."

Poteet nods but continues working on the painting.

Elliott holds up the photos and says, "I got these from Terry just now."

Poteet turns to look but doesn't say anything.

Elliott sets one of the photos on the table and then stares at the other. After a few seconds, he says, "So... You mentioned the pale horse, which you said is one of the horses of the apocalypse."

"It is."

"I'm curious. Do all four horses show up in the mural?" A grin creeps across Elliott's face as he continues, "I'm no expert on Revelations, but... I think I'm knowledgeable enough to know that there are *four* horses."

Poteet chuckles. "You're right. There are. And... All four of those horses do *not* show up on the mural."

"I didn't think so." He looks down at the photo again. "I can't see any more horses."

"Huh-uh. No... In the Bible, it says, 'Death rode the pale horse, an' hell followed after 'im.' So, I wanted the main figure to be ridin' the pale horse."

"Uh-Huh."

"An', when I was thinkin' about this—that pale horse. There's a reason why the pale horse to me is a gray horse. Because... There *is* a white horse too. So..."

"Okay. I see. By pale, you mean 'not white.'"

"Yes. Pale... Like, when somebody has a pallor of death about 'em,"

"Yeah."

"It's like a shade of gray."

"Or... I've heard it described as ashen," Elliott says.

"Yeah. That's right. So... To me... The uh... The pale horse represents sensuality, ya know. ...which is an important part of people. But if it dominates you, it'll kill you."

"In a way, I guess I can see that."

"The second horse is the red horse. An' it symbolizes your emotional state. So... Here again, it's very important that you have emotions about you. But, if they rule your life, they will also kill you. An', the third horse is the black horse. An' the black horse is symbolic of intellectualism—which means you're usin' your own understanding of things rather than God's understanding. It's thinkin' that you're, ya know... A lot of people feel that they're too smart to believe in God."

"Right. That's a tough one."

"Well, that'll kill ya, too. An' the fourth horse is the white horse. It says, 'Who sits on the white horse is the spirit with the sword.' An'... What it's basically sayin' is... If all three of these horses fall under the rule of the white horse, then you've got it all together. You let one of these horses run off on its own, an' it will lead to destruction. So... There wadn' really a reason to put those other horses in there, ya know. Because... 'Death rode the pale horse, an' hell followed after 'im.'"

As he points at the photo, Elliott says, "So, you've got the pale horse dominating the painting, and all this other is the 'hell that followed after'—the *hell* that the Indians experienced."

"Yeah. Basically."

"...like this skeleton over here, motioning the Indians to follow him."

Poteet nods. "Yeah. An' that's why I did it that way."

Elliott says quietly, "So, it's just the pale horse—the horse of sensuality. But it's Death... Because... Death rode the pale horse. And it's the Indian that's riding that horse."

Poteet walks over and looks at the photo. He says, "But I changed that for the big mural. It's an Indian, but he's wearin' a Union Army uniform. So... Now, it's the American government ridin' the pale horse."

"Okay. And I think you told me that last night. But I didn't quite get it."

"Yeah. An'..." Poteet points at the photo. "This is actually a study. Or... You could call it a prototype, I guess. But the photo was taken of the study an' not the full-size panel."

"Okay," Elliott says and shrugs. "That makes sense."

"An' I think it's..." Poteet looks away and then up. "How big *is* that thing? Yeah. I think it's..." He looks back at the photo. "I think it's nine feet—nine feet long. An' then, whatever the proportions are—height-wise. But it's an exact replica of the big one. ...Almost."

"Okay."

"An' when I find the right place for it, I'm gonna hang it."

"...you have it?"

"Oh, yeah. I got it."

"And then..." Elliott pauses and looks around at Poteet. "There's the third panel."

"Right."

"I know it's not done, but you briefly described it to me. I know what it's about."

Poteet nods and says, "Yeah... That one comes from Indian folklore too."

"Okay?"

"They say that, ya know... When the Indians come back to prominence, a woman will lead them. An' so... I was workin' on the idea for the third panel, an' I had a... She's dead now, but there was an Indian woman out here who was a judge. An' I saw 'er walk into the courtroom one day. She had on a black robe, an' she had these beaded epaulettes. An' I thought, 'That's... That's a perfect picture.'"

"Ohhh... Were you thinking about a female judge before that?"

"Yes. But I didn't have the image of the black robe in my mind."

"Uh-huh."

"I saw her holdin' a... In one hand, a book, which would be

like a law book, an' the other hand holdin' an eagle feather. But I wanted 'er to be standin', ya know. ...up above. 'Cause... I kep' thinkin' about the phrase: 'on the shoulders of giants.' An' I liked that, ya know. ...that saying. An' I wanted her to have... She'd be standin' up there. An' then, on either side of 'er would be these two warriors with their lances."

"I see."

"So, that was basically my idea for it. I think it would've been really cool lookin'—the symbolism in it an' all. But I also had all these little kids sittin' in a semi-circle around 'er—at 'er feet lookin' up at 'er. An' I did a drawing—as a prototype of it. I think Larry Hagman ended up with that one."

"Oh... And there'd be room for all that?"

Poteet chuckles. "It was a very large canvas."

Elliott shakes his head and says, "Of course."

"I jus' think it would've been a really cool painting." Poteet takes a deep breath and looks out the window. He shakes his head slowly and says, "Ya know... Jus' to finish off the whole idea of it."

Elliott strokes his beard and says softly, "Yeah."

"I would've done that one in realism, ya know. ...like the middle panel."

Elliott watches Poteet quietly.

"I... I did three of 'em."

"...three prototypes?"

"Uh-huh—same size an' everything."

"Okay."

"An' uh... Like I said, I gave one to Larry Hagman. An' then, Keith Bailey, who was the CEO of Williams... He got one. An' then I kep' one."

"Uh-huh?"

"...which Jim got."

"Jim?"

"Yeah. Jim Klepper."

Elliott chuckles.

Poteet laughs.

Elliott says, "I've got to give him credit for being on top of that."

Poteet laughs again and says, "He's been comin' out here an' buyin' my paintings for a long time."

Elliott chuckles and shakes his head. After a moment, he asks, "I wonder where Larry Hagman's is? I remember hearing that he passed away."

"Yeah. When Larry died... It's been... I don' know... Probably within the last six months..."

"When Larry Hagman died?"

"No. That's been years."

"That's what I thought."

"But, no... I had a guy call me. An' he said, 'Do you remember doin' this drawing?' He described it, an' I said, 'Of course.' I said, 'Yeah, I gave it to Hagman.' An' he uh... He said, 'Well, they had an estate sale.' An' he said, 'I bought it.'"

"Oh?"

"An' he said, 'I'm jus' curious, ya know, about what it's worth.' An' I said, 'Well, if I had it in my gallery, it'd be worth $5,000.' He's like, 'Wow.' I said, 'What'd you pay for it?' He told me fifteen hundred or somethin' like that."

"Huh. He got a deal."

"He did."

Elliott shakes his head and says, "No tellin' what that'll be worth someday—one of the prototypes."

"But, with Jim... I gave him a deal too. I mean... With somebody like him, ya know, who's bought so much from me, it's hard..." He sighs. "It's hard to say 'No,' ya know... If he says, 'I want that.' Then... 'Okay.'"

Elliott laughs and Poteet laughs.

"But yeah... I guess I did two finished sets of prototypes— the nine-foot ones an' the smaller ones. But... Doin' the prototypes helped a lot. An' so, the painting... The actual painting itself went pretty fast."

"...makes sense."

"'Cause we knew exactly what we were doin'...ya know, the exact colors we were gonna use an' all that."

"You'd probably do it the same way now."

"I would, except most of that's already been done. But... Ya know... As a painter, it was exciting to do somethin' like that, somethin' that big. 'Cause you ain't never done anything like that."

Elliott laughs quietly.

"You ain't never known anybody to do anything like that either," Poteet says and chuckles. "So..."

"Someone said last night... I think you mentioned it."

"What's that?"

"...that this might be the biggest painting in the U.S."

"It might be, 'cause it's hard to do somethin' that big." He looks at Elliott. "I tol' ya 'bout hangin' it. That's a problem, but that ain't all."

"Okay."

"Yeah. I had to use linen, 'cause it's much stronger than canvas. We gessoed the whole thing, an'... We had to do that, ya know, to get the substrate ready to paint on. An' uh... Yeah... That was work too. Gettin' all that done."

"I'm sure. Although, I have no idea what 'gessoing' is."

"It's what you put on canvas or linen to get it ready. I always do that. You brush it on, an' uh... When it dries, it creates a great surface for paint."

"I see."

"But, yeah, we uh..." Poteet chuckles. "When I had those canvases lined up there—all three of 'em..." He chuckles again. "An' I'm lookin' at 'em..."

Elliott thinks it's funny and says, "Yeah?"

Poteet scratches the side of his face. He then shakes his

head and says, "...three huge white canvas. An' I'm like, 'Holy shit!'"

Elliott laughs.

"I thought, 'What have I done?'" After a moment, he adds, "Ya know. But... There was this artist I was datin' back then. She tol' me a million times. She said, 'You know somethin'?' She said, 'You're a real artist.' She said, 'A lot of other... Like me...' She said, 'I wouldn' even dream of tryin' to do anything like that. That would never even enter my mind.'"

"I'll bet not many would."

Poteet smiles and adds, "Not many are that stupid."

Elliott chuckles.

"An' I think a lot of that—the size of it an' all—was because of Stevenson's influence."

"I would think so."

"An' I kep' thinkin', 'I can do that.' An' it seemed like the right thing to do for this project. I wanted to get everybody's attention, an' that was one way to do it."

"Sure."

"So, I did the Harold thing. I went big."

"You did. But it was much more than that, I think. An' I... I started thinking about this last night." He shakes his head. "You can't escape the significance of this thing. And you can't escape its power. That's the way it comes across to me."

Poteet takes his rag and cleans his painting knife.

"And it almost feels like it's... It's mystical or something—like it has a spiritual quality built into it." He looks at Poteet and asks, "Do you feel that way about it?"

"Yeah. I do," Poteet responds and sets his knife down. "You know that Indians are spiritual people."

"I guess I've always thought so."

"Right. Well, they are. An' I had so many Chiefs an' uh, elders of so many tribes..." He breathes deeply. "An' I always felt like I was doin' it for them an' for generations to come."

"Sure."

"Why else would I bother. Ya know... I could've stayed in Santa Fe. I had a good life. I had friends. I was sellin' everything I could paint."

Elliott strokes his beard as he listens.

"But... I wanted to do it for my people—for my father's people. An' it needed to be done. I had support from all these Indian leaders. An' uh... I had their blessings." He pauses and rearranges his painting table. "An' I thought about those Indian leaders all the time, while I was painting. An' I thought about why—why I was doin' it. An' I felt like that spiritual energy—energy from those tribal leaders—was being painted right onto the canvas. I really did."

"That doesn't surprise me. I had a sense of that—just by looking at the photo."

Poteet turns to his table and picks up his painting knife. He turns back to Elliott with his knife in hand and says, "On that third panel... I don' know... I want it to be done, but I don' know if I wanna do it."

"I understand," Elliott says as he sits up straighter. "You're older now. You like it here in Santa Fe. Life is good."

"It is. An' that's it—exactly. I've already given five years of my life to that project."

"Of course."

"But I wanna tell ya about the support I got from the tribes while I was doin' it."

"Okay."

"It's when I was at OU. It's one day when we were doin' a photo shoot. Over a hundred Choctaws came up to be a part of it."

Elliott nods.

"They came all dressed up in their traditional clothes."

"That's great."

"An' uh... This one Indian guy come up to me, an' he said,

'We want to do somethin' for you.' An' I said, 'Yeah. Well, what is it?' An' he said, 'Well, we wanna sing you this song that we haven't sung in a hundred years.'"

"...a hundred years?"

"Yeah. An' they did. They sang it."

"Wow!"

"So, that was a real honor, ya know," Poteet says with the hint of a smile.

"I'm impressed. I mean... With you, it's just one thing after another," Elliott says as he shakes his head.

Poteet chuckles.

"But *that* one—the singing of the song..." Elliott takes a deep breath and then continues, "That's... It's very powerful." He shakes his head again. After a moment, he adds, "It's historic, I think."

"Yeah," Poteet whispers. "An' that's how I felt about it, too."

"I mean, they thought enough..." Elliott shrugs. "They came, and they dressed up. It was a large group."

"Yeah."

"...to be in this photo shoot for you."

"Yeah."

"And they sang a song they hadn't sung for anybody in a hundred years—a *hundred years!*"

"I know," Poteet acknowledges and pauses. After a moment, he nods and says, "There were plenty of other reinforcing moments through that project. Ya know, it happened all the time. But that one was special." He takes a deep breath. "It was *very* special."

"It had to be."

Poteet grabs his cup and asks, "Can I make you some coffee?" He looks toward his kitchen. "I've got a new machine back here that makes really good coffee."

"Sure. I'd love some."

Poteet grabs another cup and heads for the kitchen. He soon returns and says, "It won't take long to brew." He turns to inspect the painting on his nearest easel.

Elliott asks, "Does talking about the mural and some of those validation things make you uncomfortable?"

"Kind of... 'Cause, they paid me a great honor, ya know—a *great* honor. An' by not finishin', I don't feel like I've earned it. So, yeah. It makes me a little nervous."

"With what you gave of yourself and the talent you brought to the project, I think you *did* earn it."

"Thanks. But..." Poteet shakes his head and walks back into his kitchen. He yells, "...jus' black?"

"Yeah."

Poteet returns with a cup in each hand.

He gives one to Elliott, who smells the fresh coffee and smiles. Elliott closes his eyes as he savors the aroma of the brew and takes a sip. He says, "Yeah. That's good coffee."

Poteet takes a sip and sets his cup down. He says, "The fact that the mural's unfinished bothers me."

"I can understand," Elliott responds and takes another sip. As he's enjoying the taste of his fresh brew, he's thinking that the unfinished mural bothers him too. He wishes he knew what to do about it.

CHAPTER 40

Roy Masters

With the coffee and a break in the conversation, Poteet stares at his partially finished canvas silently. He's wondering what pieces of his life story have been left out. Actually, he knows of one and is thinking about bringing it up. He turns to Elliott to say, "I think we should talk about Roy Masters."

"So, who's that?"

"He's the oldest... Uh... He's got the longest runnin' radio talk show in America. He's been on the air for sixty-some years."

"And he's still on the air?"

"Yeah... He lives out in Oregon. He does the show when he can. He's old, ya know. ...ninety-somethin' now. An' he's missed quite a bit lately."

"So, what does that have to do with you?"

"It's funny how that started. It happened as I was goin' back to OU one night. I was drivin' back from Santa Fe. An' that was before XM Radio or anything. An' I'm channel surfin', ya know—jus' tryin' to stay awake. I finally got a clear channel, an' it was this guy talkin'."

"Okay."

"An' he was talkin' about the very thing I was havin' a

problem with. An' then... I mean... It hit me. It hit so close to home, I almost had to pull off the damn road. Because it was... He said a lot of things. But he said that women were inherently evil. An'... From what I'd been through, that hit home with me."

Elliott raises his eyebrows but lets Poteet continue.

"An' I thought, 'Wow.' I thought, 'I gotta meet this guy.' An' so, I found out who he was, where he lived... An' I went up to Oregon to see 'im. We had a good conversation, an' I started doin' his type of meditation."

"That sounds like a spiritual thing."

"It is."

"So, Roy Masters is a spiritual-type guy."

"He is. But he's hard to define like that."

Elliott cocks his head and wrinkles his brow. "What do you mean?"

"He talks about spiritual things, but he's also written a book on physics."

Elliott closes his eyes and shakes his head in disbelief before repeating, "Physics?"

"Right."

"But getting back to how he's helped you?"

"Okay."

"He has a church?"

"No. There's no church. An' he tells ya, 'I don' have anything you can join.'"

"Hmm."

"An' he says, 'But, I'm here to help you.'"

"...interesting."

"He says, 'I will talk to you, an' I will tell you what I think. Then, *you go*. You leave. Like, see ya later. Adios. An' if you have problems, you can call me up an' talk to me about 'em.' An' uh... Boy, he's brutal with ya too." Poteet chuckles. "But that's the way you have to be. He tol' me... He said, 'Ya know, a lot of times people think that I'm mean.' He said, 'I'm not mean at all. I don't have a mean bone in my body. But I'm not gonna sit here an' listen to how fouled up you are an' then jus' pat you on the head an' send you on your way. No. I'm gonna tell ya what's wrong with ya. Then, it's up to you. You have to find your own connection to the universe.'"

"Okay?"

"Yeah. He says that to everybody. Uh..." Poteet chuckles. "I've listened to his radio show, ya know. An' uh... Many times, somebody'll call up, he'll just say, 'Your problem is, you're just a no-good person.'"

Elliott and Poteet laugh.

"Okay... So... If you're the caller, and you agree that you're a 'no-good person'... Then what?"

"You gotta change. If you wanna solve your problem, then... You've gotta change."

"Do people really change?"

"I did."

"Really?"

"Yeah. What I learned from Roy Masters changed *my* life."

Elliott nods slowly and says, "I think you're right."

"...about what?"

"Roy Masters. I need to know more about him."

"He's a really smart guy."

"You say he's on the radio and lives in Oregon."

"Right. An' his organization is called The Foundation of Human Understanding. An' uh... After I found his radio show, I tried to listen to it every day. I was meditating every day too. An' uh... It helped me a lot, 'cause I could see a practical application. When he says somethin', it's not jus' words. He explains it. It's..." Poteet points and says, "If you do this..." He moves his hand to point in a different direction. "Then, *this* is gonna happen."

"Is this foundation a church?"

Poteet shakes his head and says, "No. Roy dudn' think you should be in church."

Elliott cocks his head and looks away for a moment before asking, "Did the Roy Master's stuff become a disruption to your progress with the mural?"

"About the only thing that disrupted my schedule, which really wadn' a big deal, was, uh... David Boren had asked me... He said, 'We have a lot of groups from all over the world that visit the campus.'"

"Mm-hmm."

"An' he said, 'We like to take 'em around an' show 'em different things.' An' he said, 'Would you be open to lettin' 'em come in here an' see this?' An' I said, 'Sure,' ya know. An' so, we did have people from all over the world come in there."

"That seems like more evidence of university support for your project."

"It was. David Boren was totally behind what I was doin'."

"So, what happened?" Elliott asks in a way that shows his own frustration with the way Poteet had been treated.

CHAPTER 41

...back to Idabel

"So... Where was David Boren when they kicked you off campus? He should've been right there behind you."

"I don' know. An' I've often wondered about that myself. Surely, he knew. He must've been aware that I was no longer a stop on their tour." Poteet shakes his head and says, "I don' know."

"I think that's strange."

"But I had a guy who would come by. He was my original contact there. His name was Michael Mares. He was the director of the museum, an' uh... He would come by an' say, 'This is really fantastic.'"

"...because it was going to hang in his museum?"

"Oh yeah."

"...in their art museum?"

"It was gonna hang in their Natural History Museum."

Elliott nods and says, "I guess it still could."

"It could, but we didn' end on the best of terms, ya know."

"True."

"But... That last time, when I talked to Michael... Uh... He was very appreciative of what I was doin'. But he got replaced. An' then, everything changed. This woman came in an' took the directorship, an' she'd never done that before."

"Sounds like she might have been over her head."

"She was. But that was also when nine-eleven happened."

"Okay. And that affected what you were doing?"

"It did. Because the support I was gettin' from Williams dried up."

"Why?"

"They took what they were givin' to me an' sent it to New York City instead. Ya know, that happened to a lot of charities. All their donations went to New York, an' uh... It was completely understandable. New York City needed the help, but it was tough on me."

"Yeah," Elliott says, "I'll never forget where I was when I first heard about it. I was in my car driving to the studio. When I got there, everybody was walking around like zombies."

"That's the way I felt too."

Elliott shakes his head. "It was a shock."

"Yeah... So anyway... Williams quit donatin' to the university, an' *that* made a difference. But it wadn' the only thing. That lady came in, an' there were issues. She was gettin'... Ya know, people were talkin' to her about the mural. I had the middle panel almost done, an' it scared the hell out of 'em. It really did."

"That middle panel is a very bleak picture. And the message of 'Death' is really clear."

"It's supposed to be. So... With all that, it wadn' long before she came over to reject the mural, an' send me packin'."

"In my opinion they haven't paid enough of a price for doing that to you."

"I could've gotten more out of 'em, if I'd pushed. Our contract was very clear on what they had agreed to do."

"So, you had a contract?"

"We did. An' *they* even wrote it."

"And I suppose they fell short..."

Poteet chuckles.

"So, was it mostly about money?"

Poteet shrugs. He then looks toward the window and takes a deep breath. He shakes his head slowly and says, "Yeah. It was partly that. But... It was controversial. It had been controversial. There'd been protests. I'd been on the news. Certain journalists were payin' attention an' writin' about it."

"It would have taken some courage to stand up to that kind of pressure."

"Yeah. An' she wouldn' do it."

"So, that was that, and they kicked you out."

"They did. But... I had a contract. I hadn' had a problem with it. I'd signed it."

"It must've been written totally in their favor."

"It was, but I didn' mind. They'd been fair to me up to that point. An' so... When she came over, she said, 'Well, pursuit to such an' such.' An' I said, 'Look. You don' have to do that.' I said, 'If you wanna reject the painting, just go ahead an' sign off on it.' An' I said, 'Ya know, it's fine.' An' so, she signed off on it. An' I told her. I said, 'Well, I wanna thank you for that.' An' she said, 'Why would you do that?' An' I said, 'Because you jus' gave me a four million dollar painting.' She said, 'I did, didn' I?' An' I said, 'Yeah, you did.'"

Elliott chuckles.

"Of course, that was based on what they made me insure it for."

"Huh."

"An' she said, 'Well uh... Uh... Would you, uh...'" He imitates her clearing her throat. "'Would you leave that painting here?' An' I said, 'Well, hell no. Why would I leave my painting in your building?'"

Elliott laughs.

"I said, 'Nope. That's it.' I think... If the director of the gallery hadn' changed, I would've finished it there, because...

I told you that the first director was seein' what I was doin'. An' he... He was just kind of in awe of it. An' he said, 'This is gonna be a great addition to the museum, an' a great gift to the people of Oklahoma.' An' that was the last thing he said to me. But ya know, he... For some reason or other, he stepped down. I don' know if he got ill or what."

"Hmm."

"But... The mural *was* controversial. An'... I'm sure the picketing caused her some heartburn."

"Yeah. The protestors..."

"But it wadn' a surprise. It was like the Chiefs tol' me. They said, 'You're gonna catch hell from both sides.'"

Elliott nods.

"An' I did. But I didn' care. I mean... Ya know, as an artist, we kind of like controversy."

Elliott chuckles.

"That part didn't bother me at all."

"I see."

"Some of the local TV stations an' magazines had been followin' the project, an' they got in touch with me after it was cancelled. They wanted to know what happened. An'... I jus' didn' feel right about bad mouthin' anybody. Because I was friends with David Boren, an' I didn' wanna cause him any trouble."

"I'd say that was a very forgiving attitude."

"I guess."

"So, when you first got started there... Did they say, 'We're going to give you 'til this date or...?'"

"Huh-uh."

"And say, you need to be done by such and such..."

"Nope." He shakes his head. "There was never a time schedule."

"You got screwed."

"An' then, I had a similar situation with Williams."

"...your main sponsor?"

"Yeah. 'Cause that woman at Williams... Ya know, the one I first talked to..."

"Right. ...who called on Christmas Eve."

"Yeah. Well... When I talked to her... She brought lawyers with 'er an' everything... Because they'd quit donatin' money. I had a contract with them too. But... Like I said, it was because of nine-eleven. An' I told 'er... We sat down, an' I tol' 'er... I said, 'Look, you don' need these lawyers.' I said, 'I'm not suin' you or anybody else.'"

"She must've thought you had grounds..."

"She did. An' I did have grounds, because they had committed to the whole damn thing. They had committed to be our lead sponsor. But I said, 'Nope. That's not gonna happen. I'm not...I'm not suin' anybody.' An' I think they went, 'Whew, thanks.'"

Elliott grins.

"So... Because yeah... They, ya know... They had said, 'We're gonna be with you an' stay with you to the end of this thing.'" Poteet nods. "But they didn't."

"Yeah."

Poteet turns to his table and starts rearranging tubes of paint. He says, "But on the other hand, they gave me over seven hundred thousand dollars. An' then, they got some of their vendors to start pitchin' in money too. It was a lot of money, but it still wadn' enough. Ya know, I probably needed another half a million to finish it."

"Seems to me like you were pretty gracious through all of this."

Poteet strokes his goatee. "I didn' wanna fight. That wouldn' a been right."

"If you could get it going again, I wonder if they would be a supporter?"

"Possibly."

"That's an interesting thought."

"It is. But all the people I knew there are gone now."

"Yeah. But... You do have a track record with 'em."

"Yeah. We have a history..." Poteet acknowledges with a nod and adds, "We tried to do right by 'em, ya know. Everything we printed... We'd put their logo right on it, an' it would say, 'Sponsored by Williams Corporation.'"

"I expect they felt like you were being fair."

"We missed a few things, but not many."

"I think... If I were them, I'd want to be on board with your project again."

"Who knows... But... A lot of these things... I jus' look at 'em like..." He shrugs. "That's the way it was meant to be.'"

"Yeah. And that probably helps your attitude."

"Maybe."

Elliott was beginning to see how Poteet's compelling story might mesh with his own intensions of "doing something." With the full story of the mural, he was seeing a story he could tell that would reflect the plight of all the tribes. It was not a new understanding, but it was a vision that was maturing in his soul. He now felt that this rejection of the mural should be shouted to the rooftops. He wanted to say boldly, "Here's a story of mistreatment of this one Native American that is the perfect analogy for what happened to *all* the tribes. This must be fixed. This must be rectified." How could the message be any clearer?

"I'm not sure I could have walked away like that," Elliott confesses.

"But ya know... People would call me an' say, 'You oughta talk to this museum or that museum.' I'm like, 'Ya know, I've given enough, an' I'm jus' not gonna do it.'"

"You were burned out."

"I was."

"So... When you think about it now..."

"I have days when I wish I could finish that last panel. It's when I think of Bear Heart, mostly." Poteet pauses and takes another sip of coffee. After a moment, he looks back at Elliott and says, "But anyway... On that third panel... We'll see what happens. But... As far as tryin' to get the word out about the Trail of Tears an' all, I don' know anybody that's worked harder at it than me."

"I don't doubt it."

"A lot has happened since... But... At that time, I didn' know of anybody else doin' much of anything."

"I'm sure you must have inspired others."

"I hope so. But I have no idea."

Elliott takes another drink of his coffee but remains quiet.

"When I look back on those five years, I see it as a good experience, ya know. I learned a lot, an' I ended up with two great paintings. An'... In my heart, I know that I gave it my best."

"So... When they shut your project down, did anybody from the tribes come around and go, 'Hey! What happened?'"

"Nope. They didn'."

"Huh." Elliott shakes his head. "That doesn't make sense to me."

"I know it."

"It jus' seems like..."

"Yeah."

"It seems like a lack of leadership somewhere."

"I know. But they never did."

"To be so supportive at the beginning..."

"Yeah."

"...an' then it goes away." Elliott shakes his head again. "An' everybody just forgets?"

"Yeah. So... I put the panels in storage an' uh... By then, I was ready to move on."

"Maybe you were somewhat relieved."

"To a degree... But I believe that the mural... It'll have a life of its own, ya know—somewhere, somehow. Maybe it'll be after I'm gone. I don' know. But... I did have a real sense of accomplishment. We'll see what happens."

"So... When you left OU, then what?"

"I went down to Idabel. I went down to my ranch an' built a studio there. An' uh... At the time, I owned the whole thing. It was a thousand-acre cattle ranch." Poteet pauses and looks toward the north window. "Well... Let's see... We came out here at the end of 2008. So, I was down there about six years."

"Did you like painting there?"

"I did. But..."

"It didn't hold you back somehow to be away..."

"Uh..." Poteet looks toward the window again. "No... But I had this dealer from New York City. He called me, an' he said he was gonna be in Dallas. He said, 'I'd really like to come see you.' An' I said, 'Well... Come on. Come see me.' Then uh... So, he did. He rented a car, an' he drove down to the ranch. An' uh... I showed 'im around, an' we talked for a while. When he was gettin' ready to go, he said, 'I jus'...' He said, 'I don' see how this happens.' An' I said, 'What?' He said, 'How does an abstract artist like you end up in the middle of nowhere on a thousand-acre cattle ranch doin' abstract work?' An' I said, 'I don' know.'"

Elliott laughs.

Poteet chuckles. "I said, 'I don' know. It just did.'"

Elliott continues to laugh as they hear footsteps on the stairs.

Terry peeks in and says, "I got those paintings packed and ready to go, so I thought I'd come see how y'all are doin'. Sounds like you're talkin' 'bout the ranch."

"We are," Elliott responds. "Poteet was telling me about painting there after the OU fiasco."

"I'm glad he did, or I wouldn't a met 'im."

Poteet and Elliott chuckle.

Poteet nods and then says, "But, it was... Uh... Ya know, I didn' mind bein' there. In fact, I liked it. It was a great place to be. It was beautiful. I had horses. An' I loved watchin' the bald eagles."

"I wouldn't have thought there'd be bald eagles in southeastern Oklahoma."

"Oh, yeah."

"Oh, there's a bunch of 'em," Terry notes.

"Hmm."

"Ya know, I'd saddle my horse an' ride to that lake I've got down there," Poteet says with a smile. "It's like a twenty-three-acre lake."

Elliott nods. "That sounds wonderful to me."

"It really is. An' uh... I was ridin' down through there one day, an' I look up. There was two of 'em—two bald eagles. It was a male an' a female. They had built a nest up in a tall tree. An' I watched 'em. One of 'em would take off, swoop down to the lake an' grab a fish. That one would land. An' then the other would take off, swoop down there, an' grab a fish. As long as I was on my horse, they wouldn' pay any attention to me. If I got off my horse, they'd fly away."

"Hmm."

"They didn' seem to be afraid. I guess I just looked like a funny horse to 'em."

Elliott smiles and says, "Most people don't get to do that."

"I know. An' that's somethin' I really enjoyed."

"And it seems like you were able to continue with your successful painting career while you were there."

"I could, but... Eventually, I decided I wanted to be back out here."

Elliott opens his arms. "And here you are."

Poteet smiles and says, "Yes. Here I am."

Elliott nods. "So... Let's talk some more about your career

successes." As he is speaking, his phone rings. He reaches into his pocket and looks at the name. His eyes focus on the phone, and he stands. Without saying a word, he hustles into the gallery room next to the studio.

With Elliott's sudden exit, Poteet turns to look at his latest work in progress. He picks up his knife, glances at Terry, and then begins working with his paints.

All the talk about the ranch was bringing back memories for Terry. Although it was short-lived, it was a magical time for her. She had been back many times, but none of her visits had been as special as those first days. She pulls out her phone to begin checking messages—trying to be as productive as possible as they wait for Elliott's return.

In a few minutes Elliott rushes back in to say, "Sorry. They had something come up on a set down in Florida. They needed authorization from me and had to call."

"Sure."

"It happens sometimes."

CHAPTER 42

The Cinderella Story

Poteet looks at Elliott. "You mentioned my successes."

"Right."

"Sometimes, somethin' subtle will hit you."

"Okay."

Poteet chuckles. He takes the last sip of his coffee and says, "It was funny. I was over... I was gettin' a colonoscopy at the hospital in Texarkana. An' uh... There was a couple of nurses..." He squints. "No, it wadn' a colonoscopy. They were doin' a heart scan, where they went up through my femoral..."

"Oh."

"...with a camera."

"Okay."

"So... I was sittin' there watchin' it—up in my heart. This thing jus' went... Ya know... Of course, my heart was fine."

"But... You must've had some kind of issue."

"Yeah. I... I still don' know what happened. But... I... These things popped up on my hands—these bumps—an' on my feet. So, I went to go see my doctor. An' he said, 'I don' know what that is.' But he said, 'I don' like it.' An' he got me in there, like that day. But they never did find out what it was."

"Huh."

"Uh... It was funny in a way."

"...your heart?"

"No. ...the nurses there."

Elliott chuckles and says, "Oh."

Terry rolls her eyes and says, "Here we go again."

Poteet smiles and looks at Terry. "She's heard this, but... Anyway... Before we started that procedure, we were talkin'. They got around to me sayin' I was an artist—a professional artist. An' I said, 'You can Google me.' So, one of 'em went over to the computer, an' she did. She Googled me. She come back, an' she said, 'You ain't married, are ya?'"

Elliott and Terry burst out in laughter.

Poteet continues, "An' I said, 'No.' An' uh... She said, 'Well, unless you've got congenital heart disease...'"

Elliott and Terry continue to laugh.

Chuckling, Poteet says, "'I'm comin' after you, boy.'" Poteet laughs and then adds. "That was funny."

Elliott takes a deep breath and utters, "Yeah."

"It's kinda stupid to think that was significant, but it sort of hit me that way."

Elliott chuckles.

"But... Lookin' back, it wadn' always that great."

"Sure. You had to work hard, and you had to get good training."

"Yeah. An' I got good trainin' in New York. ...at the Art Students League, an' it was fun. An' that was the first time I was there, ya know... I was goin' to school. I was young, an' uh... I was meetin' all the movie stars. That was a lot of fun. But... Right before I met Terry, I got hooked up... I was datin' this woman. She was a... She had just gotten divorced. But her an' her husband were Hollywood producers."

"Hmm. Maybe I know 'em."

"I'm sure you do, but I'm not gonna say her name. But, they made, like *hundreds* of millions of dollars. It was just unbelievable."

"Interesting. That narrows it down."

"Yeah. It was when I was livin' at the ranch, an'... She wanted me to come to New York City. She wanted me to live with her at the Dakota."

Elliott sits up. "...so *this* is your connection to the Dakota."

"Yeah—right next door to John Lennon's apartment."

Chuckling, he repeats, "...next door to John Lennon's apartment."

"Yeah. An' Yoko still lives there."

"Hmm."

"Yeah. An' uh..."

Elliott shakes his head slowly. He stops and stares at Poteet. He says, "I certainly didn't expect this. Actually, it blows my mind." He strokes the hair on his chin.

Poteet chuckles.

"I'm trying to understand how the rich Hollywood socialite who lives in the Dakota next to Yoko Ono meets the Native American painter from Santa Fe."

"I was actually livin' at the ranch then."

"Which makes it all the more unlikely."

"True."

Elliott laughs and continues, "This is a very unexpected twist." He shakes his head. "At the very least, it probably ramps up the significance of your story to my board and my partners. I don't know." He chuckles. "It might help my cause if you'd tell me her name."

Poteet turns to his painting table and says, "I can't do that. I just can't."

Elliott nods and then says, "You must've done it."

Poteet turns to respond, "Do what?"

"...go live at the Dakota?"

"Yeah, I did. ...for a while."

"Wadn' John Lennon killed there?" Terry asks.

"Yeah."

Elliott says, "...right out front."

"...just outside the front gate," Poteet adds. "An' uh... Practically, every time I'd walk out of there, somebody'd be takin' pictures."

"I'll bet," Elliott says quietly.

"An' they were always takin' pictures of me. They didn' know who the hell I was. But... Yeah. I ended up livin' right there. Yeah, right next to Yoko. An' right there on her door, she had a little brass plaque. It said, 'Newtopian Embassy.' An' it's still there. Yeah. At least it was when I was livin' there."

Chuckling, Elliott repeats, "Newtopian..."

"What does that mean?" Terry asks.

"I don' know. But I'm sure it's somethin' John put there. Other than that, I don' have a clue."

Terry nods.

"But... Livin' in that apartment... It was jus'... Uh... I mean... This woman had *too* much money. She was... An' uh... She said, 'You can paint here in New York City, an' uh... We'll live here at the Dakota, an' you can get a studio.'" Poteet sighs and turns to Elliott. "You'd have to see this apartment to believe it. I mean... When I broke up with 'er, she sold it for twenty-five million."

"Wow," Elliott whispers. "Even for the people I know, that's a lot."

"Yeah. An' uh..."

"So, how did you ever meet *her*?"

"Uh... It was my art dealer out in California... He, uh... She was a big client of his. An'... He knew that she had been divorced, an'... So, he tol' me... He said, 'I know somebody you might like to meet.' An' he... He told 'er about me."

"And you were living at the ranch?"

"I was. So, he called me one day. He said, 'I got this woman out here.' He said, 'She's really good lookin', an'...' He told me who she was, an' he said, 'She wants to meet you.' So, I said,"

'Okay,' an' went out to California. An' that's how we met. An' uh... Ya know... One thing led to another. So... But I just *hated* it in New York City. I absolutely *hated* it."

Elliott turns to Terry. "Do you mind hearing all this?"

"...not when he's talkin' 'bout hatin' it."

Elliott chuckles. After a moment he turns back to Poteet and asks, "Did you ever have any interaction with Yoko?"

"She was a real, uh, bitch in my opinion. Yeah. Because... Ya know, we had... jus' like I got here. We had a common area, where we'd put out the trash. An' I'd see 'er there. So... For a while, I was real friendly an' everything. But she wouldn' speak. She wouldn' respond. You could say 'Hi' to 'er an' she'd jus'... Nothin'. So, I'm thinkin', 'Who cares?'"

"Yeah."

"But yeah... I lived right there. Ya know... They wouldn' let 'er in there today."

"Yoko?"

"Yeah. 'Cause they don' want high-profile people livin' there, uh... Like, Lauren Bacall lived there. But uh... Who was it? I think it was James Taylor that was tryin' to buy an apartment there, an' they wouldn' let 'im. They didn' want celebrities."

"I can understand that."

"Yeah. It's the paparazzi."

"Sure. They don't need that."

"Right. So, I was tellin' ya about the guy that introduced me to 'er—my art dealer in California?"

"Yeah."

"She'd been a client of his for several years. An' he said she would spend, ya know, a hundred, hundred-fifty thousand every year."

"That sounds like a good client."

"Believe me. It is."

"So... What happened?"

"Well... She asked me before we broke up... She said, 'Where in the world would you like to live? Jus' tell me, an' we'll go live there. It dudn' matter.' She said, '...jus' pick a place.' An' I said... Yeah. I mean, there's a lot of places overseas that would be nice, ya know. But I said, 'Really... I love Santa Fe.'"

"Out of anywhere in the world, you'd pick here?" Terry asks.

"I would. I did." He shrugs. "I love it here. Ya know, my work fits in well an' all that. So, she bought a gorgeous place out here after we broke up."

"*After* you broke up?" Terry asks.

Poteet looks away for a moment before saying, "Yeah. It was one of those award-winning, million-dollar... No. It was more like two-point-somethin' million. An' it had an art studio."

"Sounds great," Elliott says with enthusiasm.

"It had horse stables."

"Oh, my gosh!"

"Yeah. It had everything."

"It was perfect for you."

"It was," Poteet says and nods.

Terry breaks in and explains, "Elliott... Let's get this one thing straight right now. I didn't buy no million-dollar nothin' for Poteet. I guess, he jus' decided that he liked me the way I was."

Elliott chuckles and says, "Obviously."

"An' it works better that way." Poteet says. "Lemme tell ya. But... This woman... She bought that beautiful place, even after we broke up."

"Did she keep it?" Elliott asks.

"She did for a while. But boy, she was a nut. She was certifiable. 'Cause... There was a guy... He was a builder, an' he built his house near hers. An' uh... I forget how many acres she had. I'm thinkin' it was like... I don' know. She had somethin' like 20 acres."

"Okay?"

"So... Her an' this builder had to share the same road. An' she ended up suin' 'im over it. But... She was crazy. An' he finally had to sell his place to get away from 'er."

"See..." Terry interjects. "I don' mind Poteet talkin 'bout his previous girlfriends like that."

Elliott chuckles.

Poteet smiles and says, "Yeah. She drove everybody crazy, includin' me." He chuckles. "But... After somethin' like that... You start thinkin', 'Money ain't everything.' An' she did all kinds of shit to me. She was awful. But I was always attracted to the wrong type of woman, ya know. Roy Masters pointed that out to me. 'Cause, I always thought, 'I love you, but you stay over there.'" Poteet points away. "Ya know... That's how I was raised."

"I guess so... Because your mother was..."

"Yeah. She was always somewhere else. An' after Roy said it, I started to see... 'Yeah, that makes perfect sense. That's exactly it.' 'Cause, you're sort of drawn to what you grew up with. Roy would say, 'You can be drawn to that very thing that corrupted you.'"

"It seems like Roy Masters really helped you."

"He did."

"But..." Elliott says, "Changing subjects for a moment..."

"Okay."

"Let me tell you what I've been thinking about lately."

Poteet nods.

Elliott strokes his beard and then says, "All the time... You know, I keep wondering, 'Can I make a series out of this? Or can I make a movie?'"

"Sure."

"And I think I've figured it out."

Poteet chuckles and says, "Okay?"

"It's Terry's story."

Terry sits up with a blank face and wide eyes.

Poteet turns to lean on his painting table.

Elliott looks at Terry. He says, "It's your 'Cinderella story.'"

Without blinking, Terry stares back.

Elliott sits forward and faces Poteet. "And I can't take all the credit for this. Judy and I were talking the other day. You know, I gave her the tape of"—he looks at Terry—"that conversation you and I had."

Terry nods and says, "Okay."

"And... Judy actually suggested it. It made sense to me. We'll see. But think of this." He turns back to Poteet and starts gesturing with his hands. "There's a small-town beauty shop where Terry's trying to make her way." He quickly glances at Terry and then back to Poteet. "She and her friends are looking out the window at this good-looking guy they don't know. Then, she meets this guy a few days later at the local Pizza Hut. He approaches, and they go out to lunch. And, after a few lunch dates, he proposes to her."

Covertly, Terry nods and smiles.

Elliott continues, "Have you ever heard of a story more perfect for the Hallmark channel?"

Poteet chuckles.

Elliott looks at Terry.

Eventually, she nods slowly and answers, "Not really."

"And then, she finds out from her brother at the *Thanksgiving* dinner table that this beautiful guy who's proposed to her is a *famous painter*." As Elliott speaks, the volume and pitch of his voice are rising. "Can you believe it?"

Terry raises her eyebrows and watches.

"...and she also finds out that he's *rich*."

Poteet objects with, "I wadn' 'rich.'"

Terry sits forward to say, "To me, you were. ...drivin'

around in a bran' new XLR Cadillac sports car. An' when you gave me those ten hundred-dollar bills to go take my tests. What about that? An' then, you ownin' a thousand-acre cattle ranch. I'm tellin' ya... In my book, that makes you *rich*."

Poteet and Elliott chuckle.

"And then, you bring the story out here for *Christmas*." Elliott's gestures are becoming more dramatic. "You know how they love *anything* having to do with Christmas on the Hallmark channel."

Terry nods and says, "That's true. They run Christmas stories year 'round."

"Yeah, they do."

Terry adds, "They run Valentine's Day stories year 'round too. At first, I thought it was strange. I guess I'm used to all that now."

Elliott and Poteet chuckle.

She says, "But, Santa Fe was absolutely beautiful then."

"Believe me, I've been envisioning that in my mind for several days."

Terry nods.

"Even if Hallmark didn't buy it, I'm certain one of the other channels would—Prime, Netflix, HBO, somebody..."

Poteet chuckles.

"But... The film wouldn't cost that much to make. It would be exceedingly popular. And that's just the foot in the door. How could you not want to know more about this handsome stranger, this Prince-Charming character who sweeps Cinderella right off her feet. How could you not love that? I mean... And then, you get into everything else." Elliott stares at Poteet—reaching his hands out.

Poteet responds, "I guess. If you say so."

"And... The best part..."

"What's that?" Terry asks.

With Poteet and Terry waiting, Elliott grins, nods, and says slowly, "It's true. It's all true."

Without smiling, Terry looks at Poteet with a sparkle in her eye.

Poteet watches Elliott with a hint of a smile.

Elliott looks at his watch and says, "I've got to go, but I can be back in a couple of hours." He looks at Poteet and asks, "Will that work?"

Poteet shrugs and says, "Sure."

Elliott turns his recorder off but leaves it on the table. He grabs his satchel and heads for the double doors.

Terry follows.

As Poteet listens to the descending footsteps, he's thinking about what Elliott had just mentioned—making a movie about Terry. What a turn of events that would be. But it made sense. When you think about it, it is an unusual story. And it *would* be perfect for the Hallmark channel. As he reaches for his painting knife, he's hoping to finish his painting before Elliott returns.

CHAPTER 43

"She Didn't Have the Bitch..."

Elliott sticks his head through the double doors and says, "I'm back."

Standing just a few feet away at his worktable, Poteet holds up some straight pieces of wood and says, "I've got an idea for my next painting."

Elliott points toward the easel and asks, "Did you finish with that one?"

"Essentially. It's got to dry, but..."

Having surveyed the room, Elliott asks, "Do you have that stand for my recorder? Looks like your table might be a little crowded now."

"Sure. It's in my storeroom," Poteet answers and sets the frame pieces down. He heads for his kitchen.

"Great. Thanks," Elliott says as he sets his satchel on the floor.

Poteet soon returns with the stand. He hands it to Elliott who begins to attach the recorder.

"Did you get done what you needed to?" Poteet asks as he arranges the pieces of the frame.

"Yeah. And I've decided to stay an additional night."

"I'm glad you're staying. I'll tell Terry."

Elliott nods and adds, "It's a beautiful day."

"Yeah. It's a great time of year out here."

"While I was walking, I was thinking about the support you got from the tribes and your meetings with the Chiefs. I can't get that out of my mind."

Poteet scratches his head and looks at his frame pieces.

"It's an image that's compelling to me. I can see it. I can see a table. I can see these tribal leaders in a range of garb, from near-traditional to business suits."

"It was more-or-less like that. An' there were several meetings."

"For a film, I think I would slant it more toward the traditional look." He nods and says, "It's an inter-tribal image that you don't see very often. I think they're usually fighting each other these days."

Without looking up, Poteet responds, "They are."

Elliott chuckles. "So... You got tribal support. You got OU on board. You raised some money and got started with your painting."

Still studying the frame pieces, Poteet nods and says, "That's about how it went."

"After that, was it all work? Or did you take some breaks?"

"Yeah. I'd have to stop an' raise money every so often."

"Right."

"And... I had a couple of chances to get away. One was a trip to Rome."

"Hmm."

"I was datin' this woman at the time who was a sculptor. She had, uh... She'd gotten some sort of scholarship to go over there an' study. An' uh... She said, 'Well, I'm gonna be over there, like all summer.' She said, 'Won't you please come over. It'll be fun' An' I thought, 'Yeah. Why not?' So, that's what I did. An' I'm really glad I went. 'Cause, I got to see a lot of stuff that I'd only seen in books."

"I'm sure that was great."

Poteet nods and continues, "When I got there, I hired this guide. She was an older lady from England. An' she took me to places where most tourists would never go, ya know."

"Uh-huh."

"She knew where some of the real famous paintings were that... Unless you knew, you wouldn't go there. An' she... I remember when we were walkin' down the street one time, an' she said, '...see that buildin' there?' an' I said, 'Yeah.' She said, '...you see those window treatments?' an' I said, 'Yeah.' She said, 'Michelangelo did those.' I said, 'You're kidding?'"

"Wow."

Poteet chuckles. "An' I was so amazed when I saw the Sistine Chapel, because they had just cleaned it."

"Yeah?"

"An'... Ya know... All those years with all the candles an' all the smoke collectin' on the ceiling. But... When they cleaned that thing... I mean, I jus' couldn' believe the colors that Michelangelo had used. I mean, they were just 'boom'—bright, ya know, like... I forget which figure it was. It was this sort of lime green thing on this woman... It was jus'... Like, wow! He was... Michelangelo was really into bright colors."

"What an experience that must have been for you, as an artist."

"It was. Yeah. An' the characters... They were so real."

"I guess you would notice things like that."

"I had read where he used to... Michelangelo would sit in these, what we would call a 'beer joint,' ya know—there in Italy. He would sit in there an' draw all those people that were patrons..."

"Oh...?"

"An' he would sketch 'em an' take those drawings with 'im."

"Like, to use as examples?"

"Yeah...like his models."

"I'll bet they thought that was pretty cool."

"An' they tell a story about when he'd done a big portion of the Sistine Chapel, an' it was botherin' 'im. He didn' like it. So... He was sittin' in that place where they went to drink, an' the owner opened a cask of wine. He tasted it an' said, 'Wine's no good. I gotta throw it out.' That registered with 'im. An' he went back an' tore all that out, 'cause he kept sayin', '...wine's no good. ...must be thrown out.'"

"Huh."

"Yeah. He had to throw it all out. An' in the Sistine Chapel... Those are frescos. An' the way I understand it. I've never done one. But Michelangelo would put fresh plaster on the ceiling an' paint it while it was still wet. An' then, the color would dry in the paster."

"Oh...... Okay."

"But, what's... What would be so difficult, especially if you were doin' a figure or somethin' like that... The color you put on there... It's not gonna be that color when it dries."

"Huh."

"When you first put it on, it would be dark, an' it'd dry lighter. So... I mean, if you got one half done an' had to come in the next day..."

Elliott chuckles and says, "Yeah. You'd have to match it."

"Yeah. But even *gettin'* paint back then was a problem. You didn' jus' go to the paint store an' buy it. You had to mix it yourself."

"So, what would you start with? What would you use?"

"...different things. The easiest ones were the earth colors. Oh... Like a yellow ochre... Or say a burnt umber or somethin' like that. An' those were actually minerals they would mine or find on the ground. They'd have to grind 'em up."

"Wow."

"But blue was always the hardest color to make."

"I guess not many minerals are blue in nature."

"They aren't. But, somewhere along the line, somebody found lapis lazuli—ya know, the stone? They ground that up an' made it an oil paint. It was, uh... It made a real bright, brilliant blue. An' what they would do is put their paint in these goatskin things." Poteet nods. "Yeah. You can imagine havin' to go out somewhere with all your paint in goat skins."

"Huh."

"An' I've read all these stories about artists gettin' poisoned back then," Poteet says and laughs.

"Oh really."

"Oh, yeah. ...especially with white. Because it was lead."

"Oh...?"

"The lead would make it opaque. An' so... For years, they were usin' this leaded white paint, an' all these artists were gettin' poisoned by it. They finally discovered that it was because of the lead."

"Huh."

"But most of this stuff that I use... It's... Oh, I mean, ya know... I'm not like Van Gogh who used to eat his paint."

Elliott laughs.

Poteet chuckles and says, "Yeah, he did."

"Whoo! That can't be good."

"I never tried it. I might've done it accidentally, but..."

Elliott chuckles.

"I never did it intentionally."

"I can't imagine what would possess someone to want to eat their paint."

"I can't either," Poteet says, and they both laugh.

When the laughter settles down, Elliott says, "Wow."

"But... Ya know, there's a lot of artists who've been borderline nuts."

Elliott starts laughing again, and Poteet does too.

Poteet adds, "I guess it jus' comes with the territory."

Terry pushes through the double doors and says, "I think you boys are havin' too much fun up here."

Smiling, Elliott says, "I'm trying to understand why Van Gogh would want to eat his paint."

Terry snickers and says, "Right. Poteet tol' me 'bout that."

Elliott motions for Terry to come in. He says, "This might be a good time to talk to Poteet about you."

She takes a deep breath and looks at Poteet.

He shrugs.

She says, "Okay," and goes to sit in her regular spot.

While he's deciding what to ask, Elliott loosely crosses his arms and looks in the direction of Poteet, who is arranging frame pieces. He begins to see frustration mounting in the painter's body language. Poteet finally shakes his head and says, "I've gotta leave for a minute. You two can talk."

Elliott and Terry exchange a glance.

Poteet points to the partly assembled frame and says, "I'm missin' a piece, an' I need to run nex' door."

Elliott nods and says, "...no problem. I'll just go ahead and get into the questions I had for Terry."

"Perfect," Poteet declares and walks out.

Elliott looks over at Terry.

She smiles.

He says, "Again... I'm thinking about that first day."

"Okay."

"Because... Poteet... And 'target' may not be the right word." Elliott chuckles. "But Poteet must have decided that you were who he wanted to be with."

"Yeah, I guess."

"And I'm sure..."

Terry interrupts, "An'... I don' know why."

"I think your mom was..." Elliott looks out the window and nods slowly. "I think she was probably a big part of that."

"I think my mom had the biggest influence on 'im, because

he saw what a good person she was. Now, Poteet... An' this... An' he's tol' me this. I'm jus' gonna tell you what he said. ...okay? An' ya know... He said, 'Terry, you "don't have the bitch" in you.' An' that's what he told me."

"And he didn't want any of that."

"No, he didn'. An' a lot of women do have it. Ya know... An' I've always said, 'It's hard for me to trust a woman.' An' it really is—to trust 'em very much. I have lots of acquaintances, I've got five thousand people on my page."

"Right."

"But uh... As far as a close female friend, other than my sister—my blood sister..."

"Yeah."

"I'd trust her with anything, ya know. But as far as jus'..." She stops and points at Elliott. "Now, don't put this in any damn movie. You'll hurt some feelings." She brings her hand back to her lap. "But I'm jus' tellin' ya how I feel. I mean, I love lots of people—*love* 'em. But... As far as out here, I don't have a close friend. Ya know, back home, I... I mean, I enjoy people. I enjoy people a lot. But... I don't... I've had so many things happen... You don' wanna trust—too much. Poteet says... An' this is what he tol' me." She puts her hands out in front of her in a "Stop" position. "'Keep 'em right there. Keep everybody right there.' An' I thought, 'That's a good rule to follow.' You can trust 'em, but don't bring 'em too close into your life. Ya know... An' I don't think I want to. I mean, I don'... I got Poteet. Yeah. That's how I feel about it."

"And it all goes back to the Pizza Hut."

"It does for me."

They hear footsteps on the stairs and turn to see Poteet enter.

With a smile, he holds up a frame piece and says, "I got it." He immediately gets back to building. Before anyone else has a chance to speak, he says, "Yeah. I remember that day at the Pizza Hut."

Elliott chuckles. Looking at Poteet, he says, "From Terry's standpoint, it's truly a Cinderella story."

Poteet chuckles.

"Because she didn't know you at all."

"Yeah. An' that's true."

After a long pause, Elliott says, "And in three days, you're asking her to marry you."

"Yeah... Well... Ya know... Like I said, I'd been single for twenty-two years. An' uh... Because I jus'... After that last one... That last divorce..."

"Yeah."

"Because... I remember my mother tellin' me, she said, 'Ya know, one thing I've noticed about you. You do pretty well, until you let these women start distractin' you. An' then, you lose your focus.' An' I said, 'You're right about that.' An' so, I decided I wadn' gonna do that anymore."

"Huh."

"So... Uh... Yeah, I was single for twenty-two years. An' then..." He turns to look at Elliott. "Ya know, I knew Terry's brother."

"I heard you worked out with him."

"Yeah, I knew 'im, an'... He's a nice fellow too, an' then... Ya know, I ran into Terry that day, an'... She was... I mean... If you don't like Terry's personality, there's somethin' wrong with *you*."

Elliott chuckles.

"That's the way I looked at it. She's always really friendly, an'... An' uh... Yeah. One thing I could tell about Terry right away... An' I told 'er. I said, 'Do you know what sets you apart from a lot of other women?' She said, 'What's that?' An' I said, 'You don't have the bitch in you.' I said, 'That's jus' not you.' She didn' know what I meant. But she knows that most women are bitches."

"Terry jus' told me about that."

Poteet looks at Terry.

She smiles.

"Obviously, that was important to you," Elliott says.

"Very... I wadn' gonna do that again."

They hear movement downstairs. Terry gets up and raises her index finger. She says, "Excuse me," and walks out.

Poteet continues, "But... I was at a point in my life where... An' even the guy... Masters up there in Oregon, ya know... We were talkin'... He said, 'It would be good for you to have a mate.' An' he said, 'You don't need a playmate. What you need is a workmate.' An' that made complete sense to me. It seemed like I might be able to find someone like that."

Elliott closes his eyes for a moment, then opens them and says, "So, Terry must have seemed like that type of person to you."

"I jus' thought... Ya know, I really liked Terry. I thought she was real pretty. I loved her personality an' everything."

"But you didn't know her."

"No. I didn' know 'er."

"You'd just seen her from a distance."

"Yeah."

"And you'd watched her, and you could tell how other people reacted to her."

"Well, yeah. But... Where I had never been a good judge of character of women before..." He chuckles. "I'd turned into a very good judge of women. An' I just, uh... I just sort of instinctively knew, 'Yeah, this person would be good.'" Poteet points to a shelf on the wall near Elliott. He says, "Hand me that green box right there." Poteet continues to point as Elliott reaches for the box and hands it to him.

"Well... As it turned out, she is," Elliott says.

"Because we've been together... Well, we're startin' our eleventh year together."

"Right."

"She's not demanding. An' I've been in relationships..." He shakes his head. "No matter what ya did, it wadn' good enough. Ya know... One of those things."

"Oh yeah..."

"An' uh... She's real appreciative of everything. I mean, the least little thing you do... She just loves it. She's grateful for everything she has now."

"Mm-hmm."

"An' uh... She was... Ya know, she tells me all the time, 'My life has never been better.'"

"Mm-hmm."

"Of course, I don't... I don't do any of those... She doesn't have to worry about me, an' I don't have to worry about her."

"Hmm."

Poteet uses a pulling tool to stretch a piece of canvas over the frame.

Elliott watches.

Poteet says, "I... Ya know, I made up my mind years ago. Nothin's worth bein' jealous about. I mean, it'll ruin a relationship—absolutely ruin it. An'... Uh..." He picks up his tack gun and shoots a tack through the canvas and into the frame. He says, "Yeah, we don'... We don' have to... That's not somethin' we worry about. So..."

Elliott says, "After being single for twenty-two years..."

"Yeah..."

"You must have made a decision about getting married."

"But I didn'."

"So... You just saw Terry that day and told yourself, 'I want to marry *her.*'"

"Yep. That's about how it worked. But... I said, 'Before we do anything, me an' your mother are gonna sit down an' have a good talk.'"

CHAPTER 44

Terry

"If you wanna know what a woman's gonna be like, talk to 'er mother," Poteet explains. He continues, "So... I drove down to Terry's mom's house. Terry wanted to go, an' I said, 'No, you ain't goin'.'"

Elliott chuckles.

"I said, 'This is none of your business.' An' uh... Ya know, I just loved her mother. I really did."

"Did you know her mother from before?"

"Huh-uh."

"Did you know of her?"

"Not really."

"Huh."

"No. But I'm glad I got to know 'er. She was quite a woman. She had four kids. Her husband died when he was thirty-four—Terry's dad did. An'... Her mother was a pretty woman, an' Terry looks jus' like 'er. An' uh... At thirty-four, she never knew another man. She devoted her life to raisin' those kids. An' boy... Lemme tell ya... They worshiped the ground she walked on, because she didn' let anything come before those children. An' she worked hard, too. She was one of those that could take a little an' make a lot out of it, ya know.

She built 'em a new house an' everything.'"

"It seems like that talk might have been what convinced you."

"If it hadn' a gone well, I wouldn' of asked 'er."

Elliott gazes out the west window for a moment before saying, "And then, there was the trip Terry was planning to take to Oklahoma City."

"Right."

"...for the cosmetology, whatever it was."

"Yeah."

"And uh... Before she left, you gave 'er a thousand dollars."

"I did."

"I could tell she was just thrilled."

"Well... It was comin' up on Christmas, an' I knew she didn' have any money."

"Yeah."

"An' uh... She had to go up there to take this test, an'... Ya know, there was the motel an' everything she had to pay for. So, uh... From my ranch down there... It wadn' much. But they would usually send me... Every year, I'd get like twelve hundred bucks for not plantin' somethin'. An' I'd just gotten a check. I didn' need it. An' uh... I knew she did. So... Yeah. I could tell it looked like *ten thousand* dollars to her."

Elliott laughs and says, "I'm sure."

"But, with Terry's mother... Well... She worked at the school, an' she worked somewhere else too. Her kids didn't do without. But they didn' get what a lot of the other kids had, either. She jus' didn' have it."

"She *had* to be frugal," Elliott observes.

Terry enters, and Poteet asks, "Did you sell anything?"

"No. But, I think they'll be back. They liked the abbreviated portraits. I think they'll come back an' get a Willie." She moves across the room to sit down again.

Poteet continues by saying, "She did. She had to be frugal

to raise those kids."

Terry sits forward to ask, "...you talkin' 'bout Mama?"

Elliott replies, "Yes," and adds, "...because Judy wanted me to ask some more questions about you."

Smiling, Terry says, "Okay." After a moment she continues, "An' talk about frugal. She had to... I think she got sixty-one dollars a month on all of us—from Daddy's Social Security after he died."

Settling back in, Elliott responds, "I can't even imagine how you would live on that."

"Yeah. But I wanna tell you somethin' 'bout my mama—what she did. She... She not only knew how to manage a dollar, she knew how to make it happen. Didn' she, Poteet?"

"Yeah."

"She... My daddy died in nineteen... nineteen sixty-one. An' she had four kids. Alan was the oldest, an' I was four. Tracy was three. Michael was one. Alan, I think, was... Twelve. But anyway, she... We lived in a little old house. It was jus' a little box house. An' uh... I mean... When I was born, I don't even think we had inside plumbin'. We had to go out to the two-holer."

"Yeah, we didn' either," Poteet adds, "when I was out at Grandma's."

"But we got inside plumbin', ya know. An' uh... When my daddy died... An' I have very few memories of him, but I know I was crazy about 'im. An' I know I missed my daddy. But, uh... Mama... Not only did she raise us four kids without ever knowin' another man, but she bought eighty acres an' paid it off."

"Really?" Elliott responds.

"Yeah."

"That's amazing."

"I know. Then she... She started buildin' her home, a brick home, down there on that eighty."

"And the location of the eighty acres was down there by, uh..."

"Hayworth. An' uh... First of all, she got the electricity out there, got a well dug. An' then she poured the concrete foundation. Ya know, she had to build it in stages. She didn' have a contractor. She had to do that herself. Because she couldn't afford all of it at once."

"Maybe we can work that into your Cinderella story."

Terry chuckles and stares at Elliott. After a moment, she continues, "So anyway, she... Ya know, she got all of it paid off."

"...pretty remarkable, really," Poteet affirms.

"It's another story of hard work and perseverance," Elliott notes.

"But we had to... We had to stain all the facin's an' all that stuff, ya know. ...an' do some of the work ourselves to get it done."

"The kids did some of the work?"

"Yeah. It was Tracy, my brother, an' myself. Because... Alan, my oldest brother had already moved out, an'... I got to live in it one year. We finished it in 1974, an' I got to live in it 'til '75."

"Was that when you graduated from high school?" Elliott asks.

"Yes. And then I went to college."

"Where did *you* go to college?

"Durant."

"Was that the same college as Poteet...?"

"Yes. But years later, of course."

"Right."

"But... I went for jus' one semester, an' then I got married. An' uh..."

"We really haven't talked about that marriage."

"I was a virgin the night I got married."

"Nooo..."

"Yes, I was. I certainly was. An' uh..."

"Well, congratulations for that, I guess."

Terry snickers.

Elliott chuckles.

"I'd been taught my whole life to stay with who you marry. But there was infidelity there—later on."

"...by your husband?"

"Mm-Hmm. An' it just about killed me. It did. It was just a really, really hard thing for me to go through."

"I'm sure. How did you discover it?"

"I found a sock in his laundry, when he was workin' down there in Mississippi—a woman's sock. An'... An' it just, absolutely... I mean, I went from... I went down to, like a hundred thirty-eight pounds. I lost so much weight, 'cause I was just sick." Terry turns and asks, "Poteet, you wanna hear this?"

"No."

Terry and Elliott break out into laughter.

Poteet adds, "...not really."

Still laughing, Elliott says, "Okay, he makes the calls around here."

Terry says, "Yeah, he does."

Poteet chuckles.

Terry confirms, "He really does."

"All right then, movin' on."

Poteet mumbles, "Yeah, movin' on..." but he doesn't let it drop. He explains, "It's jus' that... Well... The problem was..." He turns to Terry. "Number one, you were way too young to get married."

"I wondered about that," Elliott says.

"Yeah, I was eighteen."

"That's way too young," Poteet asserts.

"I had to worry if we was gonna have electricity. I had to

worry about food. I had to figure out how to survive."

"That's a tough life," Elliott notes.

"Yeah. An'... At one time, I had seven part-time jobs."

Elliott chuckles and looks over at her. "I don't even know how you can have seven part-time jobs."

Poteet chuckles.

"I was a rural carrier part-time. You know—a sub."

"Really? ...a rural mail carrier."

"Mm-hmm. An' I was..."

"...seems like that could've turned into a really good full-time job."

"It did. An' I was postmaster there for a while."

"Really?"

Terry grins and answers, "Yeah."

Poteet chuckles.

"Yeah. But I hated it," Terry says and laughs.

Elliott laughs and says, "Okay."

"An' I didn't do very well. It didn' really work out with the post office. But anyway... But uh... Yeah... An' at one time I was elected to be the City Clerk."

Elliott's chin drops. "You were elected?"

"Yeah. I was elected as City Clerk."

Poteet chuckles.

Elliott snickers and asks Poteet, "Did you know all this when you married her?"

Terry giggles.

"I didn' know it when I married 'er. No."

Elliott and Terry break up with laughter. Poteet joins in with a chuckle.

"I was an elected official," Terry reiterates.

Elliott continues laughing.

Terry winds her spell of laughing down and says, "Oh, goodness." She finishes with a sigh.

Elliott says, "This is a different side of you, I guess."

Elliott and Terry laugh together.

While laughing, she is able to respond, "It is. Yeah." When the laughter subsides, Terry says with a smile, "But let's get back to Poteet. He's the star of this show."

Chuckling, Elliott says, "You had a political career."

"I did."

Shaking his head, Elliott says, "You should've just kept that going."

"Oh, it was a nightmare too. An' I hated it. I jus' *hated* it. Because all my life I'd wanted to be a hairdresser."

Elliott chuckles.

"An' I didn't achieve that 'til the very end. I was actually a hairdresser for one month." She points at Poteet. "An' then, this guy come along."

"But..." Elliott grins and says, "You were all these other things... You were a postmaster. You were an elected official."

"Yeah."

"And your goal was still to be a hairdresser?"

"It was. All my life, I wanted to do hair. I was artistic, an' you need that to be a hairdresser."

"But her family..." Poteet says, "They did all right. An' every one of 'em is a really responsible person now."

Elliott asks, "Are they all still alive?"

As the mood turns solemn, Terry answers, "No, my younger brother died about five years ago."

"Yeah, Michael..." Poteet says. "He was the one I knew. But he'd hurt his back. I can't remember how he did it. An' then, he started takin' these opioids."

"Oh..."

"I know."

"Oh, that's so sad," Elliott says and shakes his head.

"An' he ended up havin' a stroke. Yeah... An' he wadn' that old."

"Do you think it was caused by the opioids?"

"I do," Terry answers. "I think he jus', ya know... He was tryin' to quit."

"Yeah. That's tough."

Terry stares blankly past Poteet—lost in her memories with tears beginning to fall from her eyes.

After a moment, Elliott offers, "Maybe it was just too much stress."

"Yeah... Apparently," Poteet says.

Elliott utters, "Boy," and starts shaking his head again.

Terry removes her glasses to begin to wipe the tears away.

Elliott sits quietly.

Terry slips her glasses back on and says with a smile, "An' now, I have grandkids."

Elliott returns the smile and appreciates the effort to move on.

"An' they're everything to me. They're just... Both of 'em are *so* precious."

"You have two?"

"Yes. I have a grandson an' a granddaughter."

"Okay—one of each."

"Yeah. An' my grandson... He loves to rodeo. An' Poteet is absolutely *goofy* about 'im."

"He's a good kid," Poteet says.

"He is," Terry adds. "He's very well mannered. Ya know... I'm tellin' you right now. If you met him, it's all, 'Yes sir. No sir.' An' Poteet is the only grandfather Brett has ever known with me."

"...Brett is his name?"

"...Brett Stuart. Yes. An' Brett... Brett is a... He's a blessin' in so many ways to me, because... I lost his dad, an' he... He favors 'im, an' he's... He's kind of got the attitude of his dad, ya know. An' he helped me through some real hard times." She stops and takes a deep breath.

Elliott and Poteet remain quiet. Poteet watches Terry carefully.

"An'... Ten years after I lost my son, Poteet come along, an' I was still greivin' so bad—so terribly bad. But Poteet... He helped me so much. My son will soon be dead twenty years. But... But Poteet... I give a lot of credit to Poteet, because... First of all, he let me talk about it, ya know. An' then, he helped me. He helped me deal with it, because I wasn't dealin' with it. I was angry. I was angry about it. But Poteet... He pulled me out of it. He pulled me out of that dark hole an' sinkin' hole I was in. He helped me, an' I give him so much credit for that."

"Well... You can't deal with things like that on your own," Poteet says. "You better ask God to help you get through it."

"Well, I *was* askin' God. An' my family was too. They were all prayin' for me."

"But you didn' give up your anger."

"I did *not* give up my anger."

"That's the main thing." Poteet says sternly, "You've got to give it up."

Terry points at Poteet and turns to Elliott. She says, "He's the one that told me what I had to do."

Elliott nods.

"...because my son was murdered."

Elliott gasps and his eyes widen.

"An' Poteet told me not to have anger an' resentment in my heart, an' I'll tell ya somethin'."

"I can't even imagine how you'd handle that," Elliott whispers.

"Ya know... There was nothin' I could do. There was nothin'..."

"You won't do it in one day," Poteet adds.

"No. It took me a while. It took me a long time. But it was Poteet, an' he encouraged me. He really... I truly... But I'll tell you right now... My family prayed for me for ten years, because I got out there. I got wild an' out there. I did things that I regret so much. I did drugs. I did things that... I didn' care. I didn' care if tomorrow came. I did not care. An' uh... I'm not that person today at all." She begins to cry and adds, "I'm jus' not."

With sadness emanating from his posture, Poteet says, "Well, now you've got Brett."

Through the tears, she responds, "Well, I got you."

"Well, you've got Brett too."

"An' I got Adriel."

"Yeah, you do."

"Adriel?" Elliott asks quietly.

"...my granddaughter."

"That's a lot..." Poteet says, "That's a lot to live for."

Elliott shakes his head and says, "Terry, I'm sorry. I shouldn't have gone there."

Still crying, she looks at Elliott. "No. It's not you at all." She says, "I just needed to tell you that, because I'm a cheerful person today. I'm happy. My life is good, but it hasn't always been that way. I mean... But Poteet... Poteet pulled me out of that dark hole. He did. God first. God did, an' then Poteet. An' then my family too. But I admired Poteet *so much*. I respected him *so much*. There's nothin' that I wouldn't do for 'im. You know what I mean? He helped me realize... You can't change what the past is. You can't... You can't go back. Because I was livin' in anger." She looks over. "Wadn' I, Poteet? I was angry. I was still angry after ten years."

"Your problem was..." Poteet explains, "It's like Roy says. You kept relivin' it."

"I was."

"An' that's where you gotta stop. That's what you gotta conquer. You gotta ask yourself, 'Why am I relivin' this?'"

"Because I was angry, an' I was mad."

"You were."

"An' I didn't know... I didn' know that I shouldn' relive that tragedy over an' over. But... Poteet helped me. He did." Terry dries her tears with her Kleenex and looks at Poteet. She says, "I very seldom talk about this, do I, Poteet?"

"No, not that much."

"I think about it. I think about my son—every day, just about. I miss 'im, an' I always will. But I'm not angry." She says again, shaking her head, "I'm not angry—not anymore. But... It just felt like my world was... I mean... I... I don't remember much about that time. I don't... Even today, I don't remember much. I know I went into shock. An'..."

"Yeah, you did."

"But... I was..." She looks over at Poteet. "I was probably still in some shock when you come along." She turns to Elliott. "But I do know that Poteet guided me through a dark, dark place in my life. An' I'm forever grateful."

Poteet watches Terry with a harrowed brow and soft eyes. He steps toward her.

She holds up her hand in a "Stop" motion and says, "No. I'll be alright." She takes off her glasses again to wipe the tears away.

Poteet and Elliott remain quiet and watch.

When Terry gets her glasses back on, Elliott says, "I'd say that's enough for today." He looks at Terry. "I really didn't mean to do that to you." He shakes his head and says, "I really didn't, and I'm sorry."

Terry stands and looks at Poteet. She says, "I'll close up downstairs. An' then, I'm headin' for the house."

Poteet nods and says, "I'll be right behind ya."

As she walks by, Elliott reaches out.

Terry responds by grabbing his hand and giving it a gentle squeeze.

Elliott watches her walk out. Shaking his head, he says to Poteet, "I'm sorry about opening that wound. I probably should've known."

"There's no way you could've known."

Elliott nods and reaches for the stand holding his recorder. He thinks about Terry's life and how tough it had been. He thinks about how fortunate she was to have met Poteet and for him to have come into her life when he did. He nods and thinks, "Whatever Poteet learned from Roy Masters seems to have worked for Terry too. And that's significant. But... How hard it would be to lose a son." He shakes his head as he thinks about it.

CHAPTER 45

The Story of Loretha and Rowland

When Elliott walks through the double doors the next afternoon, he notices a mostly-blank canvas on Poteet's easel. He says, "That must be what you put together yesterday?"

"Yeah. An' you can see I haven't gotten very far."

"...could be because you keep being interrupted by this movie guy from California."

Poteet chuckles and asks, "Anything goin' on in town last night?"

"I decided to go out for a pizza, and I saw the craziest damn thing."

Poteet smiles.

"It was when I walked by the square down there...looked like they were trying to present some entertainment for the tourists."

"They do that."

"Well... This was a band. There were probably ten of 'em up there on stage. They were dressed up in wild outfits, and it was mostly horn players. They didn't play any songs I knew. They were mostly funny, sometimes serious, but totally entertaining. They had to be locals, and they must've written the songs themselves."

"They *are* locals. I can't think of their name. But yeah, they are entertaining. I've seen 'em a number of times."

"So, I stood there and watched 'em. When they were through, they tried to get people to register to vote." He stares and shakes his head slightly. "It was bizarre."

Poteet shrugs and says, "That's Santa Fe." He then turns back to his canvas.

"I guess it is," Elliott responds and pulls out his recorder. He turns it on, sets it down on the worktable, and looks at Poteet. He says, "...about yesterday. I'm sorry I made her cry." Elliott sighs and adds, "I pushed too hard."

Poteet turns around and says, "She's not mad."

"I feel bad for ruining the mood and taking her back to a really hard time."

"Don't worry. It's not a problem," Poteet says and turns to his palette.

"I hope not."

"An' she actually wanted you to know about that part of her life. Ya know, she said that."

"She did. But... Anyway..."

With a loaded knife, Poteet turns toward his canvas and asks, "Do you know what the shortest sentence in the Bible is?"

Startled and looking up with eyebrows raised, Elliott answers, "Jesus wept."

Poteet chuckles. "Right. How'd you know that?'"

"I remember hearing that some place. It was kind of like a Bible trivia question, I think."

"Anyway, it *is* 'Jesus wept.' An' I tol' Terry. I said, 'If Jesus can weep, so can you. It's okay, ya know. It's all right. But you can't let it take you over.' An' this is what I had to do with 'er when I first met 'er. She was still really hurtin' from the death of 'er son."

"I know you helped her a lot."

With painting knife in hand, Poteet turns to Elliott and says, "I told 'er, 'God didn't mean for you to relive that pain. Ya know, there's a time for you to weep. But then, you have to get over it.' An' I had to keep talkin' to 'er—all the time. An' now, she's fine."

"She does seem to be."

Poteet turns to his table and palette. He says, "She's fine. Ya know. She'll tell ya that. An', she tells me, 'I don' know what I would've done if I hadn' met you.'"

"She said that several times yesterday."

With a loaded knife, Poteet turns to his canvas.

Elliott watches for a moment and then asks, "Do you mind if we talk more about your family?"

"No. That'd be fine."

"Okay. I know you have a sister. You've mentioned her several times."

"I do. She lives down by Idabel. She's six years older than me. An', she was pretty much on her own by the time she was twelve or thirteen. We sometimes stayed together at Mother and Daddy's house, but we didn' have much to do with each other. I guess... Everything considered, she had a pretty normal life—high school an' after. So... By the time I was about fifteen, she was datin' this guy, an' they were gonna get married. But he was from an old family who had money, like... Clarksville, Texas, was named after his family."

"Oh?"

"Yeah."

"Their name was Clark, I guess."

"Uh-huh. An' uh... So, his mother didn' approve of my sister. An' she told Rowland..." Poteet looks at Elliott and explains, "Her boyfriend's name was Rowland."

Elliott nods and says, "You've mentioned your brother-in-law, Rowland, several times too. Seems like you were usually getting into fights together."

Poteet chuckles. "Yeah, we did some o' that. But... Anyway, his mother told 'im... She said, 'If you marry 'er, I'm cuttin' you out of the will.' An' uh... Well, they had a lot of money. So, he told my sister. He said, 'I can't do it. But she ain't gonna live forever.' An' uh... So... My sister said, 'Well, I'm not waitin'.' So, she married someone else."

"I thought Rowland was your brother-in-law."

"You're gettin' ahead of me."

"Okay."

"But anyway, they had a boy."

"Hmm."

"So... They'd been married... I don' know—maybe two or three years. An' Rowland's mother died."

"Oh?"

"Yeah, she did. So... My sister left her husband—right then. She left 'im an' married Rowland."

"Oh."

"I mean, she left that guy in a heartbeat. Yeah."

"So... With Rowland, your sister married into money," Elliott concludes.

"She did. Rowland an' his brother had over five thousand acres there in Texas."

"And they raised cattle?"

"Yeah. But Rowland an' his brother... They got crossways with each other, ya know."

"It happens."

"An' so... Rowland sold his half an' came to Idabel." Elliott nods.

"An' yeah... He bought that place."

"...the ranch?"

"Yeah. It was a thousand-acre cattle ranch?"

"So, that's what he did with his money."

"Actually, I found out later... An' this was through my attorney, just recently... I found out that Rowland never put up any money."

"...to buy that ranch?"

"Uh-huh. My attorney... Ya know, he said, 'Yeah, I handled the paperwork on it.' He said, 'It was in receivership by the people that owned it before. It was government-financed, an' the government didn' really wanna mess with it. An' so, Rowland come in an' jus' said, 'Well, I'll take up the payments.' An' it was like, close to fourteen hundred acres at that time." Poteet turns away from his painting and looks at Elliott. He says, "Yeah" with notable frustration in his voice. "An' uh... He probably operated it... I don' know, ten years or more."

"Huh."

"An' then, that's when he got into trouble—mortgagin' the cattle twice."

"I've heard of people doing that."

"An' that's what got 'im. But yeah... So... When I came into it, all this money was owed on the place, which I had to pay off. An' uh..."

"...seems like it wouldn't have had a mortgage."

"That's what I thought."

"So... He must've managed it poorly. Or he just blew the money he got."

Poteet sighs. He sets his painting knife down and begins cleaning his hands with a rag. He says in a loud voice, "I don't know what the hell they were doin'—my sister an' Rowland. An' I don' know what happened to his money. 'Cause Rowland would go off an' pipeline every so often. Ya know, he went to Alaska—made a lot of money in Alaska on that pipeline."

"So, he... He would do something like what your dad did."

"Uh-huh. Yeah. An'... Ya know, Rowland did it off an' on for years. When the cattle business was good, he was in the cattle business. When it wadn' too good... Well... He'd, ya know... He'd go do somethin' else."

"So... When he got in trouble..." Elliott asks, "Could he

have gotten out of that, if he'd just paid off one of the mortgages?"

"Probably. But he didn' have the money. Huh-uh. No. 'Cause... When he called me... This was in '98. An' uh... He said, 'If you don' buy it, we're gonna lose the whole thing.'"

"Right. You mentioned that, and you bought it."

"I did."

"And you made money."

"I did."

"It's hard to be angry about that."

"I'm not, of course, but... It could've made me two million if I hadn't sold back that bottom part of it, ya know..."

"So, why did you sell?"

"It was to Rowland—after he got out of prison."

"He went to prison?"

"Yeah."

"...for mortgaging the cattle twice?" Elliott asks.

"Yeah. But... When he got out... Here's somebody that had always been a cattleman an' had land. An' he was miserable, ya know... So, I told 'im, I said, 'Whadaya wanna do?' He said, 'Well, I wish I had part of it back, an'...' I said, 'Okay, I'll sell you part of it back.' He said, 'Well, how much you want for it?' An' I said, '...jus' what's owed on it.' ...which was only, when I figured it out, about a hundred dollars an acre. So, I said, 'Just give me a hundred dollars an acre.' An' he did."

"Did he successfully manage the property after that?"

"Well, this is what I'll never understand. Uh... He... He was off pipelinin'. So, he leased it out to these farmers."

Elliott nods. "That would seem to make sense."

Poteet stares at Elliott for a moment before adding, "...with an option to purchase." Poteet breathes deeply and continues, "The last time he leased it out, he gave the man this damn option to buy it."

"Huh."

"He never told me. He never told my sister. He never... An' then when... Then he died, an' the lease ran out. There was this option to buy it. An' the guy exercised his option an' bought it."

"Well... Maybe, your brother-in-law didn't think he could lease it out without including the option?"

"No... No, he didn' have to do that. I don' know why he did it. I really don't. But, when that guy, ya know, said he wanted to buy it... Well... My sister called me. She said, 'I don' wanna sell it.' An' I said, 'You don't have a choice. This is a legal contract. You've gotta sell it.'"

"And her house was on that property?"

"No, her house actually wasn't. She had a homestead."

"Hmm."

"...of a hundred sixty acres, which she's still got."

"...which was a separate piece of property?"

"Uh-huh. It was a separate piece. I mean... It's all one contiguous piece, but the homestead was a cutout." Poteet shakes his head. "An' I still don't know why he did that. It jus' didn'... It didn't make any sense to me why he would do that."

"Hmm."

"But... He did a lot of things that didn' make any sense to me."

"Well, I mean..." Elliott shakes his head. "He started out with money and the place didn't cost him any cash."

"Right. An' I think he was makin' payments on it—yearly payments. But I remember one time... 'Cause he told me... Uh... When he took it over, there were all these government programs..."

"Yeah."

"An' I still get a check, but... He tol' me. He said, 'I can get enough money from the government each year to almost make the payments on this thing.' ...which was fifty thousand a year. An', he was gettin' thirty-somethin' thousand from the government. So... Yeah... An' these programs were... They were payin' us *not* to do somethin'," Poteet says and looks at Elliott, shaking his head.

Elliott chuckles and says, "Right."

"...not to grow this. ...not to grow that." Poteet pauses. ...then adds, "We weren't gonna grow it anyway."

Elliott laughs and Poteet joins in.

"Yeah. An' there's a lot of those ranchers down there that made their whole livin' jus' doin' that."

"Huh."

"I mean, you could go down to the Farm Service Agency. You'd see 'em. They're jus' sittin' around, waitin' for the next new program to pop up."

"Hmm."

"Yeah."

Terry sticks her head in and says, "I'll tell you a little bit about Poteet."

Elliott looks over and says, "I didn't hear you out there."

"I wore my tennis shoes today." She points to the adjacent room. "I had to check on somethin' in there, an' I heard y'all."

"Okay. So, what can you tell me about Poteet?"

She walks in and sits in her regular spot. She crosses her legs, leans forward, and says, "He has been so generous. I've never seen a brother as generous as he has been with Loretha. Ya know. He saved the ranch. He saved 'em when her husband went to jail. An' uh... He... He took over an' made the payments an' all that stuff. An' then, when Rowland got out of jail, he sold Rowland five hundred acres for a hundred dollars an acre, just so he could have his own land, ya know. He gave her horses, trailers, trucks, horse barns, their ranch back..."

Poteet nods and says, "Yeah."

"...uh, Kubotas, zero-turn mowers. I mean, it just goes on." She looks at Poteet and says, "There's no tellin' how much money you actually gave her, is there?"

"Huh-uh. No tellin'."

Elliott says, "That's amazing."

"I wouldn't be afraid to say a million," Terry speculates.

"Oh, probably more than that," Elliott suggests. "...if you look at the value of the ranch."

Poteet nods and says, "Yeah."

"He made her a millionaire," Terry asserts. "...by givin' her that land for a hundred dollars an acre."

"I told 'er I'd give 'er a horse. An' I said, 'Take your pick. You can have any horse you want.' An' uh... I had one, an' she was worth quite a bit a money. Loretha took her, an' I said, 'Well, that's fine.' An' she's been ridin' that horse for all these years now, ya know. She runs barrels. I guess she still does. I haven't talked to 'er for over a year now."

"...your older sister's still barrel racing?"

Poteet chuckles and says, "Yeah."

"...in her 70s?"

"Yep."

"Huh."

"An' winnin'," Poteet says with a smile. "She won... She was tellin' me about the... I think she was in Texarkana, an' she won that thing. An' she said... After her run, she went over an' tied the horse to the trailer, so she could go to the concession stand an' get a Coke. When she returned, somebody had hung a handicapped sticker..."

Elliott laughs.

Poteet grins and finishes, "...off her saddle horn. An' man, that pissed 'er off."

Elliott laughs until he can say, "That's funny."

"But yeah... It's been a few years since... But... There's a rodeo there in Oklahoma. It's the same rodeo that Dobson Rader an' *Esquire* come down to write about," Poteet explains and then looks at Elliott. "Remember. I told you."

"Right. The oldest rodeo or something."

"Yeah. But she entered that thing the first time when she was... I think she was fifteen. An' her husband, before he died..."

Terry stands and says, "I've got to get downstairs. I'm meetin' somebody..." She looks at her watch. "...in two minutes."

Elliott says, "Okay."

They watch Terry walk out.

"But anyway... Before he died, he said, 'Why don't you get in that rodeo again?' She said, 'Oh, I don' wanna do it.' An' he said, 'Aw, get in it.' She said, 'No. I don' want to.' Then after he died, she said, 'I'm gonna do that for 'im.' So, she did. An' before she made her run, the announcer come on an' said, 'This young lady's from Idabel, Oklahoma.' He said, uh... 'She's makin' her return trip, sixty years later.'"

Elliott laughs.

"An' people were like, 'What?'"

Elliott continues to laugh but can say, "I'm sure."

"An' out she comes. An' boy, I'm telling ya. Yeah. She didn' win it, but..."

Elliott whispers, "Wow."

"Yeah."

"People would think, 'No. I didn't hear that right.'"

"Uh-huh."

"That's what I'd think," Elliott remarks.

"I'll tell ya... She can ride the hair off of 'em."

"That's amazing. It really is. And the way it ended with the handicap sticker and then competing again after sixty years to honor her deceased husband. I like it. It's another really good story. And again, I love that it's real."

"Yeah, it's real alright,"

"It's a little rough around the edges. But I'm telling you, it's another great love story. Your sister was always in love with Rowland, even to the point of honoring his memory with the racing. The rodeo brings some great action to the story. And then, there's the part about Rowland going to jail." He looks at Poteet. "And your sister stayed with him."

"She did."

"I don't think it's quite Terry's Cinderella story, but it's a really good story."

"That may be. But... Jus' so ya know, I've still got *my* five hundred acres."

"I would guess that you're glad of that."

"I am. But I never would've bought it, ya know, except that he asked me to. I did it for them."

"Of course. Yeah. That's obvious."

"Her an' Rowland... Yeah... They stayed together for a long time—a long time."

"Until he passed away."

"Right."

"So... Can we get back to your mother?"

"Sure."

"Is she still alive?"

"No. An' I forget what year that was. She had emphysema an' COPD, probably from workin' in those cafés, breathin' that smoke, ya know. That's what I think it was."

"Okay. So... Did your relationship with your mother ever change?" As Elliott asks, his mind jumps to the relationship he'd had with his own mother. It hadn't been the best, and he'd had very little respect for her while she was alive. As he had grown older, he seemed to find more empathy in his heart for who she was, considering the problems she faced.

CHAPTER 46

...on Generosity

"I was never close to my mother. Uh... Ya know, I had a responsibility, an' I knew that. So... When she started gettin' older, I did take care of 'er."

"Like Terry said, you're a generous person."

"I saw it more as a responsibility."

"I'm sure you did a lot, and I see that as generous."

"Maybe. But I've learned some things about bein' generous."

"Like what?"

"Well... We've helped a lot of people. Ya know, we used to... It started... Uh... I tol' Terry. I said, 'I'm not goin' through this—buyin' you Christmas presents an' buyin' you birthday presents. I'm not gonna do that."

"Okay."

"It puts too much pressure on somebody.' An' I said, 'I hate it for people durin' Christmas, when they're strugglin' an' they're wonderin' what they're gonna do.' An' I said, 'No.' I said, 'I buy you stuff all the time.' Ya know... An' I do. I said, 'It dudn' have to be a certain day... I don' know... It's been about three years ago. I said, 'Well, we're not gonna be spendin' all that money on ourselves.' I said, 'There's a lot of kids down there—from home, that I know... They're not gonna have anything.' So... We, uh... I don' know. I was sendin' like... What was it? A hundred or two-hundred-dollar gift certificates to these families. Ya know... An'... I think I spent somethin' like—close to three thousand dollars. An' then, we'd get a phone call from somebody. 'Well, here's this family. They don't even have any shoes an' stuff.' An' she'd come in here... 'Can we do that?' 'Yeah. We can do that one too.' So... I think I was up to around four thousand dollars." Poteet laughs.

"Wow."

"An' uh... I did that for two years. But the last year..." Poteet sighs. "I tell ya. It's just unreal. People were callin' an' sayin' shit... They were almost like *demandin'* it."

"Oh, that's a shame."

"An' I said, '...to hell with it. We're jus' not gonna do it. ...jus' not gonna do it anymore.'"

"That's unfortunate."

"Yeah. Because we were tryin' to help some of these kids that didn't have anything, but... I'll tell ya. People down there though... The reason a lot of 'em don't have anything is because of drugs. An' they get that certificate... Hell, they'll jus' go trade it for drugs or somethin'. So..."

"Yeah," Elliott responds softly.

"So... I told 'er, 'Hell, let's jus' give it to...' Ya know, she wanted to give it to the Shriners Hospital, 'cause her son went through Shriners. I said, 'Okay.' An', we've been givin' to Saint Jude's, Wounded Warriors, these different organizations an' things. Uh... But... Yeah, I think you have to. I mean... If God has blessed you, you should give back. You really should."

"I believe that. Yeah."

"...any way you can. But you have to be careful 'bout how you do it. An' I know this firsthand too, ya know. Most people are manipulators. It's what Roy Masters calls that Dracula/Vampire thing."

"I haven't heard about that."

"Yeah. You will. It's like they live off of your life blood, ya know. A perfect example of that is my sister. 'Cause... The more I helped her an' her family, the more they resented me."

"And you think that's typical?"

"I think... Yeah. I've had it happen more than once. But... This... Tryin' to please people is the worst thing you can do. It really is. I mean, forget all that."

"Hmm."

"I got to where... An' I still don't. I mean... Every person I know that needed money has come to me, an' I jus' go, 'Nope. Can't do it.'"

"Mm-hmm."

"I'm not gonna do that. Ya know, if you... I've had people come out here. 'Can I borrow five hundred dollars?' An'... 'Nope. I'll tell you what I will do, though. I'll give you a hundred bucks to get you down the road, an' you don' even have to pay me back.'"

"Okay?"

"That's the way I handle it. An' I've... I've tried to tell Terry. I said, 'If anything ever happens to me, people are gonna be all over you.' An' I've made her... I said, 'You promise me that you'll do what I do?'"

Elliott says, "That's a good idea."

"Ya know, that's another thing about my sister. When I would be kind of down an' out... An' there were plenty of those times. She wouldn't have anything to do with me. Then... When I was doin' good an' could help 'er..."

"I guess, all the help ran one way."

"Yeah. Oh yeah. Always."

"But... Back to your mother..."

"Okay."

"Sounds like she kind of came in and out of your life."

"Yeah. After I got grown, I remember comin' to town. I

was livin' in Dallas. I'd come to town, an' I wouldn' go see 'er. An' she'd act like she was really hurt or somethin'. An' I'm thinkin', 'Well... What's the deal?' Ya know, we never had that kind of relationship. An' uh... I think she died an angry woman. My sister never helped 'er, when she got older. An' uh... But I did. I gave 'er my American Express card, an' I said, Jus'... Whatever you need, get it. Ya know, you jus' get it."

"Again, that's generous."

"I bought 'er a new car. An' uh... But I jus' felt like it was my obligation. I've always been a responsible person like that, but..."

Elliott strokes his beard and says, "We've talked about your grandmother."

"Right."

"...your mother's mother."

"Yes."

"And... She had animals. She had horses."

"Well no. She didn't have horses. She didn't like horses, 'cause the horses would bite her cows."

"Oh yeah, that's right. And she worked really hard."

"Yeah. She did. She had to." Poteet chuckles. "An' yeah, this friend of mine... It's this Israeli guy... He came in today."

"Okay?"

"An' we were talkin'. Kind of like this. He was askin' me about my family. An' I was tellin' 'im... I said, 'On my mom's side, they were Welsh.' An' he said, 'Really?' He said, 'Ya know, the Welsh are very interesting people,' an'... He said, 'They keep to themselves, an' they're the tightest people in the world.' So, I told 'im. I said, 'My grandmother wouldn' even give me a nickel.' An' he said, 'Well yeah, that's typical.' He said, 'They're very, very frugal.' An' he said, 'You notice... You never hear about people goin' to Wales. They always go to Scotland an' Ireland an' all that.' He said, 'The Welsh... They don't want you over there.'"

Elliott begins to chuckle.

"He said, 'They don't. They like to be...' He said, 'They'll be very nice to you.' But then, they want you to go." He motions with his hands. "...to go away."

Elliott laughs. And then, Poteet laughs.

Elliott says, "Huh. That's true. You don't really hear about people going to Wales."

"No, you don't."

"Yeah. But on my family... My father left when I was five. My mother died angry. I've helped my sister a lot, but she won't even talk to me."

"I think we'd call that dysfunctional."

"...or worse," Poteet laments. He then turns back to his table and his palette. "But... You've got to take into account... We lived in Idabel, Oklahoma. An' that place is jus' nuts. It was then, an' it still is."

Elliott chuckles and says, "It must be."

"Every time I pick up, ya know, these newspapers..." Poteet picks up a folded newspaper.

"So... You take the Idabel newspaper?"

"I do. An' it's always, 'This man here... He beat the hell out of somebody over there.'"

Elliott takes off his glasses and rubs his eyes.

Poteet turns to Elliott. "I thought of this, an' I meant to tell you."

As he's putting his glasses back on, Elliott says, "Okay."

"It's what I see about myself lookin' back."

Elliott nods.

Poteet sets his painting knife down and leans against his table. With arms crossed, he says, "It was the times when I was really searchin' spiritually... Those were the best times in my life. Because... There were times I wadn' at all. I mean, I wadn'. Anything spiritual was out of the picture. An' then, when I, uh... When I came to Santa Fe, that changed everything. I got back on track, an' then things worked out. But... Yeah... Back durin' the 80s. I was kind of lost—spiritually. It was in the 90s that I found Roy Masters."

"Obviously, that was important to you."

"It was," Poteet says and retrieves his painting knife from his table.

Elliott turns to look out the window, concerned about Poteet's infatuation with this man. He knows that Roy Masters was personally helpful to him, but he's afraid that this type of devotion to a spiritual leader could make Poteet less appealing. He's afraid that Poteet's beliefs could likely torpedo this project.

Elliott knows that there are many people in the country and beyond who adhere very closely to their spiritual beliefs. But he also knows that most of them aren't in southern California. Personally, he hardly knows anyone this caught up in the spiritual side of their lives. He knows some who are off the deep end in some far-out religions, but this is different. Poteet seems to hold some deep-seated Judeo-Christian beliefs. Elliott scratches his head and thinks about some of the whacky and controversial things he's heard from Poteet. It seemed like most of that was what he'd learned from Masters.

Elliott studies Poteet as he applies a layer of bright yellow paint to his canvas. Poteet moves with the fluid ease and precision of a virtuoso violinist. He has a way of letting earlier paint layers bleed though just enough to let them say, "Hey, I'm here." His technique is beautiful and provides the perfect contrast and a depth to his paintings.

Elliott is thinking he might be willing to cut this talented painter some slack. He feels like all of Poteet's focus on spirituality might be a result of his Native American DNA. He hopes his partners will see it that way too.

Elliott's attention snaps back to Poteet, when he hears him saying, "'...I know I'm not long for the world.'"

"Are you saying... Was it Roy Masters who said that?" Elliott asks.

"Yeah. Ya know, he's ninety. But..." Poteet turns to face Elliott. "Roy said, 'No matter what situation I'm in, there's always a calmness that I feel.' An' he said, 'It's not...' He said, 'It's not somethin' that I do.' He said, 'I know where this is comin' from.' He said, 'I never thought I would be what I am today—about helpin' people through God an' all.' But..."

"I have some questions about Roy Masters, based on some things you've said."

"Okay," Poteet responds as he moves back to his palette.

"I think you said..." Elliott pauses. He then continues, "...that you shouldn't be in church."

"That's right."

"And that's his point of view?" Elliott asks for clarity.

"That's exactly what he says."

Elliott massages his lips with two fingers for a moment before repeating, "...that you shouldn't be in church."

"Yeah. He... Ya know... Because he said... 'So, look at this. How many religions are out there?' He said, 'Hell... There's religions out there that are based on a misinterpretation of one verse of the Bible.'"

Elliott nods and says, "I believe that's true."

"He says, 'They all can't be right.' He said, 'I mean, that's obvious, idn' it?' He said, 'Most of 'em are up there talkin' just to hear themselves talk.'"

"Unfortunately, that may be true."

"But it's been good for me," Poteet says and chuckles. With a loaded knife he begins applying more paint. "Because... Literally... After I got into this, I could pick up the Bible an' read a verse an' see it totally different than I ever saw it before. Because..." Still facing his painting, he turns his head toward Elliott and says, "Ya know, through Roy's teachings, I could see what they were talkin' about."

"That makes sense."

He turns back and continues applying the paint. "An' if you truly believe... An' Roy does. He says 'I'm a Jew.' An' he says, 'Really, there's no such thing as a Christian.' He said, 'Jesus wadn' a Christian. He was a Jew.' It's who he was. He was a Jew."

"So, Roy's a practicing Jew?"

"He is. An' I'm sure, that's one of the reasons he opposes the Muslims."

"He opposes Muslims?"

"Oh yeah. He's against almost everything they do."

Elliott raises one eyebrow and breathes out a quick rush of air. He shakes his head and thinks, "This issue could be trouble." After a moment, he says, "But let's get back to Roy being a Jew and talking to people about Jesus."

"Okay. He says, 'People get hung up in this thing—bein' a Christian. But bein' a Christian is... You have to see what Jesus was seein', an' Jesus was a Jew.'"

"Jesus *was* a Jew," Elliott says. "I know that much."

"Right. So, I'm thinkin', 'Maybe the man's got a point.'"

Elliott closes his eyes and then looks up. He says, "Well, the hard part about what you've been saying—the part about not going to church..."

"Right."

Elliott takes off his glasses and rubs his eyes. He puts his glasses back on and says, "How do we..." He pauses again uncomfortably. "And I'm not an example of a good Christian, by any means. It's unusual for me to make more than a Christmas program and an Easter service every year."

"I don' go at all."

"I know that," Elliott responds and has a sense that he's getting in too deep. He continues anyway. "And again, I'm the wrong person to be making this point, but... How do the masses deal with this? Because... Traditionally..." He opens his palms with his fingers spread apart. "Traditionally, we think... We go to church to learn about the spiritual side of our lives and how to be better people."

"Right."

"And church is where we hear that message." Elliott can barely believe what he's hearing himself say.

"Sure. I get it. But that's not what's worked for me. Like I told you, I've spent a lot of my life searchin' for spiritual answers, an'... For me, it's been Roy Masters. He's got books. He's got a radio show. An' it's led me to a deeper level of understanding, ya know. I could read the Bible twenty years ago... Now, I pick it up, an' I look at it from a different point of view. An' I see it in a different way."

"Mm-hmm," Elliott says and has to admit to himself that much of what Poteet is saying makes sense.

Poteet continues, "I agree with Roy Masters, an' I think the Bible was divinely written. An' I think everybody, no matter what level you're at, can get some understanding of it. No matter whether you're a little kid, or what. But there's an underlying principle to what Roy teaches, an' uh... He says, '*You* can't do anything.' He says, 'If you do *nothing*—right'—which means do 'nothing'—if you do that right, you can do nothing wrong."

Elliott shakes his head and repeats slowly, "If you do 'nothing' right..." He chuckles.

"Yeah."

"I'll have to think about that," Elliott says and again looks toward the window to digest the past few minutes of conversation.

Poteet continues, "Yeah, you'll need to give that some thought. It took me a while, an' you have to understand where he's comin' from."

"Okay."

"You've gotta understand that *you're* not doin' it. You're

lettin' *God* do it. You let life flow out of you. That's what he's sayin', 'Let life flow through you.' Ya know. An' Bear Heart said the same thing. He said to stay in constant prayer."

Elliott tilts his head and narrows his eyes. After a moment he asks, "So, Bear Heart would say that?"

"Yeah. But... Ya know, it dudn' mean you have to walk around mumblin'. It's like... What Roy was sayin', an' what Bear Heart was sayin' are the same thing. Is that... Bein' in constant prayer means that you're allowin' God to flow through you. *You're* not doin' it. You're just sort of... You're just observin' this thing while it happens."

"Do you think Bear Heart affected you spiritually?"

"Of course, he did. He was a medicine man. That's what he was all about. That's how I know about 'Stayin' in constant prayer.'"

"But then you found Roy Masters."

"That's right."

"So... For yourself, you could meld the ancient Native American customs with Christian teachings as taught by a Jew."

"Sure," Poteet responds as he chuckles. "Seems kind of crazy when you put it that way, but... It's all about connectin' to the universe. Bear Heart an' my ancestors are about connectin' to the earth. That's how they've traditionally seen those relationships. Roy sees it, both as a Jew an' as a Christian. He sees it as a connection to God—the God of the Universe. They both see it as a connection to somethin' greater than themselves an' a force that can intervene in our lives. There's more commonality there than you might think."

"It's always seemed to me that humans have a need to acknowledge a higher power." Elliott finds himself revealing more elements of his own faith than he intended.

"I've always thought so, an' uh... I've always recognized that need in myself, an' I've tried to understand it. Whether a lot of that was comin' from my Indian side, I don' know."

"...interesting," Elliott acknowledges and feels that Poteet is right on track. He continues, "From what you've said, it seems like... At least some of, maybe a lot of, what Roy Masters talks about is based on the Bible."

"It is. Ya know. He says it all the time, 'I love your Jesus.'"

"Even as a Jew..."

"Yeah..." Poteet says and starts to chuckle.

"And so... He actually agrees with everything that's there."

"He does...everything. Yeah...everything."

Elliott nods slowly and says under his breath, "Yeah, wow... So..."

"I don' know how all this talk about Roy Masters fits into my story, but..."

"Well, it's... You're telling your story, and that's part of it, which..." Elliott struggles for words. "So... Does it..." He pauses and stares at the ceiling. He looks back at Poteet. "Does it somehow tie back to seeing Jesus in the closet?" After asking, Elliott is afraid that he shouldn't have gone there again.

Without hesitation, Poteet answers, "I think so. Yeah... 'Cause there was... I told you there was always that pull on me, like it was with art...to somehow know more...to have a closer relationship with it, ya know. 'Cause, I look back on it...bein' a little boy an' goin' to all the churches—different churches. Nobody took me."

"Yeah, I think that's amazing."

"I'd... I'd jus' go."

"Yeah. Because you were motivated with... I don't know... I mean, partly through that experience."

"Yeah. I mean... When the other kids... I knew they were there because their parents had brought 'em an' said, 'You're goin' to Sunday school.' They didn' wanna be there, but... I just felt like... An' I don' know. I was just pulled in that direction."

"Okay. So, fast-forward..."

Poteet nods.

"Your spiritual journey has gone from taking yourself to Sunday School to following Roy Masters."

"Yeah. That's right."

"So... For you, Roy Masters is the one who's figured it out."

"He is."

"Is there anybody else?"

"Not that I know of. An' believe me, I've... I've searched..."

"I believe you have."

"I have. An' it's jus' like... Ya know, I've done all these different meditations, like with a mantra. It's where you get into this state, an' you say the mantra. An' uh... But Roy says, 'No. Don't do that.'" Poteet chuckles. "No. When you do that, you're tryin' to hypnotize yourself."

"Oh?"

"Roy said, 'No...' An' he said, 'Jesus said it Himself: "By Myself, I can do nothing."' Roy says, 'Well, you can't either. You can't do anything either.' So, you're out there tryin' to make yourself a better person... An' I've heard 'im say this. He says, 'You think... Because you give to this an' you give to that an' blah, blah, blah, you're...' He said, 'Do you think you're gonna buy your way into this?' He said, 'You ain't.' He said, 'You cannot...'"

As he feels the vibration of his mobile phone, Elliott is nervously trying to overcome a sudden sense of guilt. He stands and stretches as he looks at his phone. He then says, "I need to take a break."

"Gettin' a little heavy for ya?"

Elliott smiles and replies. "Maybe..."

"I guess we should lighten it up and talk about Roy's theories on physics for a while," Poteet says and smiles.

Elliott shakes his head and chuckles as he walks out the door.

Poteet then turns to his painting table.

In a few minutes, Elliott returns and says, "I needed to talk to my wife. She's planning a vacation for us. It's next year, but she had some questions for me."

"Sure...no problem."

As he sits back down, Elliott says, "And... For some reason, it made me think of your trip to Hawaii."

Poteet chuckles.

"I wondered if you had ever gone on a vacation... I mean, before that?" Prior to receiving an answer, Elliott's mind jumps to his own upcoming trip. He feels like they will enjoy some extended time in Florence. He knew that he'd like the art. And the pace of life might be a little more comfortable than the time they'd spent in Rome.

CHAPTER 47

Controversy on Top of Controversy

Poteet answers, "No."

Elliott quickly recalls what he had asked and follows up, "So... You might've been thinking, 'Everybody else had been on vacations.'"

"Right."

"And, you hadn't."

"That's true."

"So... It starts bugging you, and it just keeps building up and building up, until you've got to do something about it. So... you want to go to the best place you could think of at the time, which was Hawaii."

"I guess," Poteet says and shrugs.

"So... You think, 'I can do this. I'm going to go. I'm going to have myself a vacation.'"

Poteet laughs, and Elliott joins in.

"Yeah. I didn'... I don't think I looked at it as a vacation, but... I knew when I got off that plane, an' I was broke... It damn sure wadn' a vacation then."

Elliott and Poteet laugh together.

"And from that meager start, you turned it into a thriving company."

"It was a tough beginning. That's for sure."

"And I can see you walking into Hanes," Elliott says and they laugh again. "...with that million T-shirt order."

Poteet stops laughing and says, "Yeah. Well, I think that it goes back to what Roy said."

"Which was...?"

"God has a plan for you. Just let it flow."

"Was that's God's plan for you?"

"I guess it was, ya know. Because it was the furthest thing from my mind. I had no idea how that was gonna turn out. Or the trip to New York... An' even comin' out here... Ya know."

"Yeah."

"But it all turned out good."

"It did."

"All of it..."

"Yeah. But you weren't into Roy Masters at that time."

"Right. But I was still searchin' spiritually. I think I told you about that ashram where I lived in L.A."

"You did."

"So... I mean, my spiritual journey was all over the place."

"Right." Elliott nods, mostly to himself. He had to admit that Poteet wasn't always looking for spiritual answers in the Bible or in Christian churches. Early on, it was mostly places other than that. He looks directly at the painter and says, "I feel like that's another success for you."

Poteet raises his eyebrows and says, "I guess."

"...a successful journey. I mean, you were searching at a very young age, you know...taking yourself to church...trying to figure it all out."

Poteet nods.

"And then, there was the thing in L.A."

"Right."

"After that, your spirituality went dormant for a while. And then, you wound up with Roy Masters."

"Yeah. That's about how it went."

"But Roy Masters... Just based upon what you've told me... Some of his views are very controversial."

"Oh yeah, they are. But he's been on Sean Hannity. He's been on..."

Elliott interrupts, "...Sean Hannity?"

"Oh yeah, he's been on Hannity. But ya know... They could only put 'im on there, like one time." Poteet laughs.

"I would imagine." Elliott chuckles and says, "It's like... Man, don't put that guy on here again. You'll get us thrown off the air."

Still laughing, Poteet says, "Yeah, that's about right. But... Once you understand where he's comin' from... I mean, you really can't, uh... You can't disagree with 'im too much. There was... I can't remember this famous atheist. I watched that interview. They were debatin' each other, an' Roy jus' destroyed 'im."

"Huh. I should see that."

"Yeah. Yeah."

"You'd think that'd be archived some place."

"I'm sure it is. It may be on his website or YouTube or some other website. You could call up there an' ask. ...like, 'What was the famous interview Roy did with the atheist?'"

"Yeah, I might do that."

"You'll learn, like I did."

"Seems like most of our conversations today have ended up at Roy Masters."

Poteet strokes the hair on top of his head with his fingers and replies, "I guess that's true. But somethin' else about Roy... An' I think it was back in the seventies. He was the nation's foremost expert on hypnosis."

"Okay?"

"He had a clinic in Houston, an' people would come in to get help for quittin' smokin' or other things. He'd hypnotize 'em to do that. Uh... But he said he started to notice that some people were easy. ...could be hypnotized like that." Poteet snaps his fingers. "An' others were more difficult. What he found out was that the people that were hard to hypnotize were Christians. So... He's written some books about that. He's written so many books. Uh... But he says that we can become hypnotized, ya know, even at a young age, through trauma an' different things."

"And so, he would call things like that hypnosis?"

"It is hypnosis. Yeah. He said that most of us don't realize we're under hypnosis right now."

"Okay. So... While we're still on Roy Masters, I want to follow up on something else you mentioned. But you said that he, uh... He is totally against the Muslim religion—Sharia law an' all of that."

"Yeah."

"And uh... That again is so politically incorrect."

"I know it's not PC. But, when you..." Poteet pauses mid-sentence and looks over at Elliott. "You've read those excerpts from the Quran where, ya know... If you don't believe the way we do, you need to die?"

"Yeah. I've heard about that."

"Now, how in the hell can anybody back that up? Ya know."

"They can't. But... They'll say you're a Islamophobist."

"I'd agree with 'em. I'd say, 'Yeah... I am. Sure.'"

"Being the Devil's advocate here..." Elliott breathes deeply. "What if they say, 'Well then, you're a terrible person, and there's no reason to talk to you anymore.'"

"I'd say, 'No. I jus' see it clearer than you do.' I mean... I see these bumper stickers that say, 'Coexist'—spelled out in religious symbols. How in the hell can I coexist with somebody who wants to kill me? It's a hypnotic state. That's what Roy says. I mean, they start real young programmin' their kids into this. But I also see some tenants of hypnotism in some of the Christian churches around here. I mean... If there's more emphasis on historical rituals than studyin' the Bible, you might have a problem."

"I've never thought of it like that."

"An' then... You've got the PC crowd who thinks that all religions are the same. But they're not. Then, you got all these... I mean... These young kids that are all about social-ism... It's crazy."

"I live in L.A, and a lot of my friends aren't so sure."

"Yeah. Well, they're crazy too," Poteet says and shakes his head. "No... They're not crazy. They're jus' misinformed."

"They are misinformed. And they won't allow themselves to be otherwise. It doesn't really make sense."

"For decades, it's what they've been taught. I'm half surprised you're not one of 'em."

"I had a couple of good economics classes in college and learned about 'The Russian Experiment.'" He uses air quotes. "Most of the people you're talking about are younger and were never exposed to those things. I heard somewhere that, uh... That somebody had done a poll, and they'd asked kids, college-age kids if they'd ever heard of Mao Tse Tung."

"Hmm."

"Eighty-nine percent had never even heard of 'im."

Poteet shakes his head and repeats softly, "...hadn't heard of Mao."

"Uh-huh... And then, they asked how many had heard of Joseph Stalin?"

"Huh."

"And again, it was a small percentage."

"Really?"

"Most hadn't even heard of Stalin. So..."

"I shouldn't be... But I am surprised," Poteet admits. "An' they're walkin' around with Che Guevara T-shirts on. He was a bloodthirsty murderer. That's what he was."

"Yeah. I know that, but I can't say it. If I did, my investors would walk right out the door."

Poteet shakes his head for effect. He looks at Elliott and says, "It's like this."

"Okay."

"If you've been taught that that's"—Poteet points at a splash of aqua on his palette—"not aqua but it's raw sienna."

Elliott nods and says, "Yeah?"

"An' you're talkin' to someone, an' they say, 'That's aqua.' You go, 'No, it's not. It's raw sienna.' There can be confusion about things."

"That I can understand."

"Yeah."

"But... There's the reality of the actual history..."

"You're right."

"Kids don't get very much of that."

"And they don't teach civics anymore," Poteet says. "An'... One of the great quotes from Frank Zappa is: 'How are you gonna know what your rights are, if you don' know what they are?'"

Elliott chuckles and asks, "Frank Zappa said that?"

"Yeah."

Poteet begins to chuckle too.

"...in a song? ...or what, in an interview?" Elliott asks.

"It was in an interview I read."

"Well... He was... He was like a Ph.D. or something."

"He's a very smart guy," Poteet says and smiles. "So, how're you gonna exercise your rights, if you don't even know what the hell they are?"

As Elliott says, "I think he's got a point," he turns his head to see Terry walk in.

She says, "There's a woman down there who's just crazy about my Honey Badger, an' I'm lettin' 'em bond for a few minutes, ya know. I think he might be able to help me sell a portrait." She smiles. "She's down there lookin' at 'em now."

"Good for Honey," Poteet says with a grin.

Elliott glances at his watch and then up at Terry. "It's time for me to go. But can I ask you a couple of things while Honey Badger's selling this portrait?"

Terry smirks, crosses her arms, and replies, "Sure. Whadayawanna talk about?"

Elliott chuckles. "I'm still trying to envision Honey Badger selling a portrait."

"Oh! That'll happen. You jus' watch. I know how this works."

"Well, when he can run her charge card through the machine... That's... That's when we make a movie about *him*."

All three laugh.

When Poteet and Terry are both staring at Elliott, he remembers the questions he wanted to ask Terry. He sits up to say, "I'm surprised at how much of our conversation today kept circling back to Roy Masters."

"You shouldn' be surprised," Terry says. "He studies those books, an' he listens to those tapes all the time. Oh yeah, Poteet's an expert on Roy Masters."

"Do *you* study Roy Masters?"

"No. I don't think anyone studies Roy Masters like Poteet. I like what he says, but there's a lot of it I don' understand. I'm actually more comfortable with your good-ol' southeast-Oklahoma Baptist preacher. We don' go to church here, but I sometimes listen on the Internet to a preacher I like."

"Do you understand how controversial Roy Masters is and what he teaches?" Elliott asks and then moves his eyes from Terry to Poteet—half expecting a disapproving facial expression. Not seeing one, he looks back at Terry for an answer.

"Oh, I'm aware. An' I agree with a lot of it. Most women

are evil, an' I *like* for Poteet to be the boss. Like I've said... It was the first time in my relationship with a man—for me to not be the boss. An' I like it. I really do." She smiles and points at Elliott. "I tell people that all the time."

Elliott looks back at Poteet, who hasn't changed expressions. He nods and looks at Terry. "Well... That's what I wanted to know."

Terry winks at Elliott. She says, "I think it's about time to get back."

Elliott chuckles to himself and begins gathering his stuff. He and Poteet make some tentative plans for the next morning and he heads for the stairs.

On the way out, he sticks his head into the office and sees the customer point and say, "I think I want that one."

Terry glances over and notices Elliott. He gives a quick wave as he grins and points at Honey Badger.

CHAPTER 48

"...when you tell a woman that."

The next morning Elliott walks through the double doors and takes a moment to look at Poteet's current work in progress. He's surprised at how much it's changed since he last saw it. Now, it's mostly blue and yellow. He asks, "What are you doing with this one?"

"There'll be two Indian braves inside a large circle. I'm workin' on the background now." He points. "The circle will be over here."

Elliott smiles and says, "I like those colors."

Poteet nods. "It's the colors that draw a person to a painting. So... For me, it's about gettin' that part right."

"I see."

"An' that's what sets artists apart in my book. Some can do wet-on-wet, but most can't."

Elliott points at his recorder and says, "I had a chance last night to listen to some of our past conversations."

"Oh yeah?"

"I can't decide what I think about Roy Masters."

Poteet chuckles. "I can understand that. If they don't hate 'im outright, that's the way most people feel."

"But... He helped *you* a lot."

447

"He did."

"You went up there to meet him."

"Yeah. I did. He's got a little... Oh, it's a... He calls it a ranch...no animals on it, but... It's probably... I don' know. What? ...thirty, forty acres. He's got a real nice little lake."

"Does he broadcast from there?"

"I think so. Yeah. He used to broadcast out of L.A. But I think he can do it from there now."

"You'd think he would. Travel at his age could be a problem."

"Right."

"And... As we've been discussing, there's a strong spiritual component to his teachings."

"There is," Poteet says and looks at Elliott. "An' I needed that. I still do." He turns back to his painting. "Because... I feel like... When you're young, ya know, you're workin' on a borrowed religion. I call it 'borrowed,' 'cause you're borrowin' it from other people—mostly older people. An' then you start on your own trek."

"Mm-hmm."

Poteet sets his painting knife down on his palette to continue, "Well, that didn' really answer it for me. Yeah, I've lived, ya know... I've done all kinds of different meditations."

"I know."

"But it's come full circle for me now. I've got my own interpretation of it, instead of somebody else's. Like... Who was Jesus Christ? Well... When you're young, you know all about that from Sunday School an' everything. But... Now, you have a personal relationship. An' it... It means more—somethin' totally different."

"So... It sounds like you've become a conventional Christian."

Poteet looks down and folds his arms. He looks up to say, "I'm not sure 'conventional' is the right way to describe me."

Elliott chuckles. "So, what *would* you call yourself?"

"I have a connection to the universe—an' God. I read the Bible an' other books. An' I listen to Roy. I think my understanding of all this is closer to Roy's than anybody else's."

"But... Roy doesn't have a church."

"You're right. An' that's why it's hard to put a label on what I am."

Elliott nods. "But... He must have a place where people can come."

"He does. An' when he's speakin'... Right behind 'im, there's always a sign. It says, 'Be still an' know. Be still an' know I am God.' An' that's... He really means it. You gotta get still enough, an' that's through the meditations."

"Hmm. I'm pretty sure that most Christian churches don't do meditations."

"That's true. But Roy says that you need to get still enough where you can separate from your problems."

"Huh."

"'Cause he was always sayin' about anything that's botherin' ya... If you can get still an' jus' start lookin' at this thing, it'll take off. It'll leave you."

"I don't think I get that."

"Roy says that if something's really botherin' ya..."

"Okay."

"...an' if you'll get still an' start to look at it... You don't have to think about it. You don't have to do anything. Jus' look at it. He relates it to... Ya know, turnin' on the light to a cockroach, an' it runs off. An' I've experienced that. I know what he's talkin' about."

"Huh..."

"I listen to his program sometimes. People call in, an' they'll tell 'im. They'll say, 'Well, you've just got it all wrong. I mean, you're all wrong about that. I mean...' Roy tells 'em,

'No!' He says, 'Men have to be men.' He says, 'You aren't here to love the woman.' He says, 'What you're here for is to love the hell out of 'er—not to love the hell that's in 'er.'"

Elliott takes a deep breath and says, "Again... I'm surprised he hasn't been run out of the country."

"Oh, I know."

"...for saying stuff like that."

"Yeah, I know. But... Oh yeah, there's a lot of people that jus' go nuts over this."

"I imagine."

"But he... No... He's not gonna waffle."

"I guess. If you're ninety, you don't have to."

"Huh-uh. He ain't gonna waffle. 'Cause, ya know. Most men *are* weak, an' they're weak for the woman. He says, 'Men mess with women's bodies, an' women mess with men's minds.'" Poteet laughs and continues, "It's true. It is. It's true, ya know. An' most men won't understand this. It's... 'The moment—outside of marriage... The moment that you succumb to the urge for sex, she knows right then that you're weak.' He says, 'All women know that.' He says, 'Why do you think that women like bad boys? It's because they know they're weak. That's why.' Once you start to understand where he's comin' from, you go, 'Yeah, I can see that. I can definitely see that.'"

"Well, okay..." Elliott says, "So, my question is... With the Roy Masters thing and him being so controversial with his beliefs, do you mind being associated with him."

"Huh-uh."

"...or claiming that you follow his teachings more or less?"

"I don't mind—not at all."

Elliott looks past Poteet and nods slowly.

Poteet continues, "I look back on all these failed relation-ships an' everything. An' like Roy says, 'It was the sex—the out-of-wedlock sex.' So, I decided I wadn' gonna make that mistake again. An' so... When I met Terry, I'd been celibate for five years. I jus' hadn' wanted to mess with it, ya know. An' uh... 'Cause, I thought, 'I've listened to this man, an' I believe 'im.' If you wanna have a relationship, you have to be strong. As a man, you've got to be strong in what you believe. You've got to know what you'll stand up for. An' so... Uh... Ya know, the first date that I had with Terry... I know I shocked 'er. Because we were eatin' there, an' I told her, I said, 'Well... Uh... There won't be any sex.'"

Elliott smiles.

"Ya know, when you tell a woman *that*, they're like, 'What? Wha'd you jus' say?'"

Elliott chuckles.

"I mean... Then, they're *really* tryin' to do it."

Elliott laughs.

Poteet laughs.

When the laughing stops, Elliott says, "That's funny."

"Yeah. But it's true, Elliott. It's absolutely true. But that right there... It sets you apart from every other man they've ever met."

"I believe it."

"An' it's all worked out for me. It has. An' I told Terry this, ya know. I said, 'Life is so much simpler for me now—bein' married. It's been good.'"

Elliott smiles and nods.

"I mean, it really has."

"That's great."

"But... That's when you have a good marriage. Now... If you have a bad one, which... An' I've been in those too. That ain't no fun."

They both turn at the sound of a knock on the door. Terry peeks her head in.

Elliott says, "Poteet tells me that he likes being married to you."

"Well, he'd better say that."

Elliott grins. "So, what about his work schedule? How's that for you?"

"He's a workaholic."

"Is that a problem?"

"No... I'm tellin' ya. He said some of his wives used to fuss about 'im workin' all the time."

Elliott chuckles.

"I thought, 'Man, I'm tellin' ya right now. I ain't gonna fuss.'"

Terry and Elliott laugh together.

"Some of the dudes I hooked up with wouldn't work."

"So... You've seen the other side."

"Yes, I have."

"So, how were you first introduced to Poteet's art?"

"It was at the ranch—there in Oklahoma. It was when we jus' first started seein' each other. I'd told 'im I'd marry 'im. An' he'd asked me to come stay out there with 'im."

"Right."

"So, I did. An' I sat down to put some makeup on. I was sittin' beside the original paintings of Marilyn an' Howard Hughes. An' this was when Poteet was first gettin' started with the abbreviated portraits."

Elliott chuckles.

"I was puttin' my makeup on, ya know. I knew the paintings were there. I mean, they was on kind of like a gurney thing. It was a place where he'd set his paintings. I was seein' 'em, an' I loved 'em. But I didn' understand 'em. But, when he explained what he was doin', I thought, 'He's jus' so smart an' so creative.' It made me even crazier about 'im."

Elliott asks, "Can we go look at 'em?"

"Sure," Terry says, "I've got all the small ones down in my office on the wall."

"Y'all go on. I wanna keep working on this," Poteet says as

he points to his painting.

Elliott stands. He and Terry head downstairs.

As they look at the wall of portraits, she says, "Before we left Oklahoma, he did Elvis, the black one with the pink." She points. "It's down there."

Elliott moves to the Elvis print.

"You see those lines. They represent Elvis's legs—the stance, ya know."

"I can see that."

"The lines goin' across... To me, they look like a Cadillac grill or the shirt he wore in *Jailhouse Rock*. ...the black an' white shirt he wore. Like I was sayin', Poteet painted that at the studio, before we come out here."

Elliott points at the line of paintings and asks, "Was that the order that he painted 'em in?"

"Uh... Marilyn was first. ...Howard second. ...Elvis third. Uh... An' then, I think it was... After we got out here an' got kind of settled in, I believe it was Paul Newman. That was the next one an' then Lucy."

"Paul Newman...?" Elliott asks, as he looks down the line of portraits. "I don't think I see him."

She points. "This is it right here. Can you see the iris of the eye? You can see the beautiful skin tone—the blue denim shirt that he always wore."

"Oh yeah."

She moves to her right and points. "Lucy was the next one, an' then it was John Wayne. Uh... I'm not sure if I got that right, but... I should've cataloged 'em. I should've put 'em in order as they were painted. An' then, there was, uh... Jack Nicholson. That was before too much longer. But, uh... Ya know, Poteet has to get in a certain mindset to paint these."

"Sure. Of course."

Terry sits down at her worktable.

"Do you think he's through?" Elliott asks.

"Oh no. Huh-uh. An' I don' want 'im to stop. 'Cause, I see it every day. I see people's enthusiasm every day. An' uh... I see that this is gonna be his legacy, ya know."

"Huh."

"The Trail of Tears mural is amazing. It's amazing that he even thought to do that."

"Mm-hmm."

"But... He stepped way out of the box with the portraits. An'... Like I say, I see it every day."

"Mm-hmm."

"An' uh... I mean, he will someday go down in history as the first artist that ever did that. Because he was. No one else had ever done that."

They turn to see Poteet walk in.

Elliott declares, "Terry thinks these portraits will be your legacy."

"I do," Terry says as she looks at Poteet with a smile.

Elliott turns to Poteet and asks, "How did you...? What made you think of doing these?"

"I kind of got on this train of thought, because... I used to do research, ya know—studyin' ancient art an' stuff like that. An' I started to see that all these designs, no matter where they were from... They were very similar. Even, ya know. Like... From the southern tip of South America up to Norway an'..."

"All these things bein' done in the same time period is what he's talkin' about," Terry clarifies.

"Sure," Elliott says and nods.

"Yeah. That's..." Poteet says.

Elliott interrupts, "I think I get where you're going with this. I think you've been searching for a commonality, art-wise, that runs through the human race, maybe."

"Yeah. I think that's it. An' I think it's there."

"Hmm."

"It's like the pyramids, ya know. The pyramids in South

America were built simultaneously with the ones in Egypt. But they didn' know about each other. There wadn' any communication between 'em, of course."

"Yeah."

"But... An' then I read... Uh... It was Thomas Edison that said he didn' really invent anything. He said, 'It's hangin' up there. You jus' have to reach up with your mind an' grab it. You have to grab it an' pull it down.' An' I started thinkin', ya know... There is a... At certain times, I think there's a burst of energy that comes out in the universe. An' if you've got your mind open to it... Uh... These new ideas an' all... If you're lookin' for 'em, you'll find 'em. It's like I say. I wadn' thinkin' about textin' an' everything in terms of painting, but... Inevitably, it had to be that way. I mean, because that's what I do. It's gonna come out, somehow."

"...interesting."

"An' it was partly Warhol's influence, I think. Ya know. Because I was intrigued by his portraits. They were jus' snapshots. He'd snap a picture, break it down to jus' black an' white, an' silkscreen that on—different colors an' everything. ...very simple to do. But... I was intrigued by that. An' I kept thinkin' that I wanted to do some sort of abstract portrait work. But... Every time I'd start on an idea, I'd go, 'Oh, I don' like it. I don't like it.' An' so I'd jus' abandon it. An' then I got... Then I started gettin' fascinated with everybody an' their damn cell phones. Ya know, I don' even carry one. But..."

Elliott says, "You know... Only the very elite don't have to carry a cellphone."

Poteet grins and says, "Yeah. I know."

Terry says, "I mean, I don't like to be without mine. So, I'm not very elite." She laughs.

"They don't carry money either," Poteet adds.

Terry chuckles.

After a moment Poteet continues, "But I started seein'

everybody textin'. An' sometimes I can't even read 'em, because they're so abbreviated."

"Mm-hmm," Elliott mumbles.

"But... To me, it was fascinating. It was like... I know that's what that word's supposed to be, but it don't look like it."

Elliott chuckles.

"Ya know. 'Cause, I remember the one that got me was 'later.' First time I saw somebody... I mean... Yeah... To write 'later'... It was an L-8..."

"Uh-huh."

"...E-R. An' so... I was jus' thinkin' about that, ya know an'..."

Elliott nods and thinks about how long it took him to understand those text-type abbreviations himself. He still doesn't get them all.

CHAPTER 49

The Abbreviated Portraits

"So, I'm down there at the ranch. An'... I wadn' even... I wadn' gonna do a portrait at all. I was jus' gonna do a painting. I was gonna do a white painting with a red center. An' I'm paintin' this thing, an' I jus' had an epiphany. I jus' saw it in my head. An' I thought I would go over there an' put the beauty mark on it. An' I thought, 'Well, that's it. That's Marilyn Monroe.' 'Cause, that's how I see her—standin' over that grate in New York City, with that white dress on, red lipstick, beauty mark... An' that started the whole thing. An' it... We've actually had people come in here that had never seen these... An' they'd see that painting an' go, 'That must be Marilyn Monroe.'"

"Really?"

"Uh-huh. Yeah. So... Ya know, as an artist, we're always workin' in a vacuum somewhere—alone, isolated." Poteet chuckles. "Or there I was on a thousand-acre cattle ranch."

Elliott smiles and nods.

"I did Marilyn."

Terry says, "You did Elvis. Uh... Howard Hughes."

"Oh yeah. It was Howard Hughes."

"...an' then, Elvis."

Poteet repeats, "...an' then, Elvis."

457

"An' then, we moved here," Terry points out.

"But... Stevenson... He was in Idabel. An' he come out to my studio one day. An' I had these paintings hangin' up, ya know. An' he'd always been real supportive. But he said, uh, 'What the hell are those?' An' so, I told 'im this whole thing, an' he went, 'Really?' An' I went, 'Yeah.' An' he couldn' quit lookin' at 'em. An'... He... He looked at 'em a long time. An' he come over an' told me. He said, 'Ya know, you have done somethin' here that destroys modern art.' He said, 'This is a totally different thing.' He said, 'It's absolutely amazing.' He said, 'You have to keep doin' these.' He said, 'Whatever you do, don't you stop doin' these.' An' I thought, 'Well, it was kind of a good idea.' But he said, 'No, no, no. You don't...'" He said, "You... You... You don't understand what you've done.' So, I've continued to do 'em. An', they really have become a phenomenon."

"Would you call those modern art?" Elliott asks.

"Oh, yeah. ...definitely modern art. Uh... Yeah... Because it is a new way of lookin' at a portrait. Because... To me, they *are* portraits. They're just... Like, when I'm thinkin' about doin' one, an' it hits me... It's like, 'BOOM,' ya know. An' I know I got it. 'Cause... I don't try to make it up. I'm thinkin', 'What do I actually see?' I'm seein' somethin'."

Elliott points to a painting on the fireplace hearth. He says, "That's Clint Eastwood."

"It is," Terry acknowledges.

Elliott looks at Terry and says, "We were just talking about that one, but I don't think it's the original."

"Right," Poteet responds. "No. What I do is... When I get ready to do one of these portraits, I always do one *that* size to work it out."

"...like a prototype?"

"Yeah. But I call it a study."

"Okay. So, that's the original study for your Clint Eastwood portrait."

"It is."

"Well... Does that give it some special value?"

"Yeah. I think it does. So... What I was doin' when I started these... I was keepin' all of these studies for myself, jus' for my own collection." He laughs. "An'... I had two of 'em in here. One of 'em was the Beatles. I can't remember what the other one was. An' this guy come in an'... He said, 'Well... Would you sell that?' I said, 'I don' wanna sell it. I'm keepin' it for my collection.' He said, 'Boy, I really want those.'" Poteet chuckles. "An' I said, 'Well... Ya know... Naw...' An' uh... So, he come back two or three times—askin' me that. So... One day he asked me. He said, 'What would you take for 'em?' I said, 'ten thousand a piece.' He said, 'I'll take 'em.' So... Then, I started sellin' 'em."

"It seems like you would have asked for more."

"Well..."

"...seemed right at the time, I guess."

"Yeah. I jus' thought... At ten thousand... It'd scare 'im off."

Elliott chuckles and nods.

"But it didn'."

Elliott points to a painting at the end of the row. "That one of Donald Trump has to be one of your most recent."

"Yeah. An' it's one of my favorites," Terry reveals.

"It's a good likeness. But I wouldn't be interested in buyin' it. I couldn't put it up."

"I understand."

"You'd have to be a Trump fan to get that one."

"I actually had somebody buy one who didn' like Trump," Terry explains.

"Really?"

"Yes. An' they bought a large one, because they were just amazed at how Poteet brought it out. An' they weren't Donald Trump fans. An' I thought, 'That's real unusual.'"

"I would agree."

"I mean... It gets more reaction than any of 'em. An' uh... A lot of the time it's negative. Sometimes, they just laugh. Ya know."

"Yeah."

"Usually, I get the laugh, but uh..."

"Well, it is such a good representation of 'im," Elliott notes.

"It is."

Elliott moves closer to the print and says, "I mean... That hairline... I don't know. It's just perfect. An' then, when you put that red tie on there..."

Nodding, Terry agrees, "He captured it."

"He did."

"When you see most photos of Donald Trump... It's in a blue jacket an' the white shirt an' a red tie."

Poteet explains, "On any image or picture, your mind has to read some of it into it."

"On this one, it's pretty easy," Elliott affirms.

Terry smiles and says, "Yes, it is."

Poteet points to the wall of portraits and says, "Because... As a neuroscientist explained to me... He said that we don't store images in detail of people in our minds. I look at it like a screensaver. Ya know. With a screensaver... Soon as you hit that mouse, then 'BOOM.' So, that's kind of my... That's what your mind is doin', because... When I see people, an' they're lookin' at one of these paintings... Once they realize it's Marilyn Monroe, then they see Marilyn Monroe in their minds."

"Yeah. That's the way it seems to work for me," Elliott agrees.

"An', it's not just an adult that can figure it out," Terry adds.

"No," Poeet confirms.

"We have kids come in, an' they get it."

"I'm not surprised," Elliott says.

"Speakin' of kids... Poteet was Artist of the Year back in 2012," Terry says and looks at Poteet. "Weren't ya?"

"Yeah."

"An' uh... Well... Tell 'im what you had to do—goin' out to the school an' all."

"Yeah. Well, uh... They asked me if I'd get involved with the kids...if I'd donate twenty hours of my time to teach art to these high school students. An' I said, 'Yeah. Sure.' So... I went out there an' showed 'em some things. I had a film. I showed 'em these portraits an' told 'em the whole concept behind 'em. An' I said, 'Now... This is what *you're* gonna do. I want you to come up with somebody. An' then, you create an abstract portrait of *them*.'"

"Huh."

"An' it was amazing. It really was."

"You should've seen what they came up with," Terry says.

"Oh, really?"

"Yep." She looks at Poteet. "What's the Blue... One of 'em was..."

"...Blue Man Group," Poteet says. "An' it was really cool."

"Hmm."

"It was like... He did three ovals, like egg shapes."

"Yeah."

"An' then, everything was all blue. The guys were a little lighter blue than the background. An' then... Ya know. Because they beat these drums, an' all this stuff flies up. So, he had that. An' I thought, 'That's perfect. That's really perfect.'"

"An' then, there was the one that had the unibrow," Terry remembers.

"Frida Kahlo."

"Yeah. That was a good one too," Terry says.

"An'... After the kids finished all those, we had a black-tie affair out here, an' uh... Ya know. People bought tables—expensive tables. An' these paintings were the centerpieces for each table—the portraits."

"That's great," Elliott responds.

Poteet smiles and says, "An' uh... All of 'em sold."

"Yeah," Terry says softly.

"Everybody's... Every one of 'em sold. Yeah."

Elliott smiles and says, "Sounds like it was a great experience for those students."

"It was. I'm tellin' ya," Terry affirms.

Elliott turns again to look at the portraits. He asks, "Who's missing?"

Poteet chuckles.

Terry says, "There's a lot of 'em missin'."

"I just read an article on Muhammad Ali," Elliott interjects. "I think he's missing." He turns to look at Poteet. "What do you think?"

Poteet steps closer and offers an observation, "Muhammad Ali was an amazing person. He really was. Not only gifted... He was the most gifted boxer I'd ever seen in my life."

"You were a boxer at that time too," Elliott recalls.

"I was. Yeah."

"Would you consider doin' a portrait of Muhammad Ali?" Terry asks.

"I've already done it. I did one forty years ago."

"Really?"

"Yeah."

"...an abbreviated portrait?"

"That I haven't done. But yeah. I know what the other one looked like. An' I could... I could take some of those pieces an' do another one. Yeah."

"That's a good idea, Poteet," Terry concludes. "You should..."

"Ya know, I met 'im one time."

"You did? I didn' know that," Terry says, drawing back.

"Oh, I met 'im. Yeah. If he'd a been a movie star, I'd go,

'Fuck it. Who cares?' But... This guy... I knew this guy was special. He was a special person."

"Mm-hmm," Elliott says.

"He had it. An', it wadn'... To me, all the braggadocios was like, with a wink, ya know."

"Yeah. It seems like that was mostly about promotion," Elliott suggests.

"All of it was with a wink."

"Mm-hmm," Terry agrees.

Poteet mimics Ali, "I am the greatest in the world."

They all laugh.

Poteet continues, "Yeah. But he was. An' he was the one that said, 'Well it ain't braggin' if you can do it.'"

"Yeah, that's true," Elliott concurs.

Terry says, "Kid Rock wrote a song about that."

Elliott looks over and asks, "Kid Rock?"

"Yeah. He wrote a song. 'It ain't braggin' if you can back it up.'"

"That's right," Poteet agrees.

Elliott chuckles under his breath.

Poteet tells Terry, "I've got to run upstairs for a minute."

She nods, and he walks away.

Terry points to a chair at her table and says, "You're welcome to sit."

"Okay," Elliott says and sits.

"I'm absolutely amazed at how many young people come in here an' get these portraits. Because... I mean... A lot of 'em weren't around..."

"Uh-huh."

"These younger people weren't even born. So..."

"And they can still figure some of 'em out?" Elliott asks.

"Yeah. Oh yeah."

"But they probably don't have the emotional connection that we do."

"No. They don't."

Elliott points at one of the portraits. "Like, *Lucy*..."

"But everybody, pretty much, has seen an episode of *I Love Lucy*."

"I guess so. I'm sure they haven't seen as many as I have."

"I bet they haven't seen as many as me either," Terry says. Elliott laughs.

"Because... I loved it. I loved *I Love Lucy*."

"Me too."

"Ya know, Pam's wantin' Poteet to do Elizabeth Taylor—really bad."

"...seems like a good idea."

"It does. It really does. Those violet eyes."

"Yeah."

"Those distinguished eyebrows that she had. I see all that."

"But she's even old for my generation."

Poteet walks back in and asks, "Who's old?"

"I told 'im about Pam wantin' you to do Elizabeth Taylor."

"Yeah. She is old—or was. I think she died about ten years ago."

Terry smiles and says, "I'm tryin' to get Poteet to do some younger people, ya know. ...to bring in the younger generation." She looks from Elliott to Poteet. "...but he's got to be inspired."

Poteet smiles and says, "That's true."

Chuckling, Terry points at the line of portraits and says, "An' these are the people that have inspired 'im so far."

"Yeah," Elliott says.

"An' Michael Jackson isn't one of 'em," Terry adds.

Elliott chuckles.

Poteet sits in the chair opposite Terry and says, "I think you're gonna see a lot of this in painting an' in an art."

"I think the abbreviated portraits are just brilliant... absolutely brilliant," Terry observes. "Because... Everybody...

I get so much response from these things. I get so many people. They jus'... I mean, they'll bring people back. They might not purchase one of 'em, but they'll bring people back to see 'em. Ya know... They do it all the time."

Poteet nods.

"An' we see other artists tryin' to do this same thing, don't we, Poteet?"

"Yeah."

"An' I don' really like it."

Elliott chuckles.

"But... That's another thing Stevenson taught me," Poteet points out. "I had said somethin' to 'im about another artist copyin' my art, an' he said, 'Well, you want 'em to.' An' I said, 'Really?' He said, 'You don' know that?'"

Elliott chuckles again.

"I said, 'No.' He said, 'Ah. Good. I get to teach you somethin'.'" Poteet chuckles. "He said, 'Think of one person out here.' Because, I was in Santa Fe. He said, 'Think of one person—an artist that's really, really famous.' An'... The first person that popped into my mind was Allan Houser, the sculptor—the world-famous sculptor."

"...an Oklahoma guy, wadn' he?" Terry asks.

"Yeah. He was born in Oklahoma. An' uh... I said, 'Yeah, I can think of somebody.' He said, 'Okay.' He said, 'Are all the young sculptors, Indian sculptors, tryin' to emulate this guy?' An' I said, 'Yeah, they are—every one of 'em.' An' he said, 'Okay.' He said, 'I'm gonna tell you somethin'. Before they started doin' that, he wadn' famous, was he?' An' I started thinkin', 'Yeah, you're right.' He said, 'That's why museums love for people to copy paintings that they have in their collection. Because it's advertising.' He said, 'No, you want people to copy you.' He said, 'That'll be...' He said, 'Because... No matter who copies you, they still know who the first guy was to do it. An' all they're doin' is bringin' attention to you.'

So... I thought, 'Yeah. Yeah.'"

Terry looks back at the wall and says, "An' another thing with the abbreviated portraits... Ya know, when they come in here, I get 'em involved. An' it's not hard, 'cause everybody wants to be a part of somethin'. An' when I, ya know... I start askin' questions. I ask 'em, 'Who do you think this is?' Well... Then, they're involved. I mean, I can..."

"I'm sure that's fun," Elliott says.

"Yeah, it is. I've seen it many times," Poteet adds.

"I watch 'em, an' I can tell, ya know. Because they're... While they're talkin' to me, they're lookin' at the next one. They're tryin'... Especially if there's more than one..."

Elliott begins to chuckle.

"Because they're tryin' to outdo the other one, ya know."

"Sure," Elliott says.

"It's like a contest. That's how it works. But yeah. Uh..."

Poteet leans forward to say, "But what's funny, though... I'll watch people come in here, an' they're... They're lookin' at 'em. They don' know what they're lookin' at. But once they figure it out, they always smile. Because, then they see it. It's just human nature."

"Huh."

"An' then, there's the business reason for doin' these."

"Okay."

"I've always heard artists say, 'Multiples. If you wanna make money, the money is in the multiples.'"

"Hmm."

"An' I found out, yeah. You're right. It is."

"...makes sense."

"'Cause all I gotta do is sign 'em."

"That's a good deal, but... Do you think that's affected the sales of your paintings? ...your original paintings?" Elliott asks.

"Naw. Because... The people that like these..." He looks

away for a moment and then says, "I don' know. Some of my collectors have bought these too."

"Mm-hmm."

"But... In general, it seems to be a different type of client."

"Okay. I think I can see that."

Poteet shakes his head. "I jus' wish I could solve the black piece thing..."

Elliott chuckles and asks, "What in the hell is that?"

Poteet points at the portrait wall. "Ya know, I did Elvis..."

"Right. Terry and I were just looking at that."

"I did 'im in black, because that's how I remember 'im— when he wore the black leather an' all."

Elliott stands and walks over to the Elvis portrait. As he looks more closely, he says, "That's how I remember 'im too. And his were the first records I ever bought. I think I was just five or six years old."

"Yeah. But... It's the color."

"What do you mean?"

Poteet shakes his head. "For some reason, black paintings are the hardest thing in the world to sell. An'... You would think that the Elvis portrait would be one of the favorites. But it isn't."

Something catches Terry's eye, and she stands to look out her window. Without saying a word, she hurries out of the room.

As Elliott continues to look at the Elvis Presley print, Poteet says, "Ya know, Elvis came by Mother's drive-in one time."

Elliott turns away from the print chuckling and says, "Nooooo."

"He did."

"I didn't know she had a drive-in. I knew she had the café."

"Yeah."

"The cafe was down on... Uh..."

"Skid Row," Poteet answers the unasked question.

"Right. Skid Row. I guess it was actually a café and a beer joint."

"Yep."

"And she had a drive-in too?" Elliott asks.

"She did. She actually had the drive-in first. An' then... After several years, it burned down. But, uh... Back then... An' this was in the early sixties, ya know."

"...seems like that would've been before there were many drive-ins. I mean, that's..."

"Well, drive-ins kind of got started about then, with the carhops an' everything. ...remember A&W Root Beer."

"Oh Yeah. I remember going to A&W with my family. I was just a kid."

"Yeah."

"That would've been in the fifties."

"Right. An' so... That little ol' place that she had—that little drive-in... Uh... You could go an' drink beer there, an' it was like a little fast-food place, too."

"Okay."

"Most people back then... I remember... That parkin' lot would jus' be packed with people out there drinkin' in their cars, ya know."

Elliott chuckles.

"An' uh... Oh yeah... An' they had the carhop runnin' all over the place."

"...running beer everywhere, I guess," Elliott suggests as he tries to understand.

"Yeah. But... Elvis an' Colonel Parker pulled up there one day."

Elliott chuckles and shakes his head.

CHAPTER 50

Who's Next

"I wadn' there. I didn' see it. But Mother tol' me 'bout it. She was there." Poteet uses his hands to describe the layout. "The building was up high, so you were actually lookin' down on the parkin' lot. An' then, where the carhop was... She had a little thing about the size of a tollbooth, an' they called that the doghouse. An' so, the carhop would stay in there."

"I see."

"So... From there, she could get out real fast. There was a window right there where she'd order, an' Mother'd fill the order. But, when Elvis an' Colonel Parker drove in, she said she saw 'em. I think they were in a baby blue Cadillac—brand new. She couldn't tell who it was. But... When the carhop went out there, they ordered a coke an' a beer. A beer was a quarter, an' a coke was ten cents. Mother said she saw the carhop go out there. Her name was Dawn, an' she had no sense of humor at all. She was just, ya know, matter of fact on everything. An' she said she saw Dawn talkin' to the driver, ya know. An' she saw these guys laughin' an' everything. So..." Poteet chuckles and continues, "When the car drove off, Dawn come back, an' Mother said, 'What happened?' She said, 'Well, when I went out there, I told 'em it'd be thirty-five cents.' An'... The one man... We found out later it was Elvis. He was the passenger, an' he leaned across there an' had a five-dollar bill. An' she tried to grab it, an' he kept pullin' it back, ya know. An' she didn' think that was too funny."

Elliott chuckles.

"An', the driver, Colonel Parker said... He was laughin' an' he said, 'Do you know who that is right there?' She said, 'No.' He said, 'That's Elvis Presley.' She said, 'I don't give a damn who it is, it's still thirty-five cents.'"

Elliott breaks up.

"Both of 'em started laughin'—Elvis an' Colonel Parker. An' Elvis jus' told her to keep the five dollars. Yeah. An' when Dawn tol' Mother 'bout it, she went, 'Oh my god, was that Elvis?'"

Elliott laughs harder.

"Yep, sure was," Poteet says and laughs. "Yeah. 'Cause you didn' see brand-new baby-blue Cadillacs around Idabel back then, ya know."

"Huh..."

Poteet chuckles.

"Wow. So... Did that have anything to do with you wanting to do Elvis for the abbreviated portraits?"

"Oh... I dunno. I grew up right durin' that time when he was becomin' famous."

Terry walks back in and sits down. She says, "They like the landscape with the horses. I think they're about fifty-fifty."

Poteet nods at Terry. He looks over at Elliott and continues, "So... When I think of Elvis..."

Elliott turns to look again at the Elvis portrait. He says, "Looks like your colors are pink and black for this one."

"Yeah. Those were his colors. 'Cause, I see the young Elvis, ya know, when he had the dyed black hair...

"Oh yeah."

"...an' black leather."

"Oh yeah. Those were his best days in my book," Elliott discloses.

"I should probably do another one. An' I've thought about it."

"Mm-hmm."

"...the white jumpsuit Elvis."

"...seems like that would sell."

"But yeah. I mean... 'Cause, like I say... When I do these portraits, I'm not tryin' to make it up. I ask myself, 'What am I actually seein'?' What are the pieces of images that are floatin' out there?"

"Mm-hmm."

"I know that I'm relatin' it to somethin'," Poteet explains as he looks at the Elvis portrait. "But... With this one, ya know, that's... I mean, that's what I saw. An' what I didn' know but found out after I did it... His favorite color was pink, an' most all of his jackets an' everything were lined in pink satin or whatever. Yeah."

"I was a fan," Elliott reiterates.

Poteet points at the wall. "I've got two black paintings up here. One of 'em is Cher, an' the other is Elvis. Then I thought of all these other people I could do. An' people said, 'Why don't you do Johnny Cash? Why don't you do Frank Sinatra? Why don't you do Michael Jackson?' Well, I'll tell you why. It's because every one of those is a black painting to me. They are. I mean, Johnny Cash..."

"Yeah. The 'Man in Black.'"

"That's right."

Elliott chuckles and says, "How else can you do him?"

"Yeah. An' Frank Sinatra..."

"Hmm. Frank Sinatra..."

"I see 'im in a black suit, white shirt, fedora..."

Elliott cocks his head for a moment and then says, "Yeah."

"An' Michael Jackson—same thing. I see him with those

black pants, white socks, black shoes..."

"Uh-huh."

"So, that's why I didn' do 'em."

"...because they're mostly black?"

"I don' wanna do a lot of black paintings. I don't. But yeah, I'd love to do Johnny Cash. But... I jus'... No... I've gotta do somethin' with color in it. I started to do Winston Churchill, an' I ended up with the same thing—black an' white."

"Hmm."

"But I had an idea for an abbreviated portrait that *would* be different."

"Okay?"

"It was like, Custer's last stand—with arrows an' everything."

"Huh... But you haven't done it yet?"

"No. That was one of those that... Ya know, you get in a place, where you're lyin' in bed. You're half awake, half asleep..." He turns to Elliott. "I've done this a lot—where you get a good idea. An', of course, for me it's usually a painting."

"Sure."

"I don' know where it came from. But yeah... I saw these... They weren't particularly shaped like arrows, but... They were more of a Chevron design, ya know—blue ones an' red ones. An' all the blue ones were on the ground an' the red ones were..."

Elliott begins to snicker.

"...stickin' out of the blue ones."

Terry and Elliott laugh.

Poteet chuckles.

Terry says, "I hadn' heard about this."

Elliott says, still laughing. "It seems like a good idea."

Poteet says, "Maybe..."

"But it's not a portrait," Elliott notes.

"No."

"Maybe then... It's an abbreviated something else," Elliott suggests.

"...could be. It could be what we'd call 'an abbreviated event.' Whadaya think."

Elliott grins and repeats for consideration, "...an abbreviated event. I like it. ...could be a whole new thing."

"Yeah," Terry says, chuckling.

"With a Custer painting, you might gin up some new controversy."

With a straight face and a low monotone voice, Poteet responds, "Oh, good."

Elliott and Terry howl. And then, Poteet laughs too.

When he catches his breath, Elliott asks, "Isn't that what you want?"

Dead pan, Poteet says, "Oh, good."

They all laugh hard again.

When it dies down, Terry says, "That'd be great." She looks at Poteet. "But I want you to keep goin' with more portraits." She motions with her right arm toward the wall. "I love these."

Poteet crosses his arms.

Terry and Elliott turn toward Poteet.

Poteet studies the wall and says, "I think it's partly the 'black thing.' An' it's partly... Ya know. I don' know how many of these I *should* do. Is there a right number? I don' know. Can there be too many?"

"I don't think you're nearly to that point," Terry says. "I wanna see more of 'em."

"Maybe Muhammed Ali will get the juices flowing," Elliott suggests.

Poteet chuckles and looks back again at the portraits. "My plan has been to keep the originals together. The more of these I do... Ya know, it's gonna be harder."

"It seems like keeping them together is a good idea," Elliott says.

"I'd like to see some museum buy 'em or some collector buy 'em an' keep 'em all together. They'll be worth so much more that way."

"Mm-hmm."

"An' I might not sell 'em in my lifetime. But ya know... It's somethin' Terry'll have."

They both look at Terry.

She sits forward, points at Poteet, and says, "You quit talkin' like that."

"Well..." Elliott says, "I'm going to hope you have plenty of time to add many more portraits to your collection."

After a moment, Poteet says, "But... If somebody walked in here today an' said, 'I'll take 'em all at a hundred-fifty thousand a piece,' I'd sell 'em."

Elliott asks, "And there's like twenty of 'em?"

"No. I've done nineteen."

"Oh..." Elliott says. He glances at the wall and repeats for his own benefit, "...nineteen."

"Yeah."

"Well, that's close to three million dollars."

"I'd take it."

Terry says, "An', ya know, we've had people come in here that actually... They got angry at us, 'cause we wouldn't sell the originals."

"Really? Angry?"

"Mm-hmm... An' uh... Well... This one man... He said, 'Why do you have 'em on the wall, if you're not gonna sell 'em?'"

Elliott chuckles.

"That's what he said, ya know. He was somewhere from up north—New York or someplace. He wanted Marilyn, an' I think... He wanted Paul Newman too. But I said, 'We can't sell you those.' I showed 'em the prints an' I told 'im, 'We can sell you these.'"

"Uh-huh."

"But I told 'im. 'You can't have the originals.'"

"I understand."

"With the prints... I do forty-nine of 'em. My editions are small. There's forty-nine of each one of those." He points at the portrait wall. He then points to the larger print of Willie Nelson by the fireplace. "An' uh... We start *those* out at a thousand dollars, an' every time we sell ten, they graduate up two hundred-fifty dollars more. So, they keep goin' up as the edition gets smaller."

"Uh-huh."

"I think, when you get to the end of the edition, they're like three thousand apiece. An' I sold out of... Oh... I sold out of Marilyn a long time ago. An' I started a second edition. I sold out of the Beatles too. We'll sell out of all of 'em—eventually."

Elliott points at the print of Willie. "So... Those prints, the larger ones, start at a thousand?"

"Mm-hmm."

Elliott turns to look at the wall of portraits. "Okay, because I thought the smaller ones..."

Poteet interrupts, "Yeah. The smaller ones don't graduate up in price. I've got 'em stable at... I think we said, fourteen hundred."

"Right," Terry verifies.

"So, if you've got an early number of the big ones..."

"Yeah."

"Then, you got a pretty good deal."

"Yeah. Ya know... Like I say... I've started a second edition on Marilyn."

Elliott nods and says, "And I assume, a second addition print would be worth less to collectors."

"It usually works that way," Terry confirms.

"I had a guy..." Poteet explains. "He'd bought a Marilyn from me for a thousand dollars. An' so, when I started the second edition, well he... He called me up, an' he said, 'You told me that you're jus' gonna do forty-nine of those.' An' I said, 'Well, that's right I did—in the first edition.' I said, ya know... 'Doin' these is not unlike a book. A book has a first-edition, an' it sells out. Then, you start a second edition.' An' he was like, 'Well... Then... Dudn' that lower the price of mine?' I said, 'Absolutely not.' I said, 'It actually makes it worth more.' An' so... He kep' on an' kep' on. An' I said, 'How much did you pay for that?' He said, 'I paid a thousand dollars.' I said, 'Well, I just sold the last Marilyn at three thousand dollars. Why don't you jus' lemme give you your money back, an' you send that print back to me?' He said, 'Oh... Oh no...'"

Elliott and Poteet laugh together.

Still laughing, Poteet utters, "He changed his mind."

"Yeah."

"No... These portraits have been good for me—and for the gallery."

"Sir Anthony Hopkins called us one time," Terry tells Elliott. "He wanted to talk to Poteet, but he wadn' here. Sir Hopkins was at Ojai, at Poteet's art dealer out there. An' actually... Khaled was the one that called. She said that Sir Anthony Hopkins was wantin' to speak with Poteet."

"About what...?"

"He wanted Poteet to do a portrait."

"...of him?"

"Yeah."

Elliott looks at the wall. "Well, I don't see him up there."

Poteet clarifies, "I haven't done one."

"I see."

"I've thought about it."

Terry smiles and looks at Elliott. "When you think of 'im, what do you see?"

"...when I think of Anthony Hopkins?"

"Yeah... Is it the mask?"

Elliott tilts his head and looks away. "No. That's not the first thing that comes to mind for me."

"So... What is it? ...the motorcycle?"

"No."

"Uh-huh," Terry says quietly.

"I see his face."

"Really? I see the mask."

"An' the mask is white. I see black an' white." Poteet says, shaking his head.

Elliott chuckles and says, "With Anthony Hopkins making the effort to call..."

Poteet turns to Elliott. "Do you see color? When you think of Anthony Hopkins, does any color come to mind?"

Elliott pauses and then answers, "Not really."

Poteet chuckles and says, "That's what I mean. But I hope he will come by. We can talk about it. An' I've been around plenty of celebrities, ya know. They're jus' people."

Elliott nods. "They are. In my business, I'm around actors all the time. They aren't my best friends. They come and go. But some really are great people."

"Sure. I tol' you 'bout Larry Hagman, didn' I. We became friends, an' he was a great guy. He was a funny guy."

"But..." Elliott explains, "And I know you're not surprised. A lot of 'em have big egos and are really hard to be around."

"Sure... But they tend to lose some of that when they come in here."

"What do you mean?"

"From the ones I've met, I think they look at artists differently."

Elliott blinks and cocks his head. He says, "How's that?"

"Yeah. I think they do. 'Cause you're... You're doin' somethin' that they can't do. Ya know. They seem to be kind of in awe of somebody that can create a painting an' get an emotional reaction from people."

"It is very different from what they do."

"Anyway, that's the feelin' I get."

Elliott sits back and adjusts his glasses. He says, "You may be right. I don't know."

Poteet shrugs and says, "That's the way it seems to me."

After a moment, Elliott looks at Poteet and says, "I've been thinking about the mural again."

"Okay," Poteet responds as he shakes his head.

Elliott takes a deep breath and articulates, "I know it's in the past, but... There was some unfairness there that makes me want to do something about it. I don't know what—but something."

Without moving or showing any emotion, Poteet says, "To tell you the truth, I'm tired of tryin' to get support."

"I know you are, and I don't blame you. You've given so much of your time and your talents."

"I'm worn out from tryin'. I jus' can't do it anymore."

Elliott sits forward and says, "But it's a tragedy, and I can't get it off my mind. It's that third panel. It's the panel of hope. It's the panel of achievement. It's the panel of competence. It features the next generation of American Indian children who are interested and paying attention." He looks at Poteet. "Like you say, it's about the tribes coming back into prominence."

"That's right."

"And it's terrible that this uplifting painting of a bright future was cancelled. One day, out of the blue, you were kicked off campus, and you had to quit."

"I did. I had to take down those big easels I'd built."

"And you even lost your place to hang the finished mural."

Poteet looks down. "I did." He looks up to add, "An' that hurt too."

"To me, it's just another sad tale of mistreatment of the Indians. It's another broken promise. The contract you had and all the agreements... They, evidently, meant nothing. And all of that seems like a validation of the very theme of the mural. It's ironically so very appropriate," Elliott says and shakes his head.

"It's always seemed that way to me too."

"It's not right, and it shouldn't be that hard to fix."

"I don' know about 'not bein' that hard'... Believe me, I've tried."

"I know that. It was a bad choice of words. Sorry. It just seems like there should be a way to fix it. That's all."

"I understand, an' I agree. But... An' I've said this. Uh... To me, it was always about education. I jus' think people should know what happened. It was a tragedy. It was terrible. It wadn' right, an' the people of this country should know about it."

"Yes, they should," Elliott says. He looks at Poteet, then Terry and back to Poteet. "Bill O'Reilly's book, *Killing Crazy Horse*, ya know. It's done a lot to get that story out."

"It has. It's good. I've read it."

"But... Bill O'Reilly's narrative pretty much stops with the *killing* of Crazy Horse. But your message doesn't stop there, and it shouldn't. O'Reilly did what he intended. He told the history and revealed the awful details. But he's not American Indian. He lives in New York. His ancestors weren't touched by the pain and the death. They weren't forced to live under the terrible conditions of the reservations. They didn't have their food and meager subsistence stolen by corrupt bureaucrats—decade after decade. But now, it's a new day, and there's hope. I don't think that Bill O'Reilly will do a follow-up book about the successes of the tribes and the successes of the tribal members. But... Your plan has been to get *that* message out there too."

Poteet nods but without energy.

Elliott looks at Poteet. "I believe as you do that your mural will hang somewhere—someplace very prominent. It could be at OU."

"I doubt it."

"It could be at a Native American museum someplace. It could be the Smithsonian. It could be one of the tribes that will take up your cause and help you get that panel done. They could feature it in one of their properties. Or it could be another university. I don't know. But it will be somewhere."

"I believe that, an' I've told you."

"Right," Elliott says and nods. He then adds, "Unfortunately, Bill O'Reilly stopped at the total submission part. Anyone who's been around the tribes knows that their leaders and their customs are being respected now. Prominent individuals, like your friend Bear Heart, are being discovered and celebrated outside the Native American community."

"That's true."

Elliott smiles—looks at Terry and then Poteet. He says, "I've gotten on my soapbox here about this, but the unfairness of what happened to you..." He shakes his head.

"I've gotten over it. An' I think I tol' you that. I had to. 'Cause it was eatin' me up."

"I understand, and that's an important part of your story. You've learned to deal with your anger."

"I have. An' it was Roy that helped me with that."

Elliott nods.

"But... If the right person... If the right situation came along, I'd... I think I could come up with a way to paint that third panel. At least, I already know what I want it to look like."

Elliott looks at his watch and asks, "Do you mind if we have a bit more conversation this evening? I've got some work I've got to finish today."

Poteet looks at Terry.

She gives a slight shrug.

Poteet says, "Sure. We don't have any plans."

CHAPTER 51

The Galleries

As Elliott crosses the Santa Fe River, approaching Canyon Road, he wishes he'd worn his heavier jacket. Temperatures had been dropping steadily since sundown. He increases his pace and soon he is through the parking lot of the plaza and knocking on the gallery door. Within seconds, he sees Terry coming through the darkness of the front room. As she unlocks and opens the door, he says, "Thanks. I appreciate y'all staying late."

"It's no problem. I've got some paperwork to catch up on, an' Poteet would be fine to paint twenty-four hours a day, I think."

Elliott chuckles and says, "I'm sure that's true." He points toward the top of the stairs. "Is he up there?"

She nods and points to her office. "I've got to finish an invoice. An' then I'll be right up."

Elliott nods and says, "...sounds good." He turns and heads up the stairs. At the double doors, he pushes through slowly and says, "I'm back." He sees Poteet turn toward him with a smile.

"Well..." Poteet says, "What do you wanna talk about?"

Elliott begins digging into his satchel, and Poteet turns to inspect his painting in progress.

After setting up his recorder, Elliott turns to look at Poteet's painting before asking, "Do you sell out of other galleries now?"

"Mm-hmm. I show..."

Poteet stops to watch Terry walk in and sit.

She apologizes for interrupting.

He continues, "Well... When I got this place, Chris was my business partner... He wanted me to be more localized, because I was showin' in Florida, showin' in New York City... Uh..."

"Sojai," Terry adds.

"Yeah, California, I was showin' in Colorado. An' so, I pulled out of those galleries."

"It does seem like you would sell out of New York or L.A. or..."

"Yeah. But I'll tell you why I don't. Dealin' with New York is like dealin' with a foreign country."

Elliott's brow wrinkles, and he tilts his head.

"I've done it twice. An' both of 'em were bad experiences for me."

"Tell 'im 'bout the last one," Terry says.

"Yeah. Well, I was showin' in a gallery at the new Time Warner building, ya know—real prestigious place. An' uh... So, I get a call from my business manager, an' he told me what happened." Poteet turns to look at Elliott. "...you know who Patricia Cornwell is, don't you? ...the author?"

"Sure."

"So, what happened was... I had three paintings in this gallery. An' she goes in, an' she sees two of 'em that she wants to buy. An'... So, she leaves an' sends her assistant back over there to buy 'em. Well, when the assistant gets back over there, both paintings had gone up five thousand dollars apiece. An' I jus'..." He shakes his head. "'Cause that's a terrible thing to do in the art business. But what those idiots didn' realize is... There's a thing called the Internet."

Elliott chuckles.

"So, Patricia Cornwell gets on the Internet. She finds my business manager, tells 'im what happened... He calls me. An' uh... I was jus'... I called the gallery, an' I was jus' so pissed off. An' uh... I said, 'No. What you're gonna do is... You're gonna take the two paintings she wants, an' you're gonna sell 'em to 'er at that original price. You're not gonna jack 'em up five thousand dollars apiece.' An' I told 'im, I said, 'An' then, you jus' send me that third painting. I'm done.' An' uh..."

"I see what you mean."

"No. There's more," Poteet says and chuckles. "So... From that point, there was only one way for 'em to screw this up. An' I know they did it on purpose. They sent one of the paintings she wanted to 'er—an' the one she didn' want. So, she called about that. An' I said, 'Look, I'll get this straightened out. Don't worry about it. I'll get the painting that you want.' An' she said, 'That's okay. I'll jus' take all three of 'em. Tell 'em to send the other one.'" He looks over at Elliott and continues, "She bought all three of 'em, an' then she told me... She said, 'I really appreciate you helpin' me.' An' I said, 'Well, 'It was the right thing to do.' An' she told me... She said, 'I'm gonna put you in my next novel.' An' I said, 'Okay, great.' An' she did."

"She really did?"

"Yeah. An' I was out pickin' up cans in front of the ranch one Sunday mornin'. It's where people had thrown out their beer cans an' stuff. Ya know, most Sundays, I'd get on a four-wheeler an' do that. An' uh..." He chuckles. "I'm doin' that, an' this car's comin' down the road. It slams on the brakes an' starts backin' up. An' I'm thinkin', 'What the hell?' An' it was one of our local attorneys. He said, 'Whadaya think you're doin' out here?' An' I said, 'What does it look like? I'm pickin' up these cans.' He said, 'You can't do that, man.' An' I said,

'Why?' He said, 'Because I just read about you in a novel, an' it jus' blows the whole thing.'"

All three laugh.

"That's very cool," Elliott responds.

"Yeah... Yeah..." Poteet chuckles. "But. ...talkin' 'bout the galleries. I don' know. I guess if the right one come along in New York, I'd do it." He sighs. "But... The first time I tried, I was jus' gettin' started. An' uh... It was a small gallery. An' they closed down, after I'd been in there about... I don' know, six months. They closed down an' jus' took all my paintings. ...never heard from 'em again."

"They got your paintings?" Terry asks.

"...couldn' find 'em," Poteet says, shaking his head. "Nope. ...couldn' find 'em. ...never did."

"That was bad," Elliott says.

"Yeah. So, both of 'em were bad experiences in New York. An'... But... I don' know. I guess... If the right gallery approached me, I might do it. But the whole art scene has changed in New York City. ...so much. Ya know, when I was there in the 80s an' early 90s, everything was sort of centrally located down in Soho. All the galleries were down there. An' then, when nine-eleven happened... Well, everybody just vacated that part of the city, because of the poisons in the air."

"Yeah," Elliott says. "I remember Soho being the art district. I just haven't thought about that lately."

"An' so, all the art galleries moved away an' got spread out all over the city. I mean, it's so fragmented now. Most of 'em moved over to the Chelsea area, uh... Which... In the Chelsea area, there's hardly any foot traffic. You've got to buzz yourself in, an'... It's jus'... I don' know how they sell anything, to tell you the truth."

Terry stands and quietly walks out.

"But now, what galleries are you in?" Elliott asks.

"I'm in Howell, in Oklahoma City. Uh... I'm in... Now, I'm

in the Southwest Gallery in Dallas. Uh... I'm in Jackson Hole, an' here. An' uh... The guy in California sold his business. I'd been with him for twenty-five years."

"Hmm. Do you sell much out of Jackson Hole?"

"Nah. Last summer, I took four of 'em up there. We sold one. As a matter of fact, that's what I did that big Beatles thing for. They were crazy 'bout the portraits, an' I told 'em... I said, 'I'll do one for you. Which one do you want?' They told me. They said, 'If you do the Beatles, I think we've got it sold.'" Poteet looks away for a moment and then says, "I need to call 'em."

"Yeah, I have friends that go to Jackson Hole. And they love it," Elliott says.

"Oh, it's beautiful."

"I've never been there."

"I hadn' either, up until last year. Uh... 'Cause I tol' Terry... I said, 'Ya know, I think I'll jus' branch out a little bit. ...get in another gallery.' So, I started lookin' at these galleries in Jackson Hole. An' I saw the one that I liked. An' uh... Did I tell you the story about goin' down there?"

"No," Elliott says and chuckles.

"So, we go into this gallery, an'... It's a beautiful space. An' uh... This lady comes out, an'... Ya know. I asked her... I said, 'I'm...' I tol' her my name. I said, 'I'm lookin' for representation here in Jackson Hole.' She said... She said, 'You picked a really bad time.' She said, 'We've got a show openin' tonight.' She said, 'I'm so busy.' An' I said, 'I understand. I do. Believe me. I understand.' She said, 'Well, lemme take your information, an' I'll put it in the computer. An' uh... I'll get back with you.' An' I said, 'Okay.' So, I gave 'er the information, an'...' He chuckles. "She went back to the office. An' in a few minutes, I saw this guy come runnin' out of there."

Elliott laughs.

"An' she was right behind 'im. An' he grabbed me an'

shook my hand an' everything. That was his wife that I'd talked to. He said, 'Holly, do you remember me tellin' you that there's two artists that I think are jus' geniuses?' He pointed, an' he said, 'That's one of 'em right there. That guy right there.' Yeah. An' he tol' his wife, 'Sounds like he wants to sell outta here.' An' I said, 'Oh yeah... Absolutely.' He said, 'I don't care how busy we are. We're gonna talk.'"

Elliott grins.

"Yeah. But he was... It was 'cause he'd seen the portraits. He said, 'I jus' think these things are genius.'"

Elliott nods and says, "That had to be very reinforcing."

"It was."

"Which gets me to a point I've been curious about."

"Okay?"

"When did you feel like you were successful?"

Poteet turns to look out the window into the darkness of the night.

Elliott adds, "Well... You knew that you were that day—in Jackson Hole."

"I was."

"I mean, I'm sure you've had plenty of other times like that."

"Yeah, I have. Ya know, most people have to go to galleries, schleppin' their work around. An' it's great when you don't have to do that. But ya know... In reality, that's what I was doin' that day. I walked in there, jus' like anybody else would."

"But you didn't walk *out* of there like everybody else would."

Poteet chuckles. "Yeah. They treated me real well."

"That's a solid measure of your success."

"Of course. But I've sold a lot of paintings, ya know, in my life. I really have."

"Have you kept count?"

He shakes his head and says, "No."

"Do you wish you would've?"

"Yeah. I wish I had. I usually do eighty to a hundred paintings a year—somethin' like that. An' uh... For the most part, the galleries came to me. So... Yeah... It was a blessing."

Elliott nods.

"But I have a different style than most artists, an' I think that helps. I kind of sculpt a painting more than I actually paint it. Ya know, because I'm not usin' brushes. I'm usin' palette knives."

"Right."

"An' I'm always painting wet into wet. I learned how to do that at the Art Students League."

"You mentioned that."

"Okay."

"But... The Art Students League was important for you."

"It was. An' in those two years, I learned... It was less than two years. I learned so much about painting, jus' because I was workin' with some of the best artists in the world—studyin' with 'em an' lettin' 'em instruct me. So... Yeah... When I left there, I had the confidence that I could do 'bout anything I wanted to. I wadn' thinkin' about the Trail of Tears or anything like that, but I was confident that I could make it as an artist."

"I see."

"An' I think my decision to do more abstract work was important for me, 'cause I could see this comin'. Ya know, there was a time back in the 90s, when everything was Santa Fe crazy—Santa Fe cologne. Santa Fe this, Santa Fe that. An' I jus' couldn't produce paintings fast enough. But when I was workin' on that mural, I was seein' that this thing was just a fad. Ya know. I mean, the Santa Fe thing... It'll always be there. But that big boom..." He shakes his head. "An' so, I started movin' off of that, an' I loved to do abstract work anyway. So, I jus' started doin' more an' more of the abstract work, an' then, uh... I finally jus' switched completely over. Jus' doin' everything abstract. So... When I tol' the gallery I was with that I was switchin' over... I mean, they freaked out. They said, 'You're gonna lose all your collectors. You can't do this. You can't.' An' I said, 'Yeah, well... On top of that, I'm gonna double my prices.'" Poteet chuckles. "An' they go, 'Oh my God. You can't do that.'"

Elliott smiles and chuckles.

"But I did. An' my paintings jus' continued to sell. As far as how many I was sellin', it never slowed down a bit."

"Wow," Elliott says quietly. He then asks, "Do the ideas come as easily for you with the abstract work?"

"Probably not. A lot of the Santa Fe-style paintings were fairly cookie-cutter. Most of the time, I knew the elements I would be usin', an' the themes didn' go very deep. With abstract paintings... I mean, you can go anywhere you want with 'em."

"I see."

"So... When I start a painting, I'll usually have an idea. But a lot of times, I don' know where it's gonna go, ya know. I jus' start creatin' an' lettin' it go. 'Cause you can drive yourself crazy, goin', 'Oh, shit... I want it to look like this. I wanted that to happen or this to happen.' An' I said, 'No.' An' I learned this the hard way. A lot of times, I'll just say, 'Okay. You wanna go this way in the painting. Okay, that's the way we'll go.' An' that way, there's no stress. Ya know. 'Cause I've known a lot of artists that had..." He chuckles as he says, "...serious health problems, because they jus' stressed themselves out over that kind of thing."

"...interesting," Elliott whispers.

Terry walks in and says, "Those people called back on my cell phone, an' said they wanted a *Lucy* portrait."

"I thought they were lookin' at the horse painting."

"They were. But for now, they want a *Lucy*."

"With a mark?"

"Yeah," she says and walks out.

Poteet turns back to Elliott and continues, "The thing about bein' in business for yourself... There's no guarantee. You can't know if anybody's gonna walk in here an' buy a painting."

"Sure."

"But they do."

"Well, that seems to be what you're good at. You're successful at selling your paintings." Elliott quickly adds, "Of course, you're good at painting. But... You're also good at selling."

Poteet smiles and then walks around to the other side of his painting table. He opens a drawer and appears to be looking for something. He then pulls a large sheet of paper from the open drawer. He says, "Well... I've got a business mentality, an' I think that's always set me apart. 'Cause most artists aren't geared that way. But... I am—startin' from a young age."

Elliott can see that the large sheet of paper is a *Lucy* abbreviated portrait. He says, "Because of your situation back then, you had to be."

"I did. An' that's the way I think," Poteet says as he sets the print down on his worktable. He pulls out an artist's charcoal pencil and begins to draw in the outside margin of the print. He says, "An' so, ya know, when I look at a painting... Yeah. I mean, I look at it from an artistic point of view. But I also look at it like, 'Is this marketable?' Ya know. 'Cause sometimes I do things that I know aren't marketable. I jus' do those for myself."

Elliott moves closer to Poteet to watch him draw. He asks, "So, what are you doing now?"

"It's called a re-mark."

"Oh. I saw what you did with Pam's. You drew Marilyn."

"Yeah."

"That's a really nice touch."

"I think the first person to start doin' these re-marks was Whistler."

Elliott chuckles as he says, "Oh?"

"An' uh... He used to... When he figured out he could get more money." Poteet laughs. "Ya know, he would do like a little butterfly or somethin'." Poteet stands up straight to look at the print and the re-mark. After a moment of inspection, he bends back over the table and begins drawing again. He says, "I like these portraits, because... I mean, not everybody's got fifteen, twenty thousand dollars of spendable income."

"Most people don't."

"An' I know that. But most people... If they're out here, they can afford, ya know, fifteen hundred, two thousand..."

"Yeah."

"An' so... That's exactly why I do these. I like havin' somethin' that nearly everybody can afford."

"Sure."

"But... Most of my time is still spent doin' these originals."

"And... Like I try to do with film..." Elliott says and the pauses. He continues, "I expect that you want to touch people emotionally with your paintings."

Poteet stands again to look at his drawing. After a moment, he begins adding the finishing touches. He says, "I do. Yeah. An' I've seen people jus' faint, almost. Ya know, I've seen people cry in front of paintings. Yeah."

"Huh."

"I've seen it happen. Sometimes people will jus' fall in love with a piece an' think, 'I jus' can't afford it.' An' if somebody really wants a piece of my work that badly, I'll do everything I can to help 'em. I'll say, 'Look, you can pay this thing out. Ya know. Just pay me within two years. An' I'll hold it for ya.' An' a lot of people take me up on that."

Terry steps back into the studio.

Poteet points at the *Lucy* print and says, "It's ready."

She walks over and begins to roll it up.

"I had someone do that on a nine-eleven painting. She cried when she saw it, an' I worked a deal for 'er."

"He did," Terry confirms.

"I called that painting *The American State*. An' it was beautiful. It commemorated what happened that day. So..."

Terry turns to face Elliott. "I mean, it looked like an explosion. An' I mean..." She looks at Poteet, shaking her head. "You jus'..." She looks back at Elliott. "An' I mean, he did... It was an abstract painting, but it was... It was *powerful*. That one was powerful—to me. An' he's done several of 'em. They're always powerful."

"So... Do you have one of those here?" Elliott asks.

"I sold 'em all."

"He sells everything," Terry says with a hint of disgust.

Elliott smiles and says to Terry, "Yeah. But that's how he makes a living."

Without smiling, Terry responds, "But, there's some of 'em I wish he wouldn' sell."

"I understand. I know how you can fall in love with his art."

"An' I do."

Elliott says to Poteet. "We were talking about when you decided to do more abstract work."

As Poteet moves back to his painting table he responds, "Well, I've always liked to try different things, ya know, uh..."

"Sure," Elliott says softly.

"An' I've always liked art that had the loose type of look, ya know. I'm not much into the total realism thing. An'... It jus' dudn' appeal to me. When I was younger... An' I think it probably was Stevenson that said it to me. He said, 'As you age, there are those paintings you may have really liked when you were younger that you don't anymore. An' then, some that you never did like, but now you're startin' to like 'em—appreciate 'em.' An' uh... He was exactly right."

"There are some paintings I jus' wish he wouldn' sell," Terry says and shakes her head. "Sometimes he paints somethin', an'...."

"But I've got a business mentality. I paint 'em to sell," Poteet says and smiles. "An' I don't keep a lot of paintings. Uh... I've probably got more inventory now than I've had in fifteen years, but it's still not that much. But... Ya know, that art dealer that came in here to see me from New York. He come into my place, an' he was lookin' around. He said, 'Where're all your paintings?' An' I said, 'I don't have any.'"

Elliott chuckles.

"An' he said, 'What?' I said, 'I don't have any.' He said, 'You're the only artist I've ever seen that didn' have any of their own work.' An' I said, 'Well... Ya know...' An' this was before Terry an' I were married. But... 'The joy for me is to paint 'em. An' once I've painted 'em, I'm ready for 'em to go. I'm ready to start on somethin' else.'"

"Sure."

Still standing with a rolled-up *Lucy* in her hand, Terry says, "An' I'll tell you this about Poteet. He *is* business minded. Because..." She gazes around the studio. "This could be a part of the gallery."

"Mm-hmm."

"But, by Poteet bein' here... When people are lookin' for art... An' if they're interested in his art, I jus' bring 'em up here an' leave 'em." She points at Poteet. "I leave 'em with him."

Poteet smiles.

"An' he... He's sold more off of those easels..." She points at the easels.

"Yeah, I have."

"...than we've sold off the walls."

"Really?"

"Oh, yeah."

Poteet tells Elliott, "Like, you're paintin' one, an' they'll say, 'Whadaya gonna do to it?' An' we'll talk about it. They might have a suggestion. I'll probably ignore it. But they might come back in a couple of days, take another look... An' they might buy it. Yeah. It happens."

"How many have you sold like that?"

"...no tellin'"

Terry shakes her head and echoes, "...no tellin'. Yeah."

"But... Ya know, it hadn' always been this way," Poteet says.

"Sure. We've talked plenty about that. I always think about you gettin' down to your last fifty bucks."

Poteet chuckles and Elliott laughs as he reflects on that story.

Elliott thinks it's a great story and would certainly be one of the highlights of a series on Poteet. He also thinks about the fact that the story has a strong faith component and whether that bothers him. He looks into the distance to think about these issues. Does it bother him that the story was essentially about the power of prayer? He continues to think and to stare at nothing. Would that cause him to rethink his natural inclination to use the story? He looks at Poteet and wonders whether he'll have to blackball everything about Poteet having to do with faith? It makes him feel uneasy when he thinks about it that way. But... Does it? He shakes his head and utters, "Huh," without knowing it.

Poteet continues, "Ya know... Bein' poor like I was..."

"It makes an impression," Elliott says as he tries to refocus on Poteet.

Terry adds, "Yes, it does."

CHAPTER 52

The Next Level

"An' I always said, 'When I get the money, I'm gonna have every damn thing... An' I did. I finally got everything I wanted."

"It's nice to get there," Elliott says.

"I'll tell you this."

"Okay."

"I was at Stanley Korshak one Saturday, an' they had the guy from Italy that was a shoemaker. Yeah. Oh. ...beautiful shoes. I sat there an' spent almost twenty-five hundred dollars to have some shoes made."

"Okay."

"An' I've never worn 'em."

Elliott and Terry laugh. Still holding the print, Terry moves to her chair and sits.

"Yeah. I've never even worn 'em."

They laugh again and Elliott says, "...need to wear 'em sometime."

"But... Ya know, in *my* business... In what I do every day... I mean, it's jeans, an'..."

"Yeah, every day... I imagine that's seven days a week," Elliott notes.

"It is. But if I need to... Hell... I've got tuxedos an' every-thing."

Elliott chuckles.

"They're handmade. ...custom made an' all this shit."

Terry points at Poteet but looks at Elliott. "An' he trades 'im paintings for clothes."

"Yeah. An' he's got all my measurements. I can jus' call 'im up."

"Mm-hmm."

Poteet sets his painting knife down to continue, "Uh... That's what I did with that tux. 'Cause they'd already made all these sport coats an' shirts an' pants for me. An' I called 'im up, an' I said, 'I need a new tux.' 'Alright, whadaya want it to look like?' I said, 'Well, I kind of... Maybe, somethin' with a little Western theme... Maybe... a yoke in the front an' back.' An' uh... He said, 'Oh, Okay.'"

"Hmm. ...a western-themed tux."

"Yeah."

"That's cool."

"He sent it to me, an' I jus' love it. Every time I wear it, people go, 'I love your tux.'"

"Oh. I'll bet they do."

"Yeah."

"That's so different. ...so Santa Fe."

"Yeah. He's... But... I mean, you can't get any better, 'cause he's... Ya know, he tells me, 'The materials I use...'" Poteet shakes his head. "He goes over to Italy an' France an' picks out the best. Because he does dress the who's who in Dallas."

"Sounds like it works for both of you."

"But... He's a crazy bastard."

Elliott laughs.

"...absolutely insane," Poteet says and laughs. "He's funny. He's real funny. But he's crazy."

"He is," Terry affirms.

Poteet chuckles. "He's like a lot of my friends."

Elliott grins and then looks down at his notes. After a moment, he looks back up to ask, "What about awards. I know you've won some awards. There were some photos I saw down in Terry's office the other day..."

Poteet asks of Terry, "Is he talkin' 'bout that legislator who was out on The Fourth of July? Is that the photo?"

"Hmm... I don't think so." She points at Poteet. "Tell 'im 'bout Bartlesville."

"Okay... Well... Uh... This was in 2007, when they did this. The state of Oklahoma put on this huge art show over in Bartlesville. An' they had everybody from the humanities—dancers, singers, everybody in the arts. But you had to have been born in Oklahoma an' been into art for some number of years. An'... So... They called Harold an' wanted him to be in the show. An' so, Harold said, 'Well, yeah... I guess I'll do it.' But he said, 'Who're the other painters?' An' so they told 'im. An' he said, 'You don't have Poteet Victory in there?' An' they said, 'Well, no.' An' Harold said, 'Are you crazy?' He said, 'He sells more paintings in a year than I've sold in my whole life.'"

Elliott chuckles.

"An' so, they invited me."

"Huh..."

"Yeah, they did. An' I had one of the artists come up to me at the show. An' he said, 'I jus' wanna tell ya...' He said, 'You've got the best painting in here.' He said, '...by far.' An' that was an artist named Otto Decker. Otto Decker is a *great* painter. Yeah."

"Well, that's great recognition of your art."

"An' I've got some great collectors. I think you know about my Israeli friend, the billionaire."

"Right. *Moe*, I think."

"Yeah. Well, he was tellin' me 'bout bein' in the Six Day War in Israel. He was in a tank. An' he said, 'By the time the battle ended, they were firin' within ten feet of each other.' He said everybody in the tank that he was in got killed but him, an' he lost ninety percent of his hearing. An' uh... But he made it. An' he said, 'After that, I realized how precious life is.' An' he said, 'I was determined to make somethin' of myself.' So, he came to America. An' uh... An' he was a machinist. He took a job as a machinist. He'd work durin' the day an' go to school at night. An' uh... He got his degree an' then went on an' got a master's degree. An' then... Uh... An' then he started this company. Him, bein' the brain that he is, kep' comin' up with all these different inventions, an' he made a ton a money."

"That's an impressive story."

"It is. But anyway... I made a trip with 'im to London. We walked into the gallery over there, where he was introducin' me to some people. I mean, it's probably the biggest, most prestigious gallery in London. An' uh... I asked 'im, I said, 'Do you...? How well do you know these people?' He said, 'Well, I've bought over a million dollars from 'em'"

Elliott grins.

"I said, 'Well, that's... I'd say you know 'em pretty well.'"

Elliott chuckles.

"So, we walk in an' everybody's like, 'Oh, there's Mr. Madar.' An' uh... One of the owners said, uh, 'Moe, before we get started on this...' He said, '...gotta show you my new Renoir.' So, we go into this office, an' there's this Renoir there. He said, 'Do you like it?' An' Mo said with a shrug, 'Yeah. Well... I like mine better.'"

Elliott laughs.

"I mean he collects art from all over the world, ya know. An', he already had a Renoir."

"I'd say he's very serious about collecting."

"He is. Ya know, he mainly stays in Miami. An' I know he's got a place in London. An' then, uh... He an' his wife have a place in Albuquerque. She jus' likes it out here. But yeah... He was supposed to meet me there in London, an'... He said, 'I'm stayin' at the Four Seasons.' An' he said, 'Our appointment's at two o'clock.' He said, 'I'll be there by one.' I said 'Okay.' Well, I get there a little early. I thought, 'I'll jus' hang right here.' An' uh... So... But I had asked this concierge. I said, 'Is Mr. Madar here?' 'Oh no, Mr. Madar's not here.'" Poteet chuckles and says... "So, he asked me, 'Are you waitin' for 'im.' I said 'Yeah.' He said 'Well, follow me.' An' he took me over to this lounge. He said, 'Do you like coffee?' An' I said, 'Sure.' So here comes this lady with coffee an' cookies. She asks, 'What newspaper would you like to read? We have papers from anywhere.' An' I said, 'Oh, ya know—anything.' So, they were jus' treatin' me like a king, an' then..."

Poteet looks squarely at Elliott and says, "I don't carry a cell phone."

"We've talked about that," Elliott says and chuckles.

Poteet looks away and continues, "So, I'm sittin' there, an' it's... Ya know, it's after one o'clock, an' I'm thinkin'... An' so, this lady comes back in there with a cell phone. She says, 'Mr. Victory, this is for you.' An' it's Moe. An'... He said, 'Poteet.' I said 'What?' He said 'Ya know, when I get there. I know some Chinese guys.' He said, 'I can get you a cell phone for twenty-nine dollars.'"

Elliott, Poteet and Terry all laugh.

When the laughing stops, Poteet says, "I don' know why. He jus'... He really likes me. But Moe came in yesterday. I was sittin' down. He come over an' kissed me on the cheek."

"Well, that's kind of a European thing, isn't it?"

"Yeah. Well not from Moe. He's not European."

"Oh yeah, he's Israeli."

"Well... He actually didn' kiss me on the cheek. He kissed me on the head."

Chuckling, Elliott says, "Okay."

"When he was here, Terry was watchin' us. When he left,

we were talkin' 'bout it. She said, 'He looks at you like a brother.' An' I said 'Yeah, I guess he does.'"

"Huh... Well, he appreciates you—as an artist for sure."

"Yeah."

"Tell 'im about the guy in New York," Terry suggests.

"Yeah. 'Cause that guy an' what he tol' me reminds me of Moe. It's when I was workin' for that company an' paintin' in New York City. There was a Jewish guy. An' he asked me one day. He come in. There was a bunch of us in there. He come over an' talked to me. He said, 'You wanna go to lunch?' I said 'Yeah, sure.' ...get to go to lunch with the boss, ya know. An' uh... So... An' we were talkin' there, an' he said that he was raised in a very orthodox Jewish family. An' he said 'We were always taught that we should be professionals, ya know. ...doctors, lawyers...' An', he said, 'We were encouraged to do that, because our position is to help artists.' Yeah. He said, 'We were always taught to help people in the arts, 'cause that's a very important part of life. An' uh... An' so, Moe... That's exactly what he does."

"I didn't know that about Jewish traditions," Elliott reveals.

"I told you, I think, that the Cherokee people are Jewish."

"No. I don't think you did," Elliott counters. He cocks his head and looks confused.

"Hmm. Well... Their creation story... The creation story of the Cherokee people is about comin' from the east on floating islands."

Elliott perks up and points at Poteet. "You did mention something about 'floating islands.'"

"Okay." Poteet smiles. "So... The floating islands could've been ships. Ya know, an... It's in this book called *Out of the Flame*. It was written by this Jewish guy that lived with the Cherokees back in the 1600s. An' he started seein' that a lot of their celebrations an' ceremonies coincided with the Hebrews—

the Jewish people. An' uh... Yeah. I mean, when I got through readin' it, I was totally convinced. I mean, how could it be otherwise? It's jus'... All this stuff couldn't be a coincidence."

"I'll admit it's an interesting theory."

Poteet chuckles and continues, "So... Ya know. When I went over to the Cherokee headquarters one time, an' I was lookin' at some of these photographs of Cherokee people—old photos, goin' way back. They had photos of Chiefs an' people like that. I started thinkin', 'These people... They don' look like Indians to me. They look like white people.' He chuckles and adds, "Ya know?"

"Well, that would make you like a quarter Jewish," Elliott notes.

"Yeah. An' that's what I told Moe."

Elliott laughs, and Terry smiles.

"I said, 'Jus' remember one thing. When you start tryin' to beat me down on price...'"

Elliott and Terry both laugh.

"I'm Jewish too.'"

Elliott roars.

"He got a kick out of that."

Elliott continues laughing, and Poteet chuckles.

Elliott says, "That's funny. And... Obviously, Moe's a great friend."

"He is."

"And he believes in your art."

"He does," Terry says. "He's bought a lot of it."

"All this makes me think about the arc of your life."

Poteet tilts his head and squints as he looks at Elliott. Terry sits back.

Elliott proffers, "You know... Most people... And I would include myself in this. When you were left alone at such a young age, and you were essentially abandoned..."

Poteet straightens up and nods slowly.

Elliott pauses and looks toward the window. He breathes deeply then continues, "We would normally consider that a bad thing."

"Yeah?"

"But... In your case, I'm not so sure. Because... It... It has a lot to do with who you are today."

"Oh yeah. I think it has everything to do with it. Uh... I jus' never think about it too much."

"Uh-huh."

"I mean, I could. But ya know, talkin' an' discussin' with you like this..." He shakes his head. "But otherwise, I probably..." He shrugs.

Elliott leans back.

"It's jus' the way it was. But... I look back on my life, like... My twenties were a successful time for me. My thirties— sucked. They really did. An' then, uh... In my forties... I started becomin' a little bit more responsible, ya know. An'... That's when I came out here. So, by the... I'm tryin' to think. When I was probably about what? ...forty-five. Uh... Then, this thing started to work, ya know. An'... Yeah, by the time I was fifty, I started to feel like it was successful."

Terry sits forward. She looks at Elliott with a big smile and points at Poteet. "Regarding his awards..."

Elliott chuckles and responds, "Yeah?"

"Well, I gotta tell you this..."

"Okay."

Terry says slowly, "Poteet was the first non-Western artist to ever show at the Prix de West."

"Yeah. I was the first at that."

Elliott crosses his arms and asks, "And what is the Prix de West?"

"It's a western art show at the Cowboy Hall of Fame in Oklahoma City," Terry responds. "Now they call it the Western Heritage Museum or somethin' like that. But the art show is still the top western art show in the country."

With arms still crossed, Elliott cocks his head and squints at Poteet. "I don't really see your art as western."

"It's not."

"I guess. Early on... In your 'Santa Fe' period, you would have been considered 'western,' maybe."

"I suppose." Poteet nods. "I don' really know. But I *was* in the Prix de West."

Terry leans forward with her hands on her knees and says, "It's a big deal."

Poteet adds, "The other artists... The traditional ones... They didn' like it. But I didn' give a damn whether they liked it or not. But... Uh..."

Still leaning forward, Terry points and says, "'Cause you were the one who was sellin' paintings."

Elliott uncrosses his arms and responds, "Of course. Yeah."

"An' they weren't."

Poteet gives a hearty, "Hell yeah."

"So, there was a protest about Poteet bein' there," Terry explains.

"Yeah. But I didn' care. I mean, it's on my resume. Ya know, I did it."

"It's kind of a pain to fool with," Terry adds.

"Really?" Elliott asks.

"Yeah. It is," Poteet says. "'Cause they wanted... Well, you have to apply for it. But I never... I never applied. I never sent in anything. They came to me. An' then, they wanted copies—photographs of my work—like six months before the show. An' I'm thinkin', 'I don't paint that way. I'll paint these things the week before or somethin'.' An' I did."

Leaning forward, Terry looks at Elliott and affirms, "Yeah. He did."

Elliott and Poteet chuckle.

Poteet looks at Elliott and says, "But... One of my collectors... Have I mentioned Hank?"

"I don't think so."

"Well, he's one of the biggest... I saw a thing one time in a magazine. Of all the art collectors in America, he's one of the top twenty."

"He's number eight," Terry clarifies.

Elliott responds, "Wow."

"He would go to the Prix de West every year to buy somethin'...every year. An' he's got, I don' know, how many of my paintings. An' uh... When he found out that I wadn't gettin' invited back. Boy, he wrote 'em a letter. He sent me a copy. An' he said... 'I'm there every year. I buy every year, an' I bring people with me that buy. I will never come back again for what you did.' Uh... He said, 'You finally wised up an' got a great painter in there that's different from everybody else, an' that caused excitement. An' now, you won't bring 'im back?' He said, 'I'm finished with you.' An' he said... An' he tol' me. He said 'Man, they called me. They sent me letters an' all this stuff.' Ya know, like, 'Please come back. Please come back.' An' he jus' said, 'No! I told you. I ain't comin' back. ...you bring Poteet Victory back, then, I'll come back.' I told 'im. I said, 'Well... Hank, you didn' have to do that.' He said, 'Aw, fuck 'em.'"

Elliott breaks up laughing.

"At the Coors show... An' we jus' got back from there." Poteet explains, "It's kind of like the Prix de West, except it's a smaller venue. But boy, my paintings didn' look like anybody else's. I mean, nobody's..."

"Because it's mostly western art there too, I guess?"

"Yeah. ...western, an' other forms of realism—that sort of thing."

"Mm-hmm."

"Plus, I had the highest priced painting in there."

All three chuckle.

"If I did it again, I wouldn't do that. I'd put some smaller pieces in there that would sell, but..."

"It's not over yet," Terry says as she puts her hand up optimistically.

"But... I took two pieces. One was a six foot by six foot, an' the other was a four foot by four foot. An' uh..."

Terry interrupts to clarify. "The six by six is seventy-two thousand dollars."

Elliott whispers, "Seventy-two thousand..."

"Yeah. An' the forty-eight by forty-eight is...?" Terry pauses.

With uncertainty written all over her face, Terry looks over at Poteet, who touches his fingers to his lips and answers with his head cocked, "...eighteen?"

"Yeah. ...right. ...eighteen." Terry accepts and stands. With the *Lucy* abbreviated portrait in hand, she explains, "I gotta go get this boxed up—might as well do it now."

As she's walking out, Elliott bends down to look in his satchel. He says, "I brought you your copy of *Oklahoma Today* back."

Poteet chuckles and says, "It's about time."

With a furrowed brow, Elliott stands and shows the magazine to Poteet. He says, "Sorry. I didn't mean to keep it..."

"Hey. That's okay. I've read it," Poteet says and shrugs.

"I still think it's funny that they're missing Harold's portrait of you in that collection of a hundred."

Poteet chuckles.

"Have they called again about it?"

"No—not since the article."

Elliott flips through pages until he finds the article.

Poteet moves over to look with Elliott. He points and says, "I've seen that painting there. It's the ol' State Theatre. He painted that in 1947."

Elliott brings the magazine closer for a better view and asks, "Where was that?"

"Idabel."

Elliott flips to the next page.

Poteet points and says, "That's the eye. I've got that painting too." He points at the closet next to his kitchen.

Elliott draws back and asks, "You've got that?"

"Uh-huh."

"It's big."

"Yeah. I know. It's like ten feet tall an' fifteen feet long."

"From what they said in the article and from what I've read elsewhere, that might be his most famous painting."

"That's right."

"When I looked Harold up on Wikipedia, *The Eye of Lightning Billy* and *The New Adam* were the two they showed."

"Right."

"So, I'm surprised you have it."

"The family owns it, but I have it."

"Harold's family?"

"Yeah."

Elliott sets the open magazine on the worktable.

Poteet steps back slightly and says, "By the end... I think Harold had accomplished what he wanted. I mean, the list of the people he associated with an' hung out with is unbelievable. I mean, I saw... One of his nieces put a photograph of him an' Nelson Mandela on Facebook."

"Wow."

"Yeah. An'... I told you that he dined with the Shah of Iran. An' he was the guest of honor that night. At the end, he got to go pick out an emerald ring."

Elliott lifts his eyebrows and says, "Wow. He knew a lot of people."

"He did."

"And his art was appreciated, obviously."

"It was. An' I remember one time... When I went to New York in 1980, he introduced me... He had been on a cruise. ...on a yacht in the Mediterranean with this Greek shippin' magnate, who was as big as what's-his-name that married Kennedy."

"Oh yeah," Elliott says softly while trying to think of the name.

"Uh..."

Elliott whispers, "Oh, I can't think."

"Yeah."

"I know who you're talking about."

"Yeah. Aristotle..." Poteet recalls.

"Yeah."

"...Onassis."

"Onassis. Yeah."

"Well, this guy was just about as big as Onassis. An' he was... He loved... Harold was such an entertainer. Of course, you'd want 'im on a yacht with ya. Ya know... He was funnier 'n shit."

Elliott chuckles.

"He called me to meet 'im one day. He said 'Come go with me. I'm goin' up to the Cathedral of Saint John the Divine in New York City.'" He looks at Elliott and asks, "...you ever been there?"

"No. It's a landmark, and it's beautiful. But... I've never been there. It's an Episcopal church, I think."

Poteet nods. "It's an amazin' place. I mean... It's huge. An' when we first got there, he was tellin' me about it. He said... They would have these pageants at certain times every year. An' they'd have elephants an' all this in there. Yeah... An' this Tassos... That was this Greek guy's name. He commissioned Harold to do the Stations of the Cross. They might still be hangin' there. I don' know."

"Hmm."

"An'... Then he commissioned Harold to do, uh... Harold took me down there too. It was the Greek Ear, Eye, Nose an' Throat Hospital. An' for them, Harold did this huge painting. It was for their lobby. I mean, this guy was commissionin' Harold to do all kinds of paintings for charities an' all, ya know. He made a lot of his money doin' that kind of thing."

"I see."

Poteet looks down and points again at the magazine article. He says, "This is that one that I gave to the Supreme Court."

"Oh... Wow..."

"Yeah. That was... That's real typical of what I did when I first started that sort of work. It's mixed media." He points. "All of this is an oil painting." He points lower. "This part is all sand."

"Huh."

"An' these are beads."

"It's very different."

"It's really a pretty painting."

"It is. It looks big. How big is it?"

"Yeah. Uh..." Poteet turns to point at a painting that's setting on the studio floor and leaning against the wall. He says, "That size."

"Okay."

"No... Actually, it was... I think it was bigger than that. Yeah. It was actually bigger. Uh... Maybe it was five foot by five foot. It's hangin' right there when you walk into the Justice Department buildin' in Oklahoma City."

"So... How'd they get it?"

"Uh... Ya know. That Justice... She was... She was jus' houndin' me for a painting."

"Yeah?"

"An' uh... So, I thought, well... 'If it's gonna be there

permanently, ya know. ...out in perpetuity. Then, let's get 'em a good one.'"

"Sure."

"An'... That was a good one."

Still staring at the magazine, Elliott says. "It's so unique."

"It's the mixed media that makes it stand out. Not many can do that."

"Huh. It reminds me of the bottom part of that painting Judy likes. You know, the one about your family—with the Indian and the red over his eyes."

"Right. Yeah. I called it *Renegade*."

"That's it. I remember the name now."

"Yeah. The bottom part of that was sand."

"Huh."

Poteet grabs his cup and says, "I think I'll make some coffee—you want some?"

"No. It's a little late in the day for me."

Poteet says, "Okay," and heads to his adjoining kitchen.

Elliott checks his recorder and picks up his satchel from the floor. He looks through it and pulls out a notepad.

When Poteet re-enters the room, Elliott looks down and says, "Okay. You were also talking the other day about some legislator who was out here for the Fourth of July."

"...good memory," Poteet says and grins.

He holds up his note pad and replies, "...good notes."

"Yeah. Well, she... When I was in London, she called me over there. She tol' me who she was, an' she said 'I've been followin' your work for a long time, an'...' She said 'It jus'... It really kind of irks me that Oklahoma dudn' pay enough attention to our talent—especially artists that have come out of here.' She said 'Ya know. Like in Santa Fe, they really promote their artists. You can see it. You can go downtown, an' on the sidewalks there are those plaques, ya know, commemoratin' all the artists.' An' she said, 'Oklahoma dudn' do anything like that.' An' she said, 'So... We created this award to give recognition to our top artists.' She said, 'An' you're the first recipient.'"

Elliott's eyes sparkle and he says, "And that was Oklahoma."

"Yeah."

"Awesome."

"An' that's... So, I went over an' addressed the House of Representatives, an' they gave me this award. An' uh... An' when... When I got ready to leave, she said 'I wanna ask you.' She said, 'Who... Who else do you think is deservin' of this?' An' I said 'Well... Harold Stevenson, if it's anybody.'"

Elliott nods.

"Ya know." Poteet looks at Elliott. "It's gotta be Harold."

"...would seem so."

"An' so... The next year, he got the award."

"He was alive?"

"Uh-huh. Yeah, he was alive. He was already in a nursin' home. But his whole family showed up an' received the award for 'im."

"Wow. That's wonderful."

"Yeah. An' so, I've become friends with 'er, ya know—the legislator from Oklahoma. An' she was out here for the Fourth of July."

"Right. That's what you were saying."

"She come over to the house with us. She brought this other woman—a friend of hers. An'... We cooked stuff. I forget—burgers an' stuff. She got drunk, an'..."

Elliott laughs.

"Everybody got drunk." Poteet chuckles and adds, "Yeah, we did."

Elliott winds down with a loud sigh.

Poteet says, "An' 'er friend bought one of my paintings."

Elliott chuckles and says, "Oh, even better."

"Yeah. But she was sayin' when she was out here that night... She said, 'We've been talkin' about your life an' all this.' She said, 'Somebody...' She said, 'Y'all really should write a book.'"

"Yeah. Maybe somebody should make a movie," Elliott says sarcastically.

"An' I said "Well... As luck would have it, ya know, we might be doin' somethin' like that.' So, she asked me more about it. She knew who you were, of course."

"Hmm."

"An' she said, 'That's great.' She said, 'That really needs to be done.' But... I told 'er we were jus' talkin' for now."

Elliott shakes his head. "I see more possibilities all the time."

"The only thing..."

"What?"

"She's a Democrat."

Elliott laughs, and Poteet chuckles.

Elliott eventually says, "Well, did you... Did she leave on good terms?"

"Oh yeah. She came in... Before the whole party started, I said 'Okay. Rule number one in this house... We're not talkin' politics.'"

Elliott chuckles, nodding.

"I said, 'We will not talk politics.' An' everybody agreed. She said, 'Okay, fine with me.'"

"And Terry agreed?"

"Yeah," Poteet says as he walks back into his kitchen.

Elliott stands and walks over to the wall next to the double doors. He looks at a framed letter hanging on the wall.

As Poteet emerges with his cup of coffee, Elliott points and says, "I've been meaning to ask you about this."

Poteet steps over to look and says, "...the guy that wrote the song, 'Live Like You Were Dyin'.'"

"I've heard it."

"He was over at Charlie an' Mol's house one evening."

"Oh! Okay. Was it Tim McGraw?"

"Well... No... The guy that wrote the song was Tim Nichols."

"Okay. It was recorded by Tim McGraw."

"Yes. Tim Nichols wrote the song for Tim McGraw, an' it was a big hit for 'im."

"I see."

"Well... Mol wanted us to talk. So, we sat down an' started talkin'. An' uh... I asked 'im. I said, 'How do you go about gettin' an idea for a song?' He was goin' 'How do you get those ideas for paintings?' An' we started talkin'. Ya know, the creative process is real similar. 'Cause I told 'im, I said, 'Well, ya know, I'll see somethin' somewhere. An'... Since I'm, ya know, a very visual person...' I said, 'I'll see somethin', an' it'll stay in my head. An'... It'll sort of... Ya know. It starts to build on itself.' An' I said, 'Then, pretty soon it comes out in a painting.'"

"An' he said, 'I do the same thing.' An' he tol' me about that song. He said a friend of his asked 'im to go over to meet with this boy's dad, who was dyin'. An' he said he was listenin' to 'im. The boy told his dad. He said, 'Why don't you jus' go out an' do all the things that you've always wanted to do?' He said 'Live like you were dyin'. Jus' do this an' do that an' do this.' An' Tim said, 'I thought about that.' He said, 'I thought about it for a few months. An' then, one day I sat down with a pencil an' a piece of paper. He said, 'I wrote it in fifteen minutes.'"

"...interesting."

"An' uh... So... Yeah, after I met 'im that night... Uh... That was in... around Thanksgivin', I guess. An' so... Uh... I got this package from Nashville. An' I thought 'I didn' order anything from Nashville.' But I opened it up an' it was that." He points at the wall.

"What a nice gift."

"He'd written out the lyrics an' had 'em framed for me, which I thought was pretty neat."

"Very..."

Poteet chuckles and adds, "Yeah... Pretty neat."

Elliott looks at his watch and says, "I've kept you late enough."

Poteet turns to straighten up his painting table as they hear steps on the stairs.

Terry enters.

Elliott says, "It's time to go. I know."

"I'm tired. It's been a long day," Terry responds.

"I've kept you late, but I'm not sure when I'll be back."

Terry moves toward Elliott and grabs his hand. She says, "Well, don't stay away too long, Darlin'."

Elliott smiles and gives her a hug.

CHAPTER 53

"His name was Darrell Keith."

As he is being driven up to The Victory Contemporary Gallery, Elliott is wishing he could've gotten here earlier. He'd had a hard time getting away from his office. He was also thinking about some of his most recent conversations with Poteet. In preparation for the visit, he had listened to some of the recordings Judy had picked out for him to hear. They both knew that Poteet's life was worthy of a film—and in so many ways. But they wondered how they would handle the controversial topics. Clearly, it was the stuff about Roy Masters that was causing their heartburn.

He knew that mostly it was Roy's statements about women and his statements on religion that bothered him. He recalls Judy's first reaction to those conversations, and he shakes his head. Could the controversy get more eyeballs? He didn't know. He had been thinking about Andy Warhol and his ability to generate controversy. It had worked for him. But... Would it work for a film? Elliott thinks that he should know the answers to questions like those by now—at his age and level of experience.

He and Judy had also been discussing the significance of Poteet's life. It had taken him a while to see the full picture, but he had formed some opinions. Judy had been a good sounding board and a way to better organize his thoughts. As he climbs out of the car, he thinks he'll want to bring some of that up with Poteet. Once inside the gallery, Terry's assistant walks out to meet him. Recognizing who he is, she points upstairs and says, "He's here."

Elliott thanks her and heads up to the studio. As he walks through the double doors, he stares at the easel where Poteet is working and says, "I like that. It's very 'Santa Fe.'"

Poteet smiles and says, "You're back."

"I am. I had a couple of days. So... Here I am." Elliott sets his satchel down and walks over for a closer look. The painting is beginning to show three vertical panels in the center portion of the canvas. The panels have round faces at the top surrounded by different patterns of feathers. Most of the colors are shades of brown and very earthy. Elliott points and says, "The blues in the background here look very much like the color of the sky on a bright summer day. Is that what you had in mind?"

"You know that artists aren't supposed to answer questions like that about their work. It's whatever you think it is," Poteet says with a grin.

Elliott chuckles. "That's really nice. I like it." He continues to stare for a moment before moving to the worktable and digging out his recorder. After turning the device on, he pulls out a notebook. He says, "It's beginning to feel like fall out there."

"Yeah. Fall comes early in Santa Fe. We'll begin to have snow in a month or so."

"Looks like it could snow out there right now."

Poteet walks to the west window to look out. "...pretty dreary day, I'd say."

"Yes, it is."

Poteet moves back to his painting table as Elliott positions his recorder. He says, "By the way, Terry an' I are meetin' the Kleppers for dinner in just a little bit."

"Oh, I had no idea they'd be in town."

Poteet chuckles and says, "Yeah, they're here. So, why don't you come with us. Terry will be comin' by soon."

"Sure, if you don't mind. I'd love to."

Poteet goes to his phone, dials, and says, "Can you change our reservation to five? Elliott's gonna go with us." After a moment, he replies, "Oh. Okay, thanks."

Poteet turns to Elliott. "Did I tell ya I'm in negotiations for a building?"

"No. Here in Santa Fe?"

"Yeah. It's downtown."

"Are you looking for a new place for your gallery?"

"Yeah—an' my studio."

Elliott nods and says, "...exciting."

"I'm talkin' to the historical review committee now. They've got to accept me, before I can buy it."

"I see. You'll have to give me that address. I'd like to go by and take a look."

"Sure. Before we get through today, I'll get that for you."

"Great," Elliott says and checks his recorder. He repositions it slightly and asks Poteet, "Are you ready?"

"Sure. Whachagot?"

Grabbing his notebook, Elliott studies it for a moment and then says, "In the past month, I've been thinking about your life and your story."

"Has it been a *month* since you were last here?"

"Yeah, just about..."

Poteet pauses for a moment before turning back to his painting.

"I've been thinking about the way life started for you. Uh... It could give hope to a lot of people."

Poteet nods and says, "It could. Ya know. 'Cause, I think...

My story is... Jus' don't give up, ya know. If..." He chuckles. "If you have a dream, which I always did. How bad do you want it? Are you willin' to sacrifice all this other stuff? Like I say, when everybody else is out partyin', an' you're not. An' then too... Instead of doin' the easy thing, you follow your dream. I could've had a really good life by jus' doin' what my cousin wanted. Ya know, the guy that was head of Conoco. I could've gone to work for him."

"...and gone in the engineering direction."

"Mm-hmm. I could've done that. But... I didn' want to, 'cause I had a different vision for myself." He smiles at Elliott with a gleam in his eye. "But, don't ever get into this business thinkin' you're gonna make a lot a money. If you do, you're one of the fortunate few, an' I have been. But... I didn' expect it."

"I don't doubt that."

"But... I've never been one to... Ya know, I've always lived within my means. An'... It was about... I don' know. ...two or three years ago. My business manager... An' he's been with me for twenty years. He called me one day, an' he said, 'Do you have any idea how much money you've got in the bank?'"

Elliott chuckles.

"I said, 'No, not really.' He said, 'You better do somethin' with this.'" Poteet chuckles. "He said, 'It's gettin' to be too much.' He said, 'You need to get into somethin', ya know. ...do *somethin'* with it.'"

"...a good place to be."

"Yeah. I never really thought about it, because... I mean... If I needed somethin', it was always there. But... I've managed to spend quite a bit of it since, because... We did all this work over at the house." He shakes his head. "But, what's the difference? I could have it in a money market account, or I could make improvements to our home."

"But, when you do things to your home, you get to enjoy it."

"Yeah, that's right. So... When I bought the house an' made the improvements, I didn' have to borrow any money. An' yeah. I've been very fortunate."

Elliott rubs his hands together and looks out the window. He takes a deep breath and says, "There's something else I'm thinking about."

"Alright."

"And... I don't know if you would claim this. But I think you ought to claim a piece of it—which is all related to the Trails of Tears Project."

"Okay?"

"You met with historians, tribal leaders..."

"Yep."

"...and elders."

"I did."

"So... You were meeting and talking in order to raise consciousness about the Trail-of-Tears issue."

Poteet nods and says, "I was. ...an' to see how they all felt about it."

"And you got positive feedback."

"I did. ...from all of 'em—every single one. They all knew that somthin' needed to be done."

"But... Maybe their intensity had been fading over the years?"

"Not *these* leaders—not at all. Their concerns were that the issue was fadin' on the part of everybody else. An' it was mine too."

"And, you were saying, 'Okay, we need to get this history in front of people. We need to educate them.'"

"Yeah. Essentially. An' they all agreed. No. There wadn' one of 'em that said we should jus' let it go."

Elliott nods. He then bows his head and closes his eyes for a moment before looking up. He says, "And I've been thinking about this..."

"Okay?"

Elliott sits back, takes off his glasses and rubs his face. He finally says, "It seems to me that... And I don't know the right word. ...that you're one of the most, uh... Appreciated... Uh. ...honored. I think 'honored' might be the right word. Um. ...of the American Indians."

"Hmm."

"I think specifically... I mean... I think you said once that a large group of Choctaws, dressed in their traditional clothes, came over while you were painting the mural."

"Yeah, they did. An' that was to support what I was doin'."

"And they sang a song that they hadn't sung for anyone in a hundred years."

"Yep. ...a hundred years."

"Well, I mean..."

"Yeah. It was quite an honor."

"That's pretty special."

"It was. It really was."

"To me, that says that no one in the hundred years had been worthy of that. But then, you came along, and you were."

He nods. "When they tol' me what it was they were doin'... They wanted me to know that it was an honor, an' that's how I took it."

Elliott nods, looks at Poteet, and says, "That made an impression on me. It says something."

"Makes me think of a funny story."

Elliott chuckles. "That's probably not where I was going with this."

Poteet grins. "An' it has nothin' to do with the mural an' what you're talkin' about."

"Why does that not surprise me."

"But I think you'll want to know about it. I thought it was funny."

"Okay."

"I used to have this... I don' know if he's still alive, but... He was a big-time lawyer in Texas—a personal injury lawyer. An' five of the biggest personal-injury suits in Texas history were his."

"Wow."

"His name was Darrell Keith. He had come out here to Santa Fe—come into the gallery where I was showin', an'... An' uh... He brought a friend. An'... He said, 'I don' know if it's gonna work.' He said, 'I'm buildin' a new office in Fort Worth.' An' he did build it. It was seven stories—right close to downtown. An' uh... So, he said, 'I wanna decorate it.' Then he said, 'I think this will work for me,' an'... He kep' sayin', 'If it dudn' work, can I bring it back?' Ya know, I was there, an' I said, 'Sure. You can bring it back. ...no problem.'" Poteet chuckles. "So... He took it. An' about a week later, he called. An' he said, 'I wanna do some more of your paintings in my buildin'.' He said, 'I want you to come down here an' look at it.' So, I said, 'Okay.' So, I went down there. He ended up spendin' almost three hundred thousand dollars on paintings from me."

"Wow."

"So..." Poteet chuckles. "An' he was so worried about that thousand-dollar print, ya know, in the beginning."

"Huh."

"An' uh... So... He called me one day, an' he said, 'I'm gonna be honored by Baylor University.' Ya know, he's an alum at Baylor. He said, 'It's at Colonial Country Club—down in Ft. Worth.'"

"Yeah?"

"He said, 'We're havin' a dinner later.' He said, 'I want you to be there.' I said, 'Okay, I'll be glad to do that, Darrell.' Ya know. 'Cause I'd gotten to know 'im pretty well by then."

"Mm-hmm."

Poteet chuckles and continues, "An' uh... So... The keynote

speaker was Roger Staubach."

"Hmm."

"When I got there, I was seated at the table with Roger. An' Darrell got up in front of the audience, an' he said, 'There's a couple of people I want to recognize here, an'...' Of course, ya know... One was Roger. There were a couple of other people. An' then, he said, 'Mainly...' He said, 'The person that I wanna honor right here...' He said, '...is the greatest Native American painter in the country. An' I started lookin' around— thinkin', 'Who else did he invite?'"

Elliott laughs.

"I mean, I really did. An' he said, 'Poteet, stand up.' So, I did, ya know. It was like, 'No shit.'" Poteet laughs and joins Elliott who is continuing to laugh.

Still chuckling, Poteet says, "An' Roger... When I sat down, Roger... He looked at me, an' he said, 'I thought I was the famous one here.'"

Elliott roars.

"He really did. Yeah."

After recovering, Elliott says, "So... Based on that and every other thing... *Obviously, you're a notable American Indian painter.*"

Poteet chuckles.

"But I want to get back to my point."

"Okay."

"I think you're probably one of the most-honored American Indians of the past century. And I'm not just talking about what you've done as an artist—a painter. I'm saying, 'one of the most-honored American Indians.'"

"Huh."

"But I don't know how you research that."

"I have no idea."

"I tried doing searches on Google, and nothing really made any sense."

"Hmm."

"But... Coming back to who you are now. You've sold thousands of paintings for millions of dollars."

"I have," Poteet says and then pauses. "I have no complaints. 'Cause... Once this thing got cranked up really good, which was in the early nineties, it wadn' unusual for me to have sold out shows in one night. An' it's been goin' good for that long."

Elliott chuckles and says, "Yeah. That's amazing."

They hear Terry calling out from below, "Poteet, we need to go."

Poteet looks at Elliott and yells back, "Okay. We're comin'."

Elliott grabs his satchel and begins to collect his stuff. He reflects on the issue he had just mentioned. Working across all the tribes put Poteet in a unique position in that regard. Elliott thinks that he'll probably bring it up with Pam and Jim tonight, hoping to get additional input.

When Elliott looks around, Poteet is standing by the door. They head out.

CHAPTER 54

Most Honored?

The Kleppers had already been seated when Poteet, Terry, and Elliott walk into the La Fonda Restaurant. When the new arrivals get settled, Elliott says, "I had a question for Poteet today, which was: Is he the most-honored American Indian?"

Elliott looks first at Poteet, who furrows his brow. Elliott then looks around the table, holding out his hands for a response. He finishes the question by asking, "...ever? ...alive today? ...in the last century?"

"Is he the what?" Terry asks.

"Most-honored..." Elliott repeats.

"...American Indian?"

"Yeah."

"In my eyes he is."

"Well..." Elliott chuckles. "I mean, in a more general sense. And the... The points I would bring up in that regard, would be: The large group of Choctaws that showed up in full dress—traditional dress." He looks at Pam and Jim. "It was a gesture of honor and support when Poteet was painting the mural at OU."

Jim says, "Okay," and Pam nods.

"And they sang a song which hadn't been sung in a

hundred years. And this was for Poteet, because they appreciated what he was doing."

Jim says, "That's a big deal."

"It was. Another is: Bear Heart, the beloved, celebrated—"

"Yeah," Poteet affirms.

"—the medicine man who adopted Poteet as his grandson. Think about it. *He adopted Poteet as his grandson.*"

Pam smiles and says, "I didn't know about that."

"It was a big deal. Bear Heart was very famous. He supported Poteet completely and would be supporting him today."

"He would be," Terry confirms.

Poteet echoes, "You're right."

"And then there's the ceremony where Bear Heart gave Poteet the name, which means, 'Does not hide the truth.'"

"Yep. He did," Poteet says.

"How significant is that? Just think about it—*'Does not hide the truth.'* It's so profound. It says so much."

"It does," Jim says. "How hard is it these days to get the truth, especially out of our politicians."

Everyone at the table nods and chuckles.

Elliott continues, "And there's more—the support of all the Chiefs and the Tribal Elders for his mural project."

"Yep," Jim agrees.

"These are all signs of great respect for Poteet. I mean, so... Who else can claim such a thing?"

Poteet shakes his head and says, "I don' know."

Jim shakes his head and shrugs.

Elliott looks around the table. He repeats, "Who else?"

Terry says, "I don't know anyone."

Jim says, "I couldn't tell you." After a moment of consideration, he continues, "And then you think about Geronimo and all of these big-name Indians we're familiar with—from our youth."

"Mm-hmm," Elliott says.

"...because they were on television."

"Mm-hmm. Right. And I mean, I came up with some. One was Jim Thorpe, but I'm not sure he's a good comparison."

"He was certainly honored by America..." Terry says.

"Yeah. And primarily because he was a good athlete."

"Yeah."

"Of course," Poteet says.

"There's Sequoyah," Elliott suggests. "...and Will Rogers. I know they have statues in the capitol building in Washington, D.C. I've seen 'em."

"Was Will Rogers Native American?" Jim asks.

"Yes. He was Cherokee," Elliott quickly answers.

"I guarantee you that Sequoyah was celebrated an' honored for what he did for his people. He's got to be right on up there," Poteet observes.

"...very near the top, I'd say," Jim notes.

"Will Rogers... I don't know. He was famous and beloved by the American people, but was he... Was he honored by the Indians for his achievements?" Elliott asks.

"I expect they took pride in what he did," Jim responds.

"And they should've."

Pam says, "I know that each tribe has their own heroes."

"Right," Jim says. "...like warriors from famous tribal battles, their favorite Chiefs from times past..."

"Yeah."

"...stories handed down for generations."

"Sure. But they have their present-day heroes too," Pam points out. "Since we've been talking about Poteet's mural, I've looked into this. I've watched some videos online, and I've read some articles too. And what I've seen is..."

Jim chuckles, looks around the table, and says, "Who knew?"

Laughs are heard from everyone.

Without cracking a smile, Pam leans forward and continues, "There are many renowned tribal leaders right now. I'm tellin' ya. Many of the tribes present awards to their people for outstanding accomplishments." She pauses and nods. "Some really great things are being done to support the tribes and also to help them preserve their history."

Elliott asks, "Like... What have you seen?"

"I was impressed by what's being done at some of the universities. I read about this one program at the University of Oklahoma that seemed to be doing a really good job."

Poteet nods. "I'm glad to hear that."

"And I've seen this... A lot of books are being written by Native American authors to memorialize their history. And they're winning awards."

"Sure," Jim says. "And they should be. I've seen articles about those kinds of things myself."

Pam turns to Jim to say, "But most of the awards are given by the tribes to their own people, I think."

"From the research I've done, I believe that's right," Elliott says and nods, "...but not always."

"With the successes of the tribes, they can do more of that now," Jim notes.

"I guess that's why I keep coming back to these gestures of great honor that were done for Poteet years ago," Elliott says. "...back when the tribes were just finding their footing and only beginning to emerge."

"Yes. And that's important. I would also think that Poteet's *leadership* with his Trail-of-Tears project set an example for others to follow," Jim suggests.

"I think..." Pam says, leaning forward. "What you just said is the key." She repeats the word, "leadership." She pauses before adding, "It was monumental. I'm sure Poteet's *leadership* in this effort made a huge difference—more than we'll ever know."

Elliott turns to respond to Pam. "It was significant that he was willing to force the issue."

"It was. And that's what I'm saying. Poteet had the meetings when little else was being done. He took the arrows"—she pauses and then says—"no pun intended."

Chuckles are heard around the table.

She continues, "He took the criticism, and he even had protestors."

"That's true. I did," Poteet affirms.

"It's like a lot of things. Someone had to be the one out front, and Poteet was that guy in this case." She turns to ask Poteet, "When you were having all those meetings, did anyone ever tell you to *not* do the mural project because *they* had something else going?"

"Not once..." Poteet answers and chuckles. "Not a single time did that happen."

"That's what I mean," she says, looking around the table. "But Poteet did it. He had his project. He took the criticism, and it made a difference."

"It had to have," Elliott agrees. "And with my point about the 'honors'... And I don't mean to say that he's the only Native American who's ever been honored. Of course, he's not. And I really don't want to get into an argument about who's number one. I'm just saying that Poteet has been highly honored by the tribes and has to be considered as one of their upper echelon in that regard. I don't even see how that's debatable."

Sitting back, Pam shrugs and says, "I think you're right."

"And I'm sure Poteet never thought about being honored like he was," Elliott suggests.

Sitting forward and with everyone watching, Poteet responds, "...not at first. But... When these things started happenin'—like Bear Heart comin' up an' all. Then I really appreciated what him an' the others were doin' for me."

"How could you not..." Elliott responds. "But, one of the

biggest things you did was you crossed tribal lines to get support."

"He did," Pam leans forward to say. "And that was important."

"It was," Elliott agrees and then turns back to Poteet. "You talked to all the tribal leaders you could. Many came to your meetings. They all gave you their support and blessings. We've talked about the *Choctaws* and the hundred-year song. Bear Heart was *Muscogee (Creek)*. You've said that the *Chickasaws* were big supporters. In fact, you told me that all five of the 'civilized' tribes were behind you."

"They were. Most of the tribes I talked to gave us some financial support. Like I say, every one of 'em said it should be done."

Elliott sits back.

As everyone is nodding their agreement, the waiter appears, and the attention of the group turns to Mexican food.

As Elliott sits and reflects on the conversation they'd just had, he's glad he brought it up. He knew that Jim and Pam couldn't be totally objective, but he felt like they would be honest. And they certainly knew more about Poteet and his history than most.

Elliott was confident that his board and his partners would be impressed by the Native American honors bestowed upon Poteet. That was something he hadn't talked about with them. He hoped it would sway them toward supporting Poteet in a project.

CHAPTER 55

The Story is Your Life

The next day, Elliott pushes through the familiar double doors and sees Poteet applying paint to his latest creation. He says, "I enjoyed dinner last night."

Poteet smiles and says, "Yeah. You can never tell about that Pam."

Elliott chuckles. "By the way, I want to get the address of your new building before I leave today. I'd like to go by and see it."

"Okay. I'll get that for ya as soon as I get through with this layer."

After setting up his recorder, Elliott sits, crosses his arms, and says, "I hope you don't mind that I brought up the 'most honored' question with the Kleppers last night."

"No. That was okay," Poteet says. He turns to Elliott. "But... Because of that, I couldn't sleep. I jus' lay there thinkin' about it."

Elliott nods as his smile disappears.

"So... I got up an' started doin' some Google searches."

"Oh...?"

"An' what I found was that there's a Native American Hall of Fame."

"Huh."

"An' it's an impressive group of individuals in there."

"I don't doubt that, but were they honored by their people for what they did?"

"Some of 'em. Jus' bein' inducted into the Hall of Fame would've been an honor," Poteet says and turns to his palette for more paint.

"It would've been. That's true. But it's one thing to be successful... It's another to be honored by the leaders of all these tribes."

"An' I appreciate that. But... There're war heroes in there too."

Smiling, Elliott says, "Well, you weren't one of those."

"I was terrible in the Army," Poteet says. And they both laugh.

Elliott continues, "But... Let me say this. And I want to defend my arguments from last night."

"Okay."

"Your honors came to you without your seeking them, and that's significant."

Skillfully spreading the paint with his knife, Poteet says, "I'll accept that."

"You were honored by tribal members who came up with special and unique ways to show their appreciation for you."

Poteet turns to Elliott. After a moment he responds, "Yeah. They did. An'... Ya know, I was grateful for these things they were doin' for me—all of it. An' uh... Bear Heart... He was very famous and highly respected when he walked up to the podium that night. An' I didn' even realize how much until later, but... Ya know, he gave me a new name, an'... It was such a great honor what he did. An' he adopted me as his grandson..." Poteet shakes his head. "That was... An' the Choctaws... When they sang that song... They meant for it to be a sacred honor, an' that's how I took it."

"Of course..."

Poteet turns to his palette for more paint and continues. "An'... Listen, I'm proud for the Indians who've been recognized in this Hall of Fame. I am. To me, it's all part of the re-emergence..."

"It's the third panel," Elliott says with energy and a smile.

"It is," Poteet agrees. "It really is."

"You took on a lot with that mural."

Poteet points at Elliott with his painting knife and says, "That much is true."

"And all of it is important to who you are today."

"...you mean the neurotic part?"

Elliott chuckles. "You're not neurotic. You're extremely stable." After a moment, he continues, "But... I'd say that the mural project was a huge success—and for all the reasons I gave last night. It *probably* got the ball rolling on the Trail of Tears and educating people about that."

"Maybe."

"But at the very least, it added momentum."

"I hope so. That's what I was tryin' to do."

"I know. And that's why it was another successful chapter in your life."

Poteet tilts his head for a moment to look at Elliott. He then straightens up before saying, "If I added momentum to the movement, I'd call it a success."

"You should."

"And I appreciate that point of view. But ya know... It'll always feel incomplete to me—because of that third panel."

"I know," Elliott says as his smile fades.

Poteet goes back to his palette, stirs his paint with his knife, and continues, "It's a wonder to me that I was even established enough to take on that mural project. 'Cause... After a couple a years of bein' out here, it would've been easy for me to say, 'I'm too old to do this. I got a late start, and it just ain't workin' out.' It would've been easy to quit, an' I came pretty close, ya know. I told you about that, I think."

"...the prayer?"

"Right."

"But you didn't quit. And eventually, you were able to compete with the younger artists who'd been at it for a while."

"I was."

"And speaking of age, one of your best ideas didn't come along..." He looks away. "I'm trying to do the math in my head. Um..."

"Yeah?"

"...'til you were sixty years old."

"...the portraits?"

"Yeah."

"That's true."

"I find that to be inspirational. And I'm sorry to keep using that word, but it's a theme here. And I mean... Sometimes people look back and think that life has passed them by."

"Sure. I've been there."

"So... Those same folks can be encouraged by your story."

"I guess so."

"They really can."

"But... Ya know, age in art is almost meaningless," Poteet says. "Because there are so many artists that did some of their finest work in their later years."

"I expect that you'll be one of those."

Poteet chuckles and then adds, "I had an experience at the Vatican..."

Elliott smiles and chuckles as he says, "Is this when you met the sculptor you'd been dating over there?"

"Yeah. But she didn' get to go on *this* tour. They took me down to the basement."

"I've never been to the basement."

"I didn' think so. My travel agent worked it out, because I

was a professional artist, ya know."

Elliott nods.

"An' where I went... That room was the size of a football field. An' it was jus' stuffed... Oh! ...with all these antiquities an' art, ya know. It was like, 'Oh my God.' An' uh... I was walkin' around lookin' at these sculptures. I had a guard with me. An' uh... I came up on this white marble piece. An' it was a very abstract lookin' piece. It was a... I think the main body of it was probably about five an' a-half feet tall, an' it was white marble. An' it was cut in all these different planes. An' there were two bars stickin' out of it—two iron bars, an' another smaller piece of white marble that was cut in these different angles. An' it was jus' beautiful."

"An' uh... I asked the guard. I said, 'Whose work is that?' He said, 'That's Michelangelo,' an' I said, 'You're kiddin' me?' He said, 'No. That was...' He said, 'Michelangelo did five pietas in his life. Most people are jus' familiar with the one. It's one of the centerpieces of the Vatican." Poteet looks at Elliott and asks, "Do you know what I'm talkin' about?"

"Let me think."

"It's a... It's the Virgin Mary holdin' Jesus after his death."

"Oh. So, that's a pieta?"

"Yeah. An' the guard tol' me. He said that Michelangelo did five pietas, an' *that* one he did when he was eighty-nine. An'... I thought, 'Wow. He became an abstract artist.' Because... When I think of Michelangelo. I think of realism."

"Yeah," Elliott says and nods. "I can see that. I've seen some of his sculptures, and that's how they are. And the Sistine Chapel..."

"Right. He used some imagination there to tell a story, but it's painted in a realism style."

"So... Seeing that abstract pieta was significant?"

"Oh yeah. I think it probably influenced me to do more abstract work."

"...makes sense."

"But... You look at Monet when he did those waterlilies, he was a pretty old guy. Even Picasso... Ya know, Picasso lived to be, I think, ninety-two. But... Ya know. Artists... Age dudn' mean a thing."

"Mm-Hmm."

"Makes me think of what Terry tol' me the other day." He chuckles. "Ya know, she listens to this preacher called Jeff Schreve. ...lives in Texarkana. She always goes online and listens every Sunday. This Sunday, I was doin' somethin' else. But... When I came in, she said, 'Ya know, he was talkin' about Caleb today.' An' she said the whole thing about Caleb was... He was an older man when God told 'im to do whatever it was he wanted 'im to do. An' he was like, eighty-five years old, an' uh... He was still strong, an'... Ya know, she said the whole message was to stay strong, don't... Don't withdraw from life."

"Yeah?"

"An' uh..."

"I think that's a good message," Elliott observes. "At my age, I can appreciate that."

"An' she was sayin'... She said, 'All the time I'm listen' to it, I'm thinkin', "Yeah. That's... That's what Poteet does."' She said. ...talkin' 'bout me. She said, 'You ain't afraid of nothin'.'"

Elliott laughs.

"An' uh... She said that he told the story about Clint Eastwood. Ya know, Clint Eastwood is like, eight-nine now."

"Right."

"An' uh... He was out playin' golf with Toby Keith. An' Toby was tellin' the story. He said that the next day was gonna be Clint's birthday. He said, 'What are you gonna do for your birthday?' He said, 'Well, I've gotta get down to Florida. We're shootin' this movie. It's called *The Mule*.'"

"Yeah?"

"He said, 'I gotta get down there.'" Poteet starts to chuckle.

"He said, 'Clint, at your age, how do you... How do you keep doin' all this?' Clint said, 'I jus' don't let the old man in.'"

Elliott smiles and nods.

"...pretty good answer."

"Yeah... Well... I think most people don't do that," Elliott suggests.

"I think you're right. An' ya know, this whole thing about retirin', it... Uh... It dudn' register with me. I could... Uh... 'Cause, I think art really helps keep a person young. Like I was sayin', Michelangelo was almost ninety. Picasso was in his nineties. An' they were still workin'."

"And, at that time, ninety was *really* old."

"Yeah! Life expectancy back then was like, forty or somethin', ya know. An' he was a hell-raiser too."

"Michelangelo was?" Elliott asks and then chuckles.

"Uh-huh. Well... Ya know, we were talkin' 'bout Willie the other day. Willie's what? ...eighty-three, eight-four."

"He is?"

"Yeah. An' uh... He's still up there playin'. An' I'm sure he'll never quit, until he jus' can't do it anymore."

Elliott nods.

"So... I don' know what the hell I'd do with myself, if somebody said to me, 'You can't paint anymore.'" He looks at Elliott and asks, "What the hell would I do?"

Elliott chuckles and says, "Fortunately, you're in a place where there's nobody who can tell you that."

"That's true. I can stay focused on painting. But I've also learned to let life flow through me—take it as it comes, ya know. Enjoy the moment."

Elliott cocks his head and looks at Poteet. He asks, "You've said that before. What exactly do you mean?"

"It's like... You're doin' somethin', but you're thinkin' about what you're gonna do next. An' then you get into that, an' you're thinkin' 'bout somethin' else. Ya know. Of course, you plan. You have to make some plans to live. But, uh... Generally, it's jus' lettin' life unfold before you, instead of tryin' to *make* it happen. It's jus' like... When I'm paintin', I'm into that. I'm not thinkin' 'bout what I'm gonna do in an hour or whatever. I'm right there. ...in the moment."

"Mm-hmm. I know what you mean. It's that way with film for me."

"I'm sure. 'Cause you're workin' in the moment. Uh... 'Cause... You're not thinkin', 'What are we havin' for dinner tonight?' An' it's like, you're eatin' dinner. You're eatin' a salad, an' you're thinkin', 'Oh... Oh, I'm ready to eat that main course.'"

Elliott snickers.

"An' you're eatin' the main course... I can't wait to have that dessert," Poteet says and chuckles.

"Yeah," Elliott says. "You should be livin' in the moment and appreciating it. It's a good lesson."

"I think I'm much better at it now than I used to be. An' then, ya know, there's the ambition part. 'Cause, along with ambition comes fear. You're fearin' this. This is gonna happen. You're fearin' that. An' uh... Ya know, that's real stressful. So... When I see it, I can see it for what it is, an' I jus' try to let it go. I think it was Mark Twain that said... He said, 'I'm an old man now, an' I've seen many horrible things in my life—most of which never happened.'"

They break up laughing.

Elliott says, "I hadn't heard that."

"It's the damn truth."

Still laughing, Elliott says, "That's a good quote."

"Yeah. I know when I read that I just thought, 'Boy, that's the absolute truth. It's just the way it is.'"

"I'll have to remember that."

Poteet says, "But, one day it'll happen.'

"What's that?"

"I'll paint my last painting."

"Yeah."

"An' they won't be makin' any more of 'em. That'll be it."

"And of course, who can say that about their job or their work. And also... Who can say that their previous work will increase in value, because they're through?"

Poteet nods and says, "Not many..." He chuckles and leans against his table. After a moment, he looks at Elliott and asks, "So, what else you got?"

Elliott looks down at his notes. "Here's a question."

Poteet smiles and says, "Okay?"

Terry walks in and asks, "Is it okay for me to join y'all?"

Elliott beams and answers, "Sure. Please come in."

She walks across the room and sits in her spot by the fireplace.

Elliott turns back to Poteet and says, "This could be tough. It's about your painting career."

"Okay."

Elliott takes a deep breath and slowly says, "I'm wondering what status you would claim."

"I'm not sure what you mean."

"Well... Like... I think you could easily say you were one of the top-selling Native American contemporary artists."

"Oh yeah. ...for sure."

"You might say you're *the* top-selling Native American contemporary artist."

"There really aren't too many of us."

"So... you *could* be the top."

"...could be."

"You might say you're the top selling Native American artist."

"Maybe... I don' know."

"Or. ...the top-selling American contemporary artist?"

"I don' know. I'm one of the top."

Elliott bounces his fingers on his leg and says, "I'm impressed by that."

"We'll, I had... I think it was back in..." Poteet looks away and strokes his goatee. "When was it? I think it was around '96 when I was showin' downtown. They would do ads for my work. An'... So, I picked up a magazine. I saw my ad, an' it said, 'Santa Fe's Most Collectible Artist.' An' I thought, 'What?' So, I called 'em up, an' I said, 'What'd y'all put that in there for?' An' they said, 'Well, it's true.' An' I said, 'Well, how do you know it's true?' They said, 'We get these reports, ya know—city reports an' stuff.'"

"...you mean like in sales?"

"Yeah."

Elliott chuckles.

Poteet says, "I didn' know it at all."

"It's significant when it says 'collectible,'" Terry points out. "Because... We have collectors who come in here all the time. They like his paintings. But they're... Some of 'em are collectin' 'em, because they think they'll increase in value. They're collectin' Poteet's paintings as an investment. An' like I say, we see it all the time."

"That seems like a powerful endorsement."

"You think about it..." Poteet tells Elliott, "Here in Santa Fe, the population's what? ...seventy thousand. ...somethin' like that. An' there's, I think, sixteen thousand registered artists in this town."

"That's amazing."

"Yeah. It is. An' to go from that up to... Ya know, about three years later bein' the 'most collected.'"

"...in three years?"

"Yeah."

"That seems impossible."

"That's what I thought, too."

"But... Most artists are *not* business-minded," Terry says.

"We were talking about that recently."

"Right. An' Poteet is. An' that helps in a lot of ways."

Poteet nods.

Elliott says, "And about not being business minded... There's Harold Stevenson..."

"He wadn'," Poteet says. "If he had of been, he could've done so much better. In fact, he used to ask me... He would say, 'You are so smart in these areas. What should I do?' He... He asked me that a hundred times. But one thing he did do right."

"Oh?"

"Yeah... The Guggenheim Museum eventually purchased his painting, *The New Adam*, for their permanent collection. They paid 'im five million for it."

"...five million dollars?"

"Yeah. An' he used the purchase to get some publicity goin' for himself. He said, 'This was the painting that was rejected, blah, blah, blah.' An' he... An' he tol' me there was a line all the way down the block to see the painting when they previewed it."

"He owned it, and he sold it for five million dollars?" Elliott questions.

"Yeah."

"So... I mean... He should've been in good shape financially."

"Yeah, but he... He wadn'. I mean..."

"Huh?"

"He'd give it away to these lovers of his an' all this shit. It's jus'... It's jus' crazy. But... Like Harold said, 'Gettin' rejected sometimes has a way of comin' back around.'"

Elliott takes a deep breath and replies, "...sounds like it did for him."

"It did. An' Picasso too."

"Picasso? I guess I don't know about that."

"Yeah. It's when he painted the *Guernica*."

"Okay?"

"The Spanish government had commissioned him to do a painting to memorialize the bombing by the Germans of the town Guernica in Spain. I think it was in 1938 or somethin' like that. An' so... He did the painting."

"Okay."

"Are you familiar with it?"

"No."

"It's all done in black an' white, an' it's these Picasso-type figures. I've seen the painting. The Museum of Modern Art in New York City had it for forty years, because the Spanish government rejected it. They hated it."

Elliott chuckles.

"...didn' want it. So... The Museum of Modern Art said, 'Well, we'll show it.' An' they did. They kep' it for forty years, an' that became the most famous painting Picasso ever did."

"Yeah?"

"An' then, the Spanish government said, 'Oh... Wait a minute. We... We kinda want our painting back.'"

Elliott and Terry laugh.

"An' they built a whole wing to the Prado Museum, an' brought it back to Spain."

"Oh... I guess it cost 'em a lot to get it back."

"No. It was *their* painting."

"Oh. They commissioned it and paid for it, so it was still their painting."

"Yeah. They just put it out on loan."

"...for forty years."

"Mm-hmm. An'... The Museum of Modern Art, they were... 'Cause, uh... They didn' wanna give it up," Poteet says and chuckles.

"Yeah?"

"They tried everything to keep it, but... No... I mean, that

painting is... I mean, you couldn'... I mean, what would that...
That painting is worth, probably a billion dollars."

Elliott chuckles and says, "Oh my gosh."

"Yeah. It's his most famous painting. I mean, the painting
is twenty feet long..."

"Oh."

"...an' ten feet high. It reminds me of the way Harold liked
to paint."

"Right."

"But... As time went on... With Harold, uh..."

"He got a little dark with his paintings," Terry says.

"Well, he got so homoerotic," Poteet clarifies.

"You mentioned that," Elliott notes.

"Ya know, I had gay guys tell me, 'Hell, I wouldn't hang it
in my house.'"

They all laugh.

"But the last big painting that he started was down at the
ranch at the studio. I had that big easel. It was that one I
brought back from OU, to finish the third panel. An' I had a
big canvas on it, an' he'd come out to visit. He kept lookin' at
that thing...lookin' at that thing. An' I said, 'You wanna paint
on that, don't ya?'"

Elliott and Terry begin to chuckle.

"An' he said, 'I'd love to paint on that.'"

They continue to chuckle.

"An' I said, 'Okay. Whadaya wanna paint?' An' he said,
'You.'" Poteet grins. "An' I said, 'All right.' So... I had a saddle
in there, an' he was lookin' around. An' he said, 'Go get that
saddle.' So, I brought it over, an' he said, 'Okay now... You lay
that saddle here. Take off your shirt an' then... Lay on the
floor... Put your head in that saddle.' An' I think I had one arm
behind me or somethin'. An' he said, 'Yeah, that's it. An'... This
canvas was so big. An' Harold was small an' old. So, I had a..."
Poteet points at a box of cardboard mailing tubes. "I said, 'Can

you use one of those tubes right there to help you?'"

"Huh."

"So Harold... He said, 'Let's tie a big piece of charcoal on the end of that.' So, I did. I tied up a piece. An' he started sketchin' this thing out, ya know. I couldn't see it, because it was behind me. An' uh... He did that for about twenty or thirty minutes. An' he said, 'Okay, I think that's a good start.' An' so, I got up an' looked at it. An' I was like, 'Wow.' It was perfect, ya know."

Elliott and Terry chuckle.

"Yeah. He was somethin'."

Elliott says, "Yeah—like the portrait he did of you for the one hundred."

"It didn' take 'im long either—twenty, thirty minutes."

"To me, that just shows his level of talent."

"Like I say, Harold could capture a person really quickly. An' this big one, the one he didn' finish, it's beautiful too."

Elliott nods.

"It is," Terry agrees.

"But... Ya know, he..." Poteet chuckles. "When he tol' me to take off my shirt, it wadn' anything new. 'Cause he said, 'I hate paintin' clothes.'"

All three laugh.

Elliott gives a last gasp and asks, "Do you still have that one?"

"Yeah."

"How much did he get done?"

"You can tell it's Poteet." Terry answers.

"Oh yeah. I don' know. He probably got about halfway through it. Yeah, about halfway..."

"Would you consider finishing it, Poteet?" Terry asks.

"No. Oh no. No, no, no."

"You wouldn'?"

"No. That's sacrilege."

"That's what I was thinking," Elliott notes. "But even so, it could still be a great work of art."

"I'm tellin' ya. It is," Terry says.

"Actually, I kind of... I kind of like it that way," Poteet adds. "Ya know, it's the last one that he started."

"Yeah. Seems like that's very appropriate—as his last painting," Elliott says.

"It is. I mean, especially with the subject matter bein' me."

"He painted a lot of you. Y'all were close."

"Yeah, we were. I liked seein' 'im."

"Uh-huh."

"So..."

"What do you think you'll do with it?"

"Shit. I don' know. I have no idea. I guess it'll jus' be another thing in the storage unit. It'll be a treasure trove for somebody at some point in time."

Elliott looks away and hopes he'll have a chance to see the unfinished painting someday.

CHAPTER 56

What Success Looks Like

Elliott asks, "Does Harold's family have quite a few paintings of his?"

"They've got some. Uh... What Harold did, ya know, the last years of his life, was really weird to me. I mean... He lived with this guy. ...had been livin' with 'im since the '70s. But then, he hooks up with this psychopath up in New York. An' this guy stole... I don' know how many paintings from Harold."

"Really?"

"Yeah. An' Harold would never do anything about it. I mean... An' he was... This guy was a heroin addict. An' Harold's nephew told me that somebody told 'im... He said, 'He sold those damn things, like in garage sales—jus' to get any kind of money at all.' Ya know. So... Some of the great pieces that he had were lost through this guy. Because... I would ask Harold. I'd say, 'Whatever happened to so an' so painting—this painting or that one...?' An' he'd say, 'I don' know. I have no idea.' Anyway, he got to where he didn' even care anymore."

"Huh."

"It got to the point where... Ya know, life was over for him. He didn' care."

Terry sits forward and says, "But, Harold was so..."

Elliott interrupts and asks Terry, "Did you know Harold?"

"I did know Harold. In fact... When I'd go home, before Harold went to the nursin' home, I would always go see 'im. An' I would take 'im a bottle of vodka. He loved his martinis."

"He did," Poteet agrees.

"Well, awesome for you—for doing that."

"An... An' he loved sweets. An' I would go buy 'im sweets. An' I would buy 'im vodka. An' I'd take it to 'im. An' one time... I remember, he had this dog named..." She turns to Poteet to ask, "What was that dog's name?"

"Saffo."

"Saffo. It was a... It was like a..."

"...a whippet," Poteet answers.

"Okay. An' I went out there an' I took 'im the sweets. An' I took 'im the vodka. An' this dog was as poor as a drink of water."

Elliott chuckles.

"I mean, that dog was poor. I mean he was skinny, skinny poor. An' that dog was wantin' somethin' to eat. So, I went to the store, an' I bought a big old sack—a fifty-pound sack a dog food. An' I took it back out there, an' I set the dog feeder up— in his house. Ya know."

"Of course," Elliott responds thoughtfully.

"But I had to do that, 'cause I couldn'... I couldn' rest knowin' that that dog was so hungry."

"I can imagine you would do that."

"But yeah..." Poteet says. "His father was a character too. He was an alcoholic, an' I was livin' out there... I had come back from New York. An' Harold had given me his old studio an' house out there to use." Poteet turns to Elliott. "Ya know, I told ya 'bout that cool studio he'd built. But anyway... Ol' Doc... He'd show up in the mornin' 'bout seven o'clock. An' Harold wadn' there—jus' me. An'... Of course, I'd let 'im in, an'

I'd say, 'You want some coffee, Doc?' He'd say, 'I want you to take a drink of whiskey with me!'"

Elliott chuckles.

"I said, 'Damn, Doc. It's seven o'clock in the mornin'.'"

Elliott and Terry laugh.

"An' he said, 'Well, I ain't leavin'.'"

Elliott and Terry continue to laugh, and Poteet joins in.

Still chuckling, Poteet says, "I said, 'Well, give me the damn bottle then.'"

All three laugh.

Elliott says, "Wow!"

"Yeah, he... He was a character," Poteet explains. "But I liked 'im, He was funny as hell."

"Huh. Well, something I read said that he was eccentric."

"Mm-hmm. He was."

"And uh... And so, Harold was eccentric too."

"Mm-hmm."

"Makes me think about my family," Terry says.

"...because they're eccentric?" Elliott asks.

"No—not that."

"...all this discussion about Idabel?"

"Yeah. An' I mean, when mamma was alive... An' even now, ya know. I have to go see my family."

"Mm-hmm."

"Of course, Mamma... She would come out here an' stay with us some. An' Poteet jus' thought the world of Mamma, an' Mamma did Poteet."

"Yeah. Well, that's the reason he married you, I understand."

Terry giggles and says, "Yeah. An' see... He'll tell anybody to this day. He'll say"—mimicking Poteet—"'Don't go to the Pizza Hut. Whatever you do, stay out the Pizza Hut.'"

They all laugh. Terry ends with a sweet, high-pitched sigh. They laugh some more.

Poteet chuckles and confirms, "Yeah, her mother... She jus' thought the world of me."

"Hmm."

"Uh... She'd always take my side."

They laugh.

"She would."

Elliott chuckles.

"'Course, I was good to 'er, too. I'd... I'd give 'er money. An' uh... She was... Like I say, she spent all those years pinchin' those pennies, ya know... For 'er birthday or somethin' I'd give 'er a thousand bucks. Oh, my gosh. ...jus' thrilled 'er to death."

"I'm sure it did."

Terry stands and says, "Yes, it did." She walks to the double doors and says, "I think I hear somebody." She looks at Poteet and points. She says, "Tell 'im 'bout Moll an' Charlie. They might be comin' by today."

Poteet nods and says to Elliott, "Yeah. She's talkin' 'bout Moll an' Charlie Anderson. I guess they've said somethin' to 'er 'bout bein' in town."

"They're collectors of yours?"

"Yeah. They've been buyin' my paintings for years, an' we've become good friends. You'll love 'em. An' I've done some commissions for 'em, too. An' it's like... When they bought that penthouse at the Ritz Carlton there in Dallas... That's one of the first things she did. She's an interior designer, ya know. Matter of fact, the last book she did was a Number One New York Times Bestseller—non-fiction. She's also got a TV show in L.A."

"Hmm. I wonder if I've seen it?"

"It's about interior designs."

"That's not what I usually watch. My wife may know of her."

"But anyway, one of the first things she did, when she bought that penthouse... She said, 'I need this huge painting for this.' So, I painted 'er one—jus' like she wanted."

"I wonder if my wife would want to commission you to paint something for her?"

"I'd be glad to. She can talk to Moll about it—or others, if she wants to."

"That *would* be fun. I'll have to ask."

"Sure."

"But you were saying about these collectors, this couple, the Andersons..."

"Yeah. An' I think I tol' ya 'bout not givin' paintings away."

"Right. I think that was Harold's advice to you."

Poteet nods and then looks up with a smile. "But... For me, there's always been one exception to that rule."

"Oh yeah?"

"An' it's Moll Anderson."

Elliott chuckles.

"Yeah. Because she's given us so much, ya know."

"I see."

"So... Every time I do a portrait of someone new..."

"...an abbreviated portrait?" Elliott asks.

"Yeah. I give her the number one."

"I see. She must be very special to you."

"She is. An' she's got 'em all—all the number ones. An' she hangs 'em—in her home." Poteet looks up with a wrinkled brow. He says with some urgency, "Yeah. Matter of fact, I owe 'er one." He looks away for a moment, then continues, "But she's an exception to the rule. She's the only one."

"Huh."

"Yeah. An' about Charlie, her husband... He told me his story. An' it's a great story. His grandfather started out sellin' newspapers an' magazines from a lean-to—on the street, ya know. An' as time went by... Well, his son got involved with 'im, which was Charlie's father, an' they started placin' magazines in different stores. An' they ended up with a

Walmart contract—magazines, books, music, an' uh... So... Charlie said that... After a time that the people at Walmart came to 'em an' said, 'We've watched you people, an' you're really good at marketing. How would you like to own the music section in Walmart?' An' so, Charlie bought the music section in every Walmart in the world—every one of 'em."

"Wow! That's huge."

"Yeah. An' Moll told me about when they got married... When she met Charlie, she said, 'What do you do?'"

Elliott grins.

"He said, 'Well, I'm a distributor for Walmart.' She was, 'Oh, really?' She said, 'I could jus' see us goin' down the road in a truck, ya know.'"

Elliott laughs.

"She said that her first year... The first year they were married, Charlie made sixty million dollars—in that one year."

Elliott breathes out a high-pitched, "Whew..."

"I mean, yeah... He's... He's a brilliant business guy. He really is. An' they bought a place here not long ago."

"...in Santa Fe?"

"Yeah. An' she's redecoratin' it now. She's havin' me do a commission for *it*."

"Obviously, she was pleased with the last one."

"She was. So anyway... A couple of months ago, I went to Moll's house here in Santa Fe, an' all her decorators were there."

"Okay?"

"When she introduced me, she said, 'This is, ya know, Poteet Victory.' She said, 'He's, uh, one of the most important artists in America.'"

"Nice."

"An' then, uh... She said, 'I think *he's* the best.'"

They both laugh.

Poteet says, "They have a mansion in Knoxville."

"Hmm."

"...a house in Nashville an' a house in L.A. But this... This place in Knoxville... It's like a palatial estate. It looks like a castle that was built by some magnate many years ago. An' Charlie was tellin' me. He said, 'Ya know, I tol' Moll...' He said, 'We can build anything you wanna build,' an' she said... She told 'im, 'I want that'—talkin' 'bout that palatial estate."

Elliott chuckles.

"An' Charlie said, 'Okay.' An' he tol' me. He said, 'Moll was able to exceed an unlimited budget.'"

Elliott and Poteet laugh hard together.

"That's funny," Elliott says.

"When Terry an' I went to Knoxville, we stayed with Moll an' Charlie. It's when Reba was there."

"Reba?"

"Yeah. Ya know, Reba McEntire."

Elliott drops his chin, and his eyes widen.

"Yeah. Reba was there. 'Cause... Each year, they do a fundraiser for Habitat for Humanity. An' it's only fifty people. It's held there at their place. An' it's a black-tie... It's like, ten or fifteen thousand dollars a plate. An' Charlie said, 'I have to turn people away.' So, when he said, 'I want you an' Terry to come,' I said, 'Well... I'll tell ya Charlie, I'm not payin' ten thousand dollars a plate.' He said, 'No, no, no, no, no. You're my guest, an' y'all are gonna stay with us.'"

Softly, Elliott says, "Wow."

"An' he said, 'We'll jus' send a plane out there to pick ya up.'"

Elliott chuckles and says, "...good folks to know."

Poteet turns to Elliott and says, "I'm sure it's not that big a deal for you, but for us..."

"I get it."

"An' he did. He sent it. Yeah. ...jus' me an' Terry on that big Learjet," Poteet says and laughs.

"That's very nice."

"An' I mean, it was a beautiful plane. You get in, an' it's all white leather, ya know, an' all this stuff. So, Terry an' I are sittin' back there, an' they kinda taxi out—we're sittin' on the runway. An' this pilot is turnin' around, lookin' back at me. I thought he was jus' bein' friendly, so I'm sittin' there. I give 'im a little wave an' say 'Hi.'" Poteet chuckles. "An' the pilot said, 'Say when.'"

Elliott grins.

"An' I said, 'Go.'"

Elliott laughs and shakes his head.

"But... Ya know, my sister an' Reba were friends a *long* time ago."

"Huh."

"...before Reba was Reba. An'... The way Reba got discovered was... They used to have the National Finals Rodeo in Oklahoma City. So... Reba used to get up, an' she would sing the National Anthem—acapella. An' she could make the hair stand up on your neck. She's just so good. Somebody in the audience jus' happened to see 'er one time an' thought, 'Boy, ya know, that girl, uh... That girl's terrific.' An' that's how she got started."

"Huh. Wow."

"An' when she first went to Nashville, my sister gave 'er clothes. She didn' have the clothes to go."

"Huh. No kidding."

"An' when I met Reba down there... Well, Charlie got me aside an' said, 'I want you to meet Reba before everybody gets here an' jus' surrounds her.' Ya know. I said, 'Okay.' So... Uh... He took me back there. An' my brother-in-law had jus' died. An'... So, when Charlie introduced me to Reba, I told 'er, I said, 'Reba, I'm Loretha Clark's brother.' An' she looked at me. An' she said, 'You are.' She said, 'I was so sorry to hear about Rowland.' She said, 'I can't believe you're her brother.' So, I kind of had a connection with 'er, ya know, right off the bat."

"Yeah. Well, that's very special."

Poteet nods and says, "She was in rodeo. That's how my sister got to know 'er. Both of 'em were barrel racers."

"Huh..."

"Yeah."

"Well, I knew Reba was from southeast Oklahoma somewhere," Elliott notes.

"Yeah—a little place north of where we were brought up. It's called Stringtown."

"Well, I've never heard of Stringtown."

Poteet chuckles and responds, "I'm not surprised."

"But I love Reba."

"Yeah. I'm tellin' ya."

"So, she did a show that night?" Elliott asks.

"Oh yeah."

"And I guess her band was there."

"Yeah. They were all there."

"Man, oh man..."

"But yeah—jus' for fifty people." Poteet points at a spot about ten feet away. He says, "I mean, she was this close."

"How long did she play?"

"...'bout an hour, I guess."

"Wow," Elliott says, chuckling.

"Yeah."

"...probably never get a better concert than that."

Poteet chuckles and says, "Probably not... But Charlie's mother..."

Elliott smiles, knowing another story is coming.

"He'd always ask his mother to come up for it, an' he told 'er he wanted 'er to come up for this year. An' she said, 'Oh, Charlie, ya know, I really don't care anything about goin',' An' he said, 'Mama, Reba is gonna be the entertainment.' She said, 'Really?'"

Elliott chuckles.

"She said, 'Well, I'd *walk* up there for that.'"

Elliott breaks up.

Poteet joins in the laughter and adds, "Yeah... But... With Moll an' Charlie... You would think, ya know... People that rich an' everything... But they're jus' as good a people—down-to-earth... Ya know, when I was that Artist of the Year, we had a banquet here, an'... An' so, I invited 'em. I said, 'If you're around, I'd love for you to be there.' Well, they weren't around, but they showed up for it anyway. It was a fundraiser, an' I had this one... I had donated this one painting. It was... I don' know. It wadn' that big. It was like sixty-five hundred bucks—retail."

"Okay."

"My painting was the last one that they auctioned off, an' people were biddin'. An'... I'm watchin' 'em out there, an' Charlie an' Moll are sittin' at the same table. An' I figure out that they're the ones biddin'. They're biddin' *against* each other."

Elliott chuckles.

"They ended up payin' sixteen thousand dollars for it."

Elliott laughs.

"An' I said... After it was over, I said, 'Charlie, what were y'all thinkin'?' An' he said, 'Hell, man... We came out here to make you famous.' I said, 'Well, thank you.'"

Elliott laughs hard again and finishes with "Wow."

"Yeah."

Elliott says, "...great folks."

"Yeah, they are."

"You've got some great friends."

"We do, an' you hope that the people you meet... You hope that you'll be a blessin' in their lives—a good thing in their lives. An'... I always hope that, anyway. An' it's not that I want somebody to... I ain't a people pleaser, an' I don't really care if you like me or not. But... I would hope that through our connection that maybe I could be a blessin' in your life, somehow."

"I like that. More people should look at life that way. I should look at life that way."

Poteet nods slightly. "It's Roy Masters. It's what I've learned from him."

Elliott nods and grins. He says, "There's a lot about your life that's inspirational. And then... There are all the stories."

Poteet and Elliott laugh together.

"Speakin' of stories, did I tell you about Lyle Waggoner?" Poteet asks.

Elliott chuckles under his breath and asks, "...from the *Carol Burnett Show?*"

"Yeah."

"You knew 'im?"

"Yeah. I did."

"I heard that he died recently."

Poteet sighs and says, "...just a few months ago."

"Yeah. But..." Elliott says, "We bought some trailers from his company. For a while he was setting the standard for mobile dressing rooms. I mean... The stars were demanding those trailers."

"Right. He was tellin' me about that."

"I think it was a good business."

"I think it was. But... We were talkin' one day. An' I was askin' about the show."

Elliott grins and says, "Oh, yeah. We used to watch that all the time with our friends. We were younger then."

Poteet nods. "An', ya know, I was askin' about this an' that."

"I guess, this was after..."

"Oh yeah. The show'd been over for years."

"Okay."

"An'... Uh... I'd say. 'What kind of person is so an' so?' I said, 'What kind of person is Tim Conway?' He said, 'Oh, my God.'"

Elliott begins to chuckle.

"He said... He said, 'Yeah. He's funny. He damn sure is.' But. he said, 'That shit never stops.'"

Elliott belly laughs.

"He said, 'It's jus' twenty-four hours a day.'"

Elliott sighs as his laughing dies down.

Poteet chuckles.

After regaining his composure, Elliott says, "You know... I think I can see that."

"Me too."

CHAPTER 57

Telling the Story

Elliott shakes his head. After a moment he chuckles and asks, "Do you mind if we get back on track here?"

Poteet shrugs and says, "No. Whadaya wanna talk about?"

"I want to get serious about this film I hope to make."

"Sure. Of course. Whatever..."

Elliott chuckles and looks at Poteet. He says, "It's hard to not get sidetracked with you."

"That's true. I'll try to focus."

Elliott turns to the window and takes a deep breath. After a moment, he turns back to Poteet and says, "You deserve a film—at the very least. Your life deserves to be exposed, and... When I first came out here, I had no idea."

Poteet reaches up to stroke his goatee.

"And... Although I think it's about your life *now*, your life accomplishments still need to be known—by everyone." Elliott takes a deep breath and continues, "The honors given by the Indians... Your success as a top-selling artist..."

Elliott looks at Poteet, who nods slowly.

"Your Trail of Tears mural and what they did to you at the University of Oklahoma..."

Poteet raises his eyebrows and watches Elliott.

"It's your intellect and the buzz your intelligence brings to your story. It's your connection to history through Harold Stevenson, and that's really important. It's almost a second thought in this, but it shouldn't be. That history... The seeds of the sixty's culture... That's all stand-alone-worthy stuff." Elliott shakes his head. "And then, there's your love life."

Poteet grins.

Elliott chuckles and adds, "And that's what gets us an 'R' rating."

They laugh.

After a moment, Elliott continues, "It's your spiritual journey."

Poteet nods.

"It's the rags-to-riches thing—the abandoned-child thing. It's the feel-good story-could've-fallen-off-the-rails thing. It's 'How did you do it? How did you overcome? How did you survive? How did you achieve all this?'" Elliott pauses and looks around the studio. He then continues, "The word I use is 'inspirational,' and I keep saying it. But that's it. Your life is inspirational, and I think people like to see that kind of thing. They really do."

Poteet remains silent.

"I don't want to get ahead of myself, but I've been thinking about how to present this story. And I think it begins mid-life somewhere."

"I thought you liked some my stories about when I was a kid."

"I do. And, I didn't say not to show 'em. I said, 'It begins mid-life. And..."

"Okay."

"We reveal your early life experiences as flashbacks."

Poteet cocks his head and squints as he continues to watch Elliott.

"This was done very skillfully in *Arrow*. Did you see that?"

"No."

"It's been a very successful series, with lots of episodes and running for ten seasons."

"Okay."

"But the technique has been used a lot. Another one I saw recently was *The Queen's Gambit*. The opening scene is actually from the very end of the story. In that one, they give you a taste of where they're going to take you and spend the rest of their time getting there. Also, they used that a lot in *Breaking Bad*, if you'll remember."

Poteet nods.

"It's just another way of presenting a story, and I know we have enough good material on you to do that. It could start with you going to New York and art school... Or... It could start with your fairytale courtship with Terry. In that case, the flashbacks could be the bulk of the story. I can see that—flashing back to the childhood raids at the bootlegger's house, or ringing a doorbell asking for food, or some of the touching moments with the people you met at your mother's café." Elliott looks toward the west window, raises his index finger to his lips for a moment. He then drops his hand and continues, "I actually like the thought of starting with that bull-riding contest you won. You know. ...when you were thirteen. I love that story."

Poteet smiles but remains quiet.

"In the series *Arrow* I mentioned..."

"Yeah?"

"It has a lot of fighting and violence in it. You know, people like some action. And... You've got plenty of that in your history too. Living on the street... Hanging around your mother's beer joint at night, you saw plenty of fights. Not to mention, plenty of your own fights. When I think back on your early life, there's a richness to it that's almost limitless."

"It was somethin' I had to deal with."

"It was," Elliott says and shrugs. He nods and then adds, "I think it would make a great series. I really do."

Poteet raises his eyebrows and then looks down at his painting table.

"And... You deserve it. Like I was saying. You're a hero."

Poteet looks up to say, "I'm no hero."

"People should know of you. And we all should take pride in your accomplishments."

"Seems a bit over the top to me."

"...not really. It's a factual account of your life story. I'm just telling you the way it hits me. It might hit others that same way. But... I know my board's not into it like I am." Elliott looks at his watch, opens his eyes wider, and says, "Time to go—got some calls." As he's putting his notes and recorder away, he says, "Can you write down that address for me?"

"...on the building?"

"Yeah."

With frustration in his voice, Poteet says, "Sorry, I forgot about that earlier." He reaches for a pencil and jots it down.

Elliott grabs the note and heads for the double doors but stops to look back. He asks, "Will tomorrow afternoon be okay?"

"I'll be here."

CHAPTER 58

Sand, Beads, and a Building

As Elliott walks into the studio, Poteet hands him a large poster. He says, "Terry thought you might wanna have this."

"What is it?"

"It's that painting I did for the Oklahoma Supreme Court Building."

Elliott opens the poster, looks, and says, "It's the one that's in the magazine."

"Yeah. Well... They had these made, an' they gave us some."

"Okay. Great. It's very cool."

"Oh, by the way, Moll an' Charlie came by yesterday, jus' after you left."

"Sorry I missed them. From the stories you've told me, I'd like to meet them."

"Sure. An' I told 'em some about what we're doin'."

Elliott nods and says, "What'd they think?"

"They're curious. An' they hope somethin' comes of it."

Elliott chuckles.

Poteet says, "I'm curious too."

"By the way, I went by your new building last night."

"What'd ya think?"

"I just walked by. I tried looking in but couldn't see much."

"Yeah?"

"And it's..."

"It's a neat old building."

"It is," Elliott says and starts unloading his satchel. He looks up to say, "It's in a great spot. What? ...a block and a half off the square."

"It's really cool inside. I think."

"Yeah?"

"Because it's all... Ya know. Like the banister, the railing, an' all that stuff... That's all from 1880."

"Wow."

"Yeah. I mean... An' the walls... The walls an' the ceiling are pretty tall. Uh... I mean, most of 'em are at least this tall." Poteet points to the ceiling, and they both look up. "An' some of 'em are even taller."

"Hmm."

"An' uh... I mean, it's in good shape. It really is. An' the walls are adobe inside. Ya know. There's no sheet rock."

"It's definitely an art-gallery street."

"Yeah, it is."

"If you're downtown and wanting to see art galleries..."

"Yeah."

"You can go right there."

"Ya know, right next to it..." Poteet explains, "When you go past it from the square... The next gallery is Sherwood's. An' what *they* have is Indian artifacts."

"I looked in there, and I wasn't too sure what they had."

"Yeah. They're Indian artifacts."

"For sale?"

"Yep. They've got some really expensive stuff."

"Huh."

Elliott starts his recorder and sits in his usual spot. As he sets his notebook down, he says, "I checked out the Native

American Hall of Fame last night."

"And..."

"It's like you said. The honorees are very impressive."

"They are."

"They all had great careers, and some have been honored very publicly—especially the war heroes."

"Of course..."

"But even so... I wouldn't back off the significance of the honors given to you."

"I can't. I wouldn'. But I don' know how you compare somethin' like that."

"I don't either—really."

"I jus' know how I felt when all the tribal chiefs gave me their blessings. An' then Bear Heart..."

"Right. It was important to *them* to let you know how *they* felt."

"That was it—exactly."

Elliott reaches for his notebook and asks, "...changing subjects?"

"Okay."

Elliott looks away for a moment and then turns back to Poteet. "When I was on the Internet, I stumbled upon the strangest thing, and I don't even know how I got there."

"Okay."

"I think I must've seen the name 'Jackson Pollock.'"

"Okay. So, what was that about?"

"I read an article that said something about American modern art being promoted by the CIA—starting in the '40s and continuing for decades."

"Huh. That *is* strange," Poteet responds. He pauses for a moment and then asks, "So... They actually mentioned Jackson Pollock by name?"

"Yeah. It mentioned several artists I didn't recognize. But we've talked about Jackson Pollock, so his name naturally caught my attention."

"So... What about 'im?"

"They spent a lot of money promoting his art—and these other artists too."

"Really."

"Yeah. A lot has come out recently, because the CIA declassified some of their old files." He shrugs. "So... I thought it could be true, and it kind of made sense to me. And I read some other articles that said the same thing."

"Huh."

"Yeah. They spent millions and millions and millions of dollars promoting these artists."

Poteet continues to stare for a second and then says, "But... When I think about it... It makes perfect sense. How else could someone like Jackson Pollock have become so famous?"

"I wondered about that."

"I'm sure Harold didn't know anything about it either. He would've told me. Like I said... An' Harold thought the same thing—about modern art."

"Right."

"It was a hoax. That's all it was. An' that's all it will ever be," Poteet proclaims. He then smiles and tells Elliott, "An' now you've got me all stirred up."

Elliott chuckles as he responds, "I'm just telling you what I read."

"I'll have to look into it."

"I'll let you know if I find anything else."

"Okay," Poteet says. After a moment he adds, "I had somethin' I wanted to tell *you*."

"Okay. Let's hear it."

"I thought I could go ahead an' install the first two panels."

With the swift change of subjects, Elliott has to ask, "...of the mural?"

"Right. An' then, I could paint the third one on site."

Elliott nods and says, "I see what you're saying now, and it seems like a good idea."

"So, people could actually come by, an' watch what I'm doin'."

"That'd be cool."

"Yeah. It would be. An' I think it might even be fun for Terry an' me. I'd have to install the first two panels, which would be expensive. I'd have to paint the third panel, an' install it too. If I did it on site, there'd be livin' expenses for a year or more. An' then, there'd be the expense of keepin' this place open somehow. All of that would cost some money."

"And it would be a sacrifice."

"I know. An' I'm not gettin' any younger."

"But, hey... With the kind of money that some people have nowadays..." Elliott pauses and nods slowly. He then adds, "Somebody ought to do it."

"An' who knows. In a hundred years... I mean, that thing could be priceless."

"Oh yeah. I expect that it *will* be. It really is an incredible opportunity for whoever wants to step up. You're right."

"An' what I told you about people not knowin' our history. That's still very important to me."

"I know."

"'Cause... Terry an' I were at that Cowboy Poets thing in Colorado."

"I don't think you've mentioned that."

"Oh... It's up at Durango. It was just a few weeks ago."

"Okay."

"They used my image to promote the show, so they paid our way up there an' all."

"Alright."

"So... We were sittin' in this hotel. It had been an ol' bank, an' there were all these murals—Indian murals. It was a cool place. I think I told you about that—where we asked several people, an' nobody'd heard of the Trail of Tears."

"Right. You did mention asking some people about the Trail of Tears."

"But anyway... It was just... They said, 'No, what was that? ...never heard of it.'"

Elliott nods.

"Besides the Civil War, it was the single most important event in the history of our country."

Elliott crosses his arms and looks out the window.

Poteet watches Elliott for a reaction.

"I don't think most people would agree with that. I think they'd say, '...one of the world wars or the depression or maybe something else.'"

"Given the state of our education on this subject, I would agree. But I'm not backin' off on the claim. Because... Durin' the time of the extermination of the indigenous people, millions an' millions an' millions of people died. An' that's a fact."

"I know that's true. I've done some of my own research."

"An' most people don' know a thing about *any* of it."

"I would agree with that."

"An' it's a damn shame."

Elliott nods respectfully. He eventually says, "I think you're still very determined to do something about that."

"I am."

Elliott breathes deeply and says, "For what it's worth, I hope you can finish it someday."

"Well... If somebody paid me enough..." He pauses and shakes his head. "I ain't doin' it for nothin'. I ain't gonna lose money doin' it."

"Sure."

"An' nobody can finish my vision of the thing."

"Right."

"They'd just have to put it up unfinished. ...or somethin'."

"Yeah. So... What about the tribes? I think they were interested at one time."

"Right. They're talkin' a good game, but nothin's happenin'. I think if I was on the tribal rolls, it would help. They're pretty focused on helpin' their own people, which is what they should be doin'."

"...doesn't sound like they were that worried about the tribal rolls when you were getting the project going."

"You're right. They weren't."

"If that's really a problem, it's unfortunate."

"Yeah. My cousin was gatherin' documents an' information about that. She wanted to pursue it, but she died before she could get it done."

"That's too bad."

"It is. She was the one who was the judge, ya know. An' she was great. She went to Oxford."

"Oh really?"

"Yeah. She was smart as hell."

"Okay."

"An' she called me one time. She had already been to Oxford for a year or so. An' then, she..." He chuckles. "She'd come home for the summer or somethin' an' was goin' back." He shakes his head. "An' she decided to go via *Africa*."

Elliott and Poteet both laugh.

"So, she called me an' needed money. Like, she was in Morocco. An' uh... Anyway, we got 'er out of there, an' she gets on up to Europe—to Germany. An'... I talked to 'er, an' she said, 'Well, I was over in Germany, an' I was playin' these chess masters for money.'" Poteet looks at Elliott and says, "Yeah. She was that good. That's what she tol' me. An' she was beatin' 'em."

Elliott chuckles and asks, "So, when was this that she called you for money?"

"I wanna think this was probably '76, '77."

"And you were in the T-shirt business then?"

"Yeah."

"...and had some money?"

"Mm-hmm—a little. I was makin' money, yeah."

Smiling, Elliott continues, "And, she was beating the chess masters..."

"Uh-huh."

"I think brains must run in your family."

"I don' know. Uh... We jus' had a natural connection, ya know, right off. 'Cause she was wild, an' so was I."

Poteet and Elliott laugh together.

The joviality drains from Elliott's face as he says, "But... She died before she could address the tribal-rolls issue?"

"That's right. Her mother tol' me that she'd gotten married over in Europe, an' she was workin' for some oil company in the legal department. An' uh... Her husband was drivin' the car. An' I don' know what they hit. But he told her mother that Beth was asleep, an' she died instantly. She never saw the accident comin' or nothin'. An' he was injured, but I don't think seriously."

"That's sad. So, did she go to law school at Oxford?"

"Yeah. Then, she worked her way into bein' a judge in Oklahoma—at a young age." Poteet turns to his painting table and picks up his painting knife. He says, "Because, ya know, this tribal-rolls thing is a big deal now. The tribes realize that there are some Indians that couldn' get on the rolls for one reason or another—like our family. An' they know that there're a lot of white people that have no business bein' on there." He begins mixing paint on the sheet of paper that is his palette.

"I imagine that's true."

"An' so, they're cleanin' that up."

Elliott nods.

Poteet turns to his painting and begins applying the paint.

He says, "Terry's got a cousin. Her name is Julie, an' she's right in the middle of it. She said that she's had to give several folks some bad news." He moves back to his palette for paint. "An' she said, 'Man, they're in shock.'" Poteet looks over at Elliott and says, "...all the benefits they were gettin', ya know, an' they can't get 'em anymore."

"Mm-hmm. Yeah—that'd be tough, if you were used to that."

Poteet moves back to his painting and says, "I think I tol' you... My mural was insured for four million when I was doin' it. President Boren made me get it insured."

"...Boren, the university President?"

"Yeah. An' I mean... It's almost impossible to get anything insured that dudn' exist." Poteet chuckles and adds. "You probably didn' know that."

"I guess I never thought about it."

"Yeah... But through Williams, my sponsor... With their help, we got it insured—for the four million. So..."

"Who came up with that amount?"

"They must have," Poteet says and shrugs. "We had some rough figures about the cost. So... I guess, they doubled or tripled that. I don' know. But... I'm sure they thought it would be a valuable painting. But... Those paintings at The Cowboy Hall of Fame... I think I told you about Wilson Hurley."

"Right. Yeah."

"Anyway... They paid him five million to do those."

"I think that's what you told me."

"An' that's been... What? ...twenty-five, thirty years."

"Hmm. I guess I need to make a trip out there."

"An' also... There's another great piece they've got. Balciar was the sculptor that did it. It's white marble—with a huge mountain lion comin' down a cliff. It's absolutely magnificent."

"I probably need to see that too."

"They're in the same place, an' you do need to see 'em." He turns to Elliott. "Maybe you can see the First Americans Museum too. It's all about American Indian history."

"Oh?"

"Terry an' I went by there a few months ago. An' the guy I was talkin' to... An' I knew 'im. He said, 'You know what your problem was?' An' I said, 'What?' An' he said, 'You were fifteen years ahead of your time.' He said, 'What we're doin' at this museum is exactly what you did in that painting.' An' he knew the whole story behind the mural, 'cause he was there at the beginning. An' he said, 'Because we're callin' it, ya know, the American holocaust.'"

"Oh, they are?"

"Yeah. Ya know, I was quoted in the newspaper callin' it that."

"Right."

"An' I was gettin' all kinds of hate mail. They'd say, 'How dare you. You can't call it that.'" Poteet turns to his palette. "...course I told you what Steven Spielberg said."

"Right. He used that same phrase."

"An' when I heard what Spielberg said, I knew they shouldn' be mad at me for sayin' it. "But..." He moves to his painting. "Ya know, what Stevenson always told me when I was doin' the mural..."

"Right. ...about creating controversy?"

"Yeah. He said, 'You'd become famous, ya know.'" Poteet turns to Elliott and shrugs. "But... When I left OU, I didn' want any bad feelings, with OU or anybody else."

Elliott nods slowly.

Poteet turns back to his painting. "An' so, I had magazines. I had TV stations. They kept callin' me, 'What's the deal? What's the story?' An' I kept sayin', 'I'm not gonna talk about it right now.'"

"And that was probably your chance to become famous."

"Well, it probably was. Because... It's like Harold said... He said, 'Ya know, you start that up...' He said, 'Nobody's seen your mural.' He said, 'If you ever displayed it, you'd have a line ten miles long—people tryin' to see it.' It's the ol' Andy Warhol trick, ya know. Start raisin' hell with *everybody*."

Elliott chuckles.

"I jus' didn' wanna cause bad feelings," Poteet says as he trades his painting knife for a brush and starts working with his paint again.

"Do you think it's too late for you to make a big stink?"

Poteet turns to his painting and begins to paint the sand. He replies, "I don't think so. I mean... I could bring it back up, talk to some of the newspapers there in Oklahoma an' to some of the magazines an' say, 'The university jus' sort of said, "You're fired."' An' I could tell 'em the whole story. I mean... How it got started. What it was about. An' why OU rejected it."

As he turns back to his table, Poteet says, "But that kind of goes against the grain of who I am now, I think."

"You're right," Elliott says. "I also think you're gonna stay busy doing more paintings like this. It's like, 'I gotta have that. I *gotta* have it.' This thing with the sand and all."

"I decided to use some beads with the sand on this one."

"So... Sometimes you do beads, and sometimes you do sand."

"Yeah—or both. Like that one I did for the Supreme Court Buildin' in Oklahoma City. That one had sand an' beads both. I think it's beautiful."

"From seeing it on that poster, it is beautiful. It's so different."

"But..." Poteet says and turns back to his palette. "Ya know, I've been paintin' for so long. I've done so many different things that... I've never seen anybody do what I do..." He points to the painting against the wall. "...like that painting..." He points to his easel. "...or that painting. It's the sand and the beads. I want people to get the spiritual significance of those things, an' I hope they do."

"You may have to do some educating on that."

Poteet chuckles and says, "Yeah, I may..."

Elliott starts gathering his stuff and says, "I've got to go, and I'm not sure when I'll be back."

"Well, don't wait too long."

Elliott nods and smiles. They move together to shake hands. Elliott then leaves.

Once outside, Elliott thinks, "Yeah. I really like the sand and the beads."

CHAPTER 59

The Movie

Poteet yells out, "...just black?"

"Yeah," Elliott yells back, after being gone for a month.

Speaking loudly, Poteet says, "Did I tell you about my buildin'?"

"...the one you wanted to buy?"

"Yeah." Poteet pauses and then says, "Oh, I remember. You went by to check it out."

"I did."

"Well, I got it."

"Great."

"So, now we're makin' plans. Once I'm in there, I'd really like to carry more Indian art an' some pottery."

"Really?"

"Oh yeah. I wanna really branch out."

"Huh."

"Man, I'm tellin' ya. I'm spendin' so much money."

"It's a good thing you're loaded."

Poteet comes out holding a cup and smiling. He says, "...not loaded enough."

Elliott chuckles as he reaches for the cup in Poteet's hand.

"Ya know, it cost me a lot," Poteet elaborates.

"I'm sure. I don't know about the cost of real estate in Santa Fe, but"—Elliott takes a sip and continues—"it's in a great location. It's historical. It's a large space. It's cool. It looks like it has a yard behind it."

"It does. We'll make that into a really nice garden where we can display sculptures from some of our artists."

"I mean... With all of that... It's got to be expensive."

Leaning on his painting table, Poteet says, "But... Ya know, I jus'... Like I was tellin' Terry. I said, ya know, 'We jus' need to thank God I had the money to do it.'"

"I have to think it's a really good investment."

"I agree—obviously."

"It's hard to think of a better place to put your money, especially if you can use it. Which... In your case... You can make great use of the space."

"Exactly," Poteet says and nods. "It was gettin' to the point for me... An' I guess you know that I don't own this buildin'." He lifts his hand and glances around. "I have a lease."

"Which is why this other deal looks so good."

"It does. It was like... As much money as I'm spendin' here, it didn' make any sense. But... I jus' think it was a godsend when Chris, my ex-partner, came up here. He was tellin' me about that buildin'."

"Yeah?"

"An' I'm thinkin', why in the hell didn' *he* jump on that deal? He was like, 'I don' know.' Then he said, 'I'd have to come up with all this down payment.' An' I said, 'I'd a loaned it to ya.' Ya know. To get that buildin', I would've. An' uh...'"

"...because he was offered the building?"

"The thing is... His wife is a realtor. So, her company had the first look."

"Yeah?"

"An' she told 'im about it. But he didn' do anything, 'cause... That was a Friday. He come in here Monday mornin' talkin' to me about it. An' I said, 'Well, is it still available?' An' he said, 'Naw, it's already under contract.' So... As luck would have it, I went down to my bank to make a deposit. I'm talkin' to this loan officer, an' I was tellin' 'er 'bout it. An' I said, 'Boy, that was a deal. I wish I'd a known about it.' An' she was sayin', 'Yeah. That was a great deal.'"

"Hmm."

"An' she tol' me... She said, 'Well, if anything comes up again like that, I'll let you know.' I said, 'Okay. Great,'" Poteet walks back into his kitchen.

Elliott takes another sip of coffee and adjusts the position of his recorder.

Poteet soon returns holding his cup of coffee. He takes a sip and says, "A couple days later, she sends me an email, says, 'That deal fell through. You call this realtor right now.' So, I did. An'... He was kind of half-ass arrogant about it. I said, 'Hey, look. I'm a buyer.' He said, 'Yeah. You an' a lot of other people.' An' I said, 'Well, I jus' wanna tell ya... If somethin' happens, you give me a call.' An' he said, 'Okay, I will.' A couple days later... Sure enough, he called me. But what I didn' know was... Everybody who wanted to buy that buildin' had to interview with this historical board."

"Yeah?"

"An', ya know, my expert realtor... Pam..."

"Pam Klepper?"

"Yeah," Poteet says and sets his coffee cup down. "I called Pam about it, an' she said, 'Don't you dare go down there without your realtor. Don't you do it.' An' she was absolutely right. So..." He chuckles. "When I interviewed with that board, ya know... I shook their hands an' everything when I was through. An' that guy at the historical board tol' my realtor. He said, 'That's the guy. That's the guy that can buy it. I want him to have it.' So, that's how that went." Poteet chuckles again.

Elliott smiles at Poteet and says, "You're a salesman. That's one thing I know about you."

Poteet takes another sip of coffee. He looks at Elliott with a grin and says, "An' this, you will absolutely not believe."

Elliott rolls his eyes and smiles. He says, "I think I can believe just about anything—when it comes to you."

"Okay. So, just a few days after we closed, I get a call. It's from a movie director."

"Really? About your life story?"

"Well…"

"Did somebody beat me to it? You should have said something."

"No. That's not it."

"Then what?"

Poteet chuckles, takes another sip, and says, "This movie director… He said, 'We're shootin' this movie with Tom Hanks.'"

"Noooo…"

"Yeah. An' he said. 'We were out scoutin' the other day…'"

Elliott interrupts, "That's big time."

"I know," Poteet says and chuckles. "An' he said, 'We came across this buildin', your buildin'. An' I understand you jus' bought it.' An' I said, 'Yeah, I did.' An' he said… Uh… He said, 'That's a really interesting building.' An' he said, 'The movie we're shootin'… The setting is in the 1870s.' An' I said, 'Really?' An' he said, 'Yeah. We're lookin' for a buildin' we could use. It's gonna be in the movie as an old lawyer's office.' An' I said, 'Well, you could not have picked a better place.'"

Elliott grins.

Poteet chuckles and continues, "I said, 'Do you realize this buildin' was built in 1880.' He said, 'Really?' I said, 'Yep. An' every feature on the inside is original.' I said, 'Because, ya know… The historical society took it over, an' you can't change anything about it.' An' I said, 'The old banisters… All the old fireplaces...' I said, 'Even the transoms above the windows are original.' I said, 'You can see it's got that wavy glass from 1880.' An' he said, 'You gotta be kiddin' me.' He said, 'Well, that'd be perfect.' I said, 'Yeah. It'd be perfect for what you're lookin' for.' An' uh... I said, 'You pay anything?'"

Elliott laughs.

Poteet grins and continues, "He said, 'Oh yeah, we'll pay ya.' I said, 'Yeah? How much you gonna pay me?'"

Elliott and Poteet both laugh.

"An' he said, 'Well, we... We would, uh, take one day to prep.' An' he said, 'That's about thirty-five hundred bucks.' Ya know. 'The next day, when we shoot,' he said, 'It'll be five thousand or six thousand.' He said, 'We're into you for about ten thousand dollars...'"

Elliott cocks his head and looks toward the window. He muses for a moment before saying, "...for two days?"

"Yeah."

Elliott nods and says, "...seems fair."

"An' I said to 'im, 'You got a deal.'"

They laugh.

"An' I said, 'You're not gonna try to change anything or tear up my walls, are ya?' 'Oh no.' He said, 'The only thing that we would wanna do...' He said, 'We might wanna paint one wall sort of an earth-tone brown.' He said, 'But if we paint it, then we'd paint it back.' An' I said, 'I don't think you're gonna even have to do that, once you see it. Because the walls *are* brown.' He went, 'Really?'"

Elliott chuckles.

"He was like, 'I can't believe this.'"

"I guess he hadn't had a chance to go inside yet." Elliott asks.

"No. He hadn'. He said... He told me. 'We're really busy tomorrow.' He said, 'I would like, if I could, to get with you maybe on Wednesday. I wanna bring the director by, an' we'll go look at it.'"

"So, they're here in town now?"

"Mm-hmm."

"Checking the whole town, I guess, for other locations."

"Yeah. They are."

"Huh."

"I said, 'All right. Come on by. We'll go check it out.'"

Elliott's phone rings. He listens and nods. He looks at his watch and says, "I can do that. I'm on my way."

As he is picking up his recorder, Elliott says, "Yeah. That's what making a movie is all about. I've done a lot of that kind of scouting. There's always a lot of work involved before you ever shoot anything."

Poteet nods and says, "Looks like you're headin' out."

"I am. It had to be quick, and my ride will be here soon. Unfortunately, I've got to get back."

Elliott steps just outside the gallery door to watch for his car. As he looks out at the street into the small plaza of galleries, he can't help but smile and shake his head. He thinks, "Who but Poteet Victory could buy a building and then have a movie company call—especially, in just a few days? ...and for a Tom Hanks movie! Wow."

CHAPTER 60

The Movie

Elliott walks carefully along the sidewalk trying to avoid the patches of ice. It's cold, and he's glad he's got his heavy winter coat on. He's wishing he'd thought to wear boots.

Once inside Victory Contemporary, he heads right for the stairs. He gives a slight wave to Terry's assistant who had walked out of her office to see who had come in. At the double doors, he knocks softly and pushes through. He holds out his hand as he approaches Poteet with a smile. He says, "Good to see you."

"How long's it been this time?" Poteet asks.

"I think about six weeks."

"Glad you're back."

"It's turned into winter out here."

Poteet chuckles and says, "...gettin' there. We've had a couple of light snows. We're due for somethin' heavier here pretty soon."

"So... How've you been?"

"I've been good. But I wanted to tell ya. They're workin' at our buildin' today—the movie people. An' they're supposed to be filmin' tomorrow. So... You wanna go over?"

"Sure."

"We can jus' jump in my pickup."

Elliott says, "Let's go," and they head for the door.

After a short drive and a search for a parking spot, they're on the sidewalk and heading for the building. A rental truck is parked out front. When they walk in, they can see at least ten people working in the front two rooms.

As Poteet is looking around, he says, "They've done a lot here."

A woman approaches wearing a scowl.

Poteet explains, "I'm the owner of the buildin'."

She nods and turns away.

He points at the stairs and says, "I had the stairway recarpeted. They had an ugly ol' gray carpet on there, so I changed it an' put in a red one. It looked really cool. So, this producer... He said, 'Can we...'"

Elliott chuckles.

"'Can we take that carpet out?'" Poteet says and smiles. "I said, 'Yeah, but it'll cost ya 'bout two thousand dollars.' 'Well, we wanna take it out.' So... I said, 'Go ahead.'"

"Yeah?"

"But they... He came by here Friday an' gave me a check for twenty-one thousand..."

"That's more than you thought you'd get."

"...'bout twice as much. An' then he said, 'We're actually gonna need it about three more days.'"

"Really?"

"Yeah. He said, 'So I'll owe you some more money, ya know.' An' I smiled an' said, 'Okay.'"

"What a deal."

"I said, 'I'll loan it to you every day if you want me to.'"

"...beats selling paintings," Elliott says and chuckles.

Poteet grins and responds, "...most days. Yeah."

They walk down the main hallway to the back door and look out. Some workers are out there.

Elliott says, "When I walked by here the last time I was in town, I could see the yard. I was able to kind of peek in through the gate over there..." He points to the left.

"Uh-huh."

"I don't suppose they're using the yard for the movie."

"No. Actually, those are my guys out there, startin' to do some landscaping."

"Oh, okay. Because it looks like it's been cleaned up."

"It has."

Elliott turns away from the door. After a moment, he asks, "What have you heard about the movie they're shooting here?"

"Not much. It's supposed to be really good."

"Well. If they've got Tom Hanks..."

"Yeah. The name of it is *News of the World*. Terry an' I got the book, an' I'm readin' it. It's a good story—very unusual."

"Unusual can be good. It's what I'm always looking for, and it's what I like about your story."

"Well... One of the producers... I was talkin' to him. An' he said, 'We've already filmed a lot of it. ...what you call the dailies."

Elliott nods.

"An' he said, 'We've been watchin' the editing an' everything.' He said, 'This really is Academy-Award-worthy stuff.'"

They walk back toward the front of the building. Poteet points to the room on the right and says, "This is the lawyer's office."

Elliott looks in.

Poteet continues, "I'll bet it looked jus' like this in 1880."

"So, this is pretty well set up."

"Yeah." He points at the room across the hallway and says, "...an' that room over there."

Elliott looks in and says, "Okay?"

"When they're finished, we're puttin' a kitchen in there."

"Yeah?"

"...gotta have a kitchen."

"Sure."

He points down the hallway. "...storage will be back there."

"Okay."

They walk up the stairs as Elliott takes it all in. At the top of the stairs, they turn left. They take a few steps down a short hallway and into a large room. A young woman is in there working. Poteet says, "Hi."

She responds, "Hi there."

Poteet turns to Elliott and says, "I think I'm gonna use this room as my studio."

"Oh, okay."

The woman says, "Oh... It'll be a great studio."

"Yeah."

"...even more space than you've got now," Elliott observes.

"Yeah, it is."

The woman says, "It's got some of the best light..."

"Yeah. Exactly," Poteet says, "plus, there's *some* view." He moves to the window and looks out. "You can see the mountains."

"That's true," Elliott concurs. "Oh yeah, I like this." He points. "I love that fireplace."

"I do too," Poteet says as they walk out.

Back on the street, Elliott notices, "They cut down the parking meters."

"Yeah, they did."

Elliott chuckles as they move away from the activity.

"I don' know if they needed to or not. 'Cause they were gonna cover this whole thing with dirt. An' now, they've decided they're not gonna do that."

"Oh?"

"They did it up on Canyon Road."

"...cover it with dirt?"

"Yeah, an' they've already shot that."

"Okay. There're going all out."

"Seems like it."

They watch the truck as it's being unloaded.

"Will they let you take any pictures tomorrow?"

"I asked 'im, an' he, uh... He tol' me. He said, 'You can't bring a photographer down here.' He said that they wanna have complete control."

"Sure. We'd do the same. I just wondered."

"They don't want any shots gettin' out before the movie's released."

"Of course."

"An' uh... He said, "Now, if you wanna take some pictures with your phone... Well, you can go ahead."

"I'd sure do that."

"Yeah. He said, 'But you can't, uh... You can't shoot Tom Hanks.' An' uh... But he said, 'I think I can get 'im to take a shot with you,'" Poteet says and turns to Elliott. He continues, "An'... I think they will, 'cause Terry told 'im that I wouldn' sign the contract unless she got to meet Tom Hanks."

They both laugh.

"Well, that was a good idea," Elliott says.

One of the workers stops unloading the nearby truck and says to Poteet and Elliott, "He's a really nice guy. He'd probably come out and just do it for you."

"Well, I hope so," Poteet responds.

"No, he's a great guy."

"Well, that's good to know. It really is."

Poteet and Elliott walk across the street to watch the activity from there. Another bystander walks up and asks, "Do you work for the movie company?"

"No. We're just hangin' out," Poteet answers.

"...just hangin' out, huh."

"Yeah." Poteet nods toward his building and says, "No, I own that place right there. So..."

"Oh, awesome! That's the Delgado House."

"Yeah."

"That's yours, huh?"

"It is. An' this movie came along at the right time. 'Cause I'd just bought it, an' so it was totally empty."

"...perfect timing, like 'Can we pay you for your empty building?'"

Poteet chuckles and says, "Yeah."

"And you're like, 'Whadaya know!'"

Poteet and Elliott laugh.

The bystander says, "That sounds like a great idea."

Poteet says, "That's what I said. Yeah. Absolutely you can."

"Sweet."

"You can rent it for as long as you want to."

"Yeah."

Elliott chuckles.

Poteet says, "...for the prices they're payin'."

The bystander says, "Yeah... No, the film industry will surprise you. That's for sure."

"Yeah. Because they first quoted me a price... The director said, 'This is what we'll pay.' An' then they came back an' doubled it."

"Nice. Now. ...you gonna play hardball with 'em?" the stranger asks.

"I didn't have to do anything, an' they gave me a great deal."

"Oh... Out in L.A., they have to pay for everything. But... Here in New Mexico, we're just happy to get anything."

"Yeah, ya know. No kiddin'—brings in a lot of money to everybody."

"For the past few years, this industry's been great for New

Mexico. I mean, I can't complain. They've been payin' me."

Poteet turns to the bystander and asks, "So, you're workin' for 'em."

"I am. I'm a Teamster. I'm just waitin' for 'em to tell me where to drive that truck."

"I see," Poteet says and points down the street at his new neighbor's shops. He says, "Ya know, they went down through here an' paid every one of these businesses."

"Yeah. ...to buy their parking spots an'..."

"...for the inconvenience."

"Yeah—for the inconvenience."

Poteet points to his building and says, "I need to ask 'em somethin' about tomorrow."

Elliott nods and Poteet heads back across the street.

The bystander points at Elliott's recorder and asks, "What's that?"

"I've been doing a series of interviews with Poteet. We may want to make a movie about his life."

"Who is he?"

"His name is Poteet Victory, and he's one of the most successful Native American painters in the world. He's lived in Santa Fe for many years, and he's had a very interesting life."

"Is it mainly about his paintings?"

Elliott cocks his head. "There's really so much there. It's hard to say. But... Intellectually, he's a genius. He's a successful painter. He's sold thousands of paintings for millions of dollars."

"Whew!"

"His passion is educating people on the Trail of Tears."

"Yeah. I know about the Trail of Tears."

Elliott turns to look at the truck driver and asks, "Really?"

"Yeah. It's where they forced all the Indians into Oklahoma."

"That's right. Well... Poteet gave five years of his life to promote a project and paint a giant mural depicting the Trail of Tears."

"I see. He's into helpin' the Indians."

"He is. But there's more. He's also connected to some important counter-culture history of the 1960s. He's had successful businesses. He grew up as an abandoned child. There's that part. And he's had five wives. And his spiritual journey is important as well."

"...five wives?"

"Yeah. And then he was single for twenty years. It was important to him to figure out what went wrong before he got married again. And he finally did."

"Maybe I need to know more about that myself."

Elliott shrugs and nods. "I'm trying to convince my partners that it would be a good movie."

"With that kind of life story, I expect it would be. There's some individuals out there that just have more life experience in their toenails than most people will ever..."

Elliott laughs and says, "I hadn't heard it put that way."

The driver chuckles.

"But that's a good way to explain Poteet."

Something catches the driver's eye. He then turns to Elliott and says, "I gotta go. It was nice talkin' to you."

Elliott nods as the driver steps away.

Within seconds, Poteet walks out of the building, gets Elliott's attention, and points at his pickup. They both head toward it.

As they're climbing in, Elliott says, "I enjoyed seeing your building."

"Yeah?"

"It's a great building. It really is."

As they pull away, Poteet says, "I've got to be back over here in about thirty minutes. I'm sorry 'bout that, but I don' really have a choice."

"I understand. Will you be available tomorrow?"

"Yeah. We can get together in the afternoon."

"That works."

"They've got some questions for me. An' while I'm here, I'm gonna see if I can't talk 'em out of those lamps they've got on the wall."

"Yeah?"

"They look great in there. So, I asked 'im. I said, 'Where do y'all get all this stuff?' They said, '...from a prop house in Hollywood.'"

Elliott grins and says, "Sure. That's how it works. Those places have a little of everything."

"I guess they do."

Elliott chuckles. "And, you know that guy we were talking to there—the Teamster?"

"Yeah?"

"Uh... And I can't quote exactly what he said, but uh... He asked me what I had in my hand, which was the recorder."

"Oh?"

"And we started talking about doing a movie. I wasn't ready to mention an on-demand series. But anyway... I said, 'He's just led a really interesting life.'"

"He was a friendly guy, wadn' he."

"Yeah. An' he said, uh... He said, 'There are some individuals who just have more life experience in their toenails...'"

Poteet chuckles.

"'...than the rest of us.'"

"Really."

"I thought, 'You know, that's a quote we should probably use.'"

Poteet chuckles and nods.

The conversation stops as they cross the traffic onto Canyon Road and then turn into the gallery parking lot.

As they walk toward the front door, Poteet says, "Yeah. That building... I think it'll be a lot better for us over there." They walk into Terry's office, and Poteet picks a book up from her worktable. He shows it to Elliott and says, "This is it."

Elliott looks and reads, *"News of the World."*

"Right. It's like, back in the late 1800s... An' it's a true story."

"Huh."

"This guy travels around, from town to town, readin' the news. An' so... In the book, he starts up around Wichita Falls an' goes all the way to San Antonio—which, by buggy was a long way back then."

"Yeah."

Poteet sets the book down, and they head upstairs.

Before they're even settled in, Poteet glances up at the clock on his computer table and says, "Sorry. I gotta go."

Elliott nods and reaches for his recorder. He quickly gets everything into his satchel and asks, "Tomorrow?"

Poteet nods, and they both head for the stairs.

CHAPTER 61

Finding God in Physics

By mid-afternoon the next day, Elliott is knocking on the double doors and pushing slowly through.

Poteet says, "Come on in."

"Did you get 'em straightened out over there yesterday?"

"...enough, I guess. They haven't called yet today."

Elliott smiles and begins to set up. With the recorder going and notebook on the table, he says, "We have an issue at the office today, and I can't stay long."

Poteet nods and says, "I understand."

"But... There's something I've been thinking about."

"Okay."

"It's your 'Jesus in the closet' experience."

Poteet narrows his gaze and cocks his head. He responds, "Yeah?"

"Since you had that experience, uh... Does it make you feel like you've got a special purpose?"

After a moment, Poteet answers, "I think so. I... Yeah, I think so. Uh... Sometimes, I still think there's somethin' else for me to do."

"...something's still out there for you?"

"Yeah. But I don' know what it is. I keep thinkin' about, ya know, what Harold said many years ago. He said, 'I think everybody is given time to do what they were put here to do.' He said, 'Whether you be a poet, an artist, ya know... You have somethin' that you need to express.' An'... He said, 'My whole thing is to express beauty.' An' the interviewer said, 'Well, what'll happen when you get to the point where you can't?' An' he said, 'Well. Then I'll die.' An' that's exactly what he did. That's *exactly* what happened. So... Yeah... So, I don' know."

"You feel like you haven't accomplished that yet."

"Huh-uh. I don't think so. I still think there's somethin'. I jus' don' know what that would be."

"Maybe it's the Trail-of-Tears mural."

"Maybe."

"I hope you still get that chance."

Poteet shrugs and says, "I am concerned about our country. I don't know what it has to do with the Trail of Tears. But yes, we're very divided."

"Yes, we're divided."

"Like... Everything that was good is now bad, an' everything that was bad..."

"It seems a lot like that. Yeah."

"An' everything's been flipped on its head."

"...seems so," Elliott says and nods.

"Ya know, when I started listenin' to Roy Masters, it changed my life. An' we've talked quite a bit about that."

"We have, and I've done some of my own research on Roy."

"So..." Poteet asks, "Are you ready now to talk about his theories on physics?"

Elliott's head cocks to the side, and his brow wrinkles. He replies, "Really?"

"Ya know, he taught himself."

Elliott straightens up, and he asks, "How do you teach yourself physics?"

"For one thing, he's brilliant. An' I'm sure he studied everything there was out there. An' then... Bein' the brain that he is, he came at it from a different point of view."

"And so... What he came up with... That makes sense to you?"

Poteet nods, cocks his head slightly, and says, "Yeah, it makes sense."

"I just wondered."

"An'... He's been sayin' for the last few years. He says, 'They're finally startin' to listen to me.' But he was sayin', uh... 'There's an infinite amount of energy that can be tapped into, an' it's gravity.' An' he..."

"I saw something about gravity. Like, one of his books is about gravity or something like that."

"Oh, it's that book, *Finding God in Physics*. That's a really interesting book."

"Okay?"

"...a really, really interesting book."

"And that's where he presents these theories?" Elliott asks.

"Yep."

"And he feels like he's ahead of the current understanding of science?"

"Yeah. He said, ya know, 'For years, they jus' laughed at me, 'cause I didn' have any background in it. But they're finally startin' to see it. They're sayin', 'Hey, he might be onto somethin' here.'"

"Do you know what that is?"

"It all goes back to... Ya know... People talk about the 'big bang.'"

"Sure—the moment of creation."

"Right. But Roy says, 'There was no such thing as a 'big bang.'"

"Oh Really?"

"Yeah..." Poteet chuckles. "Roy says it was more like a 'big whoosh.'"

Elliott finds the statement comical and repeats, "...a 'big whoosh'?"

"Yeah," Poteet says and laughs.

"Looks like I need to do *more* research on Roy Masters," Elliott says as he looks at his watch. He then looks at Poteet. "I've got a conference call in about twenty minutes. I need to go."

"Okay."

Elliott picks up his notebook and then stops. He gives Poteet a hard look and says, "I expect for this to be my last trip to Santa Fe for a while."

Poteet nods slowly and says, "Okay."

"If we decide to go with your story, there'll be others who'll want to come out, meet with you... And they'll have questions."

"Sure. An' I'll look forward to that, if that's where this goes."

"So... I'll want to get back here as soon as I can, but it could be a while."

"Are you stayin' overnight?"

"I am. I told 'em at the office I needed to give myself one more day, especially after this short session."

Poteet nods.

"I didn't want to rush this final trip. Will you be available tomorrow?"

"Yeah. We're not goin' anywhere." Poteet raises his hand with his index finger extended. He says, "Lemme see if I can find my copy of Roy's book on physics."

"I'd appreciate that."

"It's small."

"Maybe I can read it before tomorrow."

"I had to read parts of it two or three times before it started makin' sense to me," Poteet says and heads for his kitchen.

"I'm sure I'll have to do the same," Elliott says loudly, as he reaches for his recorder.

Even before Poteet gets back, Elliott is having second thoughts about promising to read something. He begins reviewing in his mind all the work he already has to do.

Poteet returns with a book in hand and gives it to the movie producer.

Elliott is relieved to see that the book is small and not many pages. He decides he'll try to take a look.

By mid-afternoon the next day, Elliott is back at the double doors.

Poteet welcomes him warmly and asks, "Did you get to read some of that book?"

Elliott is glad he can answer truthfully, "I did." In reality, he's anxious to discuss Roy Master's theories with Poteet. He adds, "I guess, we can just jump right into that, if it's okay with you."

"Sure. An' I'll admit that there's a lot of it I still don' understand."

"There's a lot I don't understand either. But I can tell you at the most basic level what I think he means. And I'm talking about the creation thing—the beginning of the universe."

"Okay."

"But, let me get my recorder going here first."

"Sure."

As Elliott is setting up, Terry appears at the double doors. She says to Elliott, "I hear that this is your last day."

He looks up to respond, "It is—at least for a while. With my partners, I've got to make some decision about the projects we're going to fund next quarter. I've got to get back."

"In that case, you've got to come out to the house when y'all are through. We've got some celebratin' to do. If it's your last night, you gotta do that."

Elliott grins and nods. "Okay. I've got to get going in the

morning. But sure, I'd love to come out."

"Okay then. That's what we'll do." She gives a sharp nod to seal the deal and heads for the stairs.

Elliott chuckles. "So, where were we?" He quickly adds, "Oh yeah, I was about to explain the 'big whoosh' to you."

Poteet chuckles and says, "Okay. Let's hear it."

After a moment, Elliott clears his throat and says, "The 'big whoosh' is where it starts."

"Right."

"According to Roy Masters, it wasn't a 'bang.' It was a 'whoosh,' and time began." He uses his hands to help illustrate. "Energy began to flow out from the source of the 'whoosh' at the center of the universe at the speed of light."

Poteet smiles and responds, "Yeah."

"And then some pieces of the energy began to gather in pools, like in a stream."

"Yeah."

"And that began to form..."

"...matter," Poteet says.

"Right. And matter started bunching together and forming more things."

"Yeah."

"And... To me... That all seems similar to the theories on evolution we've always heard. Little things form bigger things. Simpler things evolve to form more sophisticated things. But... What's so different about his theory is the 'whoosh' part."

"Exactly."

"A 'Boom' kind of indicates 'BAM.'" Elliott uses his hands to indicate an explosion. "And that's it—a one-time thing."

"Yes."

Elliott brings his hands back together and sits forward. "Roy's theory, in my understanding, is that the energy continues from the source. And it has continued that way since the beginning of time."

"Yeah."

"The way I see that, simply, is... Like... Sometimes I drive by these places, and it's usually car dealerships. To get your attention, they've got a blower on this thing. It's big, and it's moving. It's shaped like a person."

"Yeah. There's a place out here that does that all the time."

"To keep it up, you have to have the blower on. If you turn the blower off, the thing falls down."

"Yeah."

"And that's... That's what's happening in the universe."

"Yeah."

"The 'whoosh' is a continuing source of constant energy. If that energy stops..."

"Yeah."

"The whole universe collapses."

"It would. I believe that," Poteet says as he agrees with Elliott's assessment.

"He makes a pretty convincing argument," Elliott says as he leans back with his eyes closed. He strokes his beard and eventually says, "The name of the book is *Finding God in Physics*. I think that title states exactly what Roy means. He's saying that God started the 'whoosh' and he's out there all the time keeping it going. And that he's at the center of the universe doing all of this."

"I think that's right," Poteet concurs. "An' Roy says that if you believe in the 'big bang' theory, you're believin' that there was somethin' infinitely small, infinitely powerful that blew up. An' he says, 'What was that thing? You never get that far in your explanation. You say that this one thing blew up. Well, what was that one thing?' But ya know, physics dudn' explain that."

"Yeah. So, Roy is asking, 'What was there before the bang?'"

"Yeah. What was the one thing?"

"And then..." Elliott continues, "Roy says that the thing before... It was God. I take that to mean he finds God at the center of the universe. Some would say that it didn't take God to set off the 'big bang.' That it just happened. Roy would say that God is continuing to put that energy out there—every split second of every day. And He's been doing it for millenniums."

"Yeah, I think that's what he means."

"Okay. I just wanted to check in with you to see if my understanding was similar to yours."

"Yeah. That's how I see it."

"But there was so much more, like his theory on gravity and those kinds of things."

"Yeah."

"I don't quite get all of that," Elliott admits.

"Well, I don' know if I quite get it either. But... Ya know, even Einstein... I read this, an' I've heard Roy talk about it. He says, 'The secret to our energy needs... It's all in gravity.'"

"And you say Einstein said that too."

"He did. But nobody has figured out how to capture it. But it's an infinite amount of energy. You would never need any other kind of energy, once you could harness that."

"I read that part, but I don't understand it."

"But... I mean... Isn't it interesting reading?"

"It is. And it's actually causing me to think about a lot of things differently."

Terry shouts from below, "Poteet, I'm headin' home."

Poteet moves to the double doors and shouts down. "Terry..."

She shouts back, "Yeah?"

"Can you come up here?"

"Sure." Within seconds they hear her footsteps on the stairs.

As she's walking in, Poteet asks, "You're leavin' early?"

"I've got some things to get for tonight, an' I asked Teal to come in."

Poteet nods.

Elliott moves forward to say, "They're picking me up at my hotel first thing in the morning."

"Okay. You can ride with Poteet, an' we'll get you back to your hotel later."

Elliott nods and says, "Okay."

Terry points back and forth between the two men. "I'll see y'all at the house about five thirty. Will that work?"

Elliott smiles and says, "...works for me."

With that confirmation, Terry turns and walks out.

As they hear her descending footsteps, Elliott is back on point as he says to Poteet, "I'm looking at the world differently now."

"Oh yeah?"

"I'm thinking about this source of continuous energy and how that affects things."

"Yeah. But what is so amazing to me is that Roy Masters comes up with this stuff, an' he never had any formal training."

"Yeah."

"He was just... He's just... He was born a genius, ya know."

Sitting forward and nodding slowly, Elliott says, "Yeah. I think so."

"I mean, he's just a damn genius. How else do you explain how somebody comes up with this stuff..."

"I don't know."

"...out of the blue like that?"

"Yeah. But... It was like you said. I had to read most of it multiple times to make sense of it."

"Uh-huh."

Elliott nods. "At least on the 'big whoosh' thing, I feel like I pretty well understand where he's coming from."

"Yeah?"

"And it makes perfect sense to me."

"Me too."

"Um... And you just wonder why it's not being seriously discussed," Elliott says and shrugs. "...and even celebrated."

"I know. It's a funny thing."

"It's just like... It seems like the science world should be talking about these concepts."

"I agree. But you've got to be a certain type of person for this to sink in. I do believe that."

"Because... I mean..." Elliott explains, "He gives examples of nearly everything. And I can't tell you the names of scientists over the decades..."

"Uh-huh."

"...and maybe even centuries who subscribed to the theory of a continuing source of energy. And that's what Roy Masters calls 'the big whoosh.'"

"Exactly."

"So, it's not like he's the only one that's ever thought of it."

"Right. Yeah."

"And it sounds like 'continuous energy' was even the prevailing theory at one time. Einstein came in and said it was a 'big bang' instead."

"Yeah."

"...which then became the mainstream way of thinking for the past several decades."

"So now, everybody believes in the 'big bang,'" Poteet summarizes.

"But..." Elliott sits forward with his hands together. "To me, that's what's hard to believe."

"Mm-hmm."

"When you're... When you're forced to think about... Okay, it could be this way. It could be that way." He sighs. "And for some reason..." He chuckles. "I was thinking about a trip to Hawaii that Sharon and I took recently."

"Okay."

"We were there just a couple of weeks ago with some friends. And... I remember looking out at the ocean and watching those waves just keep crashing and keep crashing on those rocks. ...with such a ferocious intensity. I was struck with the power of the waves."

"Yeah. I lived there for a while..."

Elliott smiles and says, "I know you did."

"...an' I know what you mean."

"And so... This morning... I'm thinking... How can the tremendous power behind those waves continue like that— over *billions* of years?" Elliott holds out his hands in a questioning gesture.

"Yeah."

"...all of this energy from a single event that happened so long ago? Really? I mean, a single blast, billions of years ago would keep those waves crashing with such force? I don't know."

Poteet takes a deep breath.

"Can you think of anything that just keeps going without additional input of energy? No. It eventually comes to rest. And it seems to me that the energy in those waves would have to lessen over time as well." Elliott concludes and shrugs. "It would. It's just the nature of things."

"You would think so."

"But that's not what's been happening. The power in those waves continues to pound the rocks, just as it did a thousand years ago. Or, a million years ago. It continues."

Someone walks in and says, "Hi."

Poteet looks over, smiles, and says, "Hi," but doesn't engage.

Elliott continues, "Yeah. It never stops. It doesn't even slow down. And you think about global warming with the temperatures rising. So... I've looked into that some. I've got charts of the temperature of the world. One of the friends I went over to Hawaii with is a geophysicist."

"Oh yeah?"

"So, you know... We've been several places together, and we talk about geology. I find it fascinating. He explains the time periods when certain things happened on the earth. A lot of it has to do with the temperature of the earth at the time."

"Yeah?"

"So, he gave me this chart that's really the history of the earth from a geophysical standpoint. And so, temperatures go up, temperatures go down, CO_2 goes up, CO_2 goes down. Well... Relating it to the 'big whoosh'..."

"Okay?"

"How can the temperature of the earth be maintained around a historical average, if it was just a big bang—just a one time thing? I mean..."

"Right."

"I'm saying the same thing over and over, I guess. But..."

"Yeah."

"That's what doesn't make sense to me and is the harder thing for me to believe—that there was this one big blast of energy and it's been sustaining the universe ever since."

"Yeah."

"...from the beginning for billions of years."

"Yeah."

"That's what I find hard to believe."

"An' the universe is still expanding," Poteet notes.

"Yeah."

Poteet continues, "It's still expanding. But ya know, I think everybody, even Einstein, said that once you start understandin' it, you know that there's got to be a God. There has to be. Ya know. There has to be. But... There's so many people that are agnostic or atheists or whatever that don't believe that God exists. But... Einstein said, 'God without science is lame. Science without God is blind.' That was a quote from him."

"Einstein... Yeah... I think I've heard that. But it was some time ago."

"But Roy talks in that book about everybody at one time thinkin' that the earth was flat."

"Right."

"An' Columbus said, 'I don't think so.'"

Elliott laughs.

"Ya know... An' so... He wadn' really afraid of fallin' off the edge. Yeah, an' it's funny. Copernicus, uh... He said that the earth wadn' the center of the universe. Hell, they tried to hang the son of a bitch."

"Oh?"

Poteet laughs hard.

"That's kind of what happens with new ideas."

"I find it all fascinating. I really do."

"Oh, I do too," Elliott says and nods. "I swear, I'll think differently about the world now."

"Yeah?"

"It *was* a 'big whoosh.' And it continues. That energy is constantly being pumped out. That's what makes sense to me."

"Yeah."

"But ya know... The concept of time was a hard thing for me to wrap my mind around. So... How does it change? How does it move? Why does speed have anything to do with time at all?" Elliott asks.

"Well, ya know... Before the 'big whoosh,' there was no such thing as time."

"Yeah. Well... And that makes sense to me. Because... The phrase... And you hear it frequently. It's, 'Since the beginning of time...'"

"Sure."

"I never thought anything about it. But... Actually, it's very insightful."

"Hmm."

"At some point there was no time."

"There wadn'. That's right."

"And... To me, that's not hard to understand."

"Right," Poteet says and steps closer to Elliott. He points generally to the north and says, "Ya know, they're still shootin' that movie over there today."

"I thought they might be."

"I've got to run over there for a few minutes. Do you mind?"

"No, go ahead. I can make some calls."

As Poteet heads past Elliott for the door, Elliott is thinking that there's a lot more to Roy Masters than his comments about men and women. Seems like he's trying to put it *all* together—same can be said about his comments on religion. Elliott wishes he could better understand all of Roy Masters' theories.

After about forty-five minutes, Elliott looks up when he hears Poteet's steps on the stairs. When Poteet appears, he asks, "...everything okay?"

"Oh, yeah. They said they needed to use my buildin' for another day. I said, 'Great!'" Poteet smiles. "That's another few thousand they'll be addin' to my check. I hope they keep needin' it."

Elliott chuckles slightly and says, "Sure."

Poteet looks at Elliott and asks, "Did you get your calls made?"

"No. I got back into this book." Elliott holds up *Finding God in Physics*. "I wanted to check out some things."

"Okay. So... Do you have a new perspective on it now?"

"No. Not really. I understand the 'whoosh' idea, and I get the significance. And I think I prefer looking at our world through the lens of 'continuous energy.' For one thing, it makes sense to me. We've already talked about that. But also, it's refreshing, I think."

"Refreshing?"

"Yeah. With the 'Big Bang,' it's a single event. It happened billions of years ago, and we're left now with picking through the debris of that blast."

Poteet chuckles. "I guess you could look at it like that."

"I think I do," Elliott says and looks at Poteet. The corners of Elliott's mouth begin to turn up, and he says, "With the 'continuous energy' concept, it's new energy all the time. Every day... Every second... Every split second, we have new energy and new possibilities. I like that."

"Hmm."

"But... In most of this, Roy Masters refers to God's role in it. I'm trying to wrap my mind around that as well. Of course, Masters blurs the lines between science and religion."

"He does, but I don' think it's that unusual when you get to the topic of creation."

Elliott nods and says, "So... Jumping over to the religion side..."

"Okay."

Elliott sighs and remains silent for a moment. He then begins, "With continuous energy..."

"Mm-hmm."

"It's coming from the center of the universe."

"Right."

"And in Roy Masters' theories, it's perpetually maintained by God," Elliott says.

"Yeah. But we can never understand it. It's so far beyond us. I mean, it's like tryin' to... With our finite mind, we can't imagine somethin' that infinite. Ya know. An' God says, 'You'll never understand.' Remember what I said about Moses..."

Elliott smiles.

"He kept wantin' to see God."

Elliott chuckles.

"He kept wantin' to see God an' he kept askin' 'im. An' God told 'im. He said, 'You can't handle it. You *cannot* handle this.'"

"Right."

"Ya know, most people have this idea of Michelangelo's God, ya know, this old man..."

"Yeah."

"...with gray hair an' all."

"Yeah."

"...which is totally wrong. Most people have a childlike understandin' of what this all is. But... If you're a searchin' person like I was, you finally end up with your own concept of spirituality. I know that I did. I tried a lot of things. But it seemed to come together for me when I started listenin' to what Roy had to say. He helped me a lot."

"Mm-hmm."

"But... Ya know... He's been around a long time, an' I don' know how many followers or how many people he's helped. Ya know, they're really not followers. He said, 'I don' want any followers. I jus' want you to listen. You jus' listen to what I'm tellin' ya. An' then, you go do it.' But I don' know what percentage of people get it. I'm afraid, not very many."

Elliott responds, "Maybe more than you think." He had decided while Poteet was gone that Roy Masters was someone who was controversial but someone who should be listened to. He was definitely a deep thinker, and his theories were worth debate.

Elliott is brought back to the moment when he hears Poteet say, "Ya know, when Jesus was killed... He said... He told God, 'I really don' wanna do this.'"

Elliott chuckles. "Right."

"An' God said, 'I want you to do it.' An' so he submitted himself to it. An' then, uh... Ya know. An' then he came back. An' Roy said, 'He came back, an' he was flesh an' blood.'"

"So, Roy does believe all that."

"Oh, yeah. He does. He said, 'He came back in flesh in blood.' An' he said, ya know... Jesus talked to his disciples an' told 'em—said, 'Now look, I gotta go now. I gotta go.' An' he said... The way Roy explained it. He said, 'They watched 'im go.' An' he said, 'That's where...' He said, 'I want to know... Where did he go? Where is he now?' He said, 'I know he's there. But where is this place?' An'... He said, 'That's what I wanna know.'" Poteet looks over at Elliott. "An' I believe... If anybody's gonna figure that out, it'll be Roy."

"Huh."

"I really do."

"Do you ever talk to anyone about the origins of the universe? Does that ever come up in conversation, like with the 'big bang?'"

"Not so much anymore."

"Yeah?"

"It used to."

"Yeah?"

"I think... Because... I was talkin' to people who were similar to my age, ya know. 'Cause I think younger people... They have a greater hunger to know those kinds of things. As you get older, you start to get kind of set in what you believe."

"Yeah."

Poteet looks around his studio and then asks, "Are you ready to go to the house?"

"Sure," Elliott says and begins to gather up his stuff.

CHAPTER 62

Friends

On the drive, Elliott and Poteet discuss the new building and the sculpture garden they'll have out back. It's obvious that Poteet and Terry are anxious to make the move and begin planning a grand opening.

When they walk in, they are greeted by the smell of melting cheese and Mexican spices. Poteet first turns to Honey Badger, who is very excited to see his "Papa." He then disappears into another part of the house.

Standing by her stove, Terry tilts her head and smiles at Elliott. She reaches out and says, "So this will be your last visit for a while."

After a warm hug, Elliott says, "I expect so. We'll review what we've got and then figure out what to do."

"We'll miss you."

Elliott smiles and says, "I've had a great time in Santa Fe, and I'll miss seeing both of you."

"You'll have to come visit."

"I will. I'll bring Sharon out here. She needs to get to know Santa Fe, and she needs to get to know you."

"Good. I'm jus' dyin' to meet 'er. I'm sure we'll get along great."

"I've enjoyed my sessions with Poteet, and I've enjoyed the times *we've* had to talk."

Honey Badger starts jumping on Elliott's leg and Terry says lovingly, "Now, you stop that."

She stoops down to discipline her dog, and Elliott says, "That's okay." He bends over to pet Honey Badger, who gives him a quick lick to the face. Elliott gives Honey a strong massage around his head with both hands and says, "I'll miss you too, Mr. Honey Badger." Elliott stands and looks at Terry. "But I'll be back. I have business reasons to be back here. And I think I've mentioned this. I may call someone I know at The Hallmark Channel about *your* story. I wouldn't mind having that be our introduction to Poteet."

Terry giggles.

"It's a true story, and those don't come along very often."

"Yeah. It's true alright."

Elliott chuckles.

Poteet returns and takes his place at the end of the kitchen bar.

Terry says, "I've got gin. I've got limes. They're already sliced, and I've got some tonic water. I've got Patron here for you, Poteet."

"...goin' all out," Poteet replies.

"Of course, it's Elliott's last night, an' I've got a nice bottle a wine for myself." She smiles and looks at Poteet. "How 'bout makin' Elliott a drink."

Poteet nods and says, "...glad to."

Terry sets a bowl of chips down in front of Elliott, looks at him, and says, "Here ya go."

Elliott takes a chip and turns to Poteet. He says, "After all this time watching you, I've learned to appreciate your art."

Poteet smiles and chuckles.

"You know, I said I wasn't an art guy."

"You did. I remember that."

"Well, I've learned to appreciate the difference between what you do and what other artists do. I can appreciate the quality of your work now. And... You see a lot of art here in Santa Fe—in hotels and a lot of other places."

"You do."

"And I can see the difference. I've seen the effort you put into each step of every painting, from making the frames and preparing the canvases to the way you finish each one."

"I had to learn all that."

"I've seen the skill you have in applying the paint. I've seen the richness of your colors and the way you use them. And... You have so much creativity in the themes you come up with."

"I'm always thinkin' about it."

"And then, there's the unique textures you can apply with the sand and the beads. It's amazing. It really is. And maybe I *am* becoming an art guy."

Terry smiles and says, "I did the same thing."

"And I've already impressed Sharon with some of my new art knowledge."

Terry chuckles and says, "See. There ya go."

Elliott nods and grabs another chip. He shrugs and says, "I just wanted to tell you that."

Poteet and Terry chuckle.

After a moment, Poteet looks at Terry and says, "They want our buildin' for another day."

She smiles and says, "...good deal. But I'll be glad to get in there to start workin'."

"I'd be glad to rent it to 'em for as long as they want," Poteet says and sets a drink in front of Elliott.

Poteet sits at the bar.

With her glass of wine in hand, Terry sits next to Poteet on his left.

They look at each other, and Terry asks, "Can I make a toast?"

"Sure," Poteet and Elliott say at the same time.

"Okay." She lifts her wine glass and says, "To Elliott. To a really fun time... An' to his movie, *The Life of Poteet Victory...*"

They touch glasses, smile at each other, and take a drink.

"Even if we do it, we probably won't call it *The Life of Poteet Victory*," Elliott explains. "That seems a little generic and dry to me."

They all chuckle.

Terry nods and says, "I get that. We'll work on the title."

Poteet lifts his glass and says, "To Elliott... To listenin' for hours an' hours about every little detail of my life."

They laugh together.

Poteet lifts his glass above his head and says, "To Elliott."

They touch glasses, take a drink, and set their glasses down.

Elliott looks at Poteet. He then turns to Terry and says, "...my turn."

Poteet and Terry both smile.

Elliott grabs his glass and hoists it. His smile disappears as Poteet and Terry watch. They slowly lift their glasses—but not as high.

Elliott says, "To our friends that we know..."

Poteet smiles and Terry chuckles.

"To our friends that have gone before..."

Poteet's smile gets bigger.

"An' to all the lucky sons of bitches that get to meet us."

They roar, and they cackle. They attempt to clink their glasses.

Terry half sings and half says a high-pitched, "Woohoo!"

Without another word, they touch glasses again and laugh some more.

AUTHOR'S NOTE

I had just pulled into our driveway when Jerry Nabors, a high-school friend, called me. I'm sure it was the first time he had ever called me, although we'd been on a trip to Arizona with him, his wife, and other friends not long before. Jerry had made a trip recently with these same friends to Santa Fe, and he wanted to tell me about Poteet Victory, a Native American artist he had met there.

I was entertained by the stories about Poteet, but I wondered why Jerry had made the effort to call. I began to understand, when he said, "Somebody needs to write Poteet's story." And then he said, "We told Poteet that we knew an author, and I told him I would talk to you."

I had other projects to finish, but eventually I met Poteet and his wife Terry in Oklahoma City. That evening, my wife Sharon and I joined them for dinner, and we got to hear some of Poteet's renowned storytelling. At the end of the night, Poteet asked me to come see him in Santa Fe.

A few weeks later, I made the trip. When I walked into their gallery, it was like "old-home week" with Terry. She's the type who doesn't know a stranger. When I met Poteet in his studio, we talked about everything but a book. I finally said, "My friends have suggested that I write your biography."

Poteet said something like, "I think we can do that."

I've since learned that Poteet makes significant commitments just that way. Poteet and Terry invited me to their home that evening, and we started making plans to create a book. Ever since that day, they have been nothing but gracious to me in every way.

I let them know early on that I wanted to record our conversations. And it's those conversations which form the dialog in this book. It has been written, as much as possible, in Poteet's own words. Terry would often come and go as we talked, but her very words are used as well.

At the risk of being confusing, I introduced two fictional characters. The main one is Elliott Jacobs, a successful movie producer. The second is Judy Hightower, Elliott's research assistant. She has only a minor role.

I also introduced two real people as characters. They are Jim and Pam Klepper, who are long-time collectors of Poteet's art and lifelong friends of mine. They actually live in Oklahoma City and not southern California.

Most of the original conversations included Poteet, Terry, and me. To be true to the dialog, someone had to be me—the third person. It could simply have been me, or it could have been a stand-in. I chose the latter, and Elliott Jacobs is that person. I wanted the book to be factual and authentic but also entertaining.

Bringing the Elliott character into the mix created a slightly different dynamic. Elliott grew up in New York City, which put him in a position to better understand some of Poteet's experiences there. Elliott's background in movie production gave him the expertise to evaluate the significance of Poteet's life story. It also gave me the opportunity to create a road map for producing a TV series about Poteet.

Elliott's words are my words except for what he says about his career as a movie producer, his life growing up in New York City, a second marriage, and being a Presbyterian.

I have learned so much from being around Poteet and Terry. Before starting the project, I knew of the differences in our backgrounds. I knew of his commitment to Native

American issues. I knew of his achievements in the art world. And I knew he was an endless stream of entertaining stories.

I didn't expect to learn about physics and the origins of the universe. I didn't expect to join him in a spiritual journey. I didn't expect to experience a life with so many twists and turns. I didn't expect to laugh as much as we have laughed. I didn't expect to be inspired so much by his hard work and dedication. I didn't expect to become a friend. I didn't expect my own life to be changed so significantly. I didn't expect to become driven by his passions.

I have felt many times that my life experiences were preparing me for this task. I have tried my best to do justice to my friend.

He calls me brother.

Thank you for reading.

A documentary has been made about Poteet's mural.

See jrobertkeating.com for updates.

ABOUT ATMOSPHERE PRESS

Atmosphere Press is an independent, full-service publisher for excellent books in all genres and for all audiences. Learn more about what we do at atmospherepress.com.

We encourage you to check out some of Atmosphere's latest releases, which are available at Amazon.com and via order from your local bookstore:

Dying to Live, a novel by Barbara Macpherson Reyelts

Looking for Lawson, a novel by Mark Kirby

Surrogate Colony, a novel by Boshra Rasti

Á Deux, a novel by Alexey L. Kovalev

What If It Were True, a novel by Eileen Wesel

Sunflowers Beneath the Snow, a novel by Teri M. Brown

Solitario: The Lonely One, a novel by John Manuel

The Fourth Wall, a novel by Scott Petty

Rx, a novel by Garin Cycholl

Knights of the Air: Book 1: Rage!, a novel by Iain Stewart

Heartheaded, a novel by Constantina Pappas

The Aquamarine Surfboard, a novel by Kellye Abernathy

ABOUT THE AUTHOR

J. Robert Keating is married with two children and three grandchildren. He grew up in Oklahoma and now lives in Fort Worth, Texas. After years of writing in the cyber-thriller genre, he turned to the challenges of documenting the life of a truly inspiring individual. He says of Poteet and his wife, Terry, "I was very fortunate to have gotten to know them and to have enjoyed their hospitality. As we shared our histories, our thoughts, and our feelings, we became like family. It was an honor and a joy to be allowed into their lives."